THE
GRAVE AT
STORM'S END

Katashi took his bow from his back and brandished it in the man's face. "You know what this is?"

The messenger blinked raindrops out of his eyes. "A bow."

"No, *my* bow." Katashi drew an arrow slowly and took a few steps back. "You have perhaps heard of my skill."

More sniggering, and the soldiers spread as Katashi took more steps back, ready for a show.

"Now, you tell me where you were going and what message you were carrying, or I will prove just how good I am even in this rain."

By Devin Madson

THE GRAVE AT STORM'S END

THE VENGEANCE TRILOGY:
BOOK THREE

DEVIN MADSON

www.orbitbooks.net

ORBIT

First published in 2016
First published in Great Britain in 2020 by Orbit

1 3 5 7 9 10 8 6 4 2

Copyright © 2016 by Devin Madson

Map by Charis Loke

Excerpt from *We Ride the Storm* by Devin Madson
Copyright © 2020 by Devin Madson

The moral right of the author has been asserted.

A CIP catalogue record for this book is available from the British Library.

ISBN 978-0-356-51532-8

Orbit
An imprint of
Little, Brown Book Group
Carmelite House
50 Victoria Embankment
London EC4Y 0DZ

An Hachette UK Company
www.hachette.co.uk

www.orbitbooks.net

For Chris.

Without you, this book would have been moved onto a memory stick, stomped on, screamed at, set on fire, and finally had its charred remains thrown in the sea, never to be seen again.

Thank you.

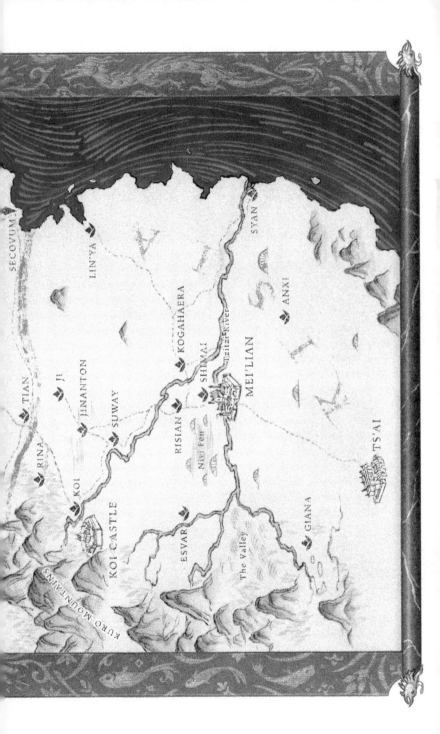

Character List

Ts'ai

Honour Is Wealth.

Emperor Kin Ts'ai .... Emperor of Kisia

General Esta Rini .... General of the Rising Army

General Hade Ryoji .... General of the Rising Army. Head of the Imperial Guard

General Jikuko .... General of the Rising Army

General Yi .... General of the Rising Army

General Vareen.................................. Commander of Mei'lian's standing battalions

Commander Rusaka........................... Commander of the camp at Kogahaera

Captain Dendzi................................. Imperial Guard

Minister Bahain .... Minister of the Right

Master Yara .... Imperial Secretary

Councillor Gadokoi........................... Of the Imperial War Council

Governor Ohi.................................... Of the Imperial Council

Father Kokoro .... Court priest

Father Hoto...................................... Priest of Kuroshima

Brother Jian...................................... Priest. Endymion's former guardian

Master Kenji..................................... Imperial Physician

Apprentice Yoj.................................. Master Kenji's apprentice

Raijin .... Kin's brindle horse

Otako

We Conquer. You Bleed.

Emperor Lan Otako .... Deceased. Eldest son

Emperor Tianto Otako...................... Deceased. Youngest son

Empress Li .... Deceased. Mother to Hana and Takehiko

Emperor Katashi Otako, *"Monarch"* ..... Only son of Emperor Tianto

Hacho .... Katashi's bow

Lady Hana Otako, *"Regent"*........... Only living daughter of Emperor Lan

Tili... Lady Hana's maid

The Traitor Generals .... General Manshin, General Roi, General Tikita

Captain Terran.................................. One of General Manshin's captains

Pike Captains .... Captain Tan, Captain Chalpo, Captain Roni

Shin Metai .... Deceased. A rebel and Lady Hana's protector

Wen .... A Pike and healer

Laroth

Sight Without Seeing

Lord Nyraek Laroth .... Deceased. Fifth Count of Esvar

"Malice" "Whoreson" Laroth .... Illegitimate son of Nyraek Laroth

Lord Darius Laroth .... Legitimate heir of Nyraek Laroth

Lord Takehiko Otako, "*Endymion*" ..Illegitimate son of Nyraek Laroth

Kaze.. Endymion's horse

Vices

Vice Without Virtue

Lady Kimiko Otako, *"Adversity"* .... Katashi's twin sister

Avarice .... Once employed on the Laroth estate

Lord Arata Toi, *"Hope"* .... Vice

Vices .... Spite, Conceit, Ire, Parsimony, Apostasy, Folly, Rancour, Enmity, Pride, and Envy

When gods walk, the ground trembles
When gods cry, the skies weep
When gods love, the world sings
When gods fight, empires fall

DAY ONE

1. HANA

In darkness we waited. Silent. Tense. A group of imperial guards on the east bank of the Nuord River, watching for the flash of a lantern.

It was a starless night, and under layers of leather and mail, I carried my weight in sweat. Especially beneath my helmet where my hair stuck sodden to my head, but how else could one hide blonde curls? *No one can know*, Kin had said. *You're just another soldier.*

Beside me, General Ryoji shifted his weight. He was little but an outline in the darkness, yet the blended scent of leather and sweat and cedar oil was impossible to mistake. There were traces of Katashi in that smell, and I wavered between wanting to move away and draw closer, fighting with my own instincts. My own memories.

The general shifted again, letting out a short huff of air. We had been waiting too long.

On my other side, a whisper warmed my ear. "Are you all right, my lady?"

Tili's voice trembled. General Ryoji had cautioned against her involvement as he had cautioned against the entire mission, but tradition dictated the presence of another woman, so another woman there would be. Kin would risk no mistake.

I nodded. "You?"

Despite the darkness, I was sure she nodded back, but when I felt for her hand, I found it tightly clenched and shaking. I squeezed it and wondered how much more strongly an Empath could feel her fear.

For weeks, there had been nothing but bad news. First, we had lost Risian. Then Lotan. News no longer arrived from the north, and heavy losses stalked the heels of every victory like a plague we could not shake. We held Kogahaera, but only thanks to the Nuord River, its roar even now cutting the silence of an oppressive night.

"We need to move," Kin said in a low rumble.

"There's been no signal, Majesty," General Ryoji returned.

"If they're dead, they can't signal."

"If they're dead, we should turn back."

General Ryoji seemed to hold his breath, statue-still as he waited for a reply to such brazen honesty.

"It's too late for that," Kin said. "We go to Kuroshima without them."

The general bowed, and again I wondered what Malice or Darius might read in his rigidity that I could not. More than fear? More than the ill ease of a man ordered to act against his better judgement?

"Ji. Tanner," Ryoji said, speaking over my shoulder. "Stay with . . . her."

"General," I began. "I am armed and quite capable—"

"Yes, my lady, but they have their orders."

Ji and Tanner filled the space he left behind. They were often with me, but though I knew their names and their faces, I trusted neither the way I had come to trust Ryoji—the ever-present sentinel who had saved me from the pit a lifetime ago, whose loyalty to Kin seemed to know no bounds.

We started to move, and Tili remained pressed to my side as we climbed the gentle curve of the bridge. At the peak, my sandal caught an uneven stone, but the press of soldiers was so close I could not fall, could only jog on as we descended into enemy territory—Otako territory. For years I had carried the name with pride, but tonight I would give it up to become Kin's wife—Kin's empress.

I had always dreamed of sitting on my father's throne, always dreamed of ruling. Tonight that dream would come true, but it was a very different wedding to the one I had planned when I had asked Katashi to marry me. Fate had allowed me mere hours of such a joy—a joy so great the world had seemed to break beneath the strain of it.

Perhaps hearing my trembling breath, Tili pressed closer, but although she hampered my movement, I could not push her away. Her presence was the only comfort left.

We slowed as we gained the far bank. Ahead, light flickered through the dense shield of soldiers as it might through trees, glinting off buckles and patches of leather worn shiny with use.

"Spread out."

Drawing weapons, they fanned out.

"No, not you, my lady," General Ryoji said, once more appearing beside me.

"How can we maintain the ruse if I do not do my job?" I said.

"This is not your job, my lady, but keeping you safe is mine."

Again a hint of Katashi's scent—some oil perhaps, or just a cruel trick of memory—and though Ryoji could not have seen my expression in the darkness, I turned my face away. Ahead with his own escort, Emperor Kin led the way toward Kuroshima village.

It lay about a mile from the river, a gathering of small houses in the lee of the mountain. At this hour, they were shadowed and silent, the only light a lantern at the base of the climb that led to Kisia's oldest shrine. There, two men in priest's white were waiting beneath an arbour of becalmed leaves.

Leaving me with Ji and Tanner, General Ryoji hurried to join Kin, his hand as close to his sword as could be considered polite in the company of priests. I made to join them, but Tanner blocked my way with his arm. There was tension in every line of his body and his eyes darted, watching the soldiers move about the silent village. Without lanterns, the distant buildings melded into the trees. Dark. Lifeless.

Tili huddled closer still, as though I were a fire by which she could warm herself. Seconds dragged by, until at last General Ryoji made a sign, and Tanner lowered his arm. "My lady," he said and bowed.

Tili and I joined them at the base of the mountain. Other soldiers gathered.

"What's going on?" I hissed at General Ryoji. "What of our scouts?"

He glanced at the two priests. "It seems they never arrived."

"But they were experienced soldiers."

"Yes, my lady," he said.

"They can't have just gone missing."

The general pulled at his bottom lip for a troubled instant. "No, my lady."

"It's quiet. Is the village empty?"

"All but, like we expected. The war is too close. Even at the base of the old mountain, no one is safe."

"We are not alone here, General, the risk—"

"The risk of being attacked while retreating is just as high, my lady," General Ryoji said, and I wondered if they were Kin's words. "With none of the benefits of success. We go up."

He moved on with a nod not a bow, maintaining the pretence that I was a mere soldier. I liked the informality, taking what small joys I could in being treated, for once, like just another man.

A flotilla of paper lanterns spread light through the group, and I took one, thinking of another time I had gathered in the dark with a group of men in imperial uniforms.

No, don't think about Katashi.

I edged toward Kin. "It worries me that the scouts have not been seen," I whispered. "We should leave."

"No, we proceed as planned, a group on each branch of the stairs just as tradition dictates."

"Are you sure it's wise?"

He grimaced at me. "I am sure that anyone who wanted us dead could have killed us by now. Take what comfort from that as you will."

"Very little!"

"We have no choice. We have to do this right or risk losing all legitimacy."

He was right, but I hated it. Hated the silence and the darkness, the still press of the air and the nervous looks of the soldiers. Hated to have found myself here at all.

No, don't think about Katashi.

General Ryoji ordered half the men to remain behind and split the other half into two groups, one to accompany His Majesty up the right branch of the stairs, the other up the left branch with me, braving all one thousand four hundred and forty-four steps to the Kuroshima Shrine.

The forest into which we climbed was thick and dark, our winking lanterns the only stars, our steps and huffing breaths the only sounds. One thousand four hundred and forty-four stairs, one for every day the goddess Lunyia had waited for her husband. She, the goddess of loyalty and fortune, to whom all Kisians prayed upon their marriage. I counted them to give me something to think about other than what awaited me at the top.

At 210, General Ryoji stopped a few steps ahead. "Lim."

"General?"

I turned, swinging my lantern so fast the flame drew dangerously close to the paper. Behind me, the guard identified as Lim touched a hand to his sword.

"Run back down," the general said. "Tell Rashil to send for reinforcements."

"But General, there's no sign of enemy movement, and His Majesty said we could not risk—"

"Send for reinforcements. There was nothing before the skirmish at Cherry Wood either," Ryoji said. "Or when they hit us south of Risian. If the bastards want to play games with us, then this is the place they'll choose. Send for reinforcements."

"Yes, General."

Fast footsteps faded away down the steps, and I turned back to see the general's features screwed into a scowl.

"You would think by your expression that you *want* to be attacked, General," I said.

His eyes darted to my face and a rueful smile dawned. "Not exactly want, my lady, but I don't like uncertainty."

"Surely even if they know we're here, they don't know we are doing this. We were careful."

The guards behind me stood silent to listen, and I winced at how desperately hopeful I sounded.

"Yes, my lady," the general agreed. "But Lord Laroth has a habit of knowing things he ought not. I cannot say I liked the man, but only a fool would not respect his skill and take it into consideration."

Darius and I had argued often, but never had I thought to find him truly my enemy. Even after what he had done, and the passage of weeks in which I had called him so, it still felt wrong.

A grimace crossed General Ryoji's face. "Apologies, my lady, I did not—"

"You expressed no thought I have not had myself, General," I said. "And if you're right, we had better keep moving."

The whole procession lurched on, climbing faster now as though our enemy were right behind us. I tried not to think about the burning in my thighs or the fate that awaited me at the top of the mountain, and instead stared all but unseeing at the novice leading the way. His white robe eddied, ghostlike, about his feet. White robe, white sash, and plain reed sandals. It was an impractical colour for all but those who spent their lives in pursuit of piety.

I had stopped counting the stairs, but my legs ached enough that we must surely have passed 1,444 and missed the shrine entirely. Absently, I wondered where the path would lead us, it seeming to own no end, when at last the novice turned his head to say, "We are almost there, my lady."

I made no answer. My whole body ached. One thousand four hundred and forty-four steps from the village to the shrine had left me cursing my robe, my armour, my helmet, and the heavy soldier's sandals that were like a weight upon each foot.

My stomach dropped as the last step vanished beneath me.

"Welcome to Kuroshima Shrine, my lady," the novice said, halting beneath an arch of tangled branches hung with wild flowers. Beside me, General Ryoji's steps crunched to a halt upon the path, light spilling onto his feet. Inside, Kin would be waiting. I had asked him to marry me, but he was not the man I had wanted to rule alongside.

Don't think about Katashi.

Kuroshima Shrine was famous throughout Kisia, so I had expected it to be grand and imposing, not a cosy bird's hollow. There was no gleaming woodwork or fine art, no thick beams or broad sweeping roofs, just a simple curved wall of interlocking iron branches rising to form a low, rounded ceiling hung with paper lanterns.

Kin stood in the opposite archway, watching a priest approach across the slate floor. Every fourth tile was painted a jarring red, and whether by accident or design, the man avoided them.

"Your Majesty, it is an honour to welcome you to Kuroshima," he said, bowing very low before his emperor.

"Thank you, Father," Kin returned, gesturing for the man to rise. "I have long wished to witness so great a part of our empire's history, and what better occasion than upon the event of my marriage."

The priest wore serenity like a blanket and bowed again. "Indeed, Your Majesty. We are honoured beyond words."

Although Kin smiled, he did not speak again, leaving the priest to glance around in search of the bride. His gaze hung for a moment upon Tili, a slight frown between his brows at so curvaceous a soldier.

I pulled off my helmet. Sweat-dampened curls fell loose upon my brow, and the old priest stared, sucking in a breath before sinking into another low bow. "Lady Hana Otako, our shrine is humbled indeed."

"You are too kind, Father," I said, and with every eye on me, I hunted for something more to say. Darius, Mama Orde, and all my tutors had sought to instil in me the sort of grace and learning that would allow the uttering of pretty speeches, but until now I had only been representing myself. Now my words would reflect not only upon Emperor Kin but upon the whole of Kisia. I cleared my suddenly dry throat. "In truth, I feel there is little that could humble so old and so beautiful a shrine," I said, the courtly words not even sounding like my own. "We are transient, but it endures. Is there somewhere I can make myself presentable, Father?"

The man's eyes bulged, and he glanced at our novice guide. A silent heartbeat passed before he said, "Of course, my lady, follow me."

Once again avoiding the red slates, he led me toward the opposite archway, my armour clinking with every step. I caught Kin's eye as we passed, but though his lips smiled, his eyes did not. His attention, like General Ryoji's, was elsewhere.

The priest led the way to a small pavilion off the main path. It had a simple reed floor and walls lined with spare robes, white sashes, prayer chains, and pouches of fresh incense. Its smell filled every breath with the taste of sandalwood.

Tili followed me inside. Frowning, the father was moved to speak, but I stopped him. "My maid, Father," I said. "We could not be too careful."

Tili removed her helmet and bowed to the old priest. "Father."

His disapproval did not shift, but with a sharp nod, he left, ignoring Ji and Tanner as they took up silent vigil outside the door. There was urgency despite the calm night, and before the door closed, my sword belt and weapons hit the floor. Whatever other conventions I had persuaded Kin to set aside, I could not kneel before the Shrine Stone armed.

"Help me out of this," I said, tugging at the soldier's knot that held my crimson sash. It went first, followed by the leather tunic and its linen under-robe, gauntlets and breeches—every trapping of the common soldier had been made to size, but once more, tradition dictated I could not take my oath in it. Tili unrolled the ceremonial robe she had carried tied in a bundle, and though its beautiful silk was creased, being dishevelled was a small price to pay. No one watching our progress from the camp at Kogahaera would have reason to suspect Lady Hana made one of the party. They might recognise Emperor Kin, but what could be more natural than an Emperor making a pilgrimage to Kuroshima in a time of war?

I ran my fingers through my hair, and Tili helped me into my robe. We did not speak. There was little to say, and we had not been good at small talk of late.

A knock fell upon the door. "My lady?"

I had no mirror to be sure I was ready, but there was no time to do more. "Enter," I said, running my hands down my creased robe.

The door slid to reveal the novice who had been our guide. "I'm sorry, my lady, but Father Hoto is anxious to begin."

The young man stared directly at me as he spoke, not effacing his gaze as etiquette required.

My pulse quickened. "He sent you?"

"Yes, my lady, he is anxious to begin the ceremony." Still he did not drop his gaze, and I hunted his face for some clue of what he was trying to tell me. No fear that I could see, no meaningful glance at my sword.

"Then I will of course come at once," I said, and only then did he step aside to let me pass.

Back outside, the air was humid, the night quiet. I tried to make eye contact with Ji and Tanner as I passed, but neither was used to looking at me. All I could do was stride toward the main hollow, counting the steps behind me. Tanner. Ji. The novice. Tili at my side. No surprises, yet I was fretful with only stiff silk at my hip.

Light spilled from the main hollow of the shrine, and I strode through the narrow arch only to halt on the threshold, my heart thudding against my breastbone.

Conceit stood at the altar, a knife pressed to Father Hoto's throat. Behind him stood a dozen soldiers in Pike black, hooded and anonymous, while Kin's soldiers faced them across the red slate floor, hands tense upon their sword hilts.

"Why, Lady Hana, you have kept us waiting," Conceit said, his pretty features and malicious smile a memory from another life. "How kind of you to finally join us."

A grunt sounded behind me and Ji crumpled, his blood spraying over my feet. The novice pressed a bloodied knife to Tanner's neck. "Don't move," he quavered, his white robe splattered with blood. "Don't move or I'll have to kill him too."

He trembled, but the blade remained steady against Tanner's throat.

"She's thinking about moving," Conceit said, holding every gaze. Kin's soldiers hovered out of range like wary cats. "As you can see, your companions have not been welcoming, my lady. And to think I only came to give you this gift."

He gestured to the altar. There lay a black sash where a white one ought to be. "It's a more appropriate colour, don't you think?"

No one moved. No one spoke. All eyes were on this man. "No? You don't get it?" he said, when no one answered. "The sash of a whore instead of an innocent bride?"

"I'll slit your slanderous accusations from your throat," General Ryoji said.

The man clicked his tongue. "My, my, General Ryoji, how venomous you are toward your guests. But—" He nodded at Father Hoto. "You need him, don't you? He's the only one here qualified to perform a marriage ceremony."

Conceit laughed suddenly and removed his knife from the priest's throat. Father Hoto collapsed upon the stones, curled up like a child.

"Father Hoto." The intruder knelt at the altar. "Would you do the honours?" He didn't wait for a response but pursed his lips piously. "I, Conceit," he said, mimicking a ceremony, "most trusted of the Vice Master, pray the gods never saddle me with such a whore for a wife. I would not wish my children to be born of such loose loins, smeared by the seed of so many men as they claw their way into this world."

"Shut him up," Kin ordered. "Now."

Conceit seemed not to hear. "In the eyes of the gods," he said, "I offer the Imperial Whore this black sash—"

An arrow leapt for the unguarded Vice and hit him full in the chest. But there was no satisfying crack of bone. No gush of blood. The arrow clattered uselessly off the wall as Conceit disappeared.

From across the altar, a new Conceit laughed. "I, Lady Hana Otako, the Imperial Whore," the second Conceit continued in a high-pitched voice. "Cannot wait seven days to have my robe torn off. Take me now, commoner, give me your enormous—"

The second Conceit rolled as another arrow came at him.

"Ha! Now we're playing." He leapt to his feet. "You would kill a woman making her prayers?" He clicked his tongue reprovingly, and behind him, the small group of hooded Pikes drew their swords.

"Hold your ground," Kin growled at his men.

"Is this how you treat every guest bearing wedding gifts?" Conceit asked as he drew the deadly sickle Malice gave to every Vice in his service. The man's smile turned predatory.

"No," Kin said. "This is how I treat foul-mouthed traitors. Cut him down!"

As one body, the imperial guards advanced. I had left my weapons with my armour, but I snatched up Ji's sword and ran in on anger-fuelled steps.

"My lady, stay back!"

I shouldered the concerned guard out of the way. "Don't you dare tell me I have no right to defend my own name!"

Dark figures swarmed. Someone shouted. Another screamed. I dodged a clumsy swing and charged on, looking for Conceit. He, a flash of blond amid the chaos. Curls of incense smoke framed his tragically beautiful face.

"Why, Lady Hana," he said, arching high brows over dead eyes. "Or should I call you Captain Regent?"

"Shut your mouth or I'll shut it for you," I growled, jabbing at his gut.

Conceit danced out of the way, laughing. "I didn't mean what I said, you know. I'd have you no matter how many men had loosened you up first."

Anger took control and I thrust wildly. A lighter sword might have touched him, but I hadn't the strength to send this heavy lump of steel through his chest.

"Dressing like a man doesn't suit you," he said. "And that sword makes you clumsy. Perhaps your beloved Kin doesn't wish you well-armed. Here, have mine."

He threw his sword up and caught it by the blade. All confidence, he held it out to me. "Call it a wedding gift."

I swung at his outstretched arm, prepared to hit bone. But it was Conceit. Of course there was no resistance, no real flesh, and I fell off balance as the blade passed through him. He did not retaliate, just stood there with a hurt expression and one arm missing. "My lady, I was only being kind."

I thrust my sword into his gut. I knew there would be nothing, that I was only fuelling my anger, but rage had me in its grasp. Conceit's laughing face disappeared, yet my blade found flesh. Black sash. Black short robe. A Pike, his shocked cry like the wail of a bird.

The Pike dropped his sword, his slim hands fluttering in panic as he plucked at my sleeve. Beneath the hood his shadowed features looked youthful.

"I…I…" He gulped for breath, like a drowning man. Then a high-pitched moan and a gesture of despair that was all too feminine.

A woman. Dressed in black.

"Shit!" I looked into the dying whore's face. "I'm so sorry! I—"

Blood oozed down her chin and bubbled in her mouth as she tried to speak and only managed to spit crimson.

"I'm so sorry." I yanked the sword free and she fell to her knees. "Stop!" I shouted. "Stop! Don't kill them, they aren't Pikes!"

No one seemed to hear me, so I ran at the closest woman and threw myself between her and the imperial guard seeking to run her through. "Stop! Put down your weapons!"

"My lady!" The guard lunged, gripping my robe and yanking me forward as a blade touched my side. I overbalanced as he let me go, leaving the room spinning as pained grunts and fleshy sounds sickened my stomach.

"They aren't—" Bodies littered the floor. Most wore black, only a few crimson sashes there to break the monotony. Conceit was nowhere to be seen, but his flair for the dramatic had left behind a massacre. Only one robed and hooded woman still stood. I started toward her as someone grabbed my arm.

"What in the name of the gods do you think you're doing?" Kin demanded as he pulled me around. "How many times have I told you not to do anything foolish?"

"Foolish?" I snapped, already turning back toward the woman. "As foolish as striking down enemies who—?"

It was already too late. The last false Pike had been skewered upon the end of an imperial sword, and it was all I could do not to be sick as she slid to the floor dead. "That was unnecessary," I hissed, spinning back. "They weren't Pikes and you knew it."

"But they attacked us and did not stop even when their leader was gone. What else would you have had me do?"

A dozen things, but I could find voice for none of them. It would change nothing even if I could.

Into the silence, Kin said, "In seven days, you will be my wife, and I will not let you run unprotected into battle."

"Then as you are to be my husband, I will not let *you* run unprotected into battle either. Shall we dig out an Errant board and sit back while others fight for us?"

He gave a disgusted snort. "An emperor should always lead his men."

Kin held out his hand for the sword. My grip on it tightened. "I am the daughter of an emperor," I said in a soft growl, the words only for him. "I told you I would not sit idle and become a pretty doll for your ministers to leer at. I could have kept the title Katashi gave me, but instead I am here. You gave me your word and I expect you to honour it, *Your Majesty*."

I threw the sword at his feet, the clang of metal on stone loud in the silent space. Kin did not flinch. "I told you not to throw Katashi in my face," he said, speaking just as quietly. "There are enough whispers about you and him to fill the Valley. I don't need more."

My heart pounded against my ribs, and the shrine full of dead whores and soldiers faded to nothing but Katashi's warm body beside mine and the soft fall of his hair upon my shoulder as he held me tight.

"I want you Hana," he had breathed against my neck. *"I want this. May I make love to you? I won't without your permission."*

"I need you safe, Hana, not dead," Kin said, neatening the fall of his bloodstained robe. "The whole purpose of this night is to show the people who they should fight for, not for you to prove your bravery."

He walked away on the words, already gesturing to General Ryoji. "Keep guard in case that Vice comes back," he said. The general nodded and moved away, leaving Kin to contemplate the mess. "Father Hoto!"

The dishevelled and trembling priest peered over the top of the altar. "Y-your Majesty?"

"How long were they waiting for us?"

"S-since this morning, Your Majesty. They k-killed my novices and said that if I did not p-play my part, they w-would kill you and Lady Hana too." The man straightened, folding his hands together to hide their shaking. "I am sorry, Your Majesty, I am wholly at your mercy."

"I have no need of a dead priest," Kin said. "Do your job and you may consider yourself forgiven for your part in tonight's farce."

"My job?"

"I came here to be married, Father Hoto, and married I will be."

The priest blinked rapidly, then nodded. "As you wish, Your Majesty," he said, crushing the links of a prayer chain in his hand. "Then if you would care to...care to kneel at the um...at the altar, we shall begin."

"Clear the stones!" General Ryoji ordered, and his men began dragging away the dead, leaving bloody trails on already red stones. One was the enemy who had worn the robe of a novice and led me up the mountain.

"My lady," Kin said, indicating the Shrine Stone. "Would you do me the honour?"

I went to him, stepping over a woman no older than myself. Her throat was a bloodied mess and her limbs were tangled. Broken. The stink of blood and fluids mixed with the incense, and it was all I could do not to be sick.

Kin seemed not to see the dead. He knelt at the altar and waited until I joined him, until once again the night was silent.

Father Hoto clasped his trembling hands. "Our goddess the Lady Lunyia," he said, seeming to draw comfort from habitual words. "Mother of the moon and the rivers and the springs, turn your gaze upon us that you might hear our words and bless this union we have gathered to declare."

The black sash was gone, whisked away in the chaos, leaving a white one draped in its place.

But Conceit had been right. Had that been his purpose in coming? Merely to sow doubt in Kin's mind?

The thud of my heart drowned the rest of Father Hoto's words. This was it. From here, there was no going back. At the end of the ceremony, Father Hoto would tie the sash around my waist, and there it would remain for seven days, after which the rite would be complete and my husband would untie it with his own hands. It was tradition, just like the colour. White to mark the virgin bride. But it was not Kin's hands I knew, not his touch I remembered in the middle of the night. It was Katashi who came to me in the darkness of my tent, his naked body strong and heavy, musky and sweet. His hands on my hips, caressing, grasping, his warm breath stealing past my ear as he chuckled at my desire.

"Emperor Kin Ts'ai, first of your name, Lord Protector of the Kisian Empire," the priest said, shocking me from my reverie. "You may now speak your prayers."

Kin shifted, pulling crimson silk from beneath one knee so the skirt could spread neatly. It was the very same robe in which he had first asked me to marry him for the sake of Kisia, the very same robe I had wanted to spit on.

"I pray the gods hear my words," Kin said, his head bowed such that his neat topknot stood proud. "I, Kin Ts'ai, emperor of the imperial expanse of Kisia, pray for your blessing upon my marriage. This day, in your presence, I offer this bridal sash to Lady

Hana Aura Otako. Its knot is tied to mend what is broken, and to bring peace to Kisia. This woman I take in good faith and honour, and will protect as my own blood from this day until death."

I shivered as Kin's voice faded from the air.

"Lady Hana," Father Hoto said. "First and only daughter of Emperor Lan Otako, you may now speak your prayer."

The soldiers continued to shift bodies as quietly as they could, and I tried not to think about it, tried to breathe evenly as I spread my own skirt with shaking hands. The robe had been procured from Mei'lian especially for the occasion—pale pink and embroidered with shimmering gold threads that caught on my dry fingers.

Beside me, the ghost of Katashi edged closer through the stink of death. It ought to have been him kneeling on the other side of the altar, his single dimple peeping beside his lopsided smile.

I swallowed a lump in my throat.

"I, Lady Hana Aura Otako, first and only daughter of His Majesty the Great Emperor Lan Otako, kneel now before the gods in acceptance. In humility, I beg to be found worthy of such honour and will serve my duties with patience and fortitude."

We had fought over the words. They were traditional, like the sash and the ceremony, and as much as he had assured me equal power under the law, such changes could not be made while we were in the midst of a civil war. Therefore, as Kin's empress I would have a position of power, but as his wife I was expected to be submissive.

"You may rise."

Kin did so easily, so used to the great skirt of his robe that he neither stepped on it nor had to kick it out of the way. It wore him as naturally as he wore it.

Mine was more awkward, and Father Hoto held out a helping hand. I did not take it, just stared at the soft wrinkles criss-crossing every finger. The hand was withdrawn, and I got to my feet, standing tall and proud while Father Hoto took up the sash. Chanting another prayer to Lunyia, he passed the white silk around my waist. It tightened, as Katashi's hold had tightened, his hands skimming my naked skin like a sculptor appreciating form.

At my belly, the old man's hands moved quickly, tying the knot a woman only wore once in her life. It was commonly called the Chastity Knot, a complex little flower with long tails, famous for the difficulty of untying it. There was a trick to it, I had heard, a simple tug in the right place and it would unravel, but there were many stories of husbands left to struggle by wives who feared consummation, and I wondered if when it came to it, I would be one of them. Kin was not Katashi.

Father Hoto let the tails fall and stepped back to appreciate his handiwork. The story would be altered of course, cleaned of bloodshed, but soon every nobleman in Kisia would want his prospective bride gift-wrapped by the hands that had tied Lady Hana for their emperor.

"Under the divine gaze of the great goddess Lunyia," he said. "And in the presence of all those gathered tonight, I declare that after the sevenday, the marriage between Emperor Kin Ts'ai, first of his name, and Lady Hana Aura Otako, only daughter of the late Emperor Lan Otako, will be complete. Long live Emperor Kin."

Amid blood and lifeless flesh, the circle of guards bowed, a military witness to a marriage made in war. "Long live Emperor Kin."

2. ENDYMION

The camp was little more than an untidy jumble of tents and makeshift shacks. Dogs roamed and horses tugged at tufts of whippy grass, but the people sat sagged and silent in the evening heat. They were an ill-assorted bunch—scrawny children, wiry women, and silent clutches of men, some in robes and others in tunics, rank and wealth disappearing beneath a layer of dust and sweat.

Kaze's hooves crunched upon the track, the only sound competing with the cicadas' chorus. A man, clean-shaven despite his makeshift home, stood to greet me.

"Welcome, traveller," he said, approaching warily as Kaze slowed. "Where do you come from?"

"From Esvar," I said.

"You're a long way from home." Suspicion sloughed off him like flakes of dry skin.

"I'm looking for someone."

"We've all lost people in the war, but if we can help, we will."

Help you on your way. The last man we welcomed stole half our food.

Which had left these men, nobles and peasants together, to go in search of more. They had hunted animals on the edge of the Fen, scrounged in bushes, and picked over the charred remains of villages—anything to ensure survival.

His thoughts were as clear as memories, and I knew without touch that he was worthy of life.

"I'm looking for a young woman," I said. "She's short with curly dark hair. I think she came this way a few days ago. Travelling alone, probably on horseback."

Kimiko. The touch of her whispers lingered upon the air. I had been following her for more than a week, ever since I had discovered Parsimony and Enmity dead.

"No, I can't say that I have." The man wasn't lying but I could feel her, slipping from my grip like a ghost.

With a nod of thanks, I continued on my way. The occupants of the small camp watched me go, their thoughts chasing me out of sight.

Once the scent of their souls faded, I let my Empathy range, but Kimiko was elusive. Her whispers were there and gone in flashes, no sooner caught than they slipped free.

One million three hundred and seventeen thousand and seven. Four thousand five hundred and ninety-four. My mind would not be still. Two Empaths. Twenty-six Vices. The numbers came quicker than ever, each a truth about the world that lived beneath my tongue. And they would keep coming if I let them, keep clawing at my attention. Sixty-four. Seven. Five hundred and eighty-two. That was Risian, close enough to taste. One hundred and five. Sixteen. Two. In Kogahaera, six thousand two hundred and twelve, while Shimai, the smaller of Kisia's sister cities, dragged on my mind with its vast weight. One hundred and twenty-six thousand and eleven.

I must have known silence once.

One million three hundred and seventeen thousand and six.

With a pained cry, I wrenched myself back, dragging my Empathy across the world like a heavy anchor. "No," I said. "Not yet. Not yet."

Anxiety prickled the back of my neck. A horse appeared on the track ahead, its drooping head emerging from a stand of straw pines edged in gold.

Kaze twitched.

"Just a priest," I said as a cart followed, its wooden panels brightly coloured. I signed to him using the old merchant language the priesthood, and then Katashi, had adopted, but the man shook his head.

"Where are you travelling to, Brother?" I called instead as he came within earshot.

"To Giana," the priest called back. "The smart man is one getting out of the Tzitzi Valley, eh?"

Kaze continued toward the priest's weighty draught horse. "One might say you're late in making good your escape," I said. "We have been at war for weeks."

"Nearer two months. But when one has duties..."

He trailed off as loose thoughts leaked from his mind, leaping the gap between us like a spark.

She had been alone.

A girl. A peasant girl with her short robe ripped at the shoulder, sobbing as she ran along the road, a village behind her ablaze in the dark. She had clutched her stricken clothing and begged for help, a broken sandal askew on her foot.

I helped! I let her hide in my wagon. I let her wash. I fed her. I dressed her. I offered to take her with me to the next town. She was so grateful.

And from the darkness, a groan and a thick huff of breath. A whimper. A cry.

Oh, Wrent, what have you done?

Kaze drew alongside the carthorse. "Wrent?"

The wagon clunked to an abrupt halt. "How do you know my name?"

"You just told me." Kaze stopped, his hooves crunching on the loose stones. "And what was the girl's name?"

"What girl?"

"The one who cried with you inside her."

Wrent's lined face drained of all colour. "How do you know? Who told you?"

"You did," I said again. "You had best be careful, Wrent. Even in wartime, a priest needs his reputation. A coin for my silence?"

He did not look away, but edged his hand slowly toward his belt pouch.

"Have you seen another young woman in your travels?" I said. "Short, with a mess of dark curls, likely dressed in dark clothes and riding?"

The priest held out the coin. "Yes." His hand shook. "I've seen her. A few days ago on the road. And she asked if I had seen a strange young man, plain-faced and riding a docile animal without a saddle."

He glanced down at Kaze. "When I said I had not, she warned me to keep away from him if I did meet him." He twitched the coin. "Take it!" he said. "Take it and leave me be, by the gods."

"I am a god," I said, and took his hand. For an instant, the memory of Kimiko was there, her eyes ringed with fatigue and her dark clothes covered in dust from the road.

Well if you do meet him, keep away, she had said. But she had not known he deserved death.

Justice poured into the man's veins. His heart hammered. Hard. Too hard. His hand jerked out of mine, and the coin fell into the mud as he slumped back against the wagon. Reins dropped from his hands.

Two hundred and twenty-seven. Days and weeks were a distant memory, but I could always count souls.

"Walk on," I said, nudging Kaze with my heel. The colourful wagon remained where it was as we passed, and I once again let out my Empathy, always hunting the same target. But now as I looked for her, I knew she was looking for me.

————————◆►

The first rains fell as I stopped that evening to let Kaze rest at the edge of Nivi Fen. Storm clouds had been threatening all day, only to burst all at once like the emptying of a bucket. One moment I had been damp with sweat, the next rivers of rain ran down my face.

I sought shelter in the darkening trees, but the dense canopy seemed merely to condense the rain into fatter drops. The heavy patter cut Kisia's whispers.

Shit! That's another sack ripped. If I don't get this rice under cover, it will never dry.

Already soaked to the skin and it's only the first of the season.

I'll never make it now!

A warm snort of air brushed my cheek. "I know," I said, patting Kaze absently. "I'll find you a warm stable soon. And an apple."

Another snort, harder this time.

"All right," I said. "Two apples."

Mollified, Kaze nuzzled my ear. Joined by touch, his acute senses fed into my thoughts and I could feel the weight of the storm and smell the changing season. The sounds of the forest were like a town crier to his ears, the trees a great city so fortunate as to be devoid of human life.

Another smell joined the already dense soup. One he had no word for, but I knew well—the smell of his drug clung to Malice like a misty cape.

My Empathy sped in its direction, battered on all sides by disconnected emotions. Pikes and soldiers burst upon my awareness, their whispers coming thick and fast—all noise and no sense. Single words leapt out but they meant nothing—*tent, storm, shit, gods, whore, sick*. It was a lethargic soup, impatient and angry, the Vices alone beacons of comparative peace in the mire. I could sense them more clearly than the rest, as though their signatures were carved upon my mind. Ire. Hope. Avarice.

To nook vaest a toii.

Even his whispers growled.

And there was Darius, Errant consuming his thoughts. A dozen moves hung at the forefront of his mind: counters and options, plays to the gate, calculations, and a string of percentages for the chance that each of his opponent's pieces was their king. Unable to pull myself away, I listened to his dancing whispers, each one pulling up memories of an old game.

He doesn't like to lose men; that's his weakness. Surround him with opponents and he has already lost.

It all came at once. Like the strands of a spider's web, thoughts and memories connected—from Errant to Esvar, from Esvar to our father, to the night a frail boy had become a man in the storm. It was hard to hold on to them, hard to see more than a frame of time as his thoughts spun on. Errant. A smiling Avarice turning a king. The frightened whinny of a horse as it reared. Water flooding the wisteria court, its surface dusted with rotting petals.

My mind began to strain.

Malice kneeling at his feet. The touch of his lips. The warmth of his breath as he whispered in Darius's ear. So many words. Two hundred and thirty-nine days of the Spider's words while Darius had been confined to the silence of Maturation.

My grip weakened. Errant again. Two hundred and eighty-four games against Avarice, three hundred and nine against Malice, fifty-six with Emperor Kin, two with Kimiko, eight with me, eight with Katashi, and one thousand and fifty-nine competition matches played against different opponents, each one beginning with a single gold coin in the palm of his hand, baiting skin.

I snapped back to my own head. For a disorientating moment, everything was wrong. I was no longer crouching but flat in the mud, every muscle a string of aching knots. Steel pricked my throat.

"Good evening, Endymion."

"Good evening, Kimiko," I said, painfully aware of the bony

knees cutting off circulation to my hands. Nearby, Kaze snorted, the muddy ground muting the sound of his hooves as he stamped in place.

"I have no fire and no lantern," I said, the forming of words lifting my throat into the knife blade. It was only a nick, but I pressed myself lower into the mud. "How did you find me?"

"A man with a horse can never hide." Kimiko adjusted her weight, digging her knees harder into the crooks of my elbows. A lantern sat upon the ground, lighting her from beneath. "I've been waiting for you. I was starting to think you might have changed your mind about them."

"No, but I was trying to find you before I came here. I need your help if I'm going to have any chance at saving him."

She pressed the blade deeper, and her fingers brushed my neck. Connection flared.

Darius. His name on her tongue and his face in her thoughts. His smell. His touch. The memory was so real, the feel of his skin against hers so tangible it might have been mine he touched. Flesh and blood, he stood before me in the long gallery at Esvar while sunlight warmed the portraits of our family. There his mother, Lady Melia Laroth, her eyes the same as his, her lips, her nose, everything but the expression. *I've never told anyone else about her*, Darius told Kimiko. *I've never told anyone else how much I needed her.*

Kimiko threw herself off me and scrambled, doglike, into the shadows. "What did you just do?" she said, her knife hand shaking. "Were you just inside my head? I was thinking about... I don't know, I don't know what I was thinking about, but it was important and now it's gone."

"You were thinking about Darius's mother."

She blinked rapidly. "Why would I be thinking about that? He never talked about her."

In my head, Darius was staring out the window. *She understood me*, he was saying. *She knew me. Better even than Malice. I wish you could have met her.*

"You're not all there, are you?" Kimiko said, stepping back into the light as her panic gave way to curiosity. I tried to focus on it, on her, but my Sight kept slipping.

Can't stand these stinking fens much longer.

Careful.

I'm going out with the next skirmish whether they name me or not. I can't sit still another day in this wretched place.

Kimiko hadn't moved. She looked to be waiting. "Did you say something?" I said, pushing myself into a sitting position. I was covered in mud but it hardly seemed important.

"I asked if you were all right," she replied. "You look sick. And to think I was worried you'd harm Darius. You can't even focus."

"Darius," I said. "That's why I came. That's why I've been looking for you. You can help me save him."

Kimiko regarded me solemnly. Lit by the lantern at her feet, the rain fell around her like gold. "And I was looking for you," she said. "Because I cannot save a man if he does not want to be saved."

"But you can kill men who don't deserve to die?"

Her eyes narrowed but she did not answer.

I struggled to my feet, every muscle aching with a fatigue like I had never known. "Parsimony and Enmity were unwilling tools of Malice," I said. "They were forced into obedience. You should know that."

"I do know that, but they are dangerous, and every Vice I hunt down leaves Malice with fewer weapons. You want to save them all then kill Malice."

"That's exactly what I plan to do. The world must be put right. Justice must be done."

Her arm shot out, and I was looking right at the tip of her blade. "Yes, but that's what I was afraid of," she said. "I've seen your justice. If that's the way you save people, then keep away from Darius.

I will kill you if you touch him, Endymion, don't think I won't. If he dies, it will be by my hand and my hand alone."

" 'That is all we need, another Otako clogging the drain.' "

She froze, nothing but the rain marking time. "I said that, didn't I?"

"Yes."

"I meant it. But you're not really an Otako, are you?"

"No, I'm a Laroth, and so is that child you're carrying."

She held my gaze while a blooming myriad of emotions thickened the air. Fierce joy. Deep fear. Horror. Hope. "Child," she said. "How do you know?"

"You have two heartbeats. What other reason can there be?"

Slowly, she let her arm fall, removing the knife from my vision. She thrust it into her sash. "I've said what I came here to say," she said, snatching up the covered lantern. "Darius is mine. Leave him alone or I will hunt you down and skin you."

Illuminated from below, there was something wraithlike about the dark circles under her eyes. I stared instead of speaking as though the words were too heavy, too hard.

There was a child.

Kimiko strode to where her horse stood in company with Kaze, their manes dripping. There she paused and looked back, her hovering hand kissed by raindrops. "It is not I who made him what he is," she said. "If you want to save him, then Malice has to go. I can't get close enough, but you—"

"Tell him about the child."

"No!" She almost screamed the word. "Gods help me, no, how stupid do you think I am? I hate to think what Darius would do if he found out while in this state, let alone Malice. If I carry a child, I want it to live, Endymion, not be cut from my bleeding belly like a diseased rat. No. If you will not do the only thing that can bring him back, then at least give me your word you will not betray me. Darius will know when I can trust him with the truth and not a moment before."

"And if that day never comes?"

You would have liked her and she would have liked you. Darius's hand was on my back, tracing lines across my robe as he went on staring out the window. Long-dead Laroths watched on in silence.

How did she die?

A pause.

Childbirth.

A child. And down in the camp, Darius played on, heedless of the new life that would soon make itself felt in the whispers.

"What was that?" Kimiko took a step from her horse, an ear lifted to the rain.

I didn't need to hear, didn't even need to close my eyes—the knowledge was just there. "Ire and Hope are coming this way."

"Where?"

I pointed, and crouching low, she slunk away in the direction I had indicated. "Kimiko!" I hissed, but she just waved a hand and disappeared into the shadowy trees, leaving her lantern lighting our little clearing.

Knowing too well what was in her mind, I hurried after her. Katashi's camp was far enough away that the lantern was soon lost to the buckled terrain that circled Nivi Fen like rumpled silk around a bowl, but I didn't need light to see my route. I followed the call of their souls until a second light appeared through the trees. And there was Kimiko, her whispers a rope to which I could tether.

"Kimiko, you—"

"Shh!"

She gripped my sleeve and dragged me down into the damp undergrowth as footsteps melded with the rain and a lantern drew closer. Hope and Ire appeared behind it as little more than shapes in the storm-filled night, winding their way through the trees. If they maintained their current course, they would walk right by us, but no sooner had Kimiko drawn her dagger than the pair stopped.

Ire, easily the tallest of the pair, set the lantern down upon the ground and turned to look at Hope. A tense moment stretched.

Kimiko looked at me. "What are they—?"

I could hardly tell who moved first, perhaps they stepped in as one, all awkwardness crushed beneath a sudden flare of desire. Hope gripped Ire's tunic as he was pushed back against a nearby tree, a grunt of mingled pain and lust all the sound he could manage with their lips pressed into a ferocious kiss. For a moment, their joint desire burned like a flame, a pang of jealousy the only other emotion I could sense, until Kimiko's intent cut through it like her blade and she crept a step closer.

"No, stop, wait."

"Why? You want me to wait until they've fucked first?"

"No, I don't want you to kill them at all. I know you're angry, I know you think Malice will be easier to reach without any Vices to protect him, but you're wrong. He'll be hard to kill either way, and you'll have sacrificed the lives of innocents for nothing."

Her jaw dropped. "Innocents? Have you seen the things those men can do? The things they have done?"

"The things Malice made them do. You didn't want to steal the crown from Katashi, but you did. Remember that pain you felt when Malice made you get us into Koi? Now think about how conditioned to obey you would be if you felt it all the time."

Kimiko looked away. "That doesn't change what they're capable of. That doesn't change how dangerous they are. Just stay out of this if you don't like it."

She moved too quickly for me to grab her arm, and I ran after her. "No!"

My shout was louder than I had meant, but Hope and Ire barely had time to turn before she burst from the undergrowth into their lantern light. In a scramble of loose breeches, neither of them had a chance of defending themselves, and I threw all the emotions I had at Kimiko as she lunged. She cried out. Her feet tangled, and with all too much forward momentum, she went over like a tree and would have slammed hard into the ground had Ire not caught her.

"What the fuck are you two doing here?" he said, yanking the blade from Kimiko's hand and throwing it into the trees. She tried to pull free of his hold but, as though dizzy, fell back on her arse and stayed there, head between her knees in the mud. Ire turned his scowl on me. "I mean apart from trying to stab me in the neck."

"I wasn't trying to stab anyone," I said.

"Because you don't need to." Ire gestured at Kimiko as she retched, arms over her head. "The shit you can do is worse than getting knifed."

"Like you can talk!" I snapped before I could stop myself.

Hope stood silent, exuding as much defiant rage as embarrassment and refusing to look at me as he retied his breeches.

"I'm not here for you though," I said to Ire. "I'm here to kill Malice. And if I can't save Darius, to kill him too." I looked down at Kimiko as I spoke, but even if she heard me, she went on trying to calm the panic I had induced with long breaths. "And then I'll kill myself."

Hope stared at me then, and I wished the words unsaid so he would look away, the intensity of his gaze making my stomach twist. "Why?" he said.

When I didn't answer, Ire folded his arms. "You know the master would be very interested to know you're lurking around planning to kill him. Give me one reason I shouldn't tell him you're here."

"Because if I kill him, you'll be free."

"You can't. I've tried." Hope's quiet voice had a fierce way of cutting through every other sound. Even the rumble of approaching thunder could not dampen it.

"You what?" Ire turned on him, but though Hope looked up at him with a grimace, it was to me he spoke.

"Oh, I've tried at least a dozen times. Always when he's asleep or so out of it on his opium he wouldn't even notice. I've tried with a blade, with a pillow, with my bare hands, but even though he's not conscious to order me not to, the pain is like nothing I've ever felt, as though it's killing me even as I kill him. I . . ." He looked down at the muddy ground while the rain fell around us. "I always get to the point where I'm sure I'm about to die and just . . . can't do it and stop. Though all it takes is another few weeks of living like this for me to think dying wouldn't be so bad, and I try again."

He glanced again at Ire, only to fold his arms and glare at me. "My point being, it's impossible to do when you're marked and probably if you have ever been marked. You're better off just leaving and fast, because I don't have any more scars to give to keep you safe."

"Malice hurt you for letting me escape that outpost?"

"What do you think?"

Kimiko groaned and tried to get to her feet, only to fall back again with a hissed string of swear words.

"You should go," I said. "In case she's still feeling murderous when it wears off."

Ire laughed. "Very nice. You come screaming in here ruining our moment and trying to kill us, and now *we* have to leave."

Hope gripped his arm. "Let's just go. I'd rather not be here if the Master finds out they've come. Not with the mood he's been in."

Ire grimaced, and I envied them their moment of understanding— Hope's hand still on Ire's arm as he shrugged and turned away. "Good luck with all the killing." He picked up the lantern, and together they walked off through the rain, their heads slightly tilted toward one another in low-voiced conversation. Ire glanced back to be sure we weren't following, but it was the back of Hope's head at which I stared. He didn't turn, and soon the night and the storm swallowed them, leaving Kimiko and I in darkness.

"Are you all right?" I said, crouching beside her.

"No, that was awful. What the fuck did you hit me with?"

"I don't know, whatever I had."

She was little more than an outline in the gloom. "Whatever you had? Then why don't you run after him and tell him how you feel?"

"What?"

Kimiko laughed, and it was a shrill, almost cruel sound amid the patter of fat raindrops. "For an Empath, you're really bad at the emotions thing. So what's the plan? You follow me around and stop me killing Vices from now on?"

"No. The plan is to save Darius if we can, and to kill them both if we can't. And if I...go...you have to promise to kill me too. This is going to be a lot easier if we work together, don't you think?"

"Unfortunately. But I meant what I said about Darius. And Katashi. If they have to die, then they do so by my hand, do you understand?"

Her glare cut through the darkness and into my skin, and though I doubted she could do either, I said, "Yes. Now, how do we save Darius?"

3. DARIUS

The headache came on suddenly, its pressure that of another mind trying to squeeze into a space too small for two.

Endymion was back.

A piece dropped from my fingers. It hit the wooden board with a heavy thud and rolled onto the floor. Across the table, Katashi lifted his brows. "Ill, Master?" he mocked.

"Hardly."

Katashi placed the piece carefully back onto the Errant board. "I am more than happy to stop playing," he said. "You know I hate this game."

"Because you're bad at it," I said, moving the piece to where I had intended with a snap. "And that is why we play."

"Or perhaps I hate it because it's a waste of time when we could just discuss plans over a bowl of wine and be done."

Last time Endymion had just skimmed surface thoughts, but now he dug with the talons of a bloodthirsty hawk. He was getting stronger. I curled my fingers into my palms, but only the left hand moved, the right no longer there.

The pressure headache ceased abruptly, leaving behind the patter of rain on the wagon roof and the stink of charred cloth coming from across the table.

"You know it would be easier to kill him."

My head jerked up. "To kill who?"

"Your delightful brother." Katashi tapped the side of his head. "Just because I detest your stupid game does not mean that *I* am stupid."

He moved a piece.

"It must," I said. "Else you would not so quickly suggest ending Endymion's life. If you sacrifice a piece early, you inevitably need it by the end."

"How poetic." His strong features creased into ugly lines.

"The feeling is mutual," I said, eyeing his sneering countenance. "I loathe you quite as much as you loathe me. But why don't we pretend for a moment that it is not so. Call it novelty. How went the mission in Risian?"

"Bloody."

"Such is the nature of war."

He moved his next piece with an angry snap and turned one of mine. "I know. It was a small force, as you said, and they weren't expecting an attack."

"No," I agreed. "Risian is old ground now. Who goes back to fight over old ground?" I shifted a piece back across the board to recapture the lost soldier, white for black.

"You, it would seem, Minister."

"Me indeed," I said with a mock bow over the board. "Because I understand the importance of every single piece."

He didn't answer, just moved another piece, boredom evident in the way he sat, his hand flopped negligently off the table. I could not be so relaxed. Though it took little mental acuity to best him at Errant, it took almost all my concentration to move the pieces with my left hand as gracefully as I had once done with my right. Too often did I reach for a piece with an absent hand. And every time, Katashi just watched. I could hardly blame him for his lack of sympathy, but it did nothing to curb the anger that bubbled under my skin.

"A good Errant player," I went on, "plans as many moves ahead as they can."

He gave me the look of a man who could put six arrows through my chest without blinking. "That only works if you know what your opponent is going to do, *Empath*."

"I am not Endymion. I read emotions, not thoughts, and then only from those in close proximity. It has nothing to do with knowing what the enemy will do and everything to do with making them do what you want them to. If designed properly, one plan is all you ever need."

Katashi's stare lingered, a little smile twisting the corners of his lips. "One plan? Like the one plan that almost got you killed? You're very sure of yourself for a man who got tricked by my sister."

Again and again she had apologised as I lost the ability to speak and move and keep myself awake. I had long since forgiven her, but to admit that to anyone would mean explaining why I was still here, explaining what Kin had done. That for five years, I had worked in service of the very man who had thrown the empire into its first civil war by ordering the assassination of Emperor Lan, and worse than all—that I hadn't even suspected.

"We will leave Kimiko out of this, don't you think?"

He slammed his fist on the table. Pieces jumped and rolled off the board, and my heart leapt into my throat.

"What I think is that you're a snarky cunt and I don't trust you," Katashi said. "I'll tell you what the one plan is, oh minister of mine. It's me sitting on the Crimson Throne in Mei'lian with Kin's severed head in my lap, and if you try anything clever to protect him, you will find yourself travelling back to Esvar in tiny pieces. I might not be able to harm you, but there are plenty of men who would gladly do it for me."

I forced a smile though I seethed. "I have no intention of helping him in any fashion, *Your Majesty*. Your play."

Katashi stood with a creak of leathers and a swirl of his silken surcoat. "No. I'm done. I'm done with you. I'm done with this. Find someone else to torture with your waste-of-time game."

He strode toward the door, his heavy tread causing the wagon to groan.

"You ought to finish what you start, Your Majesty," I said over the rapid pounding of my heart. "We are not done." I moved a piece and turned one of his, revealing a blackened crown on the white face. My lead."

His fists clenched and unclenched, and he spun back, unable to leave yet unwilling to stay. I had misread him. With every day, Katashi's moods were getting harder to predict. Malice had always been a dangerous dog, but I knew how to bring him back to heel, his longing only ever for me.

Katashi remained smouldering in the doorway, real heat coursing off him. "Let me go."

I held his stare, my jaw beginning to ache from gritting my teeth. "No. You will remain when I tell you to remain."

"To punish who? Me or yourself?"

I could not keep the surprise from registering on my face, and his snarl broke into an abrupt laugh. "Still you think me a fool. You say you hate me, but really the only person you hate is you."

The nails of my left hand dug into my silk-clad thigh, the truth of his words a whip to raw flesh. "You see that because it is a mirror of yourself, Otako. I felt you fighting me. I was weak that night, half-dead with fatigue and blood loss, and it would not have taken much to resist my mark, but no. You gave in because there has only ever been one thing you truly want. I didn't make you Vengeance. You did."

His fury returned, his face as red as his crimson surcoat. "And Kin made me that." He jabbed a finger at me. "Your Kin. When this is over, I will take great joy in killing you, *Master*. That is a promise."

"I look forward to seeing you try." The words came out clipped and angry, the sort of anger that fuelled the soul. "But I think you overestimate your men. Your Pikes are getting edgy, not to mention the trio of generals who command half your force. And what happened to that last shipment of food?"

The hit registered on his face. While no ally had yet withdrawn their support from his cause, they were getting jittery and tight-lipped. Excuses, half-filled promises, even the incoming supplies dwindled day by day as talk about him spread fear.

Katashi strode back and slammed his hand down on the Errant board again, scattering the remaining pieces. "You get off on power, don't you, Laroth?" Smoke rose from his splayed fingers. "You like playing puppet master and pulling our strings so we dance." He lifted his hand, leaving a charred handprint cutting through the white and brown squares. "One day I will burn that self-satisfied smile from your face."

Fury blazed through my veins, his anger feeding mine. "Try it," I growled.

Waves of heat obscured everything behind him, and his fingers flexed, but he could not move, could not raise a hand to me while my mark remained upon him.

"You are my Vice, *Vengeance*, and you will do as I command. Sit. Down."

Katashi's glare lingered longer than due respect allowed, before he made a flourishing bow, his hatred directed at me like daggers. "As you command, *Master*."

He knelt back down across the table and brushed aside the destroyed remains of our game. "Lead away."

A heavy knock rattled the door. "Come," I said, and the door swung to reveal two figures rain-drenched upon the threshold. Avarice pushed in first.

"Master," he said, bowing only to me. "One of the patrols has caught a scout."

His companion was one of Katashi's men. "Your Majesty," he said, out of breath and with water dripping down his face. "We have caught one of Emperor Kin's scouts, although he claims to be only a messenger."

"The Usurper is sending me notes now?" Katashi laughed

harshly. "If only he would plead for mercy or give himself up, that would be fun."

Avarice didn't have to speak again. I knew him well enough to read him.

"I will see this messenger," I said, rising from my place.

A scowl slammed down upon Katashi's features, but though his displeasure was palpable, he said nothing. His man watched, but Vengeance was not foolish enough to risk another battle of wills now we had an audience. With a grunt, he strode from the wagon.

The storm had grown heavier while we played and now drowned the noise of Pikes, traitors, and Vices alike. Lanterns flickered here and there upon the plain, and a few fires had survived beneath protective squares of canvas, but for the most part the camp was dead. Servants had once carried an awning to protect Minister Laroth from the rain, and fresh sandals in case an errant puddle caught me by surprise, but here there was just the rain, delighting in the instant saturation of my robe.

Avarice fell into step beside me. "The messenger was travelling north-west, Master," he said, his voice low. "Following the road but not on it."

"That was to be expected."

"Yes, Master, and your other prediction has proven true. Conceit left this afternoon and has not yet returned. It is not being talked of."

"Oh good," I said. "It is always nice to be right."

"Yes, Master. Are you sure you don't want me to—"

"No. Let Malice make his mischief if it keeps him happy."

"Yes, Master."

Katashi and his man walked ahead of us with a covered lantern leading the way. At the edge of the camp, a knot of soldiers had gathered around a tree, dark figures upon a dark night. Laughter hung in the air, laced with cruelty. The men parted for Katashi and might have closed ranks behind him but for Avarice. He followed, glaring, daring them to shut us out, and the soldiers fell back grumbling. A man was chained to the rough tree trunk, his clothing the uniform of a military messenger and his face familiar. The man who had come to Esvar with the message that Emperor Kin wanted me back.

"A Ts'ai messenger," Katashi said, crossing his arms as he halted before the man. "What fine gifts the Usurper does send. I guess he loves me after all."

The soldiers sniggered, but in the light of covered lanterns, the messenger set his jaw mulishly.

"Why," Katashi began with mocking sweetness, "don't you tell us where you were going."

The man spat, or tried to spit, but his mouth was too dry. It got the message across, however, and Katashi laughed at the man's fear-laced loyalty. "Oh good," he said. "I was worried you might not make this fun."

Katashi took his bow from his back and brandished it in the man's face. "You know what this is?"

The messenger blinked raindrops out of his eyes. "A bow."

"No, *my* bow." Katashi drew an arrow slowly and took a few steps back. "You have perhaps heard of my skill."

More sniggering, and the soldiers spread as Katashi took more steps back, ready for a show.

"Now, you tell me where you were going and what message you were carrying, or I will prove just how good I am even in this rain."

As Katashi backed past me, he flung me a challenging look. I held his gaze but said nothing. If I knew anything of Kin's messengers, it was that Katashi's physical methods of questioning would get him nowhere.

Vengeance nocked his arrow and took aim despite the insistent rain. "Do you have something you want to tell me?" he asked, looking at the messenger along the length of his arrow.

No spit this time, just a short sharp "No."

"Where shall I aim for, boys?"

The soldiers all shouted.

"Left shoulder!"

"Kneecap!"

"Left earlobe!"

"Third toe on the right foot!"

The Pikes had played this game before.

"Pinky finger!"

This last was met with much amusement, given the man had his arms tied behind him, bent painfully around the tree.

"Third toe on the right foot," Katashi repeated. "That sounds like a good place to start. Are you sure you wouldn't like to enlighten us?"

Kin's man said nothing.

"Very well."

There wasn't even a pause. The string juddered. A sharp yelp of pain punctuated the night, but it did not last. The man clamped his mouth shut and breathed quickly, snorting through his nose while resolutely not looking down. The arrow had not only gone through the third toe of his right foot, but also through his sandal and into a tree root, pinning his foot to the ground in a mess of blood.

The Pikes crowed.

"Well?" Katashi said. "Where were you going?"

Kin's man kept his lips pressed shut.

"Kneecap! Kneecap!"

Katashi took aim amid the noise. Again no pause for drama. Bone cracked. Blood oozed around the arrowhead, and the fevered breathing of the messenger grew faster and fiercer. But he did not look down. He did not speak.

While the Pikes called out their next suggestions, Avarice leant down and spoke in my ear. "He might kill him before he breaks, Master," he said gruffly.

"I'm sure of it," I said.

"Are you going to let him?"

"I think not, but as with Malice, it is always best to let Katashi make his mischief."

Avarice grunted.

An arrow buried itself in the messenger's left shoulder. Katashi licked his lips, his eyes bright. In a circle around him, his soldiers bayed for blood.

"Left ankle!"

"Elbow!

"In the cock!"

The bowstring stretched as Katashi drew with ease.

"You have not asked if he is ready to give information yet," I said.

Katashi's eyes darted to me.

"Perhaps," I added, "you would let me ask."

It was not a suggestion and he knew it, but his blood was up. Looking at me, he let go the string.

This time, the man screamed. I gritted my teeth against the pain I could no longer ignore. Parts of my body throbbed in the way healthy limbs ought not. Now the pain of mangled flesh hung between my legs. Blood poured onto the man's riding breeches, making dark fabric darker. Thuds punctuated his screams as he slammed his head back against the tree trunk again and again.

All around us, soldiers were laughing, caught in the reinforcing spiral of their own madness.

"Be my guest, Minister," Katashi said, indicating the maimed man. "What can I say? A drawn bow must always be loosed."

I entered the circle like a player upon a stage. "I have but a few questions," I said. "Before His Majesty continues his game."

The soldiers stopped cheering and watched, some curious, others outraged by the interruption.

"I think perhaps you might remember me," I said, approaching the stricken messenger. I did not expect him to look at me and nor did he. The crack of his skull hitting the tree trunk was sickening.

"My name is Lord Darius Laroth. I was Emperor Kin's minister of the left and am now chief advisor to Emperor Katashi Otako." The rain was washing away some of his blood but none of his fear, none of his pain. "I admire your fortitude, but I have a very simple question. One you can safely answer without painful coercion. Has Emperor Kin been drinking?"

A whimper was the only reply.

"Yes, indeed," I agreed. "But I know how quickly news of Kin's mood spreads through the upper echelons, so do not lie and say you don't know."

Again no response.

"You think you're not going to talk to me, but I can guarantee you will," I said. "Because unlike Emperor Katashi, I am not going to cause you any more pain. I am, in fact, the only person here capable of taking it away."

I touched his wet cheek with the tip of one finger, and his pain flowed thick and fast into my body. I threw off as much as I could, casting it to the air like so much dross, but every second I kept it up was more tiring than a mountain sprint.

I drew my hand away, and the man leant his head forward, hunting my touch as pain returned to his broken body.

"Now," I said. "You have something to say?"

All was silent around us, no sound but the patter of rain upon leaves. "Yes," the man gasped.

"Excellent choice." I touched his cheek again, and ecstasy shuddered through him at the cessation of pain. I breathed deeply.

"I was on my way to Koi," the man said, licking his dry lips. "To announce the marriage of Emperor Kin to Lady Hana Otako."

"What?" Katashi's heat bloomed beside me. "What did you say?"

"That," I said, lifting my voice to be heard by our audience, "is old news. Let's try this again." My fingers hovered just above his skin. "You were on your way north to spread the felicitous news behind enemy lines, especially to the count of Suway. He hasn't declared for his emperor yet and that must gall, but with Hana at his side, he can claim a true right to the throne and turn the tide of support against Emperor Katashi. You see? I know this. That is not what I wanted to know."

The messenger stared at me, eyes begging.

"I want to know if Emperor Kin has been drinking."

"Yes," he said, each word a gasp. "Yes, he has."

I lowered my fingertips to his skin. A relieved sigh brushed his dry lips. "Thank you," he said deliriously as I shed his pain for him. "Thank you."

"No, thank you for your cooperation. I now know when Kin means to attack Risian."

His shock was confirmation if ever I had needed it, and he looked up into my face, eyes full of horror. I removed my touch, and his pain rushed back, wrenching a howl from his dry throat.

Katashi stood smouldering behind me, his soldiers silent watchers of my craft.

"You may finish the traitor in your own time, Your Majesty," I said, bowing to Vengeance. "And might I suggest sending more men to bolster the force at Risian. That will be Kin's next target."

Katashi gripped my arm as I made to walk away. "You said no one goes back to fight over old ground."

"It's not old ground once you've been goaded," I said. "And I doubt even Kin is aware that he drinks once he's made the decision to send men to their deaths."

"And on this circumstantial information I am to base my plans?"

"It is not circumstantial. My plans have worked for you so far, yes?"

I went to pull out of his grip but he tightened it. "You knew about Hana."

"Even a fool could have guessed they would take such a course. You are making a scene, Your Majesty. I suggest you finish off this messenger and let me deal with the plans for Risian."

I slid free of his hold and, with a bow, turned to walk away.

"You want Hana to marry your precious emperor," Katashi snarled as he followed, though nothing could more surely make his gathered soldiers stare.

I shot a look at Avarice walking beside me. "Put the messenger out of his misery and get rid of those soldiers before this gets ugly."

"Yes, Master, though they won't take kindly to orders from me."

"Can't be helped. Do it."

Avarice dropped back, his place taken by Katashi. Steam was rising from his wet clothing and he looked demonic in the faint lantern light. "Stop walking away from me, Laroth. You knew about this and you didn't tell me."

"Keep walking. If you want to have this conversation, then at least do it where no one is around to stare."

"You think I care who stares at me anymore? If you knew, we could have done something to stop it happening."

We had almost reached the tree line, were surely suffused in shadows now, but I flinched when he gripped my arm and made me turn. "Why would I stop them?" I said, meeting his fiery gaze.

"Because she adds to his legitimacy!"

"But he also adds to hers, yes?"

"I would rather burn the whole empire than let Kin have her," he seethed, more steam rising from his shoulders and his damp hair. "Hana is betrothed to me and she is mine." A tear sizzled on his cheeks, and he lunged at me, hands clenching and unclenching before my face as though seeking my throat. "I hate you. I hate you! You ruined everything! You—"

He crumpled as though struck from behind, leaving the last curls of steam to rise like ghosts. "Katashi?" I crouched in the wet grass and reached out a tentative hand to his, expecting heat but finding skin hard like stone. "Avarice! Avarice!" I shouted through the rain. "Come quickly!"

The Vice had all but dispersed Katashi's soldiers around the now-dead messenger, and he hurried over. "Master? Are you all right? What happened?"

"Look at this," I said. "He just collapsed. Feel his skin. Have you ever seen this happen to anyone else before?"

He had been travelling with Malice far longer, but shook his head. "No. He's breathing though, so he isn't dead. Shall I run for Hope?"

"Yes, yes, go, quickly. I need Katashi alive."

Avarice hurried off into the darkness, and again I touched Katashi's hand, trying to find a way in, but his skin was not skin anymore and I could not feel anything. "Damn it, you aren't allowed to get out of this that easily," I said while raindrops pattered around me. "You want Kin to suffer, then you have to stay with me."

Guilt ate at me while I waited. Vengeance had only won the night I marked him because it owned a whole lifetime of hurts, of painful memories and regrets, but perhaps even that might have been tempered in time by his love for Hana. The strength of it had shocked me, so completely did he own it without shame or embarrassment, his love strengthening him as much as his fury.

I did not doubt Hana returned his feelings, leaving guilt tearing at me all the more. But it was too late to change anything, too late to go back—even breaking my mark on him was unwise when he was capable of so much destruction.

We were both totally drenched by the time Avarice returned with Hope, the young man kneeling beside Katashi without so much as a nod of acknowledgement. He pressed his hand to Vengeance's forehead, and where I had been unable to make a connection, he did. No instant flare, no sudden awakening, but a comforting warmth bloomed that made Katashi's skin begin to soften.

"What is it?" I said when Hope went on sitting in silence, his hand upon Katashi's head.

"You mean what made him collapse like this?" Hope said, still not looking at me. "That would have been you almost burning him out, I imagine."

"He wasn't making fire when it happened."

Hope looked up then with a little sneer. "Oh, come on, like you don't know how this works. We're only able to use our abilities while we posses the emotions that make them happen. Take that emotion away and we can't do it." He gestured at Katashi with his free hand. "You can't make a Vice that lives that emotion to his core every moment and expect him to survive when you take it away."

"I did not take away his desire for vengeance."

"Maybe not. I'm not an Empath, but I can feel hopelessness when it chokes someone so completely they want to die."

I stared at the shadowy outline of Katashi's face and guilt clawed at me anew. "You mean I've killed him."

"Not this time," Hope said. "But you're going to have to be careful. Take away his reason for wanting vengeance and he'll be dead. Make him want death more than vengeance and he'll be dead. And Laroth?"

"What?"

Hope withdrew his hand as Katashi began to stir, letting out a groan like a man with a splitting headache waking from a hangover. "Even without those things happening, he's running out of time. Katashi is dying."

DAY TWO

4. HANA

Upon arrival back in Kogahaera, I wanted nothing but sleep. My saturated layers of clothing hung heavily off fatigued limbs, stinking of blood and sweat, but there was no time to wash, let alone rest.

By the time I slid from my horse, Kin had already sent someone to summon his council. They would wait for their emperor, wait even for the least important advisor, but not for me, not while my place on the council remained a mere formality. So I didn't even stop to change my clothes, just followed him to the stuffy meeting tent.

Only Master Yara was already present.

"My lady." The man recently promoted to the position of imperial secretary rose and bowed. "I have heard the gods smiled upon your prayers. They are wise indeed."

"Thank you, Master Yara, you are most kind," I said, touching the sash I could not bring myself to look at. "Smiled upon the prayers, perhaps, but not upon the journey."

"So I have also heard. Terrible that you had to witness such things."

"News travels fast, but I assure you I am no weakling to swoon at the sight of blood."

"I have always found women stronger than many believe. Any who doubt that ought to witness the birth of a child."

I gave him a short smile. I ought to have left it there, but fatigue had sharpened my irritation, and before I could think better of it, I snapped, "Indeed, we must be strong there, since bearing children is all a woman is good for." It was anger at the world rather than at him, and I regretted it immediately, but the words had been said and could not be retracted.

No doubt well used to ill tempers, Master Yara said no more. Emperor Kin might well have chastised me for it, but the smile he favoured me with as I joined him at the table was full of understanding, sympathy, and amusement—a husband's smile, so intimate that I flinched. My fingers found the bridal sash at my waist and my heart thumped its panic.

Rather than look at Kin again, I focussed on arranging the skirt of the ceremonial robe I had ridden back in, secrecy no longer important after all that had happened. By the time every crease had been smoothed, the rest of the councillors were beginning to gather, and I watched them bow first to their emperor and then to me, before taking their places at the table. There were a few generals, the local governor, the garrison commander and a handful of advisors, and General Ryoji, his ease and magnificence putting them all to shame.

Once all were gathered, Master Yara cleared his throat and unrolled a length of parchment. "The latest correspondence from General Jikuko is unchanged," he said by way of beginning. "He reports no movement in the Valley despite increasing his scouting range as per his last orders."

"Like the ruddy storm," grumbled General Rini on Kin's other side, he the second in command as Kin had yet to appoint a new minister of the left. "A skirmish here, a rumble there, always waiting for us to move before they strike."

One of the battalion boys backed into the tent carrying a tray of bowls. The councillors went on talking while the boy dispensed food, shuffling across the floor on his knees with his eyes downcast.

"Anything from General Yi?" Kin asked, and the sound of his voice beside me once more sent my hand to the bridal knot. Over and over, I had told myself it was the right thing to do, the only thing to do, but it made me ill to think what my younger self would have said about marrying the Usurper. And now it was done with no going back.

"There have been no riders from the east this morning, Your Majesty," Master Yara said, not glancing down as a bowl of shimmering soup was placed in front of him.

"And the search for Lady Kimiko?"

"Again, nothing, Your Majesty. Kisia has been quiet today."

General Rini cleared his throat. "Never a good sign."

"There are many more reports still coming in about the plague, however, Your Majesty," Councillor Gadokoi said in his always-calm tone. "It seems to be spreading faster than expected. A messenger arrived from Minister Bahain this morning to say he is being inundated in Mei'lian with reports of attacked carts and mule trains, impassable roads, thieves, bandits, and even border raids. It would appear that... Emperor Katashi and his soldiers are fuelling or allowing chaos to reign in the north, and it is more effectively cutting us off from trade than the war itself."

"And what does Minister Bahain recommend?" Kin said into the silence these grim words wrought.

"A speedy end to the conflict, Your Majesty."

A few mutters cut the silence as the serving boy placed the last bowl in front of me, before serving the rest of the food. A plate of fish fresh from the Nuord River, a dish of pickled carrots and ginger, shredded eggs, and sugared beans. It was Kin's standard fare, the simple food of an emperor who had never stopped being a soldier.

Whether it was because of this or to distract from Councillor Gadokoi's pronouncements, Kin scowled when the boy brought in a spit-roasted duck. "What is that?"

The boy attempted to bow and almost lost the duck onto the floor. "It's duck, Your Majesty," he said. "Captain Warrete caught it to celebrate your bridal prayers, Your Majesty."

"Damn right, we ought to have a toast," General Rini said as the boy lowered the duck onto the table, causing all the bowls to clatter. "War or not. Bring wine, boy. Long live Emperor Kin."

"Long live Emperor Kin," the council chorused as Rini began carving the duck. Watching him cut into the steaming hot meat made my stomach churn, and while consumption momentarily suspended conversation, I just sipped and watched, unable to look at the man beside me or the sash about my waist.

The serving boy came back with wine and a stack of bowls. Kin did not often allow wine at meetings, but he said nothing as the bowl was placed in front of him and filled. I picked mine up the moment it was full and drank half in one mouthful, though it only made my stomach swirl all the more sickeningly, and I set it down as soon as General Rini had made his toast to my marriage.

"Thank you, General," Kin said, himself taking a large mouthful of wine despite the early hour. "Do now continue with the meeting, Master Yara."

"Yes, Your Majesty." The man had barely glanced at his food. "The messengers all left in the night. To Lord Rastas, Lord Kirita, and the count of Suway, as well as another two spreading the news in the north."

"It is to be hoped they remember how well they flourished under Ts'ai rule," someone muttered.

"Indeed," General Rini agreed. "But now we can offer them Lady Hana. Ts'ai and Otako in unity. The call of peace is likely to prove the biggest attraction. We all know this war cannot be allowed to drag on, not only because of plague and trade interruption, but because the longer it lasts the more likely Chiltae will take advantage of our weakness and wipe us all out, regardless of the present treaty."

"They will not move on us until after the rains."

"Then we have a season to put the dog to rest."

Glances flicked my way as some of them recalled the "dog" they spoke of was my cousin.

No, don't think about Katashi. He is just a dog now, running on Darius's leash.

"And Risian, Master Yara," Kin prompted.

"Yes, Your Majesty. Orders have gone to pull half the standing battalions from Shimai. The lords of Risian have made good on their promise to field men under your banner. They want to retake the Willow Road. It would seem that our tales of banditry have taken well. Otako's men are becoming figures of fear."

"Good," Kin said. "We must move before they get wind of it. This has to be quick and silent."

"Yes, Your Majesty."

The councillors all nodded at plans to defeat the Otako threat that were only possible now they had Otako legitimacy, a joke only the gods could appreciate.

"Have we heard anything of Otako these last few weeks?" Commander Rusaka asked abruptly. As camp commander, he played the role of self-important host.

Councillor Gadokoi didn't swallow before retorting, "Katashi Otako has not stopped giving us grief since he took the throne at Koi. Which war are you fighting?"

"I hear the reports same as you, Councillor, but what I hear are stories of traitor soldiers setting villages on fire and ambushing our scouts, nothing of Otako himself."

Kin sipped from his second bowl of wine. "Right now I can assure you that Katashi is back in the Fen," he said. "Waiting for me to come to him."

Katashi. His name dominated every council meeting as he too often dominated my thoughts. His humour and his gentleness, his grace and his strength and the tears that had streamed down his face the night Darius destroyed everything.

Again the nausea swelled, and I put my spoon down.

"What if he's dead?" Commander Rusaka said.

The councillors froze, General Rini with a slice of duck hovering precariously.

"Isn't it possible that it's Lord Laroth behind it all?" the commander went on. "Every day, we hear about his men but not about Otako himself. If he is dead or injured, we could attack while they are vulnerable—"

"Vulnerable?" General Ryoji turned on the man, his thick eyebrows lifted high. "Are you suggesting we march toward Koi? Otako holds the north. In sixteen years, they have never given up their loyalty to the Otako name, and they aren't about to do so now, perhaps not even with proof that Katashi Otako is dead. They have a lot to fear in terms of retribution, and I am sure many would rather go on fighting. We cannot make brash assumptions when the empire is at stake."

"No, but Jikuko *is* wasted in the Valley," General Rini replied more mildly. "A smaller contingent could hold the Neck."

Beside me, Kin ate in silence, watching his advisors with the same frown he always wore. Once again, it was General Ryoji who answered. "But, General Rini, can we afford to risk next year's harvest? If we lose the Valley, the people will starve. We do not have enough rice in our stores, and this war is already draining the treasury dry. Chiltae will not feed us without extorting a higher price than we can pay."

"And if we leave Jikuko in the Valley, we could lose Shimai. Or Mei'lian. Then there will be no empire left to fight for."

"Let him march on the sister cities and see how far he gets," Commander Rusaka growled. "I will not bow to an Otako dog from the north. Shimai can—"

"Will you bow to me, Commander?" I asked. "Or am I too an Otako dog from the north?"

The man's head snapped around, anger hardening his eyes. "My lady?"

"I am Emperor Lan's daughter," I said, keeping my voice low so they were forced to remain quiet to hear me. "I would advise you to remember there are only two men who outrank me: your emperor, who is to be my husband, and your enemy, who is my cousin. Think on that before you insult me again."

My pulse thundered so hard I felt sick. I wanted him to speak, to argue, to fight, but he robbed me of all satisfaction with a simple bow of his head and a mumbled, meaningless apology.

My fists clenched into balls. "Be careful, Commander," I said. "You cannot wish an Otako away. I am here to stay and so is my cousin. I can tell you now that Katashi Otako is not dead. And he isn't fleeing north."

Commander Rusaka snorted, his fleeting glance at Kin eliciting no response. "And how do you know that, my lady?"

"Because I know my cousin better than you do, Commander."

They may as well have spoken their thoughts aloud for how clearly they rang through the tent. And they were right. I had known him *much* better.

"Believe me," I said to cover the sound of their collective judgment and my own desperate longing. "Katashi Otako is neither dead nor retreating, despite the power Lord Laroth holds over him."

"What proof?" Rusaka asked. "Intuition does not hold weight in military decisions, my lady."

"Neither does wishful thinking, Commander."

"Enough." Kin spoke quietly, no smile on his fatigue-lined features. "General Rini."

"Yes, Your Majesty?"

"Have our scouts keep an eye out for Otako just in case."

Commander Rusaka nodded his satisfaction.

"I am not yet prepared to abandon the Valley," Kin went on. "Otako has shown a penchant for fighting over lost territory, and given the state of trade, we need to hold on to every food supply we can. General Jikuko will stay where he is for now."

There was a murmured round of "Yes, Your Majesty."

"There is little else to go on until we hear more," he added.

"Make sure the men are ready to march. We will have to move quickly or Risian will be just another loss."

"Yes, Your Majesty."

Kin rose to leave. Every member of his council got to their feet as quickly as they could, though it took some of them no little effort. I remained kneeling as custom dictated, glad it was over, but when Kin did not immediately depart, I looked up to find him awaiting my attention. No appreciative smile touched his lips anymore.

"There is time to rest now, but you will dine with me tonight?" he said. "We have had a success today worth celebrating. Don't you think, my lady?"

"We have indeed. Thank you, Your Majesty, I would be honoured."

The words sounded dead on my lips but it didn't seem to matter. At my acquiescence, he strode out, followed by the rest of the council in a chatting group.

Back out in the weak sunlight, the camp stank of mud and horse dung. A gaggle of boys ran past carrying assorted sacks and crates, one with a thin trickle of millet trailing behind him. Sounds swirled around me: the murmur of conversation, distant laughter, the clatter of weapons, and the rustle of canvas. But I was the rock in the stream. My every limb was a dead weight and my thoughts were sluggish. I needed sleep. I needed to clean the stink of blood and smoke and sweat from my body.

"My lady."

A priest stood alone in the thoroughfare, bowing such that his gold embroidered hem caressed the grass. Gold thread decorated his sleeves too, and as he rose, he showed a face threaded with wrinkles. A familiar face, one that might have been handsome but for an absent chin.

"Father Kokoro," I said, memory coming to my aid. The man had offered comfort back in Mei'lian when I had been Kin's prisoner.

So much had changed since then that I could barely hold back the tears that had been threatening all day.

"I wish to congratulate you upon your bridal prayers, my lady," he said, needing no further invitation to speak than what my silence offered. "It is a joyous time for Kisia and all her people."

"Thank you, Father."

He invited me to walk with him, and having no energy to refuse, I fell in with his slow, decorous pace. Side by side, we walked along the row of tents.

"At any other time, it would have been I that performed your bridal prayers in the palace shrine," he said, nodding to a soldier who lifted his hands in prayer. "I must try not to begrudge Father Hoto the honour."

"I am sure you have presided over many such ceremonies, Father Kokoro. You have been the court priest for quite some time, have you not?"

"Long enough that it was I who brought you before the gods when you were born, my lady."

I stopped. "You were my father's priest?"

"I was, my lady, yes."

"And Kin kept you on?"

He smiled, something a little too self-satisfied in its curve. "Priests are rarely feared enough. And if we are not feared, then we are not replaced. Good priests are invisible."

"Deliberately?" I said as we started walking again.

Wrinkles formed at the corners of Father Kokoro's eyes. "One does not usually set out to be executed. Is it a crime to be careful of my life?"

"Not at all." I bit my tongue on all the questions I wanted to ask about my mother, not ready for answers that would make my tears flow. Instead I asked, "Was there a particular reason you wished to speak to me, Father?"

Another smile. "There was indeed, my lady," he said as we turned into a narrower avenue, the tents here smaller and closer together. More soldiers bowed, clasping their hands as we passed. "I think you may have some information of use to me."

Again I stopped, spinning one sandal in the mud to stare at him. "Information?"

"Do keep walking. You draw much attention when you ought to be calm."

"One of your tactics?"

"Why yes, my lady. Never show excitement."

We kept walking. "Then in my most monotone voice, I must ask what information it is you think I possess but have not shared with His Majesty, and why it is you who must ask for it."

"Ah, you suspect me of operating without His Majesty's knowledge. I do not, my lady. His Majesty has been made aware of my long-standing investigation into the Vices. You look shocked."

"I am shocked. What is your interest in the Vices?"

"As we have discussed, I have been at court quite a long time. I knew Lord Nyraek Laroth well, and more than once in his last years we discussed the intricacies of his... condition. With my teachings, he came to understand how much of an abomination his abilities were in the eyes of the gods and sought to atone. He was a very troubled man."

The solemnity with which he spoke turned my stomach. However much anger I possessed toward my former guardians, I could not hear such words without wondering in exactly what way Lord Nyraek had been encouraged, through shame, to atone.

"I thought little of it after he died," the priest went on. "Until these Vices appeared some years ago and piqued my curiosity. I had barely begun to nibble the edges of the mystery, when who should appear at court as His Majesty's newest councillor but Lord Darius Laroth, just as the Vices were heard of no more."

His gaze felt heavy on the side of my face as I kept walking, trying to show a total lack of interest in his words. "I warned His Majesty, of course, but he did not take the threat very seriously, and in all the years since, I have not been able to prove Minister Laroth's connection to the Vices, or at least not to the degree required to remove the emperor's favourite from his position."

"Did you believe Minister Laroth was endangering Kisia? I understood him to have been His Majesty's favourite because he was very good at his job."

His gaze seemed to grow sharper, and I wished I had not spoken. "Indeed he was, my lady," he said. "But while His Majesty has always prized competence over piety, I feel quite vindicated by Minister Laroth's present treason. However great the appearance of loyalty, one cannot trust those whose very souls are defective, those whose very existence is an abomination to the gods."

I kept walking, though I wanted nothing more than to spit at him and walk away. Whatever my anger at Darius, he no more deserved to be spoken of like a worm than I did. "And what," I said, cramming as much chilly reserve into my tone as I could, "is it that you were hoping to learn from me, Father?"

"I want to know how far the... infection spreads."

"The infection?"

He smiled a warm, friendly smile. "Conceit, I believe, was the name of the Vice who attacked you at the shrine, undoubtedly on Lord Laroth's orders."

That he had come to me meant he knew at the very least that Darius had been my guardian, which meant denial would only look guilty. Better to attempt chilly condescension. "Conceit does not take his orders from Lord Laroth, Father Kokoro," I said with a mocking smile. "The Vices are not, and never have been, Darius's toys. Malice is their leader."

Father Kokoro did not appear surprised. A test, then. "Ah yes, Malice, the Eye of Vice, a man with a ribbon of bone in his hair—a dramatic affectation for a man I've always thought more puppet than player."

"He would certainly not care to hear you say so, Father," I said.

"No doubt, but who leads him, my lady, who leads him? That the Vices went to ground when Lord Laroth appeared at court and only returned when His Excellency had need of their services in defecting to Katashi Otako's cause makes it appear very much like it is he who leads the infamous Malice, don't you think?"

"I understand that brothers often have much more complex relationships than that, Father Kokoro."

There was a pause and Father Kokoro frowned. "Brother? Surely Lord Darius Laroth is an only child. Or…" He smiled my way. "Only legitimate child? The final piece of the puzzle. And how obvious the answer is now it has been presented to me. Thank you, my lady." He stopped walking and bowed, suggesting dismissal. "You must be tired. I will keep you no longer."

"Why are you asking me this now?" I said, not letting him take what he wanted and just walk away. "I have been with the army for a few weeks."

"Call me a wary soul, my lady. I have always been careful on this topic and, until Conceit attacked you, could not be sure you were not still connected to them."

"And who told you that I was?"

That knowing smile was back. "No one, of course, my lady. I have merely been a long-time observer of Minister Laroth and his various moods. The risk he took for you in Mei'lian was quite something. It must have been a shock last night to have them used against you, but let me assure you, the fact that you came back alive means you still retain some value to them. I have studied the Vices for many years, and that, I assure you, was a mere stunt."

I had a hundred stories I could have told him that would make his jaw drop, but instead I forced a false smile.

"And in the end, they will all be punished for the abominations they are, for that is the will of the gods. We are but their servants upon this earth and must cleanse it of horrors for the sake of our children."

Such calm, tranquil words and yet filled with such hate that I could not speak, not then nor when he smiled and bowed and thanked me, not even when he walked away, his serene features bathed in morning sunlight.

5. ENDYMION

The sun rose upon the sodden camp full of Katashi's soldiers, but it was the wagon parked on the outskirts that drew my gaze. Dark figures gathered around it like a flock of blackbirds hunching their shoulders against the drizzle. Beside me, Kimiko sat with her chin on her knees, her hair hanging around her like a damp blanket.

"There's probably no point in waiting any longer," she said, not turning to look at me. "You'd better go before Malice comes back."

"You should let me tell him," I said. "About the child."

"No. We have been over this at least a dozen times. You don't tell him. We can't trust him yet. All you need to do is go down there and see him and see if you can do your..." She wiggled her fingers. "...thing, and talk to him. See if he can come back. See if he..."

Kimiko hugged her knees tighter.

"It would be better if you talked to him."

"I can't go down there and walk back out. And he can't lie to you."

We had talked it all over in the night, yet I could not be at ease. I could already see Darius's mind, could already feel his judgement, and there was nothing I could say or do to change it.

Kimiko is carrying your child.

I got to my feet. "You'll finish the job for me if...?"

"Don't worry," she said, still not looking at me. "I'll kill you quite happily."

Beside me, Kaze tugged at clumps of damp grass. I touched his neck. "Wait for me," I said. "I'll be back soon."

He didn't understand my words but understood their meaning, just as I understood his reply through touch.

"I know," I said. "But I have to try."

Leaving Kaze and Kimiko behind, I made my way through the thinning edge of the forest. The loud discontent of the sentries on watch had made them easy to avoid in the night, but once beyond the tree line, there would be no hiding.

"Kimiko is carrying your child."

The empty forest made no reply beyond the pitter-patter of the fading storm. It ought to have smelt of rain and mud and wet bark, but all I could smell was the stink of burned flesh.

"Kimiko is carrying your child."

In the weak morning light, Katashi's camp was a mess of wet tents and mud and subdued whispers. The first storm had passed, but more would soon come.

"But perhaps it's already too late for you, Darius."

The sharp stab of attention hit me on the muddy slope above the camp.

"Hey!"

The voice came from above, but it was a pair of roaming sentries that sped toward me, bowstrings taut before they could get a clear shot. Another joined them, his whispers gathering fast.

"Who are you?"

"Isn't he one of the Vices?"

"Really? Seems there's a lot of them around at the moment. Oh look." The man pointed down the slope where a group of black-clad figures were making their way up the hill. "They must have smelt the stench of one of their own."

Stinking Vices.

Can't stand these damn freaks. Freaks. Traitors. I signed up to fight for Katashi Otako, not this mess.

The Vices arrived silent like a shadow, and heedless of the Pikes, they spread out around me. Ire, Rancour, Hope, Pride—each of their thought patterns as familiar as their faces.

"This is one of ours," Ire said to the sentries who had kept their bows drawn. "Don't let us keep you."

"Any stranger in our camp is our business."

"Swim away, little fishy."

Avarice stepped forward, ignoring the sentries. "You shouldn't be here."

"I want to see Darius," I said.

The Vices closed in, their whispers tangling.

"No."

He's the one.

The other one.

The freak prince.

"I will see him," I said.

"Is that a threat, boy?" Avarice growled. He gripped his sickle. "You're outnumbered."

The sentries held their ground and their bowstrings, but I kept my eyes on the old Vice. In daylight, his face was deeply lined. "You told me you stole silver," I said. "But you didn't tell me it was Lady Melia Laroth's locket."

Avarice neither moved nor spoke, just weathered the storm as he always had.

"Darius caught you taking it from her room," I went on. "No one had touched it since she died. No one would miss it, and you hadn't been paid since Lord Nyraek left for Mei'lian. Again."

Some of the Vices shifted uneasily, but Avarice remained statue still.

"You had no money left, but it wasn't for you, was it?" I said. "The housekeeping money had run out, and you might as well have been stuck at the end of the world for all the help that came. How could you feed and look after Darius without money?"

"Go. Away," Avarice rumbled. "You can't see him. Leave before we make you leave."

"I'm not going anywhere until I see Darius."

"Get him out of here."

A hand closed around my arm. "Pride," I said, though I looked at Avarice. "Pride, the only Vice who sold himself. And all for the chance to lie to his wife."

Raw emotion crackled around us.

"I know what you're thinking, Ire," I said, not turning. "Ire, another son sold into slavery. But your father was happy to be rid of you, happy to sell the beast who beat his new wife until her face was black with bruises."

Pride let go, and I heard the slap as he caught Ire's arm. "Not worth it," he said.

"One of you smothered your own mother while she slept," I said. "One of you was the lover of a lord. One bore the brunt of your father's fury every single night. One of you used to be a priest. One of you wants to die. And there's one who wants to slice the throat of every Vice while they sleep."

Their whispers grew tangled and anxious. Wary. Hands edged toward weapons, and I could have set them off, but Avarice was my only way in.

"You have all suffered and you have all wronged, but none more than you, Avarice," I said. "Have you told them about the man you call 'Master'?"

Avarice closed the space between us in two steps. "You keep your mouth shut, boy," he said, his skin rippling with patches of stone. But it was not anger that sweetened the air.

"Poor Avarice," I murmured, the words for him alone. "You love him." Memories poured forth, every one of Darius. Darius, a boy crushed by his father's expectations and his father's fears, Darius, the child Avarice had never meant to have.

"It's too late," I said. "You did your best for him. You were the father he never had. You were everything. He became a monster, but you, Avarice, I judge you worthy."

"You putrid little shivat!" Avarice ripped his sickle from his belt and swung. A hurried duck threw me off balance, and I slammed into Ire before hitting the muddy ground, breath knocked from my lungs.

"I don't want to be judged worthy." Avarice advanced on me, his sickle threateningly outstretched. "I want you to take your yapping kashak and get out of my face. Master Darius doesn't want to see you or anyone, so kill us all or go away."

"I will not hurt a man I have deemed worthy," I said, struggling to my feet. "Nor those I have not judged."

"Then go away before I cut off your balls."

A slow clap cut through the morning, and I stretched my Empathy beyond the cluster of Vices clogging my Sight. Vengeance was there, his aura hot with amusement. "That was entertaining," Katashi said, bringing his hands together in a mocking rhythm. "My guess is that Hope wants to die, Pride smothered his own mother, and Ire wants to kill you all. But who was the priest?"

No one answered.

"Don't want to play?" Katashi mocked the silent Vices. "I'll go first. I'm the one who watched my father be executed by the Usurper."

He pushed Avarice aside. "How's your arm?" He gestured to the place his arrow had hit, no contrition in his soul.

"It's much better," I said. "But it hurts when I'm careless."

Katashi tapped Hacho's tip. "Give me a good reason why I shouldn't try again and aim a little left."

"Because I don't want your throne."

"No?" He gripped my chin in his hot hand.

Hana is mine. Kisia is mine. He cannot have her. He cannot take her away as he took my father. In the echo of memory, a crowd chanted, baying for blood. Kin stood on the platform, not an emperor but a general adorned in the same crimson, his expression stern and solemn. Protector of the throne, they called him, saviour of Kisia. I tried to push through the crowd, but a hand gripped my shoulder, and I turned to find a lidless eye staring at me. "It's too late, young lord," Shin said. "If you go up there, they'll kill you too."

"But they can't!" I screamed. "He didn't do it!"

"Patience is vengeance's greatest virtue," the man growled.

I hit the ground. The smell of mud cut into the lingering memory. "Patience?" I cried. "You're going to stand there and let them execute him?"

Shin bent down, gripping my chin as Katashi had. "There is nothing I can do," he hissed. "I have already done too much."

Sunlight stabbed into my eyes as I blinked rapidly. Katashi had not moved but frowned at his hand. "What did you just do?"

"Saw your memory," I said, throat dry. "I saw the day your father was executed."

"That's impossible." A deep furrow cut his brow. "I wasn't there." Katashi blurred as I blinked away tears, the tears of a boy who had watched the world change. But it hadn't been me, no matter how real, no matter how much my wrist had been bruised by Shin's iron grip while around us, the crowd moved like an animal. It couldn't have been me. The day Emperor Tianto died I was already with Jian, curled up on soft furs in the back of his wagon.

"You're all a bunch of freaks," Katashi said, turning on Avarice. "You say Darius doesn't want to see him? Then let's ruin the bastard's day. Take him down there. Give the prince his audience with the great Lord Laroth."

"I don't take my orders from you."

"No, but there are plenty here who do. You're vastly outnumbered in this camp, *Vice*, so if you want to live to do your master's bidding, then you will do this now."

Avarice snapped his jaw like an irritated dog, but hooked his sickle back onto his belt.

"Get up," he said. "You get five minutes and no more."

———————◆—————————

It was Avarice who tied my wrists and walked beside me through the camp, through the pressing crush of whispers and fear filling the air.

Katashi led the way, flanked by his soldiers, while an honour guard of Vices kept the masses at bay.

He's the bastard Otako.

That one.

This isn't good.

We should kill him before he kills us.

Malice's wagon appeared from the crowd like the prow of a ship. I could not feel him nearby, but Darius filled my future as he filled my thoughts. And still his judgement was death. Always death.

But Kimiko carried his child. If I could just use that, maybe I could save him. I could bring him back.

Katashi shouldered the door open without knocking and swept a hate-filled bow. "Master," he said. "I bring you a visitor."

There was Darius. Right there upon the divan. A book lay open on his knees, held by a silk-encased stump that had once owned a hand. Papers, scrolls, and maps covered the small table, along with an Errant board and a steaming pot of tea. He looked so much like the Darius I had come to love at Esvar that my words choked in my throat.

Those fine brows rose. "Endymion," he said, his gaze shifting quickly from Avarice to Katashi. "To what do I owe this unexpected visit?"

"Your dear brother asked, nay, *demanded* speech with you," Katashi said. "And I had not the heart to refuse such a desperate plea. Why don't you let him go, Avarice, let them sit side by side and be all brotherly."

Avarice tightened his grip on my upper arm.

He's too dangerous.

Petty payback for your precious Hana? You know I am not so stupid.

Go on, Master, *let him near enough to touch you.*

Darius closed the book slowly. War journal. Siege. Food for sixty-five days. They had catapulted plague-ridden bodies over the walls and sat back to wait.

Too slow.

Kisia would burn.

"Well?" Darius said. "What is it that's so important, Brother?"

Kimiko is carrying your child.

The words would not come.

Kimiko had begged me not to tell him, not to speak of it, but face-to-face now, I could think of nothing else to say while Darius's thoughts clogged my mind. Guilt and shame were there, but they mingled with all too much ferocious joy at the control he possessed. Whatever he had tried to be, Darius had killed too often. Destroyed too often. Controlled. Conspired. Consumed. It was death he deserved, not life. Not a child.

What had happened to the good man?

"You are running out of time, Endymion," he said, so calm, so sure, so mocking. He laughed at Katashi with his eyes and waited.

I'm the only one who can save him. I'm the only one who can save him. I can tell him the truth. The child. His child. A future worth fighting for.

A future he doesn't deserve.

What is he waiting for? He's just standing there.

I need to get him out of here. Order him out, Master.

I know you can hear me, Endymion. Or should I call you Justice now? I see you didn't heed my lessons.

Kimiko. Child. Death.

"Last chance, Endymion."

Katashi spat. "Pathetic. Get the runt out of here. Throw him in the Fen with that traitor."

"No!" The word burst from my lips as Avarice yanked me backward. "No! I can save him! Stop!"

"I don't need saving, Little Brother," Darius said as I was pulled out the door. "I'm already free."

"But your judgement is death!"

Sunlight stabbed into my eyes as I stumbled backward down the stairs, dragged by Avarice's relentless grip. Then Katashi was in front of me, so close all I could see was his face outlined in bright light. "Next time I see you, Lord Takehiko, I will kill you. Get him out of my sight."

"No! Take me back! I can save him!"

Avarice's stony grip bruised my arm as he pulled me away, the camp a blur.

"Please! Take me back!"

"Be quiet."

"Take me back. Take me back."

Avarice stopped abruptly. We were at the edge of the camp. Swampy water oozed at our feet, but it was not that I could smell, not that I could feel. Malice. He lurked at the edge of my thoughts, his presence drawing out old memories—old fears.

My mind darted, snatching at the day. Sunlight. Beads of water hanging from an overhead branch. Whispers. They gathered like a susurrus, each individual thought near impossible to discern. Four thousand five hundred and eighty-seven.

I had to get back to Darius.

I gathered anger—from the Vices, from the fading storm and the Fen, from the empire itself, trapped in a war it could not escape—and the raw emotion came to my hands begging to be used.

"You're a fool, Endymion." Malice's voice appeared before his body, a body clad in flowing dark blue silk. He was wet from the rain but as precise as ever. Every line etched upon his face held its own mockery. "You can't save a man who does not need to be saved."

The anger burned as I forced it out through my skin. Thrown to the air, it crackled like summer lightning as it spread through all who had gathered.

Avarice's grip on my arm slackened. Ire buckled. Others dropped with wet thuds. Except Malice. He remained standing, weathering the blow with a grimace.

"You need to work on your control, Brother," he said. "Anger won't harm the trees, yes?"

Fatigue weighed down every limb, dragging me to the ground. "Darius is not the man you think he is," I said, propping myself up with hands splayed in mud. "He never has been."

"Don't try your tricks on me, yes? No one understands him like I do."

She understood me, Darius had said. *She knew me. Better even than Malice.* Kimiko might not remember his words, but they lived on in me.

"We all need saving," I said. "You need to let him go."

Malice snarled. "No. He's mine."

"Then you are the reason he will die! His judgement is death, Malice. Death for what he is and what he has done and it's your fault."

"What screwed up sort of justice do you have in that munted head of yours?" he said. "Darius made *me*. Darius taught me everything I know. *He* made the first Vice. *He* started this. *He* was the mastermind behind every plan for the empire." Malice's free hand clenched and unclenched, but he did not close the space between us.

"You love him," I said.

"Is that a question?"

"No. It's the truth. But you need to let him go, or his judgement will not change. You can save him. You can walk away."

Malice crouched, his dark eyes boring into mine. "Walk away?" he repeated. "I have spent five years working to get him *back*. Darius is *mine*!"

"The man you love is a lie."

Around us, the souls of unconscious Vices and Pikes began to reignite.

"You can save him," I said, desperation spurring a tumble of words. "You can give him something to fight for. There's a child. Tell him he has a child."

"A child." Malice's voice was devoid of emotion, though he had many. Disbelief, anger, jealousy, hatred. But he was my last chance. Darius needed to know.

"Touch me," I said. "Take the memory to him. You can save him."

Malice held out his hand. The connection was instant, sucking thoughts and memories from my mind. Kimiko. The fear upon her face. The beat of new life in her belly. Justice. Two hundred and twenty-nine judgements.

Kin.

Malice pulled his hand away. He sucked in a breath, and a short bark of laughter broke from his lips. "It was Kin? Kin who gave the order to assassinate Emperor Lan and his family?" Another laugh, longer and louder. "And Grace Tianto took the fall, yes? Oh, how Darius will like that story."

"No. Don't tell him that," I said. "Kin did it for the best. He had good reasons. Tell him about the child!"

I tried to scramble to my feet, but Malice thrust me back. "Oh, you don't want Darius to know? You think it will make him angry, yes? Well it did. He already knows."

"How? No, it doesn't matter. Tell him about the child, Malice, you have to!"

"You think I don't know Darius," he said. "But it's you who are wrong about him, yes? You think a pregnant woman can change him? You think the prospect of a child can turn him into some pious hero?" He clicked his tongue. "Pity. Really, Endymion, you think it hasn't happened before? You think this is the first time Darius has taken a chance on the life of a whore?"

"He loves her."

"Love? If he truly loved her, he would never have put her life at risk."

He must have felt my confusion for he shook his head in mock sadness. "Really, Endymion, don't you know anything? Have you never wondered why there are no female Empaths?"

Malice gripped my chin and leant in as though he would plant a kiss upon my lips. And the truth was there in his touch as truly as it was in his words. "Female Empaths die in birth and kill their mothers. If the child is a girl, then Kimiko will die. How is that for love?"

6. DARIUS

Endymion remained with me long after his body had been dragged from the wagon. The boy was skeletally frail, his hair unkempt and his cheeks gaunt, yet his presence had filled the space as only Katashi's could.

I sat my book face down on the table. Its old pages crackled. He had wanted to talk, but why risk his life now after so long a silence? I had no answer, which meant he knew something that I did not.

The door opened and Malice entered, trailing raindrops. His eyes were bright. The pulse of his soul thrummed.

"I told you the boy would go mad," he said.

His suppressed excitement was like an ache.

"Spit it out," I said. "What did he tell you?"

"Oh, poor Endymion, he was so desperate to speak, but he knew his news would hurt you too much, yes?" Malice crooned. "And he couldn't bear to hurt big brother Darius."

"Are you going to tell me or not?"

"I can do better. I can show you." Malice held out his arm over the table. I stared at it, unsure. Would I regret seeing what he wanted to show me? Normally, he was so easy to read, but there was a hard glint in his eyes and a guardedness that made my stomach churn.

"You know you're going to," he said, holding his arm steady. His loose sleeve slipped back to show the birthmark he was so proud of. "You're too curious."

He was right. Self-preservation was an elusive goal.

I touched the back of his hand. Images flashed into my head and I gasped as Justice infused me to the bone.

A hand sat heavy on my shoulder. "You are welcome to stay, Takehiko," spoke a voice I had heard almost every day for five years. "But—"

I knew what would happen next, knew with every ounce of Endymion's assurance. The point of a dagger nicked my side, but my hand was at Kin's throat. My right hand. *Not mine. Not mine*, I told myself.

"No." The word came from my lips, but the voice was Endymion's. "Empaths are never welcome."

The words became a mess. The images jumbled. "Your brother betrayed me." Kin's words came fast, angry. "Tell me why I should trust you to do what you say rather than join him."

"Because I don't lie. And because I am the only one who will never hate you for killing my mother. It might have been Shin Metai's hand, but they were your orders, Your Majesty. A single order and a palace full of Otakos lay dead."

"Except for you."

"Except for me. And Hana. But it was Nyraek Laroth who made sure of that, not you."

"We all make hard choices."

I let go of Malice's hand. The tangle of words and thoughts died like snapping threads.

"That," I said, hating the anger that surged anew, "is old news and you know it."

Malice smiled. "But still so very delicious, yes? Delicious too that Endymion came to you upon such a fool's errand. So much trouble and all because a commoner had ambitions above his station."

My heartbeat sped. "How," I began, hearing the deep vibration of fury in my own voice, "did I not see it? I watched him every day for five years. I was his closest confidant, and I never even suspected."

"Because you didn't want to, yes?" Malice said. "You wanted to believe in the good man who was right for the empire. Fool."

I turned on him. "Like you knew any better. Like anyone did. Who would believe he could kill the woman he loved to take the empire?"

"It is the perfect cover. I admire his ambition."

"His ambition nearly killed you."

"No, our father nearly killed me," Malice said. "There is a difference, yes? He might have hated the world once Empress Li was gone, but there is more to the destruction of your own children than grief."

"Perhaps. But how much of it was Kin's fault? Our father could have tried to kill us anytime in those early years, but he didn't. Not until Kin ruined everything. He will suffer as I did."

"If by suffer you mean be allowed to marry Hana and strengthen his claim to the throne, then yes, he is certainly suffering, my dear."

"You are as foolish as Otako. Surely you can see that the simplest way to give Hana an unassailable position of power is to let her marry the Usurper. Oh no, obviously you did not see that, or you wouldn't have sent Conceit to play his game."

Malice's fingers stopped combing through his ponytail. "If you knew, you could have stopped me."

"To what end? Attention was just what you wanted."

It was my turn to sneer. Malice set his jaw and turned toward the mirror. I hadn't noticed he was dripping wet from the storm until he began peeling off his sodden robe. He had just returned from an evening spent plying his particular craft.

"How fared your mission?" I asked as he hung first one robe and then the other to dry—midnight-blue and tan, his favourite combination.

"How kind of you to ask, yes?" The glance he threw me was sour. "The man didn't make it."

"Unfortunate."

"Unfortunate indeed," he said, not immediately reaching for a new robe to cover his nakedness. "Since we have lost six Vices in the last few weeks, yes?"

I returned to the divan, putting space between us. "It doesn't matter," I said. "I don't need them."

Malice turned. "Don't need them? Do you plan on taking up arms yourself then, Brother?"

"I don't need to."

"No? How then do you plan to take the Crimson Throne?"

"I won't. Hana will."

"And Kin?"

"She will destroy him far more cruelly than I ever could," I said. "How well do you think she will take the discovery that Kin murdered her family in cold blood? It's a pity your play with Conceit has put us further out of favour with her, but there are always ways."

Malice stared, not seeming to recall he was still undressed. "Ways? To take the empire?"

"First Shimai. Then the empire. Katashi is the perfect weapon, and now we have Endymion too. If we play him right, he will ensure Hana is in Shimai when we attack, then everything else will fall into place."

Malice took a step forward, and though there had once been a time when such freedom existed between us, his nakedness made me uneasy. "He won't trust either of us."

"No, but he'll trust your pretty little toy, Hope."

He grinned and, with another step, knelt on the edge of the divan, ever confident of his welcome. "I love watching your mind work." He ran a finger down my cheek. It was so natural to have him in my veins that I barely felt the intrusion. "But there's something you're not telling me, yes?"

"Not telling you?"

"I know that face," he said. "You never used to keep secrets from me."

"Five years is a long time."

"So you keep reminding me. You are devising another play."

"Perhaps."

Malice sat back with a sudden snarl. "Perhaps? Fuck you and your perhaps. I thought we were in this *together*. We are brothers."

"You think I could forget?" I slapped his hand away. "You touch me, you caress me, you stare, you consume, you suffocate me, *Brother*."

He gripped a handful of my hair. "I love you, Darius," he said, his face so close that I could smell the oil on his skin and the stink of wet hair. "I love you like no one else ever could because I know you inside and out, yes?"

It was reckless to goad him, and in some sane part of my mind I knew it, but I wanted him to hurt as I hurt. "Am I meant to thank you?"

Malice tightened his grip. "Our father called you a cold, ungrateful pup," he said. "And he was right."

"You talk about him like you knew him." I licked my dry lips. "He hated you. I might have been a monster, but you were a bastard monster born to a whore he never gave a damn about. He abandoned you."

I hissed as hair ripped from my skull. Malice propped his weight on my ribcage and wormed a hand beneath my robe, his fingernails cutting into my skin. "A family tradition, that, yes? But you were crueller. You let me in. You were my world, my everything. And *then* you left!"

"You had my money."

"Damn you!" His nails cut into my chest, freeing blood. "I would have given that up for you. I would have done anything for you."

"How sweet," I jeered.

Malice let go and sat back on my thighs, his rigid cock all too close to my own. "Why do you hate me so much?" he said. "What did I do?"

"You just ruined my last good robe," I replied. "I hope one of your Vices knows how to get blood out of silk."

A laugh burst from him and his eyes danced with brittle humour. "Oh gods, I've missed you, yes? Five years. Five years without the sound of your voice, without your wit and your fire, without the touch of your skin." He tugged at my sash.

"Get off," I said, but Malice didn't seem to hear. His long fingers were already working on the ties of my under-robe. "Stop. Now."

I gripped his wrist with my left hand, but he pulled free and shuffled back, cock bobbing. I couldn't hear the rain anymore, only the pounding of my heart and our quickened breath. I wanted to push him away, to kick him, to scream, anything to get him off me, but I was not yet so mad that I had forgotten where that road led. Mastery was survival, had always been about survival.

Malice gripped my thighs. I caught my hand an inch from hitting him and placed my palm upon his cheek with a gentleness that tore at my self-control. "Stop," I said, the word quiet. "Look at me."

Through a fall of dark hair, he looked up, granting me a single moment. "What?"

"Get off," I said. "Unless you plan to rape me."

A snarl tore from his lips. "Damn you, Darius! Damn you and your cold blood. I need you!"

"That's too bad, because I don't need you."

The words were out before I could stop them. The air changed taste, became pungent with hurt. Malice's fist clenched. "You damned manipulative little shit," he said. "You're lying."

Entirely naked, he could not hide the shrivelling of his confidence any more than the shrivelling of his lust.

"No, I'm not," I said. "Now get off me."

I gathered my robe closed with my left hand, hating its clumsiness. The divan creaked, and silently Malice strode to the mirror and began to dress in the first dry under-robe that came to hand—white, such a fine summer weight it was almost transparent. He was fuming, spilling hurt and anger.

As though feeling the weight of my scrutiny, he paused in the act of neatening his ponytail, as though to smooth his hair would erase the last few minutes from history. "I once had a brother who wanted to rule Kisia as a god," he said, not looking around. "Was she really so good, my Adversity?"

"If you thought with your head instead of your cock, you might succeed in sounding less stupid," I said.

He looked around then, all anger. "Control never was my speciality, Brother, yes? But loyalty is. So when you're ready, I'll send Hope to play saviour."

I had almost forgotten about Endymion. For my plan to succeed, I would have to move fast.

"I'm going to see Katashi."

"Will dear Katashi like his orders?" Malice glanced around at the hints of carnage my Vice had left behind the night before—scattered Errant pieces and a shattered teapot spread like cerulean tears. "He has been rather…difficult of late, yes?"

"He will do what he is told."

He began tying his sash, care and precision in every movement of his hands. "I am not so sure. Be careful with him, yes? He is not the sort of stick that breaks when you bend it. He is the sort that snaps back and whacks you in the face."

"What beautiful imagery you have."

"And what a mocking tone you have, my dear."

"He will do as he is told or he will never see the Crimson Throne."

"Never is a long time, yes?"

"Not when you're dying."

Malice's hands froze upon the last twists of his knot. "Dying?"

"Yes, dying. You cannot tell me you're surprised. It is not the first time marking someone has killed them. I assume Hope is rarely wrong about such things."

He stared fixedly at me as though trying to read small words writ upon my cheek.

"The more he uses the ability, the faster it will consume him," I said, disliking his intensity. "We are running out of time. Make sure Hope overhears that we intend to burn Shimai. That should be enough to send him running to Endymion, don't you think? Likes to do the right thing, your Hope."

"You think it's wise to let Endymion go? He's dangerous enough sitting in a swamp, let alone sending him back to Kin. We should just kill him, yes?"

"No."

Malice's brow rose. "No?"

"It's too late."

"You mean you just don't have the heart to do it."

I lifted my chin. "This is the way we are doing it. You make sure Hope moves, and I will do the rest."

Malice dropped the ends of his sash and bowed. "As you command, Mastery," he said. "It will take time for me to be subtle. Don't miss me too much, yes?"

Katashi stood at the mark, his famous longbow in one gloved hand. A dozen arrows already protruded from his makeshift target—a handprint burned into the trunk of an old oak.

"What can I do for you, Excellency?" he said, not looking around as he nocked another arrow to his string. He had discarded his imperial crimson for rebels' black. It hid burns better, but even at this distance I could smell charred fabric.

When I didn't answer, he looked over his shoulder. "Do you

want to challenge me? No, wait, you need two hands for that, don't you?"

Unconsciously I wriggled my right hand, sure I was moving fingers—fingers that could not feel the caress of the air or the touch of rain.

"Amusing," I said as he drew. I had not seen him practice before and expected a moment of pause, to prepare, to aim, but as soon as the string was at full stretch, he let it go. Invisible, the arrow leapt through the air and hit the tree with such force it shuddered. The scalded palm was full, and he was now populating its fingers.

"I hear you do this every day," I said. "Are you so afraid of losing your edge?"

"I won half of my men this way," he said, nocking another arrow. "Any fool can hit a target. To be a god, I must hit where I aim every time, no matter what the challenge. Last night would have gone very differently had I missed, don't you think?"

The arrow dug into the tip of the black thumbprint.

Katashi once again looked at me over his shoulder. "You've never come to see me before, so I can only assume something exciting has happened and summoning me would take too long."

"You dawdle."

"Unfair, Laroth, I merely enjoy the scenery."

"We're going to take Shimai."

Another arrow was already nocked to the string, but he didn't immediately draw. "Our next move is Risian."

"Forget Risian. We take Shimai within the week."

The arrow tip slammed into the as yet empty little finger. "The sister city is heavily fortified. You have some grand plan?"

"Yes. My grand plan is a frontal assault."

The mocking gleam vanished. "A frontal assault of Shimai. You want me to march my army to the gates and knock? No. I will not send my men to their deaths for nothing."

"You're already losing them," I said. "They are all afraid of you."

Katashi shrugged. "Scared men are loyal men."

"Not if they are also powerful men. The three generals you stole from Emperor Kin brought with them half of your soldiers, and they will take half of your soldiers away when they betray you. You haven't hidden the fire well enough. It's time to give them a reason to love you for it, not fear you."

"Why the sudden change?"

"Because with new information comes new plans."

"New information you no doubt intend to share with me?"

I lifted my brows deliberately. "Share with you? Why would I waste my time when you are constrained to follow my orders regardless?"

Katashi set one tip of his bow on the ground and planted his chin on the other. "Constrained to follow perhaps," he said, looking at me so derisively that I clenched my fingers to keep from slapping him. "But not constrained to succeed. I could squander my army to spite you. That would leave you in quite the predicament, wouldn't it? Having in your power a powerless man." He tapped the fletching of a new arrow to his lips. "It's tempting, but I'd rather take the throne and then stick a knife between your ribs."

"Unfortunately for you, you can't kill me."

He lifted the bow, the tip of an arrow sliding into line with my eye. The bowstring creaked. A single blue eye pierced me from behind the taut string.

"I'm not the one who is dying," I said, maintaining an outward calm. "You are."

Katashi might have been a statue for all he moved. "Do you want me to put this through your eye? I assure you it would come out the other side quite easily."

"You're not going to put that through my eye," I said. "Or any other part of my body. And you can threaten me all you like, but you would still be dying."

Long seconds crawled past. A gentle breeze brought the ashy scent of him to my nose.

"The fire is getting stronger," he said.

"Yes."

He slackened the bowstring just a touch, enough that the arrow might not have made it all the way through my skull. "What will happen to me? Will I burn?"

"I don't know."

Katashi lowered the bow, an oddly twisted smile on his lips. "How poetic an end that would be. No doubt I deserve it, but I can't stop yet. I will not let Kin go on ruling Kisia. Better I burn the throne and the empire and take it all to the seven hells with me."

A new storm was moving in from the east, its rising wind sending the black tail of Katashi's sash streaming out behind him. He looked like the avenging god he knew he was.

"What about Hana?"

Again that fiery gaze pierced my skin. Katashi shook his head. "Thanks to you, she will be a Ts'ai unless Kin is too dead to untie her sash."

He drew back the string again. The sound of it tightening sent a shiver through me. "Gods, I wish I could kill you," he said. "I wish I could put an arrow through each of your cold eyes. You ruined *everything!*"

Holding back the great weight of his bowstring, his arm began to tremble. "You should have just bowed to me!" he snarled. "I might even have let you marry my sister. With your fortune, I could have bought Kin's supporters out from under him." Tendrils of smoke curled from his gloves. "I might even now be sitting on the Crimson Throne, Hana my wife, if you had just *bowed.*"

He let go. The arrow leapt. There was barely time for me to recoil, heart in throat, before the thud of it hitting wood overrode every other sound. The arrow stuck out of the trunk beside me—at head height. Katashi stared at it.

"I thought you had to hit what you aimed for every time to be a god," I said, forcing a smile through fear.

Katashi lowered his bow. "I will burn you," he said. "The day I burn I will take you to the hells with me."

"And on that day, you will be nothing but a swamp-dwelling rebel unless you order the attack on Shimai."

"Why don't you just make me order the attack, *Master*?"

"Because I don't need to. If you want the Crimson Throne before you die, then this is your only chance. If you order the attack, you will break Kin, get Hana and your revenge. And if you don't—"

His expression sank into a scowl. "You'll leave me to rot here."

He drew another arrow so quickly that fear had no time to register. It ripped past my ear and buried itself on top of the last.

Anger roiled around him. I knew it was feeding my own, but there was satisfaction in the fury.

"Which will it be, Katashi?" I said. "The Crimson Throne and Kin's head? Or a single line in the history books about an ineffectual Otako who lost his way in the swamp?"

He eyed me with such hatred it prickled my skin. "You watch yourself, Laroth. You might be able to give me orders, but don't think for a moment that I am loyal. I will fight you every step of the way, and I will kill you as soon as I get the chance."

We glared at one another until the splash of swamp water interrupted our swelling antipathy.

"Captain! Captain!"

The voice rang through the trees, preceding a red-faced Pike. He burst into the clearing in a flurry of mud and reeds and skidded to a halt before his captain, his chest heaving.

"Captain!"

"What?" Katashi glared at the man.

"It's Emperor Kin, Captain. Everyone in Lotan is talking about it."

"Talking about what, damn it?"

"His marriage. To—" For the first time, the man seemed to consider the impact his words might have, and swallowed hard. "To Lady Hana."

It was not news to Katashi, but he seethed nonetheless. "Marriage," he said, seeming to chew the word. "I've heard, and by the gods, I'll make sure he regrets it."

"The news is everywhere," the Pike said, regaining his breath. "Some are laughing that you couldn't keep even your own cousin loyal."

Once again, the Pike seemed to think only after he had spoken, and with a flash of fear, he eyed the bow in Katashi's hand. Those gloved fingers closed hard around its shapely wood. "We'll see who's laughing," Katashi said. "Send a messenger to Kogahaera. I want Kin to know the truth about his innocent bride. I want him to know that while he was in retreat from Koi, she gave me the right of a husband he now has no claim to. I want him to know we exchanged promises. I want him to know that she's mine."

The Pike hung there on the balls of his feet, unsure.

"Do it," Katashi said.

"Yes, Capt—"

"No."

Both Pike and emperor turned to stare at me. "No?"

"That is not part of the plan."

The Great Fish tightened his grip on his bow. "I don't care if it's part of your plan or not, it's part of mine. Send a messenger."

The Pike bowed. "Yes, Captain."

"No," I repeated, not taking my eyes off Katashi. "Retract that order."

His teeth clenched and his skin reddened. "No."

"Take it back. Now."

Our eyes locked. Pain grew fast, speeding through my veins as it did his. He suffered more quickly than any Vice before him, living his skill more completely.

Katashi trembled, then words burst from him in a gust of breath. "Don't send the message," he said. The pain dissipated, leaving only the ache of its memory. "I will make sure you die, Laroth, I promise you that."

In the same breath, he lifted his bow. Draw. Release. With a sickening sound, the arrow buried itself so deep in the Pike's eye that only black feathers protruded from the socket. The dead sack of flesh slammed back into the tree and slid to the ground, all tangled limbs.

Katashi dropped his bow as flames ripped up his arms. Heat filled the clearing. I backed away, but the heat only grew as his voice rose from roar to scream. Fury swallowed every shred of his breath until there was nothing but the crackle of fire.

Trees were burning. Fire crawled up their trunks. It swallowed the target Katashi had made and danced around the fallen Pike, catching upon his hair and his robe and the arrow's fletchings, making his eye bright.

"That," Katashi said, advancing on me through the heat haze, "is how you lose me my men. If they ever suspect you have power over me, each and every one will desert me in a breath. It is *me* they fight for. It is *me* they love."

"And if you had used your brain before giving that order, it wouldn't have happened," I said, forcing the words out level and calm. "If you give the whole world the knowledge that Hana is no innocent bride, then he may not fight for her. I need him to come out to play, so keep your mouth shut."

"You just want the whole world to bend over so you can fuck it, don't you?"

"How terribly crude you are, Katashi."

He snorted, not seeming to notice the flames slowly dying around him. Without his input, the trees were too damp to burn long. "I'm no finicky gentleman like you," he said, picking up his bow. "Being born to nobility just means having a name that is worth more than the ragged clothes on your back and the rotting food on your plate."

Katashi spat on the ground, and steam rose from the clump of weed where his saliva landed. "Get the generals," he said. "We'll take Shimai. I will burn the whole city to the ground if that is what it takes. Kin is mine."

———————————

I called Katashi's council, amused as always that his advisors had as little control over him as Katashi had over himself. From the Pikes who thought they knew him to the lords who thought they owned him, all were equally powerless and yet spared me no second glance. I was just another traitor sitting at a table of traitors.

The generals arrived together. Manshin, Tikita, and Roi had always been loyal to the Otako name. At the end of the previous civil war, they had been the last to bow to Emperor Kin, but sixteen years had seen them grow as comfortable with their expanding waistlines as they had with the world Kin created. Now they bowed to a new emperor—the Otako they had always wanted—but every day their fear was growing. The fear of men not used to being afraid.

Katashi held them by a thread.

"Ah, Minister Laroth, you are before us," General Manshin exclaimed, halting in the tent opening so Tikita and Roi were forced to edge around him to escape the rain. "It never fails to amuse me to see you dancing to the exile's tune."

"I do not dance, General," I said from my place at the foot of the table. "It is you, I think, who is doing that."

The Pike captains watched our interchange. Even Lord Flint trailed off in his conversation with his son, Katashi's quartermaster, to listen. Katashi was, as always, keeping his council waiting. It was one of the few powers he had left.

"Are you sure, Laroth?" General Manshin said. "I can imagine you would dance very gracefully."

He took his place opposite Captain Chalpo, the most senior Pike. Not a word passed between them, not even a look or a nod. Out in the camp, the attitude was the same. To the Pikes, the traitors were untrustworthy turncoats who had joined too late, while to the traitors, the Pikes were chaotic madmen. They enjoyed reminding everyone that the fish for which the Pikes were named ate their own kind when food was scarce.

"It must be odd to find yourself at the right hand of two emperors, Laroth," General Manshin said when further conversation was not forthcoming. "An interesting show of loyalty, to be sure."

"I was discharged from Emperor Kin's service, General," I said, watching Tikita and Roi kneel beside him. "But no doubt you have a good reason for betraying your oath."

The rest of the council watched hungrily, but General Manshin did not flinch. "Undoubtedly."

An awkward silence fell. Stiff-backed, the Pike captains stared across the table at the traitor generals, who resolutely refused to be put out of countenance.

When Katashi finally arrived, the tension was thick. Every man at the table rose to his feet, but though I stood, I did not bow with them. No one else noticed, but Katashi's eyes locked to mine as the others retook their places with varying degrees of grace.

"This will not be a long meeting," Katashi said when all was quiet but for the rain. "We have only one matter of business to discuss—the immediate frontal assault of Shimai."

Had I owned less control, I might have laughed at their faces. Even General Manshin's mouth dropped open. But it was Captain Chalpo who broke the silence first. "Shimai? The sister capital?"

"Yes," Katashi said. "Shimai."

He offered no more information. General Manshin cleared his throat. "And might I ask, Your Majesty, what you mean by 'immediate'?"

"As soon as we can march to its gates, leaving behind everything but what we need to attack a city."

Beside me, General Roi muttered, "Might as well march our men to Lin'ya and order them to leap off the cliff."

"Let's call that a day and a half pushing hard from this side of the Fen," Manshin said, ignoring his companion. "But even if Kin does not realise what we are doing, Shimai is more defensible than Mei'lian. Our minister of the left here"—he indicated me—"could tell you about the standing garrison. What is it, Laroth? One-and-a-half thousand men in peacetime?"

"You are correct, General," I said as eyes turned my way. "Set to rise to three immediately upon a state of internal or external conflict. But what you perhaps do not realise, General, is that half of them have been removed to a camp outside Risian. Kin is planning an attack. Now is our time to move."

Katashi turned his head, and I caught the malice in his aura. "Are you speaking for me, Laroth?" he said, his tone silky.

Every eye in the tent fixed on me. Let him play his petty power games. I could bow and scrape and simper as well as any other court buffoon. "My apologies, Your Majesty," I said.

A triumphant smile twitched his lips. "As my all-too-confident chief advisor said, Kin isn't expecting us to attack one of the most fortified cities in the empire."

General Manshin met his emperor's gaze with one equally direct. "That is because opportunity does not always translate into good military strategy."

Rain drummed on the tent roof. It was too much to say that General Tikita and General Roi edged away from their comrade, but they certainly took a great interest in the grain of the table. They were both younger by a decade, but all three had been honoured as heroes after the battle of Riyan Bridge four years earlier—the last time relations with Chiltae had soured to the point of war.

"Neither does fear of failure, General," Katashi replied.

General Manshin moved his jaw as though he chewed on air. His mind would be turning fast, playing the conversation in his head the same way I played Errant. Though better known for his exploits with Kisia's finest whores, he owned the sharpest mind present, barring only my own.

"Are we sure the garrison has been depleted?" Captain Chalpo asked, he the apparent spokesman for the two silent Pikes at his side. "We don't have the numbers to fight them *and* the army Kin will pull south from Kogahaera."

No *Your Majesty*, I noted. His Pikes had been with him too long for that.

"If we move fast enough, Kin won't have time to move his men from Kogahaera at all," General Manshin said. "That, I assume, is the reason for such haste. But with all due respect, Your Majesty, an attack of such magnitude requires planning and preparation."

"Only if your brain moves very slowly, General. My Pikes need barely an hour's notice."

Each of the generals made a concerted twitch as though reaching for an absent wine bowl. They were used to more respect. And they were used to being entertained in grander style, the table they had once knelt at no makeshift affair.

General Manshin took the insult with a smile as fake and calculating as I had ever seen. "You have a much larger army now, Your Majesty, and a much larger army requires more care. And attention to detail. Its every move planned." His gaze flicked to me, so quickly that to anyone else it might have appeared just an irritation of the eye. "Perhaps you already have a plan."

"Yes, General, I do." Katashi's skin was growing red with excitement. "I'm going to burn the gates down."

Silence, and out of it fear grew like rising damp.

"With what fuel?" General Manshin enquired all too calmly. "Those gates are at least four hundred years old and as dense as iron. It would take days, maybe even weeks. Not only could the defenders rain all manner of things upon us from the battlements, but it would give Kin plenty of time to move his men south from Kogahaera to pin us against the walls."

"Not weeks, General," he said. "Hours at the most, likely less."

Give them a reason to love you for it, not fear you, I had said. And what better reason than success?

Katashi splayed his fingers dramatically. "You've heard the rumours about me," he said, lighting his own flesh with a jolt of anger. "You've heard your soldiers whispering. Now see it for yourselves."

Every man leant back as Katashi pressed his palm to the table. Smoke rose in curls, filling the tent with choking grey clouds and the stink of burning wood. The table crackled. Flames leapt to life like extra fingers, and just as Lord Flint started coughing, a chunk of charcoal hit the floor.

Katashi removed his hand and the flames died, leaving behind a hand-shaped hole edged in black.

"But how?" General Tikita breathed, fanning smoke from his eyes.

"How?" Katashi got to his feet. The sleeve of his robe was charred around the cuff. "The gods gave the Crimson Throne to the Otakos, and the gods will take their vengeance. We will take Shimai. Ready your men to move out. Now."

7. HANA

Tili combed my hair, just as she had the first time I had dined with Emperor Kin—a lifetime ago sitting before the mirror in Lord Kato's guest quarters. We had talked of anything and everything, and I had been glad to have a friend. Now there was just silence. There had been a lot of that of late.

"My lady—"

"You don't need to call me that," I said for perhaps the hundredth time since I had talked Kin into letting her stay.

"Yes, I do, my lady."

More silence stretched between us, and I stared at my misty reflection in the mirror. It wasn't the finest glass, but we made do. Duplicate stars of lantern light flickered around me.

"My lady," she began again, and this time I did not interrupt. "Why is honour so important?"

I looked at her through the scratched glass, but she did not look at me, just went on combing my hair, each curl bouncing back as the comb let it go. "I suppose because in the end, our name is all we truly have," I said. "Beauty, fortune, property, power—everything else is transient. Without our integrity, we are nothing."

"But what is that? There are men who swore an oath to Emperor Kin and now fight for Emperor Katashi. And the other way around. Are they all dishonourable?"

The sound of his name triggered a flood of memories, and for a moment I couldn't speak, could only think of what might have been.

"I think as long as they made their choice for the right reasons," I said at last, "and hold their conviction to the end, then there is honour. Why do you ask?"

She seemed not to hear my question. "What about for women?"

I turned to look up at her. "What is this about, Tili? Are you all right?"

She bit her lip and didn't answer.

"You're worrying me." I gripped the hand that held the wooden comb, a hand that trembled as much now as it had on the way to Kuroshima. "Haven't we been through enough together to be honest now?"

She met my gaze then, wide brown orbs glistening in the lantern light. "I'm afraid for you, my lady," she said, her gaze flicking to the tent entrance and then back to my face. "I'm afraid of what you're doing."

These last words she whispered, fingers clamping around the comb to stop them from shaking.

I pulled back a little. "What I'm doing? What do you mean?"

"You...you haven't bled, my lady. Since we were on the road to Koi."

A shiver ran through me, equal parts hot and cold, as the meaning of her words sank into my skin. A child. A *child*. The slim possibility had occurred to me when Katashi had come so often to my tent, and yet...I pressed trembling hands to my stomach, every breath coming fast. A child. Katashi's child. I could not tell if joy or grief was strongest, grief that he might never know, that we might never again be together, or joy that now at least I might have something of him to hold on to.

Tell me that one day our son will sit on the throne when I am gone.

I closed my eyes, allowing myself a moment of exquisite pain in that memory. When I opened them again, Tili had stilled like a deer unsure whether to stay or flee. "How sure are you?"

"You are almost four weeks late, my lady," she whispered. "Even with irregularities, that is..."

"Could it be anything else?"

"The strain of war perhaps, but I have noticed you're not eating. You said the food here made you nauseous, and I began to wonder if it was not the food, seeing as you—" She broke off and lowered her gaze to the floor. "Apologies, my lady."

"We were going to get married," I said, as much to finally tell someone the truth, to make it real, as to allay some of her condemnation. "We pledged to each other that night. The night that—"

I could not finish the words, and when I pressed my hands again to my belly, it was the white wedding sash they touched, the sash that had been tied for another man.

"Oh, my lady." Tili wrapped her arms around me as all the tears I had kept myself from crying at the ceremony came spilling out.

Tili stayed there with her arms around me while I cried, stayed even when I had no tears left, when I had worn myself raw with grief and wanted to do nothing more than curl upon the new life that might be growing inside me. And so I might have done had one of Kin's men not cleared his throat outside my tent and reported that His Majesty was awaiting me at dinner.

"Tell him I will be there presently," I said and gathered my courage for what had to come next. "Tili." I set her back from me enough that I could see her face. "Did you say almost four weeks late?"

She nodded rather than speak, glancing again toward the tent flap.

"How bad is that? If Kin and I...when the sevenday is up, will people have reason to doubt this child is his?"

"Normally, I should say no one would consider it so closely, but enough people have heard the whispers and will look at the dates. You must hope they will think you and His Majesty…"

She left that thought hanging as I had, although while she had done so out of embarrassment, I had not wanted to consider what sharing Kin's mat would be like.

"That we had sex before the ceremony," I finished for her, not allowing myself to dance around the thought any longer. "But he will know that is untrue. Tili." I gripped her hand. "You cannot say anything about this. To anyone. No one at all can know, because if His Majesty finds out…"

I could not even imagine what Kin would do. His original proposal had been all about the political value of my name, and that would always be true, but where I had come to respect him, he had come to love me, and there was no saying how much the truth could destroy our future.

"Of course, my lady, I would die rather than betray you."

I allowed myself a small laugh. "I hope it won't come to anything as drastic as that. I suppose I ought not to keep him waiting much longer. Gods, I wish I could change out of this robe," I said, running my hands down the soiled pink silk I had worn at Kuroshima. "It is crinkled and stinks of horse and sweat."

"Here."

Tili reached for the chastity knot, and I stepped back, bumping my head on the tent roof. "What are you—? It can't be undone."

"I would not dare, my lady, but there is a way to loosen it. You don't think noble ladies go the full seven days without bathing or changing their robe, do you?"

I had, silently dreading how awful I would smell by the seventh day. "No, of course not."

"Here, let me show you."

Tili hooked a finger under one of the loops of cloth. "See this piece here? It slides through one of the small knots in the base. Sometimes it takes a bit of tug—"

She pulled at the silk, and the tight sash around my waist loosened. "See?"

"Thank you. But Kin will notice I have changed my robe."

"And he won't say anything, my lady. This is how these things are done. When Lady Tanike stayed at the palace for her sevenday, she wore a different coloured robe each day. Some ladies prefer to have seven the same, of course."

Feeling even more stupid, I allowed Tili to slide the sash down over my hips and pick out a new robe. She had altered a few for me as she once had back in Mei'lian, but with a plan brewing in my brain, I chose a conventional one instead.

Rain was falling when we made our way across the darkening camp to Kin's tent. Tili held a parasol to protect me from the worst of it, but by the time we arrived, it had started to seep through its fabric.

"Lady Hana Otako, Your Majesty." Kin's guards bowed as they announced me, rain rolling off their leather hoods.

Kin's voice came from within. "Let her come."

Lantern light spilled out as the tent was held open and I stepped inside, my heart already in my throat. Yet for all the fears that filled me, he greeted me with a smile. He had been frowning over a slew of maps, every line of his face etched with sleeplessness, but he pushed the lap table aside and gestured to the table upon which a meal had already been served. I lingered a moment in the entry, allowing him the chance to admire me. He did look me up and down, but if he enjoyed what he saw he made no sign.

"It has only been served a few minutes," he said of the meal as he moved to the larger table.

"My apologies for being late. I was filthy after the trip to Kuro-shima. That poor robe is quite ruined."

Just as Tili had said, Kin made no mention of the fact that I had changed my clothing, instead pouring me a bowl of wine and serving some rice into my bowl. The sight of a dish of spiced beef made my stomach turn, and almost I put my hand to my abdomen. However ill it made me feel, I would have to eat lest I arouse suspicion.

"Has there been any news since the meeting?" I said, settling myself across from him at the table.

"Nothing of note. There is no sign that Katashi intends to move from the safety of the Fen until the rains subside. At least while the other half of his army remains near Yagi, there is little reason to fear he means to march on the sister cities."

It had been a concern in the last weeks before the rains, but all signs now pointed to Katashi consolidating his hold on the north and doing little else until after the storm season except agitating along the river. It was unlike him, but then it wasn't Katashi making the decisions anymore.

I hitched a smile to my lips even as my gut hollowed. "That is some relief at least, though I cannot but fear what Darius may be planning."

Kin winced at the mention of my old guardian's name and for a time served himself food in silence rather than answer. He did not speak of it, but I wondered whether the loss of his onetime friend and advisor hurt him almost as much as the loss of Katashi hurt me.

The silence remained as we ate, each alone with our own unspoken grief. It was companionable in its way, and I wondered if companionable was the best I could hope for.

So as not to upset my stomach, I ate as slowly as I dared, and eventually he said, "You are deep in thought tonight, my lady."

"I could say the same of you, Your Majesty."

"I have been wondering why that Vice didn't stop us getting married."

I had not expected such sudden honesty, and my heart dropped, fearing all the reasons he may have considered. "Oh?" I managed. "You think that was deliberate?"

"It had to be. That he was there means the Vices knew, that they didn't send a whole army, or even just Otako to burn us out, means we were allowed to do it. I just wish I knew why. What does he know that I don't?"

Like heavy specters, Katashi and Darius lived with us every moment, their names on our tongues and their plans in our minds. I could not decide if I wanted to be rid of them or feared that a day might come when they were no longer present.

"I know who I'm fighting, and it's not Katashi," Kin went on when I made no answer. "He's just a very dangerous weapon in a very dangerous hand."

"Perhaps he thinks I am not as useful a catalyst as we have hoped."

"Or that even though you are, it will make no difference given the strength of his arsenal. Perhaps they will not wait out the season after all. Why wait when you can burn everything?"

I shivered at the thought. Too numerous had been the reports of soldiers being burned alive on the battlefield, of scouts being found charred, and though they were all just stories, the men were starting to talk.

"You have to tell them," I said.

"I know, but I don't think it's time. While Katashi is in the Fen, it is as well to hold off. Why risk panic by telling every solider that Katashi is a Vice and can create fire from nothing? An emperor cannot deal in truth, because the truth is that thousands of these men are going to die. The only thing that keeps men fighting is the possibility that they might get through today, and that every tomorrow they could be going home."

"And if you lie, they walk into every battle blind."

"Yes, but now is still not the time."

It was a topic I felt strongly on, had argued with him a number of times, and yet tonight I was too tired to even begin and just smiled. "As you say, Your Majesty."

"Now what is this?" he exclaimed. "Did Lady Hana Otako agree with me? Without argument? There must be some error. What have you done with my wife?"

Wife. With the ceremony done and one day having passed, it was closer than ever to being true, but no ceremony and no sash would ever make the child I carried his.

"Your wife," I said before my lack of response could wipe the smile from his face. "Is merely fatigued from last night's journey and in too good a charity with you to want to argue."

"You mean there is something else you would rather argue about?"

He said it with a good-humoured smile, but though I had been ready to abandon my meal and move around the table to enact my plan, his words reminded me of something that had bothered me at the meeting. "Actually, now you mention it, I do wish you'd told me just how bad the plague was getting. And the trade issues. Are we in danger of winning this war only to lose the empire?"

His smile vanished, and I berated myself for so dampening the mood. "The severity has grown steeply. It was the same last time, when it was Katashi's father threatening the empire, but we were able to win that before things could get so out of hand. This time is...different." He pushed his bowl away across the table. "I fear the Pikes have some...far less ethical means of warfare than our soldiers."

"Do you mean they are willing to starve us out?"

"I mean they have been infecting cities with plague by dropping dead bodies in the water and launching them over the walls."

For a time, our eyes met across the table, but although I could imagine the outcomes of such actions, no words came to my tongue. The people in those cities were not only innocent but the very Kisians Katashi wanted to rule.

"I'm sorry," Kin said. "I had not meant to upset you with that information, but you asked and I do not intend to lie to you."

"Thank you."

He quirked an eyebrow. "Are you sure you haven't done something with my wife?"

"Is it so rare for me to thank you?"

"Truthfully? Yes."

"Shall I come closer so you can look me over for yourself? To be sure I am me."

Steeling myself, I got to my feet and moved around the table to kneel beside him, taking my time about every movement so he might appreciate the lengths to which I had gone to make my robe more revealing. I had even asked Tili to pin the sleeves a little shorter so I might show more wrist.

Kin raised his eyebrows as I knelt down again, close enough that my knees were almost touching his leg. "You look like my wife, but I am still not sure I haven't misplaced her somewhere."

"How cruel, I am right here."

He smiled, but there was a slight narrowing of his eyes that made me uneasy. This man was no fool, I reminded myself. I would have to take care.

"So you are," he said, and touched my cheek. "And how much sweeter that will be in a few more days." He glanced down at the knot in my sash, but made no move to touch me.

"Whoever invented the sevenday must have been the cruellest person who ever lived."

"On that point I will not argue."

I touched his cheek as he touched mine and, receiving no rejection, leant in for a kiss. His lips were soft and warm and tasted faintly of broth, but they were not Katashi's.

Don't think about Katashi.

When I pressed the kiss more fiercely, Kin reciprocated, sliding his hands into my hair. He was strong and unyielding, hot, breathless, but with Katashi in my thoughts his passion left me cold. It might get better, I told myself and leant in still further, hunting the layers of imperial silk for a way to his skin. Giving up, I tugged at the intricate knot in his sash and it fell loose.

Kin pulled away. "Hana," he said, licking damp lips. "You need to leave. We can't do this."

"Yes we can," I said. "I don't want to wait."

I tried to kiss him again, but his outstretched arm jolted me back. "Hana, it matters," he said, his voice thick. "I will not stain my honour or yours, nor give any enemies a weapon they could use to annul our marriage."

"No one need ever know."

"I can't risk that."

Gently, he removed my hand from his sash and I found tears pricking my eyes, as panic poured into my body upon a tide of ice. "Don't you want me?"

"Too much." He shook his head. "But I should never have even... Hana, I..."

"Please," I said. "What difference does six days make?"

"All the difference. And we can make it all the more special for waiting."

Always so honourable. But it was his body I needed, not his honour. I loosened my own sash like Tili had shown me and it slid easily over my hips. Both of my robes dropped with it as I got to my feet, the change from fully clothed to naked barely discernible in the humid air. Kin stared, desire unmasked upon his features. His eyes ran over me like every line and limb was a worthy feast for the eye, and for a moment I was drunk on the power of the naked body.

"I want you, Your Majesty."

He looked away, hollowing me out with sudden fear. "Get dressed."

"Why?" I cried, my hands shaking. "Is something wrong with me?"

"Nothing is wrong with you, but I meant what I said. I will have you the day I untie that sash and not before."

Kin rose from his place, his expression implacably hard. The tent spun. Some sane part of my mind was screaming that I had to leave, that to push him any further was madness, but it didn't matter how I achieved my end so long as I achieved it.

He picked up my under-robe from the floor, but as he draped it around me, I thrust my hands between his legs. Despite my purpose, I was shocked by his rigidity beneath the silks and flinched.

Kin grabbed my wrist as I closed my hand around his manhood. "Hana!"

"Please," I said. "I am afraid we will not have another chance. Afraid of what may happen. I want to know what it feels like. I want a chance at carrying our child. I want to be with you tonight in case there are no more nights."

He closed his eyes a moment, his brow creased in the way Katashi's so often had when desire came upon him, and for one triumphant moment, I was sure I had him. Until he pushed my hand away and stepped back.

"How often?"

The words were quietly spoken, but I folded my arms across my stomach, clutching my under-robe closed to fight the swirling sickness in my gut.

"How often?" he repeated, though this time the level question had a hard edge and his gaze was remorseless in its intensity. And though I knew the longer I did not speak the more impossible it would be for him to accept a lie, I could not utter an answer, as trapped in my silence by grief as by fear.

"That is a clear enough answer."

"I—"

"Go." It was an order. Kin threw my robe at me. "Put that on and get out."

"No, listen, please!" I begged though I knew not what I even meant to say.

"Out! Now!"

I stood clutching the robe to my face, tears soaking the silk. I couldn't move, but there were no words that could recall the truth, the terrible aching truth that I had loved Katashi, loved being with Katashi and had never wanted it to stop.

I felt rather than saw Kin take the robe from my hands. With a gentle tug, he knotted my under-robe, then the silk was on my shoulders and I slipped my arms in like a child being dressed by its mother, hiccupping as I fought to control my misery. He even picked up the sash, wretchedly white, the knot of our marriage still tied, still full of such hope. In silence, I stepped into its circle and he slid it up over my hips.

I waited for him to look at me then, hoping to find his anger eased, but his jaw was set hard and his lips pressed tight, those thick brows frowning such that I could barely see his eyes. He did not look at me. He just stepped back and turned away.

There were no words.

Kin knelt at the table and turned his attention back to his pile of maps. "Good night, Lady Otako."

8. ENDYMION

The Pike they called traitor looked awful and smelt worse. He was covered in mud and sitting in his own filth with the leather strap of a satchel hanging around his neck like a noose.

"Morning, Traitor," said the Pike who had led the way. "We have some company for you."

The anger had left me tired and bruised, but Ire was at my back and pushed me inexorably on. On through puddles of thick mud that sucked at my feet, on through tangles of bulrushes and panna grass until we reached a thick post hammered deep into the marsh where the traitor sat.

I could have escaped the moment they had caught me, could have run, but it would have achieved nothing. Kimiko would look for me when I did not return, and until then I would stay, would let them think they had caught me, and hope to find a way to get through to Darius. Hope that Malice would tell him the truth.

"Go on, you stinking shit." The Pike kicked the prisoner's knee, but the traitor barely winced. "Bow for Prince Takehiko Otako; apologise that he's going to be sitting in your muck."

The man did not look up. Blood crusted his hair and tear tracks stained his dirty cheek. Yet it was Darius who filled my thoughts. I could not abandon him, though every attempt to make it back into his head ended in a tangle of other men's whispers.

All I needed was one more chance.

My Pike escort kicked the traitor again, then spat. The glob of saliva hit the prisoner's bare arm.

Calm, the traitor whispered to the air. *Calm. Don't let them rile you. Don't let them break you.*

Darius needed to know.

Calm.

"Go on, Your Majesty," the Pike said. "Why don't you have a seat? Wen's prepared a lovely soft spot for you."

Calm.

Wen? The name was familiar, but he did not look up. Flies occupied his hair and dotted his skin, swarming like predators. One walked across his lips, yet he did not move.

"Too proud to sit in filth?" The big Pike kicked the back of my knee, and I buckled, landing in soggy earth and faeces.

The man laughed as he hitched my manacles to the stake. "Better get used to it, Your Majesty. You're going to be here for a while."

Ire just watched as a fly landed on my nose, and I shook my head to shoo it off. Another buzzed past. They were walking freely over Wen's face now, over his lips and eyes and nose, but still the man did not move.

Getting no satisfaction from either of us, the Pike spat again at Wen before turning to leave. Ire went to follow.

"Wait, Ire!"

The big Vice stopped and half turned, glancing over his shoulder. "What?"

"Tell Darius that Lady Kimiko is carrying his child."

Confusion. Shock. I couldn't see it on his face, but I could feel it in his soul.

"Malice doesn't want him to know," I said. "But you have to tell him."

Ire grunted and turned away.

"Ire!"

He didn't look back, just took his confusion and disappeared into the trees. I tried to follow, tethering my Sight to him as he made his way back to the camp, but my focus kept skittering.

Calm. Don't let them break you. Don't let them win.

Wen's mantra snapped me back to a clearing where the sun beat down and the air was thick like soup. There was no sound beyond the buzz of insects and the concerted croaks of hundreds of frogs.

"Are you really Prince Takehiko Otako?"

The flies momentarily abandoned their quest to colonise his face.

"Does it matter?" I said. "A name is just a word."

The man looked around and I knew him at once—the Pike who had been with Hana. She had ordered him to sound the retreat.

"That isn't true." His words croaked from a parched throat. "Names have meaning. Especially *Otako*. Our gods have been Otakos for a long time." Wen licked his lips once, twice, a third time and let out a low groan. "Damn but I'm thirsty. I've tortured myself dreaming of a mouthful of this marsh water, stink and all."

"They found out what you did."

Wen licked his lips again. "You answer my question before I answer yours. I'm lord of this marsh dump, all right?"

My smile cracked the mud baking onto my face. The human capacity for survival was ever impressive. "Yes, my lord," I said. "I am Prince Takehiko Otako. I am also Endymion, bastard son of Lord Nyraek Laroth. Take your pick."

"Nobility forward and backward and shining out your arse." He laughed, a dry, delirious sound that was more a ragged breath than real amusement. "You must have done something even stupider than I did."

I stared at the swarm of marsh flies dancing in the thick air. "I tried to save Darius," I said. "But—"

I know you can hear me, Endymion. Or should I call you Justice now? I see you didn't heed my lessons.

"But?"

"I failed." I hadn't even spoken, not a word, the Empath in me usurping every instinct of compassion, of humanity, and turning it to judgement. Darius had tried to teach me how to bury my instincts, tried to teach me control, but it had been too late. Now I was running out of time.

You will need to be chained down before the end.

"I think I'm stealing memories," I said.

"Say that again."

"Katashi touched me and I saw his father's execution. He says he wasn't there, but I can hear the baying of the crowd and smell the blood like it's on my hands."

A symphony of frogs answered. Wen's fear stank worse than the swamp. "He was there. I've heard him talk about it."

And in my mind the memory played. Kin had taken everything from me.

"How can you steal someone's memories?"

"I don't know," I said.

Wen barked a bitter laugh. "Hells but there aren't many I'd fight to cling on to."

You could take the whole night. By the gods, what was I thinking?

There was a thud as Wen banged his head into the post.

I leant against it too, staring up at the black clouds gathering above the trees. "You were thinking it would help my sister and help Kisia, and you were right," I said, speaking to air empty of all but the scavenging flies. "You were thinking you would save the lives of hundreds of Pikes and soldiers too, and you were right."

"Don't waste time with my soul," came the reply. "I gave it up for lost years ago."

And through the stink of human waste came the mixed scents of a dozen drying herbs, the tang of orange and the sharp, earthy jab of waxen marshroot. It was embedded so deeply in his memory that the smells lived with him, like the smooth feel of old, worn leather beneath his hands.

He had never thought to end his life chained to a stick in the middle of a swamp. Would we drown, starve, or die of disease first? The question should have bothered me, but I felt detached. I had failed. Once again, I tried to find Darius, but the whispers grew louder and louder.

One million three hundred and sixteen thousand four hundred and eight.

I took a deep breath, then let it out slowly. I needed to concentrate on my body, on the pain and the beat of my own heart, on the thoughts I knew were my own.

"Why did you become a rebel?" I asked, seeking distraction.

"Can't you find the answer in my head? I'm not trying to hide it."

"Yes." The smell of incense. A distant horizon brimming with promise while a droning voice spoke ceaselessly. The crunch of dry herbs. Dandelion for digestive pains. Ginseng for fever. Red clover for conditions of the skin. Marshroot for binding cuts. Honey. White balen leaves. Tea. A girl in a red robe and all the smells in the world were eclipsed by blood. "Yes," I said again, pushing the images away, trying to stay inside my own head as Darius had once taught me. "I can, but I don't want to. Tell me. Talk to me."

Around us, bulrushes rustled in the rising wind.

"It's the wrong question."

"Why?"

"I'm not a rebel," Wen said. "I fight for the Emperor of Kisia."

"You mean for Katashi?"

"Emperor Katashi, yes."

"I don't care if you lie to me, because I can tell," I said. "But don't lie to yourself. You've been a Pike longer than he's been an emperor. You're a rebel. Why?"

"What sort of stupid question is that anyway?"

"It isn't a stupid question. Men fight for what is important. Sometimes it's money, sometimes it's honour, sometimes it's revenge."

A humourless laugh cut through a roll of thunder. "What about food, wine, and women?"

"If you're thinking with your stomach."

"And my cock." I knew he was grinning, the grin of a broken man determined to keep introspection at bay.

"And what if your cock was cut off?" I said. "What if there was no food and no wine? What would you fight for then? The divine right of Otakos to sit on a lump of crimson lacquered wood and tell everyone what to do?"

A new storm was coming.

"I can see why you ended up here. I'm not sure I like you myself."

"I'm a god. It doesn't matter if people like me."

No. Wrong answer.

One million three hundred and sixteen thousand four hundred and two.

I'm going to die here. I'm going to damn well die here sitting in my own mess and talking to a mad prince. What was I thinking? Of glory and gold, of fighting for something worthwhile and dying for something that had meaning. But there's no such thing. Death is just death and I don't want to die.

Thunder rumbled.

One.

Three thousand four hundred and eighty-five.

One hundred and twenty-six thousand and twelve.

One million three hundred and sixteen thousand three hundred and ninety-seven.

Wen cried.

I must have dozed, for when I next looked about me, the sky was dark and rain was falling. There was no light. No moonlight, no lanterns, just the sound of the rain and the ragged breathing of

Wen behind me. Even the whispers seemed quieter, as though the whole of Nivi Fen was holding its breath.

One million three hundred and sixteen thousand and ninety-nine.

No, don't think about the numbers.

I tried to hold my Empathy close, close to the pain in my wrists, the stink of the Fen, and the warmth from a bladder full of piss, but my Sight soon darted away unchecked.

One million three hundred and sixteen thousand and ninety-eight.

Darius's eyes had glittered. *Your Empathy isn't alive, Endymion*, he had said back at Esvar. *It doesn't have a life of its own. It does what it's told. If you want to connect to someone, it connects, if you want to hurt someone, it hurts them, if you want to kill them, they die. It is as much a tool as your arm or your leg, but just because you own a hand doesn't mean you should slap someone.*

He had learnt it was himself he hated, not the Empathy, and now, finally, I understood what he had meant.

"All I wanted was to protect you."

You have to let it go, Endymion. You have to fight what makes you angry. You have to stop caring. Don't pretend you have no heart, don't have one at all. Your compassion will kill you.

A light flickered among the trees.

"Wen?"

There was no answer.

The light shone again, hovering like a bloated firefly. A light that survived despite the rain meant a lantern.

"Wen?"

I tried to keep my Empathy reined in, but the fear that accompanied the light was so raw it stung my eyes. Melancholy. Anger. Shame. Deep and gut-wrenching.

I knew that mind.

"Endymion?"

And I knew that voice.

"I'm here," I said through a constricted throat. "Just follow the smell."

"It's hard to miss."

Beset by rain, the lantern bobbed closer.

Wen woke with a start, jolting the post against my back. "What's going on? Who is that?"

"A friend."

The figure drew closer until the golden light etched a face from the night. "Why is it always me who has to save you?" Hope said, halting at the edge of our pool. Raindrops scattered its surface.

"Because you...I..." I trailed off. Kimiko had told me to run after him and tell him how I felt, but what did it matter? I was running out of time before Endymion ceased to exist. "Because Malice doesn't own you."

A press of emotions muffled his whispers, but he laughed softly. "I'm not so sure." He set the lantern down on a rock and crouched beside it, his dark clothes melding into the night. Rain dripped from the ends of his hair.

"Did I do the right thing? Pushing you to break the mark back near Rina?" he said, keeping his distance. "I wanted you to get away, but here you are back again. Is it that hard to escape?"

The young Vice was pale, just like he had been in the moonlight when we first met atop the crashed prison cart. "Stinking prison carts," I said. "We're good at this kindness to all men thing, huh? What is he doing? Is he going to climb down or just stand there staring at me?"

"I wish you hadn't come back," he said, his melancholy deepening. "I wish you had just kept running and escaped this hell while you could. I'd tell you to do so now, but I know you're not going to listen to me."

"But you're going to let me go?"

Hope tilted his head as though examining me for the first time, and a little smile turned his lips. "I have not given up hope in you even though you have."

My heartbeat sped as much from his words as the determined way he held my gaze just long enough to make me think of what Kimiko had said. Then, the smile twisting, he looked down at the mud. "I'm going to free you, but you have to do something important for me, can you?"

"Anything for you, you know that," I said before I could recall the words, could recall my purpose in coming.

Hope's smile twisted further. "It's not for me. I overheard Lord Laroth's plans. Katashi is going to burn Shimai, and you have to warn them he's coming, warn the people to get out. I would go, but any moment, they will notice I am gone and—"

Wen's head snapped around, the lantern light searing up the side of his face. "Burn Shimai?"

"Yes. They were talking about how Kin's marriage to Lady Hana has solidified an alliance with old loyalists. They are mounting a campaign to reclaim Risian and the Willow Road and have pulled half the garrison from Shimai. Lord Laroth and Katashi plan to take advantage of this."

"When?"

Hope shook his head, sending water flying. "I don't know. But they'll travel light and Katashi will press them hard. Days."

"Then you're right, they have to be warned," Wen said. "I don't know what your name is, but if you will free me too, I'll go. I'll warn them. I will get there in time, even if I have to run the whole way without rest. Just let me out of here."

"My name is Hope."

Wen laughed a brittle laugh. "Omen or cruel joke?"

"I wish I knew. But even if I let you go, they've already removed the garrison from Shimai. There won't be enough men to defend the city."

"Then I'll go to Emperor Kin at Kogahaera."

"Emperor Kin won't listen to a Pike."

"No," Wen agreed. "But Lady Hana might."

Hope nodded, and leaving the lantern where it was, he took a step forward into our filthy pool and scrunched up his nose. "Goodwill to all men, huh?" he said, looking at me. "Is that what I said?"

"It was what you were thinking," I said. "Out loud, you said, 'I'll help you down. Give me your hand.'"

He knelt between us, his damp cleanliness the nicest smell that had ever entered this swamp. His shoulder brushed mine, his hair level with my nose as he worked.

Metal scraped, then the chains fell loose. Hope stood. "That's all I can do for you," he said, turning away. "Don't ask me for more. You're on your own now."

Wen sighed, got up, and stretched, clenching and unclenching his fists as he reached to the sky. "Gods it feels good to be free," he said, checking his leather satchel was still with him. There was love in the way he touched it, despite the covering of mud and excrement. "Thank you," he said to Hope.

"Don't thank me yet," Hope said, leaving the lantern and backing to the edge of the pool. "All my good deeds are cursed. The Master calls it balance."

He turned away, but when I made to follow him, Wen gripped my elbow. "We have to get to Lady Hana," he said, shaking despite the heat.

"No, I came for Darius."

"You would choose one man over thousands? Even a god cannot save a monster, Takehiko."

A monster. If Darius was a monster, what did that make me?

Wen caught my hand inches from his face. "What was that? Did you just try to hit me?" he said, holding my fist in his filthy hand. His memory leapt to me, spark-like, and I saw my own blank expression. My own fist. My own anger lashing out.

Wen dropped my hand. "What just happened?"

My fingers tightened upon the lantern. When had I picked it up?

"We need to get out of here," Wen said, giving up on my answer. "You can stay if you like."

"They will all suffer," I said. "They will all die."

"What?"

"He will burn for what he did to my family. My name."

The words came from my lips, but I had not thought them. They were not mine. They—

A fist smashed into my jaw, and I hit the ground. The lantern fell into the mire on a drunken angle, illuminating the underside of Katashi's chin. "You're sick," he jeered down at me. "From the moment we first met, you haven't been able to keep out of my head. No, don't even think about getting up, Endymion, or I'll burn your friend's face off."

Wen's feet were no longer touching the ground. Katashi held him up by his tunic as though he weighed nothing. "Well, well, I thought little Hope was up to something. I ought to have killed you weeks ago, but you made such a good diversion for the men. Something for them to hate more than me."

Wen spat at him.

"Well, aren't you brave." Katashi wiped his jaw with the back of his free hand. "Hoping to impress my cousin?"

"Better than impressing you." Wen's jaw jutted as Katashi tightened his grip. "There was a time I would have followed Monarch to any end. But not this end. I will not fight to see my homeland burn. May the gods judge us all."

"There are no gods," Katashi said. "There is no justice."

"Perhaps not, but by the laws of Kisia, Lord Takehiko Otako should be on the throne, not you."

Fury whipped through the trees like the slap of an invisible hand, bending rain out of its path. Katashi gripped Wen's hair and yanked his head back. "Takehiko is no more an Otako than you are," he said, his words like a hiss of escaping steam. "He is full of *spider* blood." Katashi glared at me with those fiery blue eyes. "Go on, Endymion, stop me. Give me a reason to kill you too, out here where your brothers can't save you."

Smoke curled from Wen's hair, sending terror thumping through my head.

Burn him. Burn him.

"No!" Wen shouted, half-defiant, half-pleading. He kicked, thrashed, and tried to grab his former captain, but Katashi punched him in the gut. Air burst from my lungs. Pain. The smell of burning linen. Burning hair. Fury stained every thought. I wanted him to burn, wanted him to die, the desire raging in me so strongly I could not move, could not fight. Not even when pain seared across my scalp as Wen's hair burst into flames.

I screamed as Wen screamed, owning no thought, only pain like knives slitting my scalp.

An all too familiar soul moved nearby, trailing its melancholy. Hope. I tried to call to him, to beg his help, but before I could find words glass smashed overhead. Katashi staggered, and Wen fell in the haze before me. The lantern light and the flames had died, but the agony had not.

"Wen?" I gasped. "Wen!"

The afterburn of fire flickered across my vision. The Pike was not dead, but his soul was split, pouring pain upon the world.

Katashi groaned. "I am going to *kill* you, Endymion," he promised the darkness. His anger flared as bright as his fire had, but before he could reach the level of incandescence that had paralysed me, I threw his rage back at him. Flames burst from him, and for a few long seconds, he burned like a torch, before the fire once again extinguished.

Laughter replaced the crackling. "That tickled," he said. "And now I'm all dry."

Wen jolted awake with a whimper. I whimpered too. The rain

was doing nothing to cool the burning of my skin. No, not my skin. I tried to untangle his pain from my flesh as I crawled toward him in the darkness.

A bowstring creaked.

"You can't hide from me, Endymion," Katashi said. "Pikes live in the dark."

I rolled. Rain fell into my face, and the outline of Katashi towered over me, black robe on a dark night. But something else tugged at my Sight. Another soul. I tried to concentrate on it, but panic tore at every logical thought. I had judged Wen worthy. I could not let him die.

"Fire or steel?" Katashi said. "What is the more fitting end for a spider's bastard?"

Hoofbeats.

Katashi looked up. Once again, Wen woke and pain tore through me, our cries sounding in unison.

"Endymion?"

Katashi started to laugh. "Why, good evening, dear sister," he called, slackening his grip on the bow. "What a lovely place for a family reunion."

"Katashi?"

A lantern swung into my vision, hanging from Kimiko's outstretched hand. In her other were two sets of reins. Kaze snorted and nudged my cheek, water dripping from his mane.

Wen sank once again, and his pain drained from my body as Katashi turned his bow on Kimiko. She didn't flinch. "You shouldn't have Hacho out in the rain, Brother," she said. "You used to look after her better."

"Why are you here?"

"To kill Endymion myself."

He laughed, the sound like the hiss of rain evaporating off his skin. "You think I'm stupid," he said. "If you wanted that, he would be dead already, Miko." The tip of an arrow pointed at her face. "Go away. This has nothing to do with you."

"Do you think Mama would be proud of you? Proud of this."

Katashi froze like a man turned to stone, the name a spike of hurt in his heart. Mama. Her voice deep. Her touch soft. The smell of incense caught to her hair.

Mama.

"Do you think she would take your hand and say, *Well done, brave Tashi*?"

"Kimiko." Katashi growled like a wounded beast.

"Do you think she would applaud you for selling me to Malice?" she went on. I pulled myself along the sodden ground toward Wen. By the light of Kimiko's lantern, his face looked to be smeared with mud, but the truth was much worse. He groaned, and I gritted my teeth at the stab of pain.

"Or for burning your enemies alive?"

A snort. A step beside my ear, and a wet, leathery nose nudged my cheek. The stink of burning flesh smelt ten times worse through Kaze's nose.

"I have done what I had to do," Katashi said, his arm trembling with the effort of holding the bowstring taut. "Everything I have done has been for our family. For our name and our honour. To avenge the death of our father."

"Do you think *he* would be proud of you?"

Anguish poured from his pierced heart, washing over me as completely as Wen's pain had done. Tianto Otako, tall and strong and smelling of leather and vanilla and Mama's incense. He ought to have been emperor. He ought to have lived. He ought to have seen me grow to be a man.

"Do you think he would call your choices honourable?" Kimiko said, unrelenting. "Do you think he would call you son?"

Katashi screamed. A spurt of fire erupted, leaving tears to hiss and sizzle as they ran down his cheeks. "Damn you!" he shouted at his twin. Her horse backed, eyes darting, but she managed to keep him from bolting with a hand on his neck.

"Well?" she repeated. "Do you think they would be proud?"

"Shut up!" Katashi sank to his knees. His grief poured upon the world like sticky tar, black and cloying. "None of this should have happened. I should have been a prince. An emperor. Kisia should have been ours. But this world is rotten and wrong, and I fight it and I fight it and it only gets worse."

His hopelessness was suffocating. It infused me, and I looked at Wen with new eyes. He lived, but his flesh was scorched and blistering and beginning to swell. I had judged him worthy, but saving him was hopeless.

Hopeless.

I'm sorry. I should have stayed. I'm sorry. I should have helped. I'm sorry. I know it means nothing, but I'm sorry.

Hope had stayed. Had helped. The knowledge lit my heart with a happiness I could give no voice, a tiny light with which to fight back the dark hopelessness he was creating.

Succumbing to it, Katashi wailed. It was a strange, haunting sound, and one I had never thought to hear. The cry rose, warbling, almost birdlike in its raw emotion. He had thrown Hacho aside to huddle in the mud, this strong, confident man, this leader, this emperor, reduced to a plaintive cry in the night.

"It's you, isn't it?" Kimiko said, sliding down from her horse to stand before her prostrate brother. "What are you doing to him?"

"No." I pushed the hopelessness away, trying not to swallow its poison. "It isn't me."

Kimiko shifted her lantern, scanning the darkness. "Is this what you did on the road to Rina?"

"Yes. No. It was Hope."

I can't hold him much longer, Endymion. Get out of here.

I pulled myself up, the sticky swamp as loath to let me go as I was to leave. To leave him. "We have to go. I have to get Wen to Kogahaera."

"Who did you tell about the child? I've had Vices coming after me all day. Tell me."

"Help me get Wen out of here."

Kimiko looked at the burned Pike, while in a crumpled, steaming heap, Katashi continued to cry and moan like a child stolen from its mother. "He won't make it," she said. "He'll die before you get there."

"No," I said. "He can't." Kimiko made no move to help, just kept her distance, eyes flitting from me to her brother and back. "Help me," I said. "We need to warn Hana. Katashi is going to–"

"Who did you tell?"

Go!

Katashi's wracking sobs were slowing.

Go!

"Please help me," I said.

"Did you tell Darius?"

"No."

"Malice then." Kimiko gnawed the inside of her cheek. Steam rose around her distraught brother in thickening clouds. "Damn you, Endymion." She gripped Wen under his arms and dragged him up with a grunt. "I'll help, but only because I need to get out of here. We might as well be delivering a corpse."

DAY THREE

9. HANA

I woke trapped in a tangle of sheets, my misery its own blanket. Lying still listening, there was no sign of Tili, just the gentle pitter-patter of rain upon the tent. The night had brought no solace, only painful memories. In the darkness, the ghost of Katashi had run his hands over my hips and breasts and down my thighs, while my fingers traced the smooth curve of his back.

Beneath the twisted sheets, my white sash was still there, its knot as tight as the night it had been made. White for a virgin bride—a lie I had to wear proudly.

I got up, casting the sheets aside. At the tent opening, rain was running off the oilcloth awning. Outside, soldiers were going about their business unaware that anything was amiss. Weapons, horses, plates of food, broken armour, tools, wood, sacks of rice and millet and sorghum, messages, gossip—the camp was a busy place and it all functioned smoothly because of Kin. Without me, it would not change, but without him—

"My lady."

Tili was carrying a large pitcher and froze just outside the tent as though unsure of her welcome.

"I need to see His Majesty," I said. "Take a message for me."

"I'm sorry, my lady," she said, bowing once. Twice. Her grip on the pitcher tightened. "His Majesty rode out this morning."

"Rode out? Where to?"

"I could not tell you that, my lady, I only hear gossip."

It was only then I realised she was standing in the rain, and I stepped aside. Tili bowed a third time and walked past me into the tent. "I have brought water, my lady," she said, setting the pitcher down. "I thought you might like to wash."

"I'm sure I need to." I sniffed my underarm. "Definitely."

Tili went to work loosening my sash and my robe, but not once did she meet my gaze. She had cried with me last night. There had been nothing to say then and there was nothing to say now, but the silence felt heavy.

While I washed, Tili hunted for a clean robe. "The rain looks as though it means to stay," she said. "Blue would, I feel, be inauspicious, my lady, but perhaps pink—"

"No, my armour."

Tili turned. "My lady?"

"My armour," I repeated.

Reluctantly, she unfolded the armour I had worn to Kuroshima. "Are you sure about this, my lady? It is not the done thing for a woman in her sevenday to dress as a man."

"I am not dressing as a man, merely as a woman in armour," I said. "Will the sash loosen enough to go over the top?"

"I think so, my lady."

"Then that is what I am wearing."

Tili helped me into the plain under-tunic first, then the linen and leather and mail, tightening buckles and knotting ties, loops, and buttons. Over the top of it all hung a crimson silk surcoat. It was a beautiful thing, the fabric so smooth and soft, every stitch of the delicate dragon pattern so tiny it would have taken a skilled seamstress weeks to complete.

Tili held my white sash while I stepped into it. It needed to be loosened more to accommodate my layers, but when she began to tighten it again, I stopped her. "No," I said. "Tie it at the back. It won't be in the way there."

"At the back?" Tili's soft features creased into a picture of horror. "You cannot mean it, my lady. Only old ladies tie their sashes at the back."

"And one day I plan to be very old. Do it."

"Yes, my lady."

With a sharp jerk, she turned the sash so only smooth white silk crossed my stomach. There it was yanked tight, and Tili stepped back to cringe at her handiwork.

"Lady Hana!"

My eyes did not leave Tili's face. "That's General Ryoji," I said. "But if he is here, then who went with Kin?"

"Lady Hana!"

I went to the tent entrance. General Ryoji stood in the spitting rain. His hair was stuck to his forehead and he was out of breath.

"General," I said. "If you did not ride out with Emperor Kin, then who is protecting him?"

"He has an escort, my lady," General Ryoji said. "My job now includes your protection as well as his. I'm afraid you are needed."

"What's wrong? Is it Kin? Where has he gone?"

"No, not His Majesty. Endymion."

"Endymion?"

There was an extra beat of silence before he said, "Have I pronounced it wrong? My Chiltaen is not very good. The young man who sat with Lady Kimiko when she was unwell."

"Yes, yes, I know who he is," I said, stepping out into the rain, my heartbeat speeding to a flurry. "But what about him?"

"He arrived a few minutes ago with Lady Kimiko and an injured Pike. They're asking for you."

I began walking before he finished. "They're with Master Kenji, my lady," he said, jogging to catch up. "But I must warn you it is not a pleasant sight."

I ran, rain falling like needles as I sped along rows of tents. Soldiers leapt out of my way. Some of them were preparing their mats, others rising from them, the change in watch making this hour after dawn busier than usual.

Outside Master Kenji's tent, a boy was holding two horses.

"My lady, please wait," General Ryoji called. "It is not—"

I pushed through the leather curtain and breathed in the stink of blood and burned leather, of piss and faeces and sickly-sweet honey, and I retched. "I'm sorry, my lady," General Ryoji said, joining me. "I ought to have better prepared you for the smell."

"It is...quite a smell," I said, happy to grasp at this excuse, though no smell had ever made me feel so nauseous before. I straightened to find every eye in the tent upon me. Master Kenji and one of his assistants stood at a worktable, while on the straw-strewn floor, Endymion sat hugging his knees to his chest. Every inch of him was filthy.

Kimiko sat beside him, wet and blood-splattered, the remains of her hair a knotted mess. I would never forget the smell of it burning as I dragged her across the floor of Katashi's tent.

"Hello again, Hana," she said. "I see I ought to congratulate you. That is a fine sash."

Kimiko's wrists were tied, and two imperial guards stood watching her with their hands clasping their sword hilts.

"Why is Lady Kimiko bound?" I demanded, turning on General Ryoji as he shook the rain from his hair.

"Because I'm a threat," she said, before he could answer. I looked back. Her face was pale with dark rings beneath her eyes, yet there was ferocity in her words. Even the straight-backed way she sat was like a challenge.

"What are you doing here?"

A muffled moan came from the worktable as though in answer, and one of Kenji's boys dashed past with a bowl of black water. At the table, Master Kenji was bent low over an injured man. "My lady, this is not a sight for any delicately nurtured female," he said as I joined him.

"Then it is just as well that I was not delicately nurtured," I replied. The physician was working quickly, cutting away cloth and charred leather to reveal black and blistered flesh. The burned man dug his teeth into a leather strap and stared up at me with wild eyes.

"Wen?"

"You know him?" General Ryoji joined me at the table, his voice an anchor in a world fast spiralling out of my control.

"Yes. I know him." I brushed a clump of singed hair back from Wen's brow as gently as I could, looking down into eyes that seemed to swim in and out of focus.

"Wen, can you hear me? It's Hana."

Skin tore away with the next strip of cloth, eliciting a muffled scream.

I turned back to Endymion and Kimiko. Neither had moved. "What happened?" I demanded. "Did...did Katashi do this? Why?"

Endymion shook his head slowly, teeth clenched on the answer. He was shaking.

"There's no point talking to him," Kimiko said. "He's an Empath and is feeling all Wen's pain. We almost didn't make it."

"Will he live?" General Ryoji asked, drawing my attention back to Wen.

"I have dosed him with a tincture of opium, General, and I am doing all I can," the physician said. "But I cannot lie and say I do not fear it will all soon be for nothing."

Wen's bloodshot eyes followed my hand as I gently took the leather strap from between his teeth. The rebel licked his lips. "Lady Hana," he managed in a terrible rasp. "I shouldn't have gone back. I should have stayed. I should..."

His eyes rolled back as Master Kenji pressed ointment onto his blistered arm. The ointment smelt of honey but was the colour of fresh grass, thick and sticky. One of Master Kenji's boys held the bowl and stirred continuously, not letting the mixture set.

"We're not in the hells yet," I said, recalling Wen's words from that night in the Valley.

He let out a cry that turned into a dry, breathy laugh. "Not yet," he agreed. "But soon the gods will judge me for my stupidity. You have to stop them, he's going to burn Shimai."

Burn Shimai. Exactly as he had planned to let the pirate enclave do before I had warned Kin of the impending danger. But Katashi needed no pirates now.

"They are going to what?" Ryoji stepped forward.

"Attack the city. Perhaps as early as tomorrow night."

"But Shimai is the most heavily defended city in Kisia!"

Wen shook his head slowly. "That doesn't matter. First Shimai, then Mei'lian. He cannot be stopped. Everyone who does not bow to him will burn."

As though to emphasise his words, Wen hissed and reached instinctively to grab his wounds. This only caused him to howl.

"You're sure about Shimai?" General Ryoji asked, crouching now at Wen's head.

"I'm sure." He swallowed hard, again and again, breath coming in sharp gasps. "They know about the battalions you pulled from the city and the planned attack on Risian," he went on between hissing breaths. "But that's all I know. They have—" The scissors snipped, and Wen screamed as more charred cloth was peeled away. My stomach knotted.

General Ryoji stood. "If they know he escaped with this information, they might change their plans," he said to me. "Do you trust this man?"

"I have trusted him with my life and would again, General," I said. "Where is His Majesty?"

"I don't know," he whispered. "He went on the mission to scout out positions east of Risian. It could take a man hours to find them."

"If you have a better idea, General, I'm listening. Otherwise, I think you ought to send a rider as quickly as you can."

General Ryoji stepped back and bowed. "Yes, my lady."

"Your fastest rider!" I added, but the general was already gone, disappearing through the leather curtain.

From the table, Wen watched me with bloodshot eyes. "I'm sorry, my lady."

"I think you have earned the right to dispense with such formality," I said, taking his blood-crusted hand.

Another short laugh turned into a cough. "Regent then," he said. "A man must have a captain. Especially where I'm going."

Tears dampened my eyes. I had seen too many wounds to believe anyone could come back from these.

The scissors snipped. Again Wen jerked, gripping my hand so hard I thought my bones might snap. Blood oozed through his linen bindings.

"Is there nothing more to be done?" I asked as Master Kenji snatched up another bandage. "To ease the pain at least."

"I am doing all I can, my lady," he said. "I'm afraid he's in the hands of the gods now. Xi has run for a priest."

I clung to Wen's hand, and together we waited. To keep him with me, I entertained him with reminiscences. Of the day Katashi found him chained to the fence outside a whorehouse for being unable to pay, of a narrow escape along the bandit pass in my first weeks of having joined them, and many a night telling tales around the campfire when the small rebel army had been more like a family, Katashi their god.

Throughout it all, neither Endymion nor Kimiko spoke or even seemed to move, until the leather curtains parted and Father Kokoro stepped in. There had to be more than one priest in the camp, and yet the court priest himself had come for a mere Pike. He stood a moment on the threshold, casting his gaze around the tent. Endymion flinched and looked away, and I was reminded of all Father Kokoro had said about the Vices and about Darius's family, about how they all deserved to die. Had he come because he knew Endymion was an Empath too?

If he knew, he made no sign of it as he came quickly to my side. "My lady," he said, bowing reverentially. "You wished for a priest?"

"Certainly, Father. This man needs you."

He bowed again and, without questioning the identity of the man upon the table, prepared to intercede with the gods on his behalf.

General Ryoji returned as Father Kokoro began his prayers. "Riders have gone out," he said, drawing me aside. "But there is no guarantee they will find them quickly."

"How long?"

"Perhaps not until evening. They planned to ride hard. His Majesty was . . . in a mood when he left."

"That is my fault."

"My lady—"

"Damn you and your *my ladies*!" I hissed. "I was a farmer's daughter and a rebel much longer than I have been a lady. What does General Rini say? Have you informed him?"

"Yes, my—" He swallowed hard. "Yes. He says nothing can be decided until His Majesty returns."

"Then we had damn well better hope His Majesty found the scenery so fine that he dawdled on the road."

General Ryoji agreed with a grimace and went out again. Wen watched him go with drooping eyes, paying no mind to Father Kokoro, who was chanting the invocation over him. In the old priest sign language, I said: *Your turn on watch*, and this seemed to please him, but he soon closed his eyes and lay like a man asleep.

Only once the invocation was done did Wen find the energy to speak again. "Captain?" he said in a whisper.

"Yes?"

"Thank you for staying with me."

"I would not leave you alone."

A weak smile. "Takehiko?"

Takehiko. At the sound of the name, my heart leapt into my

throat. Across from me, Father Kokoro's gaze flicked to Endymion an instant before the young man got slowly to his feet. "Yes, my friend?" he said, approaching with shuffling steps.

I stared at him. Takehiko? My brother Takehiko? He couldn't be. Could he?

Wen attempted to smile at him while my thoughts whirled on, trying to recall everything I'd ever heard about my brother. "You helped me find peace," Wen said. "Thank you."

"And to you." There was great sadness in Endymion's face, but tears did not slide down his cheeks as they had slid down mine. Right up until the moment Wen had said my brother's name. Now I could think of nothing else.

The three of us remained in silence while Wen's breathing became laboured. We were an unlikely group. Father Kokoro solemn, Endymion trembling, and I staring at nothing. I wished I could ask him if it was true, but with so many people around to hear the words, I could not speak, could only stand in vigil with a man who hated Empaths and an Empath who could be the truest heir to the Crimson Throne.

Caught in my own thoughts in that close, putrid space, time lost all meaning, and I don't know how long it was before General Ryoji returned. He entered looking grim and shook his head.

No sign of Kin. In the shock of hearing Takehiko's name, I had almost forgotten the difficulties we had found ourselves in.

"How many men do we have in Shimai?" I asked as he came to my side.

"Half the garrison," the general said. "Enough to hold a siege for a few hours, maybe days depending on what Otako throws at them, but not enough to beat him back."

"Mei'lian?"

He shook his head. "Half a battalion perhaps, most city guards, not soldiers." General Jikuko had not been recalled from the Valley. General Yi was marching east. We were closest, but General Rini would not move without imperial sanction.

"How long will it take us to reach Shimai?"

"Times and distances are not fixed in military movements, my lady," General Ryoji said. "If we push the men hard and travel light, we could be there in a day, or a day and a half. If we travel in the imperial style, then I'd say about four days."

I looked down at Wen, barely holding on to life. "It must be nearly noon," I said.

"Just past," the general replied.

"And it will take time to mobilise the men."

He did not answer. I bit my lip, gnawing on the soft flesh. "Damn it," I breathed. "We have to move. We have to move now. Give the order."

"I cannot do that. I command the Imperial Guard, not the army. The men will not take their orders from me, and neither will General Rini."

"Then damn well give the order in my name, General. Tell them their empress orders them to make ready to march for Shimai, in the name of Emperor Kin."

"And if they do not listen, my lady?"

"Then I will talk to them."

"If you could come now—"

"No. I will not leave this man to die alone."

General Ryoji lowered his voice. "One man is more important than the empire?"

"This man is. A leader who loses sight of the importance of individuals is not fit to command armies, General."

"A wise observation, my lady." He bowed stiffly. "I will convey your order to General Rini."

He left, and in his absence, I felt Endymion's presence more keenly, as though he had been listening to our conversation. Takehiko. The name gnawed at my thoughts, but it had to be a problem for another time. While Wen's breathing grew shallower, General Ryoji would be trying to convince the council that we needed to move. Kin was nowhere to be found, and under Darius's control, Katashi was going to set Shimai alight. Even my white sash seemed unimportant beneath this new weight, every second now clicking along faster and more urgently.

Wen sucked in a series of short, sharp rasps, drawing me back to the present. I squeezed his hand, hoping the end would come soon. There was somewhere else I needed to be, but I had made a promise and I would keep it. I would be loyal to him as he had been to me.

"He knows you're still here," Endymion said.

I did not look around but kept my gaze upon the broken Pike. "Is he in a lot of pain?" I asked.

"Yes, my lady."

"Are *you* in a lot of pain?"

"Yes, my lady."

"You may leave."

"No, my lady. Your grief is heavier than his pain." Endymion touched my hand. It tingled oddly and I shivered, a shiver that ran from my fingers all the way to the tips of my hair and back. He pulled his hand away sharply as though I were the cold one. Perhaps he didn't like people. Darius had never been one to touch without reason.

I looked down at the man on the table in front of us. His face was a mess. Another victim of Katashi's wrath.

"Is he dead?" I asked.

"He is nearly gone," Endymion said, the words emerging through gritted teeth. "He is finding peace."

When General Ryoji returned, he halted on the threshold, grimmer than ever. "There is still no sign of His Majesty, and General Rini is refusing to accept your commands," he said. "He says he won't take orders from a woman, empress or not."

Master Kenji shot a disapproving glare in the general's direction but went on rolling bandages.

"It isn't that she's a woman," Father Kokoro said, breaking his silence. "They are afraid of her. They can all remember swearing the oath of allegiance at Emperor Lan's feet. An oath that swore to protect and serve him and his heirs. If they will not take orders from you as Lady Hana, then give them Emperor Lan's legitimate heir instead." He smiled. "Priests see a lot of things, my lady. We hear a lot of confessions too."

"I'm sorry, my lady," Master Kenji interrupted, lifting his hand from the burned man's forehead. "He's gone."

Master Kenji was a compassionate man, but the sympathy in his expression was troubling. Why was he so sorry about a man who was unknown to me? At another time, I might have asked, but I had already lingered too long.

"Master Kenji?"

"Yes, my lady?"

"We are marching for Shimai. Bring as many supplies as you can, but be prepared to travel fast."

The man's eyes bulged from his head. "Yes, my lady." Master Kenji gestured toward the dead body. "What would you like us to do with him?"

"Why? What do you normally do with corpses?"

"Bury them."

"Then bury him."

"Er . . . Yes, my lady."

General Ryoji followed me to the entrance, where we were met by a grey afternoon lashed with rain. "General Rini has gathered the council," he said. "Shall I take a message that you wish to speak to him?"

"No, I will go to him there. If I speak to him alone, he can deny everything I say. I need an audience. Just make sure they are all present."

General Ryoji bowed. "Yes, my lady."

As he strode away, I took a deep breath and let it out slowly, listening to Master Kenji ordering his assistants to be sure to pack the bandages and the herb box but not to worry about the press. As he listed off herbs and oils, I found myself frowning at the dull afternoon, as though each word was creating an itch in my brain that needed to be scratched. I ran my fingers through my hair. Inside the tent, Endymion had not moved from the dead man's side. Had he known him? I couldn't recall. No one had said.

Father Kokoro stepped up beside me. "My lady, may I request permission to take Endymion into my custody? He is, as perhaps you are already aware, also a son of Nyraek Laroth and an Empath and is, I feel, very dangerous in the current climate."

I turned to face him and, keeping my voice low, said, "That man called him Takehiko."

"It may be that he has chosen a more Kisian name to blend in better here," he said with a broad smile and a little shrug. "He would not be the first to distance himself from any hint of Chiltaen heritage."

"But you said he is Lord Nyraek Laroth's son."

"His illegitimate son, yes. As you informed me Malice is also one, you cannot be surprised, my lady."

"No, but—" I glanced back to be sure no one was close enough to hear us. "I think there is something you aren't telling me, Father Kokoro. When that Pike called for Takehiko, you looked at Endymion before he even stood up."

Father Kokoro's smile broadened further, but it was a cold, constructed thing, a toothy curtain behind which annoyance boiled. "I cannot imagine what you are insinuating, my lady. Priests hear many things."

"Such as the fact that my brother is not as dead as people assume?"

I had chosen to attack him bluntly and was rewarded with a twitch he could not hide. "Perhaps the things you hear are why His Majesty kept you on as his priest?" He flinched and it was answer enough for me, and before he could retort, I added, "I have no time to deal with this now, Father, but no, you do not have my permission to as much as go near Endymion. He is, until further notice, under my sole protection. Now if you will excuse me, I have a meeting to attend."

And without waiting for a reply, I left him standing outside the tent, surely glaring after me.

The councillors were arguing when I arrived at the meeting tent, the noise of their disagreement carrying far into the camp. Two dozen men, their names all known to me, varying in age from General Ryoji at one end to General Rini at the other. He had served in the army so long that he had once outranked General Kin, in a Kisia that had belonged to my father.

It was General Rini who saw me first. "Good afternoon, General," I said, as a hush fell over them man by man. "I see you are wasting valuable time bickering amongst yourselves."

"We are discussing the situation, my lady," General Rini said, bristling. "And I can assure you we have it well in hand. When His Majesty returns—"

"When His Majesty returns, we will be too late. If we do not move this army now, Shimai will fall."

"Shimai has a standing garrison, my lady. It also has walls that are near impossible to breach—"

"Like Koi?" I said. "Near impossible is not good enough. Think on all Katashi has done before you decide you are safe behind your tall walls. And *when* Shimai falls, nothing will stop him taking Mei'lian."

Whispering rose over the patter of rain. General Rini stood. "And how can we be sure your information is even correct?" he said, his indulgent smile asking to be slapped from his face. "The dying words of a Pike? A traitor?"

I had every councillor's attention. In the silence, my rapid heartbeat sounded like a war drum. "If being a Pike makes him a traitor, then you are a traitor too, General."

"Me? I am no Pike!"

"No, you are worse. Pikes swore an oath to my cousin, and to him they have always been loyal. Tell me, General, when you first joined the Rising Army, to whom did you swear your oath?"

"To Emperor Lan."

"You swore an oath to my father, but you no longer serve him."

"How can I serve a man who is dead?" General Rini said.

"Did you serve his legitimate heirs? Did you serve my uncle? Did you serve my cousin? Do you serve me?"

General Rini's mouth opened and closed without sound. "I serve Emperor Kin. I am loyal to Emperor Kin."

"Then you have abandoned your oath and that makes you a traitor. My father is dead. My uncle is dead. My cousin has made himself an enemy of Kisia, but I am here, General Rini, I am here. I am your emperor's chosen bride and the last of the Otakos you swore to serve, and you will do as I command. If you don't, Shimai will fall."

For the first time, they were really listening to me, no longer just humouring a girl for their emperor's sake, and I revelled in the power. "You all know what we need to do," I said. "You all know how this works. Order your men to march and we can be in Shimai by nightfall tomorrow; waste time and you will find yourselves bowing to a different Otako. Make your choice."

In the ringing silence, all eyes turned to General Rini. He took a deep breath and nodded, just once, short and sharp. "Do it," he said. "Send out the orders." He turned to me. "I pray you are right, my lady. I do not like to make bad decisions."

"Do not pray for me, General, pray for Kisia, for I fear what tomorrow will bring."

10. ENDYMION

There was no headstone. We hadn't been able to bury his body before we left camp, but Wen had left behind more than burned flesh.

"In the hands of the gods may you find true peace," I said as damp seeped through the knees of my clean breeches. "In the hands of the gods may you find true justice." I had grown up listening to the prayers, and they came easily to my lips now. "May Qi guide you gently. His wisdom is great. His mercy everlasting."

Rain was still falling, filling the air with the scent of wet grass and pinwheel blossoms. Back up the hill, Kin's men were taking a brief respite, and I could hear their words as well as their whispers. Hana had not wished to halt at all, but she had pushed the men hard and the horses needed water.

"I don't know what else to say," I said. "I'm sorry Hana isn't here. I told you I was stealing memories and well, I think... I think she doesn't remember what you were to her. I think I took you from her, and now..." I trailed off, staring at the mud while never-ending whispers washed over me. "I can remember finding you sitting outside a brothel, but I don't remember why I was there. I can remember you bringing me a horse, but I don't remember the ride. I gave you the crown and told you to run, but I don't remember why I had it or why you had to run."

I drew the symbol of Qi in the mud. "I don't know if I knew you or if that was someone else tied up with you in the swamp. I have so many names in my head that I'm not sure who I am anymore."

A long ragged breath passed my lips and I stood.

Wen had carried his leather satchel everywhere. It had been his constant companion and now it marked his final resting place. It had been full of medicinal herbs in bunches and pouches, of crushed seeds and dry leaves, of pastes and oils and sticks. And because all good healers knew the determination of death, there had been a funerary box as well. It held candles, a miniature book of prayers, the sign of Qi embroidered on a silk square, and a tiny box full of shimmering seeds that I protected from the rain with the curve of my hand.

"Kanashimi blossoms," I said, taking a pinch and sprinkling them over the ground. "Just like the flowers planted for the fallen Otako warriors at Shami Fields." I thought of what Wen would say and smiled, despite the uneasy feeling that I was talking to a stranger. "I hope you will be grateful when I am hung for such a transgression. But they're pretty. Girls will come down here to pick them."

I stayed a while longer, preferring the peace of this abandoned glade to the buffeting of emotions back on the road. When at last the call came to march, I bid Wen farewell and made my way back up the hill through the dense growth of fleeceflower.

Kaze had wandered a short distance to follow a line of grass in the ditch. I patted his nose, my heart immediately full of yearning for the kiri-wood human with the curls like a storm cloud.

"Kimiko is with some of General Ryoji's men," I said. "I think they are more afraid of her than they are of me."

He blinked and snorted, before ducking his head back to the grass.

"I don't think so," I said. "Humans don't have your sense of smell. Or my Sight."

"Endymion!"

I had been hooked into Kaze's soul and not felt the approach of another. At the edge of the road, Emperor Kin sat astride a brindle stallion looking every bit the god he claimed to be. He was dressed for battle, a grand figure in layers of leather strapped over a skirted tunic. A curved blade hung at his side and a dagger was strapped to his thigh, another under his arm. There might have been more, but I could not see them. Unlike people, weapons did not whisper.

"Your Majesty."

He looked down at me, his inescapable ire like a stone to the head. "It seems we cannot escape one another," he said. "You show up just when I wish you farthest away."

"I go where I am blown, Your Majesty."

"Like a destructive storm. An apt analogy." He let out a snort of breath and shook raindrops from the skirt of his surcoat. From its crimson folds a golden dragon roared, its great maw open as though to swallow me whole. The same ferocious face was painted on the waxed wood of an imperial battle mask hanging from his saddle.

"You have been silent regarding our last conversation?" he said when I made no reply.

"To Hana, yes."

"You have told others? Do not lie to me or it will go very poorly for you."

I could read the emptiness of that threat in his soul, partnered with doubt. "You're right, it would be difficult for you to know if I was lying or not," I said, causing his frown to stiffen. "But I think I told you once before that I do not lie. Malice saw my memory of what passed between us. He will have told Darius."

Kin's nostrils flared the same way Kaze's did when he was excited. "I ought to have killed you when I had the chance."

"We agreed that letting me go was the only way to avoid a messy problem. You're thinking about executing me now, but I wouldn't do that either. Thanks to Katashi's little stunt, too many people know who I am. And Hana is unlikely to approve of you getting rid of another member of her family."

"A threat?"

"No, Your Majesty. The truth."

His stallion backed with a snort, and Kin loosened his tight grip on the reins. "Damn you. It's Darius I'm fighting, not Otako, and you have given him the greatest weapon against me he'll ever need."

"And you have Lady Kimiko," I said. "The greatest weapon against him. He loves her, you know. She's carrying his child."

Emperor Kin stared at me. "Why are you telling me this?"

"Because I want him saved."

"He is our enemy."

"He is my brother."

The rain had slowed to a gentle caress, its drops achieving nothing but the further dampening of a saturated day. "Brother," he said. "Tell me something else, Endymion, tell me—"

"We have company, Your Majesty," I said, looking over his shoulder to see General Rini approaching. Emperor Kin turned, his frustration forming a haze in the air around him.

"Your Majesty."

"What is it, General," Kin snapped.

"We are ready to keep moving, Your Majesty. Master Kenji has already gone ahead."

"Then go. We will catch up."

The general's expression didn't give much away, but there was shock behind those limpid eyes. "Yes, Your Majesty."

He read no encouragement to linger in his emperor's bearing and turned his horse to ride away, his mind spilling with speculation.

"He is wondering if I am really who everyone whispers I am," I said when the general was once again out of earshot, leaving us to our field of wildflowers and rain. "He's worried it's an assassination plot because his mother always told him not to trust men with only one name."

"I would be grateful if you didn't inform him that you have, in fact, two names," Kin replied dryly. "I control the available information or I don't control anything."

"Darius would agree."

Kin snorted. "I always thought we were much alike, at least the face Darius let me see. The real man I am not so sure about."

"He would say the same of you, Your Majesty. The man he bowed to was no murderer."

Emperor Kin clenched his teeth. "Be careful what you say, boy."

"You want truths," I said. "I am giving them to you. You knew from the first that Darius was an Empath, you knew his father was one, you forgave him his crimes because he might turn out to be useful, but you never meant to become friends, just as you never meant to fall in love with Hana."

"Who needs introspection when you have a mind reader?" Kin said. "I did not ask to speak to you to have you condemn every decision I have ever made."

"There are not so many to condemn, Your Majesty. You did what was best for Kisia. You've always done what was best for Kisia, in your heart."

Kin eyed me, his brows set low. "Then you are more sure than I."

He turned to survey his army, lines of infantry and riders taking once again to the road with knots of boys and grooms and packhorses carrying minimal supplies. Everything else had been abandoned to a caretaker squad at Kogahaera.

"I don't know why I trust you, Endymion, but I do," he said. "I've never told anyone why I did it. I know you won't keep my secret, but...someone ought to know." He watched his army march into the rain while he spoke, years lining his face. "After he signed the truce at Lioness Pass to end the war with Chiltae, Emperor Lan started secret meetings with the Curashi tribes west of the Kuro Mountains. The council knew nothing about it. But it was my job to protect him whatever his movements, so I saw it all.

He brought Grace Tianto in. They were always fighting, but for once they agreed on something—the need to conquer Chiltae once and for all."

He paused as though expecting outcry, but I just focussed as hard as I could on the present to keep from being overtaken by numbers and whispers and waited for him to go on.

"In the end, they struck a deal with the pirate lords of Lin'ya. Tianto was going to marry his daughter to Lord Eastern's eldest son in return for two hundred ships, fully manned. And still the council knew nothing." He looked at me then, and in his eyes I could see it all. The midnight meetings as two imperial brothers plotted to change the world by bathing it in blood. And Lan's sons had been no better. Prince Yarri was already proud and ambitious, and Tanaka and Rikk were following his lead. For weeks, Kin had watched and waited, hoping for change, while every smile Empress Li turned his way dug the knife in deeper.

"They were going to break the truce and throw Kisia back into a war she could ill afford," Kin said. "Our only allies would have been honourless thieves more likely to turn on us at the end than see the conquest through. The only way to end it was to end them. After years of draining Kisia dry of resources they all had to go."

Kin sighed, age coming to him in a breath. "I have always fought for Kisia and I will continue fighting for her until my dying breath. Have you seen the throne room in Shimai?"

I shook my head.

"It is hung with hundreds of scrolls," he said. "The wisdom of Kisia gathered in a single place, the words of its scholars and its poets, of its emperors and its orators, but it is not Kisia's voice. Kisia is out there in its people, in its artisans and its soldiers, in its children and its fishermen and its farmers. That is what the Otakos forgot, generation after generation believing they were gods, the empire their plaything. Even Hana is not immune to the entitlement of her name. It is something in their blood, perhaps, some disease of birth."

For a moment, he stared into the distance, before a gentle shake of the head freed him from the clinging tendrils of the past. "Every day since Hana arrived in my palace, I have suffered." His expression set like iron, but the soul that moved behind it was full of contradictions and self-doubt. Hana filled his thoughts. He loved her and hated her, and while he believed it inadequate, he envied her stark, naïve view of an intricately coloured world. He both wanted her to know the truth of what he had done and hoped she would never find out.

Again and again every decision came back to the same question. What was best for the empire?

Marriage to an Otako.

"Gods know why I told you any of that," Kin said with a snort. "I must be losing my mind. I made the mistake of trusting your brother too."

"No," I said. "Trusting Darius was the best decision you ever made, Your Majesty. If you hadn't, you would have been dead long since."

All afternoon a continuous stream of messengers sped back and forth from Shimai carrying Kin's orders. He rode at the head of his army with General Rini at his side—a war council on the move. Other commanders came and went, but although Hana remained close, she was not included. There was awkwardness, anger, hurt. Katashi rode with us as surely as if he had been present in the flesh.

"Endymion."

Kimiko drew up alongside, her horse snorting at Kaze. Her hands were untied, but four soldiers on horseback hovered nearby.

"I see they've set you free," I said.

"For a given value of free." She looked around to be sure they were out of earshot and edged her horse closer. "This plan hasn't gone very well. Do we leave? We could probably find them before tonight with your..." She wiggled her fingers.

"And do what?"

She looked back at the soldiers. "You think there's no hope? I... I admit this sudden attack worries me, if only because it means we are running out of time."

What are they talking about?

I'm sick of this damp. This had better be all over before the first snow falls.

What's he looking at? Is he looking at me?

He's going to tell the captain, I know he is. Fuck, what am I going to do?

"Endymion?"

I was running out of time too. "You should stay here," I said. "With Hana. I will go back." At least with them all marching on Shimai, it would make finishing us all so much easier. Malice. Darius. Katashi. Myself. And the world would be a better place for it.

"Go back and do what?"

"Kill them all."

The rain had eased off for a time, but the forest dripped with its own rhythm, its colours all the richer. Kimiko had been so sure, but there was an uneasiness in her now. "You're giving up on him? Is he really so lost that you will no longer try?"

"They are marching to attack a city with fire."

"I know that," she snapped. "I don't want to hear the facts I already know, Endymion. I want you to see the way only you can see and tell me there is no hope."

It's the will of the gods. We're all going to die.

If I make it back home alive, maybe then I'll tell him. Ha! No you won't, you coward.

"I can only do that if you give me your word you will kill me if I don't come back this time."

Kimiko patted her sash and grimaced. "I have no blade."

"I trust you're resourceful enough to find a way."

I closed my eyes and gave myself to the whispers.

11. DARIUS

Shimai sat upon the horizon, a shadowy mass beneath an iron sky. This was the heart of Kisia stretched out before me, this city that straddled the Tzitzi River and guarded its twin to the south.

"Admiring my empire, Laroth?" Katashi said, approaching through a sea of horsetail ferns that caressed his knees.

"It is not your empire yet."

Even when alone, I ought to have been more conciliating, given the short leash I held him on, but it had been a long day. The tracks over which the wagon travelled had been bumpy at best and Malice's company sullen and oppressive.

"My scouts tell me Kin should meet the Willow Road around noon tomorrow," Katashi said, joining me at the lip of the outcrop. "We can still hit them from behind; we could send—"

"No," I said. "If you want to take the hearts of Kisia's people, you have to be their saviour. Ambush their emperor before he reaches a battle and you'll be an honourless rebel forever instead of an avenging god. Besides," I added, taking a sidelong look at his profile, "it will hurt Kin more to have the opportunity to protect his city and fail."

He laughed but there was no humour in the sound. "You're good at being a bastard."

"Why, thank you."

"It wasn't a compliment. You've fucked up my life, I hope that entertains you as much."

"Not a bit," I said, allowing myself honesty in the hope it would keep him under my control longer than if I riled him. A Vengeance loose upon Kisia with no bridle was not worth thinking on. "For what it's worth, I'm sorry."

His gaze was hot upon my face. "Like hell you are."

Heat flared off him, and it seemed pointless to attempt to make him believe me, so I kept the depths of my remorse to myself. It would make no difference anyway. I couldn't change what had been done or lessen his pain, could only direct him toward the goal that would ultimately sate his lust for revenge. And mine.

When I didn't answer, he crouched to singe waving fronds of grass between his thumb and forefinger. "In my cooler moments, I know why Hana is marrying Kin." The tip of the next piece of grass set alight and he crushed it in a fist before it could spread. "We are monsters, you and I, and she cares, really cares, about Kisia. But that is the man who stole my throne. Who killed my father. Who would have killed me if Shin had not been there. To think of him having the life I ought to have had, right down to being able to touch the woman I love, is more than I can stand. And knowing it's your fault—" Another blade of grass flared to be extinguished in his hand. "So don't you stand there and tell me you're sorry, you shit."

I closed my eyes a moment in remorse I could not share, because he was right: it didn't matter what I thought or felt or said, or even what we did. Some things once changed could not be altered again, and he was one of them. Whatever Kimiko had been willing to forgive before, she would never forgive me for this. That I had ruined my chance at happiness as well as his would be no consolation to Katashi though.

Footsteps crunched through the growth behind us, and Katashi got to his feet as Captain Chalpo and General Manshin joined us. "We stop here for the night," he said.

"Did you have to bring us up here to tell us so?" I drawled, not wanting either new arrival to suspect they had missed any conversation.

"No, that is not the reason you are here," Katashi said. "Tell me, Laroth, what do you see?"

I followed the direction of his pointing finger. Through the sultry haze, the Tzitzi River was little more than a shadow, cutting Shimai in two.

"The river, Your Majesty."

"And Kin let you command his army," Katashi jeered. "Come on, think like a general and tell me what you see. What purpose does the river serve?"

"The Tzitzi River serves many purposes," I said. "It is useful for transporting goods; it is a source of water, both clean and dirty; fishermen pull some big fish out of it in the rains; and it makes interesting smells. But what you're referring to is Emperor Catuzi's theory of the second wall. He built Mei'lian south of the river, because the river itself protected the city."

"Not just a pretty face after all," Katashi said, turning to his traitor general. "And how many crossings span the Tzitzi, General?"

"Five," General Manshin said and counted them off on his fingers. "Shimai, Syan, the Fork, Mesai, and the Valley."

"Six," I said.

"Six?"

"Yes. The Span in Shimai. The Ezzi Bridge in Syan. The Broad at the Huon Fork. The Two Way at Mesai. The Zisian at the mouth of the Valley, and there is a rickety but passable footbridge in the hills south of Esvar. And every emperor since Catuzi has opposed the building of more."

Captain Chalpo cleared his throat. "Seven."

Katashi grinned. "Give the man a dukedom. There are seven crossings."

"Seven?" General Manshin scowled. "Where's the seventh?"

Katashi's grin widened. "We're standing on it."

I looked down at the grass, its long blades curling to touch the Laroth crest branded into my sandals.

"I see neither of you is as smart as you think you are," he said. "Emperor Catuzi might have built Mei'lian south of the river to guard against attack from Chiltae, but the north is Otako territory. An escape route beneath the river was invaluable."

Surprise leaked from General Manshin like sweat.

"Didn't you ever wonder how we got into Mei'lian without being caught at the gates?" Katashi went on when neither of us spoke. "It was called the Imperial Cellar. Only the members of the imperial family and the leader of the Imperial Guard knew it existed. The knowledge was passed from generation to generation. It was built in 1167 as an escape route from Mei'lian to the north bank of the Tzitzi, but it collapsed in the tremor of 1352, when I was a boy. But there are . . . ways to get through."

Vices. He had used them to get into Mei'lian to steal the crown, but Malice hadn't mentioned any plans he'd made with Katashi this time.

"A tunnel into Mei'lian does not help us take Shimai," I said, choosing my words carefully. I had not known a tunnel went right beneath the river, but it was no surprise. The Otakos had always been keen on escape tunnels. Overseeing the repair of the passage between the sister cities had been one of my first jobs as a new councillor, but surely Katashi could not know that portion of the old system had been fixed and was now usable. Would not know that Kin could make use of it.

"You have very little forethought for a man famed at Errant, Minister. Men sent through the tunnels may not help us take Shimai, but I am not planning to stop at Shimai. Are you?"

I couldn't read Katashi's face, couldn't feel anything but the vengeance that fuelled him. But I knew Kin. He would bring soldiers through the passage from Mei'lian to bolster Shimai's defenses, even if it meant leaving the capital unprotected, because Shimai was the gateway to the south. Jikuko was in the Valley. Yi held what was left of the north and the east. Fear had begun to cripple Kin's play, every piece too precious to move. General Kin had risked everything, but Emperor Kin had too much to lose.

Yet he was going to lose.

A spark of remorse flickered as I thought of the man I had called friend, broken and ruined. "Splitting your force will make taking Shimai more difficult," I said, before I could stop myself.

"Not unless you betray me," Katashi said. "Are you planning to betray me, Laroth? Do you wish all your good work undone?"

General Manshin and Captain Chalpo didn't speak, but their silent stares spoke their own words. With an audience, it was treasonous to question him, treasonous to doubt my resolve, treasonous even to admit a moment of remorse though the sight of him filled me with it.

I bowed. "Not at all, Your Majesty, but as your chief advisor, I must counsel you to discuss your plans with your generals before making any move."

"And as your emperor, I will do whatever I like, whenever I like."

He glared at me, unspoken words in his fiery eyes. *Go on*, he challenged, his lips turning into a sneer. *Force me to do your bidding here and now with these men to see.*

If they so much as suspected the truth, they would not fight. Not for me.

"You are dismissed, Laroth. I will not need you again until tomorrow."

Having no other choice, I bowed again, trying to maintain an outward assurance I was far from feeling. My control was slipping.

Tall grass caught at my robe as I started back down the hill in the half-light of dusk. My sandals were not made for rocky slopes, so I picked my way with care. I needed space to think, but before long, a bloom of amused curiosity informed me I was not alone.

"Your Excellency." General Manshin fell in beside me, his long stride heedless of the trailing undergrowth.

"General," I said.

He kept pace as though waiting for me to say more, but despite social etiquette, I maintained a discouraging silence. When I had been the minister of the left, General Manshin had taken his orders from me and been accountable to me. It was time he remembered that.

"I must confess, Your Excellency," he said when I offered nothing. "I had been trying to fathom your reason for following Katashi Otako, but you had me utterly stumped."

"Ought I to thank you for the compliment?" I enquired when he paused.

"That is, until now." He tried his own silence, but if he expected me to demand an explanation, he was to be disappointed. "You see," he continued. "I am capable of discerning subtle changes in the men I deal with, and there is nothing subtle about the Great Fish."

I had to agree but said nothing.

"And nothing subtle about the … magic that infuses him now. Yet despite the fire in his hands, there is no fire in his soul. He is silent and broody despite numerous wins and sullen though the war goes his way."

"You are very philosophical. It ill becomes you, General."

"Almost I might have said I missed your snark, but you have cured me of any nostalgia."

"Good."

We managed half a dozen steps in silence. Back in Mei'lian it would have been true silence, but here the frogs and the birds and the darting of little lizards sabotaged its gravity.

"You are pulling the strings, Laroth," General Manshin said. "And he is dancing."

I let the words float between us, unacknowledged but unfading. He was sharper than anyone gave him credit for.

"You control the Vices too," he added.

He earned my most weary expression. "You are going to get to the point soon, I am sure."

"Always, Your Excellency," he said. "Because, you see, if I am not fighting for him, you will have to give me a reason to fight for you. My soldiers are loyal to me, not Emperor Katashi, and they will go where I go. And if I remove my support from your cause, then I think the chances of my good friends Tikita and Roi following are fairly high, don't you?"

The growing shadows seemed to deepen the lines of his face— half age, half dissipation. General Manshin was the perfect example of a man who was a lot smarter than he looked but not as smart as he thought he was.

"You may leave with my goodwill, General," I said. "Although I do wonder where you would go. You see, having been minister of the left, I am aware just how much a battalion costs to maintain, and while you are a man of means, largely thanks to Emperor Kin, I know you cannot afford the upkeep on your own men for more than a month, two at the most, and then you're running up debts you'll never be able to repay. That, General, is too much of a gamble for a man like you. And even if you could do it, what would your men *do*? Soldiers without a purpose inevitably grow bored and find their own purpose. You need a sponsor, General, and unless you plan to try your men's loyalty by defecting beyond the borders, Kin is your only other option. If you think he will let you keep your head after this treason, you don't know him, yes?"

There was silence on the hillside. I stopped and turned to face him, causing him to halt a step farther down the slope. "There you go, General," I said, treating him to a smile. "I have just given you a reason to fight for me. I'm the only man who has no interest in seeing you dead."

Malice was restless when I returned. He had been fretting all day, getting so snappish that every Vice kept their distance. Even Hope.

The young man was sitting by the side of the track, pulling out grass, while Malice sat far away from the horses and the light.

"Smoke," I said, stopping in front of him. "We are halting here for the night."

"So we might be, but no amount of time will assist me to smoke nothing, yes?"

"You're out?"

"Perceptive." Hands restless, Malice tugged his ponytail. "You used to carry an extra packet for me."

"I did." I spread my arms wide and glanced down at the pristine fall of my last robe. So many ruined: one at Esvar, another at the mouth of the Valley, and three in Nivi Fen. They were getting harder to come by, opium even worse. War was taking its toll on the empire in a thousand tiny ways. "You're on your own."

He looked up at me, no scowl on his face though I could feel it in his soul. "So I see." His stare penetrated deep.

"Something you want to say?" I said.

"No, not me. I don't keep secrets, yes? I don't wander off into the forest when I think no one is looking."

I shot him a pitiful look. "You're pathetic when you're not smoking."

"Pride almost caught our rogue last night. Adversity." Malice didn't so much as blink. "She appears to be…hanging around, yes?"

"That might explain why Vices have been going missing," I said.

Malice started grinding the tip of his ponytail between his teeth. It was an old habit.

"If you keep no secrets, why have I not heard that you're planning to help Katashi get men into Mei'lian through the tunnel?"

He eyed me for a time, unspeaking.

"Perhaps that is why I have not seen Ire and Rancour around this evening."

"What is it you want, Darius?" he said, snatching the hair from between his teeth and throwing his ponytail back over his shoulder. "The throne all to yourself?"

"I don't want the throne."

"Then what?"

When I did not answer, Malice got to his feet. "What," he repeated slowly. "Do you want?" He gripped my face between his hands, so close I could taste the kiss he longed to force upon me. "Where is my brother?"

Every Vice was watching, but I did not care. "I'm here," I said. "Can't you see me?"

A bestial grunt had always been his response to unsatisfactory answers. Yet another habit long since broken that was creeping back. He let me go. "You complain about my secrets when Katashi knows more of your plans than I do, sees more of you than I do. I am your brother, Darius, yes? Your brother."

Suffocated by his touch and his words and his very existence, I pulled free and walked away. He called after me, but I did not turn, did not listen. "Freedom," I said under my breath. "All I have ever wanted is freedom."

DAY FOUR

12. HANA

The courtyard before Shimai's imperial residence was full of soldiers, of labourers and servants, of artisans and noblemen. They came to fill their stomachs and sharpen their swords, and to laugh and talk and sing until there was no time left for fear.

There I found General Ryoji, kneeling at a long table with a group of soldiers. None were guards under his command, but all were laughing. I had hoped to join them unnoticed, but the moment I stepped out into the weak afternoon sunlight, an uneasy silence spread, bow by bow. I did not slow or lower my reddening cheeks, but by the time I reached his table, General Ryoji had risen and was bowing, along with every other soldier that dined with him.

"Lady Hana," he said. "This is a great honour. How may I serve you?"

How to say I had not wanted to be alone? Even more impossible to say I had not wished to dine with Kin. With no way of saying anything I wished to say, I fell back upon annoyance.

I drew myself up, though as with Katashi, my full height barely reached his chin. "I understand you have given orders to keep me out of the battle," I said.

"It is His Majesty's wish that his empress remains safe," General Ryoji said, a sidelong flick of his gaze taking in our watchful audience.

"I don't care what His Majesty wishes; I will not hide and I don't need five guards." As I spoke, I pointedly did not acknowledge the two imperial guards who had followed me out.

"You mean seven, my lady," he corrected, and his smile was disarming. "Two were instructed to keep their distance."

"Knowing you, that probably means there are eight. I don't approve of this sudden increase in security."

General Ryoji turned to his companions. "A moment, please."

Each man bowed and silently took their half-finished meals elsewhere. Regret doused me. "I interrupted your meal," I said when they had all gone. "I am sorry."

"Not at all, my lady," the general said. "I am entirely at your disposal. But in this I am afraid I cannot help. I am responsible for your safety, but it is His Majesty who gave the order for extra guards."

Extra surveillance. I could not hold his gaze. If Kin had confided my crimes to anyone, it would be this man. I ought to have excused myself and walked away, but even if he knew the truth, I still did not wish to be alone.

I lingered, and after a few long seconds, General Ryoji motioned to a vacated place at the table. "If Lady Hana would so demean herself as to eat with a commoner, I would be honoured to entertain her. Take a cushion."

I looked at the rough stones. "Cushion?"

"I like to use my imagination." A laugh twinkled in his eyes, and though I had sought him out to berate him so I need not be alone, it felt perfidious to have succeeded in my mission so well. But again there was a hint of Katashi's charm about him, Katashi's scent, and I agreed to endure the heartbreak for the opportunity of reminiscence it allowed.

As I knelt on the stones, a fresh bowl appeared on the table before me. The cook bowed, gripping his stained apron. "We are honoured, my lady," he said, his thick eyebrows colliding between his eyes.

"Thank you," I murmured, cheeks once more burning scarlet. I was drawing much attention and tried to appear unconscious of it.

General Ryoji took up his half-finished bowl. "This is a fine mountain broth."

The soup was thick and chunky in an unappetising shade of brown. "Doesn't mountain broth have to be—?"

General Ryoji pressed a finger to his lips. "Please, my lady," he said. "Don't spoil my dinner."

"More of your imagination?"

"Every good general has one."

"Along with a good deal of suspicion, I understand."

"Oh yes, that and the compulsive acquisition of information come with the job."

For a time, Ryoji and I ate in silence, while around us more and more men from all walks of life crammed into the courtyard. Along with weapons and food they were served orders and camaraderie, and under the influence of their noise and good cheer the knot in my gut began to unwind.

"And how long have you been a general?" I asked.

"Only two years, my lady," he said. "Though I have served His Majesty for nine. I came to Mei'lian for no other purpose, an idealistic boy, you might say."

"And now?"

"Oh, now I am painfully self-aware."

"How humbling."

"Terribly. Not a day goes by that I do not sacrifice a goat in honour of my good fortune."

There was laughter in his eyes and I couldn't help but smile. "You are a strange man, General."

"I know. I hope you do not object."

"No," I said, lifting the bowl to my lips. "Not in the least. I'm rather strange myself, I think."

"Not strange, my lady. Unique."

I wiped my mouth with the back of my hand, an action that would have drawn a scold from Mama Orde. "What nice words you have," I said. "Is that why you're so popular with your men?"

"Soldiers don't care much for nice words, my lady."

"Then perhaps you practice on the court ladies?"

"No."

"Then there is perhaps a Lady Ryoji?"

"No, my lady, there is not."

I was not so vain as to believe there was anything in the conversation besides a naturally personable disposition, not so foolish as to think he would ever betray his emperor, but in that moment, I wished them both true.

For a brief time, there had been the attack to think about and the army to move. In Kin's absence I had found purpose, only to lose it again when he had returned to lead his own men south. No gratitude. No approval. Not even a look.

"Is everything all right, my lady?"

I met the general's gaze only to find it so full of concern that I looked away. "Perfectly fine, General," I said. "Are the preparations for the city's defence going well?"

"As far as I am aware, my lady. Preparations for the defence of the imperial family are more my purview, and on that head, we are ready."

Family. I had not thought of us as a family, wasn't even sure I liked the sound of the word, though in a very real sense, we soon would be when a child was added to our number. "You will be with His Majesty?"

He tilted his head a little to the side as though in unspoken question. "I go where I am most needed. I was hoping with you remaining here I would only have His Majesty to worry about, however."

"Ah, so my imprisonment is to make your job easier."

The general winced so comically that, forgetting the number of people watching us, I laughed. I might not have noticed how many soldiers and labourers turned to stare had General Ryoji's expression not hardened into a humourless court smile. "Exactly so, my lady," he said, reminding me of our respective positions with nothing but a few words and a bow.

Before I could gather the shreds of my pride and rise to depart, the general nodded at something over my shoulder. "Father Kokoro will be kept busy much of the evening, especially now the men are beginning to talk about Otako using witchcraft."

I glanced around to see Father Kokoro, bright in his white robes, speaking prayers over soldiers kneeling around him.

"You sound as though you do not approve, General."

"Of prayers? Men need prayers, my lady. I am merely unconvinced that even a Vice is capable of setting something on fire with their hands. Otako is a flesh and blood man, not an incarnation of the gods come to wreak revenge upon Kisia, whatever the common people might say. Master Kenji himself says it is not possible, that the body requires a certain temperature in order to survive. If you cool it, it dies. If you heat it, it dies. Even were it possible for a man to create fire from his hands, the heat would kill him."

Kill him. I had told myself over and over again that he was no longer my Katashi, no longer a man but a monster, but those words were too much. "I have seen him do it with my own eyes, General. It is true, whatever people would like to believe. His Majesty just does not want to make it known in case it causes panic, but better people know what is coming."

"If that is His Majesty's wish, then I will see it is not spoken of."

"Why? He is wrong."

General Ryoji winced. "His Majesty is a god, not a common man. He cannot be wrong."

I gripped Ryoji's sleeve. "You know as well as I do that he is flesh and blood the same as you. I am an Otako, but I bleed and eat and piss just like everyone else."

Across the courtyard, the group who had been eating with

General Ryoji had finished their meals and each threw a glance at the general before leaving. They were not the only ones watching us.

I let go of his sleeve. General Ryoji lowered his voice still further. "My lady, the empire survives because people believe he is a god," he said. "That the Otakos are gods. Kisia almost fell to ruin the day a common man took the throne, but that day, General Kin gave up being a common man and became the god they needed. What do you think would happen if every peasant thought themselves entitled to power and wealth? What would happen if they realised they were ruled by someone as fallible and human as themselves?"

He was right. The survival of Kisia balanced on its emperor. If the emperor was strong, capable, and infallible, then so too was the empire. Kin could never apologise, never rescind, and never change. If I wanted to succeed at being an empress, I would have to meet him pride against pride, not wait for him to come to me.

"My apologies, my lady," General Ryoji said, bowing his head. "I should not have spoken with such vehemence."

"Perhaps not, but you are right." I rose on the words. "Excuse me, General, but there is something I must do."

———————•◆•———————

The Crimson Throne reached toward the fretwork ceiling, its lacquer the dark red of dried blood. Although it was but a replica, my father would once have sat upon it, surrounded by the empire's wisdom on its myriad of panels and scrolls.

Footsteps sounded in the passage and the door slid open. Kin strode in dressed in his full armour, his dragon war mask bouncing against his leg.

"Lady Hana," he said, halting mid-floor to maintain distance between us. "It is usually I who does the summoning. What can I do for you?"

He had left his guards outside with mine, and for that at least I was grateful. But there was no friendliness in his bearing, only stiff pride, and the flickering light of a brazier served only to make the stern lines of his face more severe.

"Your Majesty." I bowed.

"What do you want?"

And that was it—no smile, no loving glance, nothing but the irritation of a busy man. "Something to do," I said. "I want to fight."

"Then I expect you shall whatever my orders," he said. "No consideration for me has ever stopped you before." The whip of the words sent my pulse racing. Already he was turning away, and there were no words on my tongue that could tempt back a man so wholly set against me.

"No." Kin spun around. "There *is* something you can do. Talk to Lady Kimiko."

"Why?"

"I need all the leverage I can get," he said. "She's Katashi's sister and Darius's lover. She's carrying his child, there has to be a way we can use her. She won't talk to me but she'll talk to you."

Sister. Lover. Child. The words washed over me. Child. *Child.* How different that word had made my world. My blood turned to steel. "No."

Kin's brows rose. "No? No, you will not talk to her? An emperor must do whatever is necessary."

"Yes, and I'll talk to her, but not until I get what I want."

"Bargaining?"

"I have to, because an empress also does whatever is necessary."

The twitch of his eyebrows registered the hit. "Very well. What do you want?"

"Truthfully? I want to know why it matters that I have no virtue to give you," I said. "No, don't look at me as though I'm filthy and should not speak of it. I want to understand why you're turning your back on me before this marriage has even been given a chance."

"I will not talk about this."

"Then I will not speak to her."

His hands clenched tight. He was dressed for battle, but this was not the battle he had expected tonight.

"Look at me," I said.

"This is ridiculous."

"Look at me."

"Hana—"

"You can't even look at me. Why?"

"Why?" He stared at the brazier, his jaw working. "Just go."

"Not until you look at me."

Challenged, he did as I bid, turning not to search my features as he had once done but to stare straight into my eyes so directly he would not see me at all.

"Satisfied?"

I shook my head. "No. You're looking but you don't see me."

"That's absurd."

It was so like him, stubbornly intractable Kin. I stepped closer and he let me stand there, let me into the circle of his warmth where his breath made my hair dance, but the moment I looked up to his face he pushed me away. "You belong to him," he said. "You've always belonged to him, and now every time I look at you, I see Katashi, owning you as I never have and never will."

"Never will?"

His features twisted. "Go! Leave before I say something we will both regret to our dying days." He flung me toward the tall doors, bordered in scrolls of ancient wisdom.

"Like your wedding prayers?" I spat, spinning back.

A short, harsh laugh snapped through the room. "The whole empire would have had cause to regret it if I had not spoken those."

"Oh yes, you've made such a great sacrifice upon the altar of duty," I sneered. "How terrible a thing to have to marry a woman who's had the audacity to ever love another."

"Do not speak of duty like you understand it," Kin said,

advancing on me with his teeth bared. "You know nothing of my suffering."

"No, I don't, because the only suffering you have communicated is how upset you are over me fucking someone else."

His hand closed around my throat and my back slammed against the wall. "Is that so unreasonable a response, my lady?" he hissed in my face. "Is it so unreasonable that I would wish my wife not to have lain with my enemy?"

Anger overrode any sensible response, and I spat back, "So many times."

Kin's hand fell from my throat to grip my shoulders, turning me to the wall hung with wisdom. A swish of silk and the clink of a buckle and I didn't need to look around to know what he intended.

My body owned no heat for him, no desire, but I was determined to stay, determined to have him, determined to win, and stood still while he pulled down my breeches. His weight was soon against me, my palms pressed to the door. Breathing heavily, he ran a hand up my neck to grip my hair and every moment I expected him to thrust into me, but he did not. For a time, I just listened to his every ragged breath, then he let go of my hair and stepped away.

"You should go."

"Before you do something you'll regret as well as say something you'll regret?" I said, gathering my breeches up as I rounded on him.

Kin had turned away and was adjusting his armour. "Just go, Hana."

"You were right," I said. "I don't belong to you"—his head snapped around—"but I don't belong to Katashi either. I belong to *me*. And if you want me, you'll have to work with me, confide in me, listen to me, *trust* me. You will have to let me be your empress, not just your wife, or we will tear each other apart before Katashi even gets the chance."

Again Katashi, always filling the space between us.

"Hana, I—"

His mouth stayed open but no words came out. The anger was gone, but something else replaced it, something far worse that tore at the pit of my stomach. His jaw snapped shut, and without another word, he strode past me to doors, pulled them open, and was gone. I could find no voice to call him back.

He is not the man you think him, Shin had said.

One of the court priests had spoken the invocation over Shin's body. I had watched them bury him, watched them dig the shallow grave and throw him in, but although they had filled the hole, although they had covered that scarred face with dirt and rice sacks and horse dung, I could see him as clearly as if he stood before me.

A man does not climb to the Crimson Throne over the bodies of thousands because of duty. He does it for power.

The guards outside Kimiko's cell bowed as I approached. It was a cell made for a nobleman, no bars and cruelty, just a simple room with a sturdy wooden door that opened with a groan. I shook my head at the guards as they made to follow. "No," I said. "Wait for me here."

Inside, the sound of the siege preparation was dimmed to the thud of running steps and distant shouting. Kimiko sat on the floor, what remained of her curls covering her like a ragged cape. She looked up as I entered, hard blue eyes peering over her knees. "Your hospitality toward your family is extraordinary, Cousin."

"I did not order you arrested," I said.

"No, your husband did." Her emphasis upon the word *husband* turned my heart to heavy lead.

Crouching before her, I answered the unspoken question. "I love Katashi. I love him so much that just thinking about him, about what he has been made, makes my heart bleed, but I am an Otako and my duty is to the empire. Katashi and Darius would burn it down. I must stop them."

"That is a very noble sentiment."

"But not one you agree with?"

She looked up at me through a stray lock of hair. "Who told you it was your duty as an Otako to do what is best for the empire?"

"Does someone need to have told me so?"

"No, but it does sound like exactly the sort of thing Kin would say. Duty is honour. But you know it is not an Otako's duty to care for the empire, it is the emperor's duty. And since he went to such great lengths to usurp us, to ruin us, to ensure our family would never rise again, let him carry the burden he did not wish us to have, not thrust it back on our shoulders the moment it suits him."

I shivered at her quiet vehemence and found I could not answer, could not defend my words or Kin's, though the weight of his arguments had settled so heavily in my soul.

Kimiko's smile was sad as she watched me grapple with thoughts I did not want to examine and questions I did not want to answer. "Why are you here, Hana?"

"To find out if you will help us."

"In what way? If my brother will not listen to you, he will not listen to me."

"You know as well as I do that Darius holds the reins. And you're carrying Darius's child."

My gaze dropped to her stomach, protected now by bent knees and crossed arms.

"Endymion told you?"

I hadn't spoken to him since we'd left the camp at Kogahaera. Too much else to worry about, I had told myself, his identity hardly important when Katashi was coming to kill us all. "No," I said. "Kin told me."

Kimiko scowled. "Your honesty does you no service."

"Then it's true?"

The stare that bored into my head had certainly been adopted from Darius's repertoire, whether deliberately or not. But I had known Darius longer than she and stared back. Without lowering her gaze, Kimiko answered. "I have not bled."

"War does that to us."

"Oh yes, but Otako women have been bearing children through war for centuries. And besides, Endymion has ways of knowing things he ought not."

Shouts echoed through the door, but here in this stuffy little room with its single sleeping mat and its lap table and its pot, it was as though the rest of the city did not exist. Not the river, not the walls, not Kin, not Katashi, not even the manor in which we stood. There was just Kimiko and the child hidden inside her.

She tilted her head to the side, a small smile dawning on her lips. "Are you...?"

I touched my own stomach, protected by layers of leather and linen and mail. I ought not to tell her, not admit the truth to anyone, but she was perhaps the only person who could understand the depths of my joyous grief. "It...would seem so, yes."

"I don't know whether I ought most to congratulate you or pity you. If it's a boy, you had better hope he grows up looking more like you."

If not, Katashi would remain a wedge in our marriage, growing ever stronger as year upon year, our first-born child bore no resemblance to Kin at all.

"I'm sorry, Hana, but I can't help you," she went on. "And given the similarity of our positions, I expect you will understand. I will never fight for Kin, and though I do not wish Kisia destroyed, while there is hope for Darius, I won't give up on him. He is a good man in his heart, just a broken one."

"A good man who has forever destroyed the man I love and my every chance at happiness, and who is mounting an attack against this city with the purpose of destroying it. How can you forgive him for what he has done?"

"Because when the world hits you enough, when the gods will not stop spitting upon you, there comes a point when all you can do is be selfish. If I can have but one thing in this life, I would ask for more time to spend with someone who loves me. Don't ask me if I care about Kisia. Don't ask me if I care about our family. I am done with caring about this empire and its throne. There is nothing you can say to change my mind."

I hugged myself as though in protection, her words cutting more deeply than any blade. "I do not have that option."

Kimiko didn't reply, just met my smouldering gaze with a pity that only fanned my grief to rage. "If you want Darius alive, you had better hope you find him before I do. He deserves no happiness after all he has done. There is no justice in that."

"Endymion agrees with you. He can hear thoughts as well as emotions, you know, can read hearts. He tells me Darius's judgement is death."

"Another Otako you will not listen to?" I snapped. "Is he my brother?"

"Your half-brother. He is a Laroth, not an Otako."

"Why didn't anyone tell me? Did Katashi know?"

"Not until the night...the night Darius marked him. Endymion lied to us for a long time; it seems Malice made him as afraid to tell the truth as he once made you."

To think there had been a time when I had feared Katashi and Kimiko more than my guardians, guardians who had only ever betrayed me for their own ends.

"Don't worry," she said. "He doesn't want the throne. And honestly, what there ever was of Takehiko in there is nearly gone. He's almost all Empath now and dying."

I hadn't known my brother was even alive and now he was dying. It ought not to have hurt to hear, so little did I know him, but I could grieve the life we ought to have had together and the kinship we might have formed in mourning a mother we had never known. Grieve the chance of an ally upon whom I could wholly rely.

"He is going to stay with you tonight," Kimiko went on. "He tells me it's important."

"Why?"

"I asked, but his answer made no sense. Just let him stay close; he's the only person who can protect you if they come for you."

They. So ominous a word, its members all people I had once trusted and loved. Malice. Darius. Katashi. The Vices. Conceit had never been a friend, but Ire and Hope and Apostasy had always been so kind. They wouldn't be able to stop themselves fulfilling Malice's orders though, even if those orders were to end my life.

I shivered. "You may think yourself well out of this battle here," I said. "But though you choose not to help him, you're Kin's prisoner. He can still make use of you."

"A threat?"

"A warning. One woman to another."

Kimiko stood and, pressing cool hands to my cheeks, said, "You do not need to worry about me. You see, Katashi gave up on me before I ever gave up on him." Kimiko leant forward, and the shock of her lips against mine held me frozen. Her kiss was soft, sweet, and lingered in a way that made me wonder how Darius had ever been able to walk away.

Kimiko pulled away just enough to speak. "Go fight your battles, Hana," she said, her breath upon my lips. "But Darius is mine, and I will not let you take him from me."

She stepped back then, and before I could ask what she had meant by so many cryptic utterances, she took another step back and disappeared through the wall, as incorporeal as the breeze.

13. ENDYMION

Shimai was quiet. Doors and windows had been barricaded, carts abandoned, and every stall and shop stood vacant and lifeless. Beyond the walls, the plain was dark. There was no moon, and the velvet night swallowed even the light from our watchfires. But Katashi was out there. Katashi and Malice and Darius.

I had looked into Darius's mind and found only pain. Anger, remorse, hurt that bled from his heart and constricted his soul, reminding me again of the man back in Koi who had been all too ready to die. And Hana. I had seen Hana, his fears and hopes for her too hazy to make out but strong enough to make me fear what they meant to do.

A gust of wind whipped along the parapet, flickering torches. Ranks of Kin's men ran the length of Shimai's massive walls, their bows ready. Waiting. Below in the city, whispers were spreading, real whispers, hissed words passing from soldier to soldier like the fire they feared. Everywhere, Katashi's name was on lips and in thoughts, the exploits of his life gaining magnitude with each retelling.

"I am beginning to agree with General Ryoji," Hana said at my side. "I do not like the silence. Or the waiting."

"It is not the waiting you don't like," I returned. "It is the lack of control."

There was something like annoyance in her expression, but it was anxiety that drenched her soul.

A light appeared out on the plain. First one, then many, until dozens of lanterns danced like fireflies. And the fear of thousands vibrated through me, their racing heartbeats filling my ears.

"The lights are laughing at us," I said.

Hana didn't answer, just watched the winking lanterns. Then: "You're my brother." The words were unexpected, cutting through a haze of fear and noise. "That Pike called you Takehiko."

That Pike. She had forgotten Wen because of me.

She leant closer. "Don't deny it. Kimiko told me too."

"Only your half-brother." I did not look at her. "I am a Laroth."

"Why didn't you tell me?"

"Because I would not burden you with a brother you might one day come to hate."

"Does Kin know?"

"Yes." And there on my tongue the truth hovered, a secret that was no longer secret. From the tower above and behind us, Kin's gaze bored into my head. But it was not fear of him that froze my tongue.

I had heard the screams, had heard the man's footsteps coming along the passage. Hana had cried. I had tried to hush her, but her infant squall had grown louder, her little face reddening. There had been a fire iron in the hearth. I had cursed my youth and hefted it as best I could as the door slid open. While behind me, Hana went on crying.

Now justice was tangling in my fingers like skeins of silk.

"Kimiko says you don't want the throne," Hana said, looking out at the gathering lights rather than at me. "If that's true, then why are you here?"

"To right what wrongs I can before I can do no more. To be the justice the gods fail to give."

I felt rather than saw her shiver, and the space between us cracked wider. If she had other questions, she did not utter them, focussing her attention upon the approaching army instead.

"The lights have stopped moving," she said after a time. The air was tense. Humid. The stink of sweat mingled with the stink of fear, and along the wall, every archer shifted restlessly. A flickering torch lit Hana's golden hair as she stepped to the edge of the parapet.

Upon the plain, the lights were like constellations, all branching from a central flame brighter than the rest.

Katashi.

"Archers, ready!"

The cry ran along the wall, its reply a cacophony of scraping as hundreds of arrows were drawn from their quivers.

"My lady," spoke one of Hana's guards, leaning forward to be heard. "We should return to the imperial residence. It is not safe here."

Hana ignored him. "He's just standing there."

The walls of Shimai have never been breached.

The gods gave the empire to the Otakos. Now they have come to take it back.

People say he can put an arrow through a man's eye from three hundred paces.

One by one, the lanterns went out, plunging the plain into darkness. Except for Katashi. He held his hand aloft, its bright flame lighting an imposing figure, broad and black-clad with the ever-present form of Hacho watching from his shoulder.

Behind us, General Rini grumbled. "Damn the man and his theatrics. Archers, nock your arrows!"

Again the cry carried along the wall, and hundreds of men nocked arrows to their bowstrings. I left mine untouched. I could not kill a man who had not been judged.

"Come, my lady, we need to go."

Hana continued to ignore her guards. "What are you doing, Katashi?" she said.

"Something is moving." A soldier pointed, and Hana leant over the stone parapet as a dark shape plodded ponderously into the light of Katashi's flame. It looked more like a palanquin than a battering ram, but without the aid of moonlight it was impossible to be sure.

"What is that?"

"It's a shield."

"It's a ram!"

"No, it's a shield."

A large, bulky slab drew into the light of our watchfires, moving jerkily toward the gate.

"It's the roof of a wagon," I said. "They're carrying the roof of a wagon."

"They're making for the gate!" Hana cried. "Stop them! Aim for the men beneath it!"

A chorus of bowstrings stretched, then loosed their flock of arrows, hitting mud and wood and men who fell with sharp flashes of pain. But the shielded mass kept walking, edging forward with an inevitability that made my skin crawl.

"Take them down!"

Arrows flew at will, but the humidity left many to fall short.

"Aim for their legs!"

"Use that damn bow, Endymion," Hana shouted at my side. "Take them down before they reach the gate!"

"No. They have not been judged."

She snatched my bow. Its string creaked, and with a grunt, she loosed the arrow into the darkness with all the rest to fall gods knew where.

"Lady Hana, we must go!"

Men fell beneath the makeshift shield only for others to replace them, a seemingly endless supply of loyal Pikes willing to die for the cause. Kin's most skilled archers picked them off, hitting knees and legs and sides, but the huddled mass moved on, leaving its dead and wounded in its wake.

Hana drew again, and again, her action swift but lacking accuracy. *We need to stop them. We need to stop them. Oh gods, what are they going to do?*

Step by step, the giant shield approached the gatehouse. Its top was the brilliant blue of a forest pool, arrows peppering its surface like reeds. A school of silver-tailed fish flashed in the firelight.

Out beyond the range of our arrows, Katashi had disappeared.

"Douse the gates!" Kin yelled from above. "Start the water chains!"

The wagon roof hit the gate with a boom. It tilted back, the blue stream lifting, reeds and all, the fish seeming to leap from the water. Pikes darted from underneath, heedless of raining arrows, until there was only enough space between the roof and the gate for just one man.

"Take him down! Take him down!"

Pitch. Arrows. Stones. Everything was thrown at the makeshift shield, but it did not move.

"He's going to burn it," I said. "He's going to breach the city without losing more than a few hundred men."

Barely had I finished the words than Hana turned, pushing through the press of soldiers toward the stairs. Her guards shouted after her, but she didn't slow, did not stop.

"My lady!"

So much of Darius's plans had seemed to centre around Hana that I could not let her out of my sight.

She was halfway down the stairs when I reached the top, and I leapt after her two steps at a time. At the bottom, an awkward landing jarred my knee, but I sprinted on after the fading clatter of her guards, past soldiers and shut-up houses, through refuse and mud, until I burst onto the main road where the bulk of Kin's army waited. Two bucket chains ran through the ranks, carrying an endless stream of water toward the gate. Steam billowed and soldiers fell back, dripping with sweat and gripping burns. The heat was oppressive, like we were being boiled in soup. Soup that stank of piss.

"More water!" Hana shouted, striding into the throng. "Form up more lines. We can stop this gate burning. We *will* stop this gate burning."

She moved through the crowd of soldiers, a head shorter than the rest yet visible all the same. Her two protectors followed, neither attempting to turn her back now.

"Faster!" Hana ordered, her blonde head bobbing through the crowd. "More water!"

A tongue of golden flame licked from the gate. Water smothered it, only for it to reappear a few inches to the right. Again it was doused, dancing away to another place. Hana shouted, but I could no longer hear her words. Another flame rose.

One by one the soldiers fell back, slowing their task as each load of water proved less effective than the last. Hundreds of eyes lit as orange flames engulfed the gate and smoke rose in thick grey columns.

A chunk of charred wood the size of a man's hand crumbled into the square.

"Form up the lines!" Hana shouted. "Hold fast!"

A soldier averted his face from the heat and thrust his sword through the hole only to pull it back clean. Dripping sweat and steam, he stepped back, and a flaming arrow appeared in his throat. No scream. No gurgle. Just the thud of dead flesh as he hit the stones.

"Hold fast!"

No more arrows came. Tension filled the square. Beside me, a soldier sucked in great shuddering breaths, shaking from head to foot, his fear like a poisonous mushroom growing in my stomach. In front of me, a man whimpered. Piss trickled down his legs to pool in his sandals, the smell wretched. The unknown. That was what they feared. The unknown vengeance of the great Otako god.

Qi spare our suffering and deliver us from evil.

He's just one man.

A god.

We're all going to die. There is no way to stop a god.

A soldier near the front broke ranks but was caught in the crowd. Another followed, screaming.

"Hold!"

The flames vanished. The world froze. For half a breath, nothing. Then everything was noise. Firelight seared my eyes as a burst of heat threw me backward. I hit the stones and skidded, skin ripping.

Pain.

Fear.

Panic.

Too much. Too much. I tried to push it away, but the pain would not be ignored. It flared down my leg as I struggled to sit, finding my hand stuck in something warm. A stomach, slit open, its guts spilling onto the stones.

Everywhere, men were running. Smoke choked every breath and screams filled the night. I shook my head, trying to brush it all off, but it all clamoured close in a cacophony of shifting whispers.

What just—?

Where is—?

Help!

One grew louder as it approached.

There's that other bastard. Malice is going to be so pleased with me.

I rolled as a spear pierced the entrails of the very dead soldier I'd been lying on. Having no other defence, I lunged for skin, but as my fingers closed around a bare wrist, it vanished like smoke.

Conceit.

Pain sheared through my leg again as I pulled myself up. Smoke lingered over a scene strewn with bodies, each crimson sash like a rivulet of blood shimmering in the torchlight. Enemy soldiers poured in through what had once been the gatehouse and was now a gaping hole, but there was no sign of Conceit.

I limped into the shadow of a shop awning and let my Empathy range. No Conceit. No Hana. Only pain came back to me. Pain.

Fear. Anger. And the stomach-turning frenzy of excitement that came with battle. Numbers leapt into my mind now, useless numbers constantly changing in the chaos.

Two. Five. Twenty. Six. One.

Blood dripped down my leg. I dared not look at the wound, but I could not bring myself to move either. Katashi's men ran through the haze, calling to one another as they spread out.

Two horses trotted past my hiding place, their hooves making no sound upon the carpet of flesh. Sickles flashed, the Vices there and gone in a blaze of determination that briefly, oh so briefly, blocked out my pain.

Vices. Mission.

Hana.

I tried to run, but the pain in my leg made every step a struggle with both mind and body. But I had to find Hana. I forced myself to run, shedding the pain as much as I could, though more came from everywhere, pressing in with the weight of screams and thoughts and numbers. Always the numbers.

Forty-two. Six. Eleven. One million three hundred and fifteen thousand eight hundred and four.

As I ran deeper into Shimai, the smoke thinned and the screams faded, but each street seemed to belong to one emperor or another as soldiers held their ground. Hana flickered at the edge of my attention. Vague but moving. I slowed. Hunted.

No, no, please don't hurt me!

I've got to get out of here.

Closer now, and brighter, Hana's soul led me into a side street. Steps creaked beneath my feet. A pair of black paper lanterns hung overhead on either side of a black silk awning.

Inside the whorehouse, a man in voluminous silks lay dead, a bunch of keys in his hand. The keeper.

He dragged her across the floor by her hair, Malice had said. *And when she shouted for her owner, he did not come.*

The keys were just tradition now, but once they had locked the women in.

Hana's voice came through the fog, and I followed it into a dark room filled with the smell of incense. And there she was, a long, curved sword in one hand and a knife in the other, slicing the throat of an enemy soldier. The slit skin parted with blood, and she let the man fall, clutching his neck in the throes of death.

"Come to save me?" she said catching sight of me. Her chest was heaving.

"It doesn't look like you need my help."

"I don't."

A laugh came from deeper inside the building, and Hana was off. I followed, shedding the pain in my leg every second like a snake sheds its skin. I would pay for it later.

I didn't see the man until he lunged at me, but Hana was there. Her sword slid effortlessly into his flesh, entering through his stomach to cut open his gut. My thanks went unheard. She was already moving again.

"Do you want to die like your friend?"

A black-sashed soldier held court in the next room, his knife held to the throat of a naked woman. Blood covered her hands and splattered her belly, and all around her men jeered. Hana stepped forward, sword ready, but it was justice they needed.

I hardly thought, hardly seemed to have a mind at all. Seeming not to need the touch of their skin, their hearts came before my Empathy, and I read them all.

Hot blood sprayed as I slit her throat. The whimpers of fear were so delicious. Back home a wife and son, no don't think about them, don't think about them.

Unworthy.

The man cried out as the river dragged him away. His body was bloated when I found it, battered, scratched, pale, cheeks sagging as though melted by the torrent.

Unworthy.

The visceral resistance as I thrust my sword through the man's back, blood spilling through crimson.

Unworthy.

Unworthy.

Unworthy.

"Endymion!"

Only the woman was left, curled upon the floor sobbing. I spun around. Hana's face was cut and blackened with ash, but her eyes stood as wide as her dropped jaw. Around me, the soldiers lay scattered as though thrown, their bodies free of wounds though they breathed no more.

"What did you do?" Hana took a step back.

"I judged them," I said. "They got what they deserved."

I could have pulled him out of the river. I could have.

I tried to shake the memory, but the pain I had been shedding hit hard and my leg buckled.

Hana ran forward, dropping her blade. "You're injured! What happened?"

"When the gate exploded," I said. "It's nothing."

"Nothing?" She peeled back the open seam of my breeches to display a bloody mess upon my calf. Stones and grit had lodged in my flesh where skin had been ripped away.

"You shouldn't even be walking. We need to get you somewhere safe."

Hana hesitated. Fear. Uncertainty. She didn't want to touch me.

I pulled myself up with the help of a broken screen. It was getting harder to shed, harder to concentrate.

"It's all right, I can walk," I said, but Hana stepped forward. I whipped my hand behind my back. "No, don't touch me." I had met him outside a brothel, but could not remember why I had been there. I had thanked him for his help but I knew not why. I would not take another from her as I had taken Wen.

"The Vices are here," I said. "They're hunting for you, just like I said they would."

A dart of fear—like a drop of water in the ocean. "Let them hunt," she said. "Where's Kin?"

I shook my head. "The whole gatehouse is gone."

She didn't seem to hear me. "He will have pulled back. We must find them."

Hana led the way to the door and together we stepped into a nightmare. Shimai was burning. Flames danced from roof to roof, licking toward the clouded sky. A man came at me through the amber smoke, but I hit him with my pain. He stumbled, and I gripped his wrist as he fell, laying his soul bare. Afraid. Grieving lost friends. Full of uncertainty. Of doubt.

I let go. The man fell to his knees pleading. His words came so quickly there was no understanding them, but the penitence was real.

"Go," I said. "Kill no more. Go home to your family." And that family was in my head now. Daughter, two sons, both big bouncing boys with mops of dark curls. Marsci thought they were so beautiful and dressed them in the sweetest clothes, but all I wanted was for them to grow up strong.

Bowing, the man kissed my sandal and scrabbled away on his hands and knees along the rickety balcony.

At the bottom of the stairs, the smoke was thick with people calling to one another. A woman ran past with a child in each arm, one bawling and the other silent.

Chaos. Screaming. Shouting. Roaring flames. Yet the barrage of noise was nothing to the pounding of my head, so much pain, so many voices, so many numbers caught on my tongue.

"Two. Fifty-five. Eighteen. Three thousand one hundred and eight. One hundred thousand—"

Hana slapped me. Katashi's smile flashed into my mind and stuck there.

"We don't have time for you to do this!" she shouted over the noise. "We need to move."

She was already striding off through drifts of smoke. Head spinning, I followed like a man in a dream. Downhill. That was all I could tell, every shred of lasting concentration pouring into keeping myself upright and walking. Even the numbers were failing now. There was only pain.

A few steps ahead, a body fell to crunch bones upon the road, almost hitting Hana. She leapt back with a gasp, only for it to rise to a shocked squeal as someone grabbed her from behind, lifting her up so her feet ran on air.

"Put me down!"

Conceit clicked his tongue as she tried to crack his jaw with her elbow. He winked at me, as his sickle winked in the light.

"Ah, Lady Hana." The voice came from overhead where a second Conceit watched from a high balcony. He gripped the edge of the railing and leapt over, landing with bent knees in the road. I reached for skin, but he twisted out of the way. "Nice try," he said, and held up gloved hands. "No skin for you."

Both Conceits laughed, and I gathered all the pain I had been shedding off my wound and cast it at them. They both hissed and grimaced, stumbling back a step as though knocked off balance by a high wind, but where any normal man would have crumpled, he stayed standing.

"Nice try," he said, more snarl than laugh now. "Vices are resistant to your shit, remember?"

Seeing no help coming, Hana tried to bite the one who held her, but he just squeezed tighter and tighter until she scrabbled at his arms, gasping for breath.

"Careful," the other Conceit said. "They want her alive, remember?"

"Let her go," I said.

"Or you'll do what, Justice? Glare us to death? Oh no, looks like you're injured, that's a pity."

Again they both laughed in unison, an eerie sound that chimed through my pounding skull.

The sword in Hana's hand twitched. She had stopped fighting, stopped screaming, at least with her lips. It was her whispers that screamed now.

You better be able to damn well hear me, Brother, she said. *I'm going to drop my sword in five, four, three, two—*

I lunged. It was an awkward catch with slippery fingers, but I brought the blade around through the nearest Conceit. It went right through him.

The other laughed and danced back, Hana still in his arms. I rushed at him and slammed into a wall that hadn't been there a moment ago. The cobblestones hurried to meet me and I hit them, dazed and winded.

"Give our love to Kin, won't you?" Conceit said. "His invitation is already on its way."

Hana kicked and scratched and swore, but the Vice did not put her down, just hushed her like a troubled child as he strode away into the haze.

Endymion! Do something!

I started to my feet, but the wall slammed a foot down onto my chest, knocking out the air. "So here we are again," it said. "I was looking forward to the day I no longer had to see your face." A hand like mottled stone appeared in my vision. "If you get to live this life over, leave Master Darius out of it."

Avarice drew a bow from his back and plucked an arrow from a quiver at his hip.

"You're going to kill me?" I managed, the words emerging strangled.

"I know how to protect him even if he doesn't know how to protect himself."

In desperation, I threw all I had at him. It hadn't worked on Conceit, but I had no option but to keep spilling emotion into Avarice's air like poison, emptying myself as I had once emptied

Darius. Thoughts of Darius followed, thrown like so much sand into Avarice's face.

"Stop it," he said, lifting a hand as though to swat it all away. "Stop. Stop!" He reeled back off balance, and I rolled free, scrabbling for purchase on the slick stones. Lunging, Avarice gripped my surcoat, tearing it from my shoulders and landing heavily in the road. He shouted after me, but though exhaustion pooled darkness around my mind, I forced myself to throw one leg in front of the other through the pain and the desperate need to sleep. Every breath was full of smoke. Every heartbeat echoed hundreds of screams pressing in on all sides. I had no idea where I was going, just ran, dragging Hana's sword with me.

Men in crimson whirled from the smoke, shouting. The ground sloped. And then there was the Tzitzi River with Shimai's famous bridge arching across its dark roaring water. The Span was wide enough for two carts and was lit like a building, with hundreds of lanterns hanging from its slanted roof. Across the river, the south bank of Shimai looked dark and calm.

Hooves clattered on the stones as a war stallion cut across my path. I fell back, heart hammering.

"Endymion! Where's Lady Hana?"

"Hana," I repeated, dazed. "I wanted to rip Councillor Ahmet's head off when I saw what he had done to her in the Pit. I wanted to comfort her. Oh gods, the way she walked behind me, a martyr, proud despite the filth covering every limb—"

General Ryoji leant out of the saddle and gripped the front of my tunic. His fingers were covered in blood. "Where is she?" he repeated, eyes burning into mine.

"They took her," I said. "The Vices."

My knees hit the stones as I slipped from his grip.

I will not let those bastards break her. I will not let them burn her.

"Where did they take her?"

I heard the question but could not answer. My Sight was so clogged I could not see her anymore.

"Carry this man to the bridge!"

I must have passed out, for the next time I opened my eyes, I was looking up at ornately painted ceiling panels set between thick cedar beams. Arguments rolled around me. "We have to evacuate the north bank, Your Majesty," someone said. "We've lost it. Pull the men back to the Span."

"Are you suggesting that we leave Lady Hana at the mercy of our enemies?"

"I regret the need as much as you do, Ryoji," the first speaker replied. "But it is madness to sacrifice half a city and half an army for one person, empress or not. She may not even be alive."

"Your Majesty! Your Majesty!"

"What is it?" Kin for the first time. The delicately painted birds on the ceiling spun gently overhead.

"A messenger. He says he is Lord Arata Toi, son of the duke of Syan."

"The duke of Syan is dead."

There were whispers. *Didn't his son die? There was some scandal, years ago . . .*

"Let him come."

I struggled onto an elbow, though at my side, someone cautioned me to remain still. Kin stood in the middle of the bridge, his armour liberally splattered with blood and the end of his sash charred. I could not see his face, or those of the two generals standing behind him, but it was not them I wanted to see. Hope stepped onto the bridge with soft steps. Our eyes met, but he did not smile, did not outwardly acknowledge me, though inside I could hear him screaming.

"I bring a message," he said, his voice dead of all emotion. The young Vice swayed on his feet.

"You will bow before His Majesty," a guard said, stepping forward.

Kin held up his hand. "No, we have no time for protocol. Let him speak unharmed. What is your message?"

"Lord Darius Laroth, sixth count of Esvar and minister of the left in the court of Emperor Kin Ts'ai, first of this name, respectfully requests that the aforementioned emperor take some time out of his busy schedule to engage him in a game of Errant."

There was some laughter among the guards but not from Kin. "A game of Errant," he repeated.

"Yes, Your Majesty. If you win, you may take Lady Hana unharmed. If you lose, she goes to Emperor Katashi. A truce will be declared while you play, allowing you time to consolidate your position and deal with your wounded and your dead."

In the pause that followed, Hope's gaze slid toward me again. I tried to focus on him, on his whispers, but there was nothing but screaming and my own seemingly endless pain.

"And if I do not meet him?"

"Then there is no truce, and your empress goes to Emperor Katashi within the hour."

"Where?"

"The imperial manor. Lord Laroth has taken up residence in your house."

Kin grunted.

"You may bring with you one guard, and neither of you will be harmed coming or going, whatever the outcome, as long as you do not bring Endymion with you. If at any time he is found within the vicinity, the game will be forfeited in favour of Emperor Katashi."

The emperor didn't look at me but said, "Make sure he doesn't move. Kill him if he steps off this bridge."

"You can't seriously be considering such madness," one of the generals cried. "They will fill you with arrows the moment you get within range. You cannot trust traitors."

"General Rini, you counselled against risking half an army for one person, whoever they might be, and that is the advice of a good general," Kin said. "But this way, I am risking only one man. I accept the challenge."

General Rini bowed. "As you wish, Your Majesty. We will hold here."

It was then that Kin looked down at me, seeming to chew on his own thoughts. His fists were clenched, his brows drawn low as fear washed off him, fear of what he might find, of what might happen, of Darius, of Katashi, of Hana discovering the truth he had been unable to tell her.

At last, he turned his gaze to General Ryoji. "You're with me, General," he said.

"Yes, Your Majesty."

General Rini was next. "I leave you in command," Kin said. "If anything happens to me, burn the bridge."

"Yes, Your Majesty."

Emperor Kin and General Ryoji stepped into the night. General Rini watched them go, every muscle strained, his jaw clenched hard.

Hope lingered.

"Are you really Lord Arata Toi? The duke's eldest son?" someone asked, drawing General Rini's attention.

"Yes," Hope said, but it was at me he looked, such fear and longing and confusion in the piercing touch of his emotions that my heart constricted and I could not breathe.

General Rini snorted. "Well isn't it your lucky day, boy," he said. "Your father is dead." He bowed at Hope with a flourish. "Your Grace."

You will be that man again.

Hope looked from me to the general. Pain was slowly growing in his bones for every moment he stayed outside of his orders. "Dead? Recently? No, no don't tell me, I don't want to know." He gritted his teeth, hands beginning to tremble as the pain grew stronger. "I have to go," he said, looking back at me. "I don't know what's going to happen, but I'm sorry. I didn't know. If…if I never see you again…know that I…"

I found I was hanging on his every word, hardly aware that anyone else was present. It was just Hope and his churning emotions and nothing else, and yet when he looked around, he saw every gathered soldier watching, and he shrank. The world rushed back, all noise and pain and curious gazes.

With a last mumbled apology, Hope turned and pushed through the gathered soldiers, leaving only shreds of pain behind. And the memory of an evening spent atop the outpost near Rina, laughing and feeling more alive than either of us had for a long time.

14. DARIUS

I watched from the window as Shimai burned. It had been here Emperor Kin had elevated me to minister of the left. He had invited me to stand at the window beside him, not an equal, but not a servant, the space in-between the treacherous ground we would tread in the years to come.

But I had knelt at his feet and kissed the hand of a liar.

Beside me now, Malice stood with his hands clasped behind his back, reading the scrolls that lined the walls. " 'Everything has its beauty, but not everyone sees it,' " he said. "That isn't particularly apt for the situation, yes?"

"Shut up, Spider," Katashi said, the tap of his sandals across the floor like a chorus of snapping beetles. "This is madness. I am winning, Laroth. I could have taken the bridge by now."

"You will take the bridge soon enough," I said, not turning my gaze from the window. It was starting to drizzle.

"What general in history ever called a truce to play a game of Errant with his enemy?"

"General Mikuzo, in the ninth century. He lost the game but went on to win the battle, I believe."

He stopped pacing, and reflected in the glass, I saw fire flare on his fingers. "Just give me Hana and be done with this stupidity. She is mine."

I turned. "Stupidity?"

"Stupidity!"

"Your opinion of my skill at Errant is not high, it would seem," I said. "Tell me, what would hurt Kin more? Losing Hana to you without having the chance to save her, or having the chance to fight for her and failing?"

" 'What you do not want done to yourself, do not do to others,' " Malice said. "Now that one seems much more appropriate, yes?"

Ignoring Malice, Katashi said, "I don't care what hurts him more, I just want him dead. I want my throne and I want Hana."

"You will get her when I say you can have her and not a moment before."

Katashi leered. "Well, aren't you snarky today. Missing the use of your hand?"

"You can do better than that," I said. "You know I would much rather stick it in your sister."

Malice cleared his throat. " 'When two tigers fight, one limps away terribly wounded, the other is dead.' I like that one. That one is very apt indeed, yes?"

"Shut it, Spider, or I'll burn you from your cock up."

"Oh yes? Why don't you try it?"

Flames roared and heat filled the room.

"Stop!"

Katashi's hand froze as though it had hit an invisible wall inches from Malice's face. Every finger was engulfed, curling as though trying to claw solid air. "You stinking shit!"

Malice took a deliberate step back, mildly smiling. "Manners, Otako. Manners."

"Put your hand down."

He did not immediately obey my command. With his teeth bared in a snarl, Katashi fought, his hand beginning to shake with the effort. He let it drop.

"As much as I am enjoying this pissing contest," I said as calmly as I could, "at least one of us ought to be alive to meet our guests when they arrive."

Katashi turned his back on me and strode to the dais, but ignoring the replica throne entirely, he sat instead upon the empress's divan. There he touched a finger to the crimson silk and watched it char.

Outside, the city was quiet, no screams, no sounds of battle, just a thin drizzle cutting orange firelight. Inside lived the smell of burning silk and the tap of Malice's sandals as he walked around the room reading Kisia's wisdom.

A search of the city had turned up only a small amount of opium.

The doors slid open. Malice turned, and Katashi looked up from the pattern of burn marks he was creating. Hana stood on the threshold, regal in her armour and crimson surcoat. She had been filthy from battle, but her maid had been among the manor servants and had done her best. Hana's clothes had been neatened, her hands washed and her face scrubbed clean of blood; even her hair was freshly brushed, with a jewelled comb employed to keep her increasingly unruly curls tidy.

She took a step in but froze at the sight of Katashi. He had leapt up from the divan, and his long stride took him quickly across the room to stand before her, no longer the irritable conqueror, no longer the monster of vengeance but a man unsure of his welcome. Unsure of his place.

Another shard of guilt pierced my conscience, buried all the deeper by the tears standing in Hana's eyes. "Hana." He made a half gesture toward her only to let his hands fall useless at his sides.

"Katashi." She took a step closer, close enough that he could reach out and touch her. Despite all she had said, Kimiko had owned more fear of me than love, a remembrance that only dug my pain deeper still.

He closed the space, and despite the heat he emanated, she did not step back, did not flinch, but lifted her face to his with the most heart-rending entreaty. He gripped her chin gently, and in silence, they stared into each other's eyes a time, before he pressed his lips to hers.

I looked away from so aching a love and found Malice watching me, amusement in his gaze. He lifted a brow, mocking what he surely saw as time granted them merely to appease my own remorse.

When I looked back, they had their foreheads resting against one another and their hands entwined as whispered words passed between them. I cleared my throat. "How nauseous you make me," I said. "As much as I'm sure our guests would be interested to find you engaged in coitus on the floor when they arrive, I don't think it would be conducive to the desired outcome of this meeting."

Hana emerged from Katashi's hold flushed, her face glistening with sweat. "You can shut up, Darius," she said. "You have no right to speak at all."

"No? I could have left you elsewhere to await the outcome of this meeting."

She scowled. "And I should thank you for the opportunity to be captured?"

"How about the opportunity to witness so momentous an occasion?"

Not taking her hateful gaze from me, Hana spat upon the floor. "That is what I think of your momentous occasion."

Katashi laughed and pulled her close again.

For the second time the door slid, and Avarice returned, bowing low. "Master," he said. "Emperor Kin has arrived."

Hana's face paled, her gaze darting from me to Malice to Katashi. "No." She squeezed his hands. "I know you hate him, Katashi. I know you must hate me for the choice I have made, but please do not do this. Kisia must have a ruler, and you—"

Katashi yanked his hands from hers as fire began to light his fingers. "And I am a monster!" He shot a glare at me full of hatred and blame. "But if I succeed at nothing else, I will set everything right, here and now, and have my vengeance."

"Katashi—"

"Now, now, Hana," I said before she could have further chance to turn Katashi from our purpose. "Surely it is the height of romance to have a truce called while we play for you."

"Play for me?"

"His Majesty comes to pit his skill against mine, and you, my dear, will be the property of the winner. Bring in the table, Avarice."

"Yes, Master."

"Avarice." Malice strode to the man's side and spoke low while Hana spluttered over my perfidy. "My Vices?"

An infinitesimal shake of the head. "Only Hope, Pride, and Conceit," Avarice said. "They haven't gone out again since fulfilling their missions."

"Keep them in. Tell them to stay together, yes?"

I shared his unease. A few missing Vices was an anomaly; so many was a pattern and a hole in our defence. We'd only had thirteen left upon arrival outside Shimai, but that would be thirteen too many for anyone who wanted us gone.

I looked at Katashi, standing so close to Hana. No Vice had ever fought back before, but then before marking Kimiko, I had only ever made one other. Whatever the outcome, there was no going back now.

Avarice departed and I beckoned to Hana. "Yes, yes, I am treating you like chattel and this is the dark ages, yes," I said, waving a hand at her protestations. "In truth I was mostly just curious to see if he would risk everything to come for you. You ought to be most gratified, I think, yes?"

"Gratified? He is a fool and so I will tell him."

"Oh no," I said and pointed to the throne. "You will sit and you will watch, but as Kin is here on my invitation, not yours, you will not speak to him unless given permission to do so, yes?"

"And if I do?"

"Things will go very poorly for your emperor. You have my word."

She bowed, haughty grace in every line of her body. Hana was shedding her wilful youth and becoming the empress that ran in her blood. Katashi could not take his eyes off her—love, remorse, and anger all bursting from a heart that knew it was running out of time.

While Avarice brought in the table, Hana went to sit upon the throne. Katashi joined her, seating himself upon the empress's divan at her side, and what an impressive picture they made. Hana sitting proud upon a twisting nest of crimson lacquerwork, the man at her side both warrior and emperor in bearing and proportion. Katashi the black to her red, the fire to her determined assurance, an image so perfect that even without the tension and love between them, it was sure to break Kin's heart.

You're going to ruin them all, Darius.

"And which one of them does not deserve it, my dear?" I answered without thinking. The voice had been in my head. I forced myself not to look up, just shifted a cushion into place with the toe of my sandal.

Justice? Or Revenge?

It was Kimiko's voice, so clear she might have stood at my side, but when I glanced around, she was not there. Malice's eyes followed me, hawklike.

Footsteps sounded beyond the door. Hana gripped the arms of the throne as the rhythmic clack of sandals grew louder. Again the doors opened. This time it was Kin who strode in without announcement or pause, owning his throne room completely. He was battle stained, his crimson surcoat choked with ash and splattered with dried blood. Close behind came his chosen guard—General Ryoji, no surprise there, but neither was armed and that was a surprise. I had given no order to have them stripped of their weapons, yet even their dagger scabbards hung empty. I looked again at Katashi, but he did not look at me, his attention upon our new arrivals.

Kin halted at the Humble Stone and surveyed the room. Katashi lifted his brows in a sort of welcome, while Hana, stick-straight upon the throne, neither moved nor spoke, barely even seeming to breathe. Her maid stood beside the dais and stared at the floor.

"Darius," Kin said, turning at last to me.

"Majesty." The name came by habit and I let it go rather than try to retrieve the slip. "It is so good of you to come."

"Somewhere on these walls it says that it is more shameful to distrust one's friends than to be deceived by them."

Friends. The word bit, and I fought the clenching of my fist.

"And General Ryoji," I said. "I think you have not been properly introduced to our other emperor, the once-exiled Lord Katashi Otako. Your Majesty, this is General Hade Ryoji, the commoner's commoner."

Ryoji neither nodded nor spoke, though Katashi sprang to his feet and bowed majestically, sliding his palms down the black leather facings of his breeches. "A great honour, General," he said, the bow bringing Hacho into sharp focus.

Neither of our guests spoke, but Kin turned his attention from Katashi to Malice, who returned his stare with one equally bold. My stomach constricted as I realised they had never met before— these two men, the two halves of my life.

"I thought you would be taller, yes?" Malice said, finally breaking the deadlock with a shrug. "No, Darius, I fail to fathom what our little Hana sees in him."

"More than I ever saw in you, Malice," she said coldly. "If you insist on going through with this farce, Darius, then dispense with the pleasantries and get it over with."

Malice took a few steps to the raised platform upon which the throne sat and there looked up to Hana. "That's it, little lamb? No introduction? You have exchanged bridal prayers with this man but you will not even introduce him to me?"

"More that I will not introduce you to him," she said.

"Careful, Hana," I warned.

"You said I could not speak to Emperor Kin, not that I could not speak at all."

Malice turned to me, dripping amusement. "Go on, Darius, give her permission to speak to him so she might introduce us properly, yes?"

"Very well," I said, amused to find myself the centre of so strange and furious a meeting. So much history. So many hurts. "Hana, you may speak."

In the middle of the floor, Emperor Kin and General Ryoji remained two stiff statues of outrage, their faces betraying nothing. But in betraying nothing, they gave away their fear that emotion meant danger.

Hana sniffed, but when she spoke her voice rang proud. "Your Majesty," she said, looking to the man whose bridal sash she wore. "Pray, allow me to introduce the bastard son of Nyraek Laroth, better known to the world as Malice, leader of the ill-famed Vices. I was unfortunate enough to call him my guardian for five years."

Grim, Malice bowed. "Most apt, little lamb," he said. "Although you might also add that I am the only reason your emperor still lives. Were it not for me, your charming cousin would have executed him at Koi, yes?"

"If you expect my thanks, you are to be disappointed," Kin said. "What a man does to serve his own ends is no virtue."

"Is that written on these walls somewhere? I have had quite a time sifting through all this wisdom, yes?"

"Then it is to be hoped you have learnt something."

Malice grinned. "I take it back. I like him."

"The night gets no younger, Majesty," I said before the conversation could get out of hand. I indicated the table Avarice had set in the middle of the floor. "Our game?"

"I am no stranger to our games lasting long into the night, Darius," Kin said. "But I would play without an audience."

"No," Katashi said. "This idiotic truce hangs upon one order from me, and I do not trust your precious Laroth. We stay."

"Your feelings are fully reciprocated," I said, smiling at Katashi and giving him a more mocking bow than I had intended, bent by anger. "The audience stays, Your Majesty." I knelt at the table and gestured to the place opposite. Kin took it, spreading the skirt of his surcoat, graceful despite the bloodstains. There was no emotion in his face, but I could feel him more clearly now than I had ever allowed myself to do before. Despite everything, the great man owned more anger than fear, more determination than pessimism, and when he looked at me with those dark eyes, I felt so much like the minister I had once been that I nearly bowed.

"Lead or follow, Majesty?"

"Lead."

He took up his pieces, and holding them in one hand, he picked through them, searching for the king. I held mine in the crook of my useless arm, spreading them out until I found the one with the tiny carved crown.

"I see you have lost your right hand, Darius," Kin said, setting his pieces with his usual promptness. "That must have hurt."

I set my own pieces on the board, but it took much longer with my left hand, practice not yet making perfect.

"And you continue to suffer," Kin said as I placed the last one, having to shake my sleeve to get it out of the way. "You have lost your grace, Darius."

"Play," I said. "I want none of your pity."

"So you said last time we played." He moved his first piece, then returned his hand to his lap. "Your turn, Darius."

I made my move, trying not to think back on the last game we had played. I had let him crush me in return for my life, always respecting him too much and liking him too well.

"Do you like what I've done to your city?" Katashi asked from the dais. "Fire is so pretty, don't you think?"

Kin did not look at him. "Have you heard the saying: 'Before you embark on a journey of revenge, dig two graves'?" he asked.

"I have, and I would give my life to end yours."

"For a quarrel of your own making?"

Katashi leapt to his feet. "Of my making? You executed my father, the *true* emperor of Kisia."

For years, I had believed Grace Tianto responsible for the assassination of his brother's family. For years, I had believed Katashi might even have known about the plot that had gone awry only thanks to Kin's intervention. And for all those years, I had been wrong.

"Katashi," I said, speaking before Kin had a chance to respond. "I want you to tell me a story."

"Going for your nap, old man?"

"Tell me about Shin."

There was the slightest of pauses between Kin picking up his next piece and setting it down. No one else in the room moved. The burning braziers crackled loudly in the silence.

"Shin Metai?" Katashi said at last. "What about him?"

"Tell me why your father gave him that scar."

I shifted my next piece. Katashi stood in front of the divan, the raised platform adding to his already great height. "What makes you think my father gave it to him?"

"Use of my not inconsiderable intellect," I said. "Disfigured so he would be less recognisable, and as punishment for a crime he ought never to have committed, yes?"

"I think it's time you shut your mouth, Laroth," Katashi growled. Doubt. Anger. Grief. Even Katashi did not know the whole truth.

"No," I said. "You're going to tell me a story. You're going to tell me, tell us all, why Shin Metai killed Emperor Lan."

Across the table, Kin did not look up, just moved a piece forward with more care as though not to disturb the silence. And made his first mistake. He had only one chance to speak first.

Katashi lowered himself onto the empress's divan, avoiding Hana's stare. "Because he was paid to."

"Shin? Shin killed my—?" Hana reached for Katashi only to pull her hand back. "Oh gods, Katashi...who paid him?"

The Errant game was playing out as well as the scene around me. Kin's next play was careless, leaving pieces vulnerable.

"Katashi," Hana said when he didn't reply. "I thought Shin was your father's general."

"Not before your father's assassination," he said. "He never paid Shin to kill Emperor Lan."

I leapt a piece from the back of my pack to the front, following deliberately laid runs that reached like webs across the board. Still Kin did not speak.

"Then who did?" Hana said.

"I don't know."

"What do you mean you don't know?"

"Shin didn't know, Hana," Katashi said. "He was hired to do the job, but when he came to it, he couldn't stick his knife through you or Takehiko. So he left the job unfinished and threw himself at my father's feet. I saw a stranger covered in Otako blood who ought to have died for his crime, but my father saw the potential for the most loyal servant he could ever have. You should appreciate that, Laroth. My father was your sort of clever."

"Not clever enough to stay alive," I said, watching Kin's eyes dart about the board as though no conversation were taking place at all. "But then General Kin was already on the offensive, telling the world it was Tianto Otako who had assassinated his brother."

Kin leapt a piece over one of mine and turned it, looking up as it revealed a blank face. "If you have something to say, Darius, I suggest you get to the point."

His second mistake. There was fear in him, yet always the same stubborn determination to show no weakness. But pride would not win Hana back.

"Was it you?" Katashi leapt to his feet, a finger levelled at Kin. "Did you pay Shin to kill them? My father suspected it, but no, you were the honourable General Kin, so patient, so good, always 'Yes, Your Majesty' and 'No, Your Majesty.' And Shin knew!" Katashi was shouting now. "No wonder he stayed to make sure Hana didn't marry you."

"Sit down, Katashi," I said.

Katashi did not obey but jumped from the platform to stalk up behind Kin, flexing his fingers. "Sit down?" he said. Ryoji took a step forward only to find his progress blocked by Malice. "Sit down?" Katashi looked around at Hana. She was pale, small, no longer the empress she had been playing. "You have pledged yourself to your family's murderer." No accusation, only bitterness and pity and heartache, and through it all, Kin kept his eyes on the game. His hand shook as he jumped a piece and turned two of mine.

"Tell me it isn't true," came the small, breathless whisper from the throne.

It was Kin's chance to speak, to move, to do anything but ignore her like a guilty man. But he said nothing. Shock filled the silence, the taste of it bitter on my tongue. It resonated not only from Hana and Katashi but from General Ryoji standing with Malice near the window. I could imagine his expression. Kin was his god as he had once been mine.

"They trusted you. *I* trusted you." Hana was staring at Kin, balled fists barely containing her anguish.

Katashi's chest heaved and his fury washed over me, hardening my own. I had taken my oath at Kin's feet, had trusted him and fought for him as my father had before me.

You can't get past it, can you? The whisper filled my head, its familiar tone speeding my heart. Kimiko. *The only man you've ever respected, and he lied.*

A piece hit the board with a snap. "Everything I have done, I have done in service to Kisia," Kin said at last. He was trying to keep the game going, but he had already lost. They were the wrong words.

"In service to Kisia?" Hana cried. "Killing an emperor? How about my mother? My brothers? How was that your duty, *General* Kin?"

He looked at her then, his expression grim. "I ought to have told you, Hana, but why hurt you when it was sixteen years done."

"Sixteen years never knowing my family. Left to the guardianship of Empathic monsters. Did you always plan for my uncle to take the blame so you could get rid of every Otako in one go?" She turned her pleading eyes on me. "How long have you known?"

"A few weeks," I said, trying not to dwell on the pain of the remembrance. "Shin told me the night I was hauled in from Esvar."

"None of it is as simple as it sounds," Kin said, ignoring all but the woman he had never meant to love. "I owe you an explanation, but now is not the time. Believe me when I say I did it for Kisia. If I had not, there would have been no future."

"An explanation? Oh dear gods, you think you can justify this? The future of Kisia was the business of no one but its emperor."

"You might look like your mother," he snapped, "but that's your father's arrogance spilling from your mouth."

"How dare you!"

"Listen to yourself, Hana. To say that the future of Kisia is only the business of its emperor is to say that Kisia exists only for its emperor. What about its land? What about its people? *They* are Kisia, Hana, not me, not you, not your father. An emperor's job is not to own, not just to lead but to protect. They need to be willing to sacrifice everything if it is required of them."

"Would you? If it was in the interest of the people would you relinquish your throne?"

"I would."

A sneer hid her pain. "I don't believe you. Shin told me no man would climb to the throne over the bodies of thousands for duty. He does it for power."

"Shin ought to know," Kin returned. "Since he's the one who wielded the knife."

A sob burst from her lips and she looked away. Katashi had been standing behind Kin, but he went to her then, his feet following the path Kin cut with his eyes. Kin was caught to the game and could only watch as Katashi touched Hana's cheek, could only watch as she gripped the dark fabric of her cousin's sleeve and bent her head against him.

I cleared my throat. "Your turn, Majesty," I said. "Do you play on?"

"Yes. I play for my bride."

With his hand upon Hana's shoulder, Katashi chuckled softly. "Your murderer is a determined man, my dear, I'll give him that."

Hana did not answer, just buried her face into his surcoat, shoulders shaking. Kin ought to have looked away, but he did not, and for an instant his features creased as the two Otakos held each other in their own forms of grief.

Kin's fingers shook as he turned one of my pieces, white for black. Another mistake, one that gave away the position of his king. With my graceless left hand, I gripped a piece and leapt it along his line, tap tap tap, not bothering to turn any but the last. It fell upon its back, displaying a white crown upon its belly.

"My round, I believe," I said.

Kin said nothing, just slid his pieces off the board and gathered them in his hand. By the window, General Ryoji stood statue-stiff, looking neither at Kin nor at Hana, not even at the game, while Malice had eyes only for me.

Kin set his pieces for the second round, the process creating a song of staccato snaps. The room was full of tiny sounds, of the tap of wood on wood and the crackle of braziers, of distant shouts and rustling silk and a heart-wrenching sniff as Hana fought to control her grief.

"All men have secrets," Kin said once he had finished. "You kept yours and I kept mine. Trust is for people with nothing to lose."

"Yes," I agreed. "And so is forgiveness."

"And friendship."

I did not answer, and in silence, he watched my left hand struggle to achieve quick finesse. Then he said, "As your guest, I must say that your hospitality is disgraceful. We have played through a whole round without refreshment."

"Avarice," I said, concentrating on the last two pieces. "What will it be, Your Majesty. Wine?"

"I think not. How about some tea, green pear, plain rice, and thinly sliced mild fish?"

My heartbeat sped and I looked up, hunting for signs that he was mocking me.

"Am I wrong?" he said. "That was always your meal of choice, was it not? I often wondered why a man who could afford so many opulent robes satisfied himself with so plain a repast."

I nodded to Avarice, who bowed and walked away. "If you were so curious, Majesty, you ought to have asked."

"And what lies would you have spun me if I had? Your play."

I slid a piece onto the field of battle.

"Who is the real Darius Laroth, I wonder?" Kin said as he sent his first piece out to fight. "I used to think I knew him better than anyone, better than he thought I did. He was the best advisor I ever had. Everyone else saw the Monstrous Laroth, but what I saw was an intelligent man who was so full of fear and hurt that the mere acknowledgement of it would have seen him drown."

I put the next piece down with a snap. "Don't try my patience, Majesty," I said. "I bowed at the feet of a man who murdered the woman he loved, the man who drove my father mad. You are the reason he left me to die in a storm."

"No." He gripped my left hand and pulled back the sleeve of my robe, revealing the Empath mark. "It was this which did that."

I pulled my hand away.

"You think I didn't know what happened? You once called me a formidable opponent. It would have been best for you if you had believed it."

My poor, sad Darius, spoke Kimiko's voice inside my head. *He's right, and you don't even see it.*

A maid placed a plate of sliced fruit and fish onto the table. I had not heard the door open or the clink of ceramic as she crossed the floor, but there she was pouring the tea, her face deferentially averted.

Despite having ordered it, Kin did not glance at the plate or the steaming bowl of tea. He was focussed on the game, so focussed that his anger and chagrin began to melt away, leaving only an intense concentration lapping at my Empathy. When he did look up, the gaze that met mine was direct. Determined.

"An interesting play," he said, so much as though I had been Minister Laroth that I expected to find myself sitting beside the Crimson Throne. For five years I had served this man, and for five years he had given the empire his all. That was no lie. Though I hated to admit it, no one who had watched him rule could deny his selflessness.

You want to hate him so much. You want to hate him because he hurt you.

"I am not so pathetic," I said under my breath.

Kin picked up his next piece, but instead of moving it forward as I had planned, he darted left into the path of my hidden king. My stomach knotted. How had I given myself away?

You think you're so controlled, Mastery.

I made my move, an unusual play, hoping to confound him, but the next time he lifted his hand, he turned my king. "My round, I think."

"What?" Katashi exclaimed, reminding me with a jolt that we were not alone. "You lost?"

"The round, yes. The game is yet to be decided."

"The game is a waste of time."

"As you are a waste of space," I snapped. "You think I care about your plans?"

I regretted the words immediately. I was cracking. Katashi leered, his eyes hungry. I held him by a thread.

"As I care nothing for yours," he said almost cheerfully. "Finish this, Laroth, before I lose my patience, or I will burn you both."

No obedience. No *Master*. He was growing too strong too fast. I glanced up at Malice, who shot me a meaningful look. *If you push it, we're dead.*

He isn't going to remain loyal to you, Kimiko warned, echoing Malice's look. *He hates you even more than he hates Kin now, and who can blame him? Kin stole his childhood, but you have destroyed his life.*

"Tell me, Katashi," Kin said, once again setting his pieces, this time without looking for his king. "What have you done with my crown? I notice you do not wear it, though you call yourself emperor."

"I can't wear it. It starts to melt."

Kin's brows shot up. "A downside to your talent to be sure." His gaze slid to Hana. She sat staring at a finely painted screen beside the throne, her cheeks tracked with tears. When she did not return his gaze, he turned it back to Katashi, standing behind her, one hand upon her shoulder, the other entwining her fingers in his. "Did you know your father was going to marry your sister to the Easterns?" he asked as though he could not see this. "In return for a secret fleet to pillage the Ribbon."

"Marry her to pirates? He would never have so degraded our family," Katashi said.

"No? I suppose you don't think he was capable of taking part in two-faced diplomatic talks with the Chiltaens either, discussing an alliance by day while planning an attack with Emperor Lan by night."

"That doesn't even make sense."

"It does for an Otako who was given the empire by gods."

Katashi spat. "Your suppositions are as insulting as your presence. If you had known my father, you would not dare speak such lies."

"And if you had known your father, you would not call them lies."

"I will take great pleasure in burning you." Katashi's bright eyes bored into Kin's skull, but Kin just pushed a piece forward to start the third and final round.

I followed his lead, all too aware of Katashi's animosity pressing upon us like coals. There was a promise in the rebel's smile. If I won, Kin was dead. But death was what he deserved for deceiving me.

Listen to yourself! Oh, my poor broken man, you're in control of nothing.

The words cut into my flesh, her voice so clear. Endymion could get inside my head, but whatever skill Malice had gifted her, Kimiko was a Normal.

If you open a door, why can I not step through it too?

But I had let her go.

And I didn't leave. You just stopped seeing me because it hurt too much, just like you stopped giving your all to Kin because it was killing you inside.

I had called him friend.

"Damn you," I hissed as I gracelessly thrust a piece forward. "Where are you?"

No one looks twice at a maid.

Like guards, servants were so often invisible. I had barely noticed the maid still kneeling beside the table, head bowed to the floor, but I looked at her now.

Kimiko.

You didn't feel me because you don't want to see me, she said. *Just like you don't want to acknowledge your feelings about Kin. If you admit you have a heart, you will suffer too much, but if you don't, you will lose everything.*

"What is it that you're afraid of, Darius?" Kin said, his gaze slipping to the prostrate maid.

"I am not afraid."

"Yes, you are," he said. "I ought to be the one who is afraid. The second largest city in my empire is burning and my army has been pushed back to the south bank. You have captured my wife and given voice to my treason. You know more about me than anyone, more about my empire, more about my army, and yet it is you who sits there sweating."

"You have a vivid imagination, Majesty."

I moved too quickly, knocking a piece over as I reached for another. I swore, but before I could right it, Kin replaced it for me.

"I don't think so."

Kin turned an unprotected piece, and I clenched the fist I no longer possessed.

Blank.

The move had opened up three pieces I could turn, three chances to unearth his king as he had tried to unearth mine. It was always safer to win any Errant game before the deciding round, as too much of it rested on luck and luck was hard to manipulate. But I could make use of his lines, a single move capable of turning half his remaining pieces.

I gripped my piece. It was a simple move, a simple leap along an obvious path, but I could not do it, could not face what would happen if I turned his king. Instead, I pushed my piece toward his gate.

Kin's head snapped up, but I could not meet his gaze. He leapt another of my pieces. Blank. Malice touched the back of my neck. I had not seen him move, had not heard him, but the connection blazed along familiar pathways. *I can see what you're doing, Darius,* he said. *You're going to get us both killed.*

I ignored him, forced myself not to glance at the still form of Kimiko, and once again made a play for Kin's gate.

His move. Two pieces this time. Both flipped fast, both blank. Kin's disappointment stank. Sweat sparkled on his brow and darkened patches of his collar.

As the game dragged on, Katashi began to pace.

I leapt three pieces, the sort that might look important to someone who knew none of the nuances of Errant. But I mentally marked every piece of his that had once been mine and knew which were safe. I knew too that three of mine were yet to be turned, and heedless of the consequences, I moved them his way.

Perhaps no more than four Vices in the anteroom. Hundreds of Pikes down in the city. This was a new game now. Like pieces upon a board, I counted them all: General Ryoji at the window, Malice behind me, Hana upon the throne, and Kimiko kneeling just out of reach. One of Katashi's Pikes stood at the throne room door, but he was the farthest away, caught between us and our Vices.

Kin gripped a piece and leapt two of mine. He turned the first without looking down at it—blank. The second, a crown.

"I think you ought to leave us now," he said, speaking to Kimiko. "We don't need any more tea."

She rose, keeping her face averted as all good maids should. "Your Majesty." Kimiko had never sounded so meek, but disobedience meant revealing her identity to those she could not trust.

"My game, I think." Kin drew a deep breath and ran his palms down his thighs.

"What?" Katashi's heavy steps caused the pieces to rattle on the board as he approached. "You lost?"

"So it would seem," I said.

Katashi glared at the board. "Your skill at Errant is better even than you boast," he said. "You wanted him to win."

The only sound in the room was the soft click of the door as Kimiko exited, her reluctance equalled only by her fear.

Don't do anything stupid, Darius, she said. *You've already done enough.*

Kin stood. "Come, Hana," he said. "I think we have outstayed our welcome."

"She won't go with you, you fool," Katashi laughed. "It's me she loves and it always will be."

"But if she comes with me, she'll be an empress. If she stays with you, she'll be a corpse."

"Shut up, both of you," Hana snapped, getting up from the throne and stepping off the platform. "Don't you dare fight over me like I am a piece of meat. I am leaving on my own, and gods help any man who tries to stop me."

Katashi stepped in her way. "No, Hana, that isn't how this ends. You stay. He burns."

"I was promised safe passage in and out," Kin said. "And I will take my wife with me."

With a snarl, Katashi advanced on Kin, fire flaring. "You will never call her so. You have no right when she promised herself to me. When she gave herself to me. I am the one she loves, and you will burn before you touch her."

"Katashi!" Hana lunged between them, throwing her arms wide. "Darius, order him to stop."

"Yes, go on, *Master*," Katashi said, rage beginning to engulf him. "Order me to stop. Order me not to burn your beloved emperor."

I got to my feet, Malice at my side, but I knew no words would be enough.

"No?" Katashi said. "That's no fun. But you're right, Laroth, you're out of time. Kill them."

The Pike by the door drew his sword. "With pleasure."

Avarice didn't slide the door, just burst through it, tearing wood and paper. The Pike lunged at him. I knew not if I shouted or froze, but Avarice's skin mottled in time and the steel chinked off his raised arm. Another Pike threw open the ruined door and met Avarice's stony fist.

More crowded into the room. Unarmed, General Ryoji dodged the first blade that attempted to disembowel him and charged at the second, throwing its wielder off balance. I had never seen him fight in such close quarters, all arms and shoulders and tight brawling, swords rendered useless.

"Kill our guests," Katashi ordered as he pushed Hana out of the way. "But leave Kin to me."

They came at us. Avarice's fist crushed another Pike's face and more Vices rushed in. Hope, Conceit, and Envy, the newest Vice of all. Then a sickle spun across the polished wood floor. Its owner's head followed—Pride, his self-satisfied expression unmistakable.

Malice gripped my hand and drained me fast. He threw the emotion out, so chaotic and hard that its recoil turned my stomach. Pikes staggered. General Ryoji, a weapon in his hand now, slammed into the wall.

"Run! Now!" Malice shouted, shunting me in the back. "Avarice, get him out of here!"

I could not move. Pain filled the room as men fought and died, as sickles ripped flesh and pierced organs, but it was nothing to the searing pain of fire upon my hands.

Hana was screaming. "No! Katashi, please!"

"Go! Get out of here!" Malice yelled. "It's too late!" Another Pike fell to Avarice's sickle, two to Malice's emotive barbs. General Ryoji tried to force his way through the massing Pikes, but even if he reached Kin, there was nothing he could do but die.

Thrown, Hana skidded across the floor in a cloud of smoke. Katashi had Kin backed up against the dais. Fire ripped along his arms, and with already blistering hands, Kin caught Katashi's arm inches from his face.

My knees buckled under the pain, the burning, blistering, scorching pain that engulfed my hands.

"No!" Hana was up again and charged at Katashi through the growing flames, clawing and biting, breaking his concentration as he struggled not to burn her too.

"Darius!" she cried, and once again Katashi threw her from him. She landed hard, her hair smoking. Her maid darted from the shadows, tears streaming.

Kin ducked as Katashi lunged at him, all fire and hatred, but there was nowhere to go and the flaming hand grabbed hold of Kin's topknot. Smoke poured from his hair as screams poured from his lips.

And mine. I got up, vision red with pain, and ripped the bandage from my severed wrist.

All I needed was skin.

"No!" Malice snatched at my arm, but I pulled away and ran at the monster I had created. Flames leapt from Katashi's flesh as he delighted in his revenge, but I averted my face and thrust my useless arm into the fire. At his neck I found skin and pushed through everything I had. So much guilt. So much anger. So much fear. So much grief.

The flames died. Katashi hit the floor like a sack of meat, his bow smoking as it skidded from its holster.

Kin stumbled. Half his face was blistered, one eye staring from a burned socket.

"I knew I was not mistaken in you, my friend," he said, the words less than a whisper, just breath passing his lips.

He fell to his knees. I wanted to speak. I wanted to move, but there was nothing left in my limbs but pain and a dreadful lassitude that edged me toward sleep.

You stupid, broken man, came Kimiko's words, catching on a sob.

And with the darkness, the Pikes closed in.

15. HANA

The last piece of paper was torn, but I folded it anyway. Leaning close to the dim lantern, I turned it over and pressed each fold, trying for crisp edges despite the humidity. Beyond the open window, drizzle blanketed the eerie city.

"You are very industrious, my lady." Father Kokoro stood in the doorway, a sheaf of prayer paper in his hand. "It seems I will soon be sent in search of more."

He nodded toward the pile of lotus prayers covering the low table. They were not neat, some folds so weak they were coming undone.

"They don't take long," I said. "My foster mother taught me how."

"Sad that so few keep up the old ways. Most would rather buy a prayer than fold one with their own hands. Meanwhile, a novice folds the prayers of the world. And if he ceased to do so? What then?"

The words washed over me with little effect. Every inch of my body screamed at me to rest, but I could not stop. Inactivity would give me time to think.

"Sometimes tradition is worth keeping."

A cry ripped through the screens separating this room from the next. My stomach turned. I kept folding.

"Perhaps it would be better if you removed yourself from here, my lady," Father Kokoro suggested. "This must be distressing for you. The sounds—"

"A man who screams or yells or grunts or swears cannot be dead."

"Wisdom worthy of Bishani himself, my lady. You are a very brave young woman, truly an emperor's daughter. Your father would be proud."

My father.

"Thank you." The words stuck in my throat, but if he noticed, he said nothing and went out, leaving me alone with my prayers.

A low groan came from the adjoining room. Silhouettes shifted beyond the thin paper, one of them Master Kenji, the other unknown to me. While my fingers moved, I watched them, trying to make out their words, trying to discern some sense from the nightmare that had engulfed me.

Time passed. It may have been minutes, it may have been hours, but I could only count it in prayers and screams. Tili entered with a tray of tea, neatly sliced fruit, and miniature plum cakes drizzled in syrup. I resisted the urge to throw it back in her face, and when she asked if I was sure I would not change my clothes or lie down, I just shook my head. I would not change. I would not move. I would not retire to another room and wait for someone else to decide what I should and should not know.

Tili went away, her face a pale mask. She had stayed at my side through every disastrous word of that meeting, and yet I could find none to thank her.

Barely a prayer was folded before the doors slid open again, and I prepared to order her out. The words died on my lips. General Ryoji stood in the doorway, thick bandages covering his torso like a makeshift tunic, wrapped so tightly every movement made him wince. A sword had cut into his side, glancing off bone, another into his left arm, now caught to his body with a sling.

For a long time he just stood there, the enormity of everything seeming to defy words. Somehow we had made it out of the imperial manor alive, Kin wedged between Tili and I while General Ryoji cut a path. Again and again, Kin had seemed to slip away and I was sure he was dead, but his determination knew no end.

Once outside the manor it had become easier. The city was still under truce, and uninformed, the Pikes had just watched us warily. At the bridge, our burden had been taken from us.

"My lady," Ryoji said at last. "Forgive me, I did not realise you were here or I would not have come so ill-attired. Is there news?"

"No news," I said. "But for now he is alive."

"Then you have seen Master Kenji?"

I shook my head but did not need to explain. A low keening filled the room, punctuated with sharp crackling gasps. Ryoji's jaw tightened. "Have you not been tortured enough? This house is no palace, but it has many other rooms. Please, allow me to—"

"Many other rooms in which I can be forgotten while men decide the fate of Kisia? No, I thank you."

He bowed. "As you wish, my lady."

"I swear, if you call me 'my lady' one more time, I will scream."

He stepped inside then and slid the door closed behind him. "Are you all right?"

"Don't you dare ask me that question." He had been there, had heard it all, had seen it all. How could anyone be all right?

General Ryoji winced as he knelt opposite me at the table. I took up a fresh piece of paper and began folding, pressing each crease so hard my hands shook.

"Hana—"

"Did you know?"

Of course he hadn't. Even Darius hadn't known, yet I needed him to tell me so, needed to be sure. He shook his head. "No, I did not."

Part of me didn't want to believe him. I needed an outlet for all the angry words banking up on my tongue.

"Hana." He clasped his right hand over mine, gifting me a moment of reassurance amid the chaos of my thoughts, but it was so much the gentle gesture Katashi had once made that tears pricked my eyes. "I'm here if you need me," he said. "In the circumstances, I don't think it's wise to confide in anyone else."

I laughed, the sound bordering on hysterical even to my own ears. "Confide in someone else? Admit that I married the man who killed my family and tried to kill me?"

"Hush!" He turned toward the screen doors, beyond which the physicians were conferring over a rhythm of long, drawn-out hisses. "You cannot say it, you cannot even think it if there is a chance we are not alone. Kisia is built on the strength of its emperors."

"So you said. You need not worry, I cannot bear to think about it let alone talk about it." I drew my hand away, trembling fingers reaching for another sheet of paper. "I keep telling myself I will wake up, but this nightmare seems to have no end."

He watched in silence as I folded another prayer, working mindlessly, fold after fold.

"What are you praying for?"

I looked up. There was pain in his face, pain that mirrored mine, and I knew I was not the only one who suffered. Every man who fought for Kin fought for a lie.

"I don't know," I said. "Sometimes I pray that he will live. Sometimes I pray that he will die and I will be spared the necessity of facing him. Sometimes I pray that I will die, because that would be the easiest of all."

"You don't mean that."

"Don't think you know how I feel just because you bent your knee to a traitor."

"I don't. But you're a fighter. Giving up isn't in your nature."

"Everyone breaks."

He reached again for my hand, squeezing it as though to convey a wealth of emotion he could not utter. All pity and sorrow and the great weight of the secret we now both had to carry. In a swift gesture, he then lifted my hand to his lips and pressed a kiss upon it—something else Katashi had so often done that it tore my heart anew. Such joy I'd felt in seeing him again, kissing him again, being able to sit side by side with him at the head of the throne room, trying to bury the knowledge that it would not last, that it was a future forever lost to me. "I won't let you break," Ryoji said. "We need you."

Before I could answer, the screen door slid and Ryoji dropped my hand like a hot coal, twisting to see Master Kenji enter. The healer bowed solemnly, and my heart constricted as I realised how quiet it had suddenly become.

"Lady Hana," he said. "I was not aware you were here."

"Is he dead?"

"No, my lady, at least not yet." His eyes caught the pile of lotus prayers, each a different colour and size, the irregular paper all Father Kokoro had been able to find. "I see you understand the severity of the case. His Majesty is…" He trailed off, looking acutely uncomfortable and avoiding General Ryoji's stare. "Unwell."

"Unwell? You speak as though he had a mere malady of the stomach!"

"Apologies, my lady, but I am not used to discussing such matters with your sex. I do not wish to overwhelm you."

Across the table, General Ryoji made to speak, but I beat him to it. "If I could have ceased to be female by choice, Master Kenji, I assure you I would have done so long ago. As it is, forget that I am endowed with hips and breasts and tell me if he will live!"

Master Kenji's cheeks flushed. "His wounds are… extensive."

"Get to the point!" Ryoji growled. "We were there. We saw him burned. Give us details or we will march in there and see for ourselves."

The Imperial Physician looked outraged and might have protested had Ryoji not lifted his brows in challenge. "Well?"

"His Majesty has suffered burns to the side of his face and neck, his hands, and both his shoulder and his stomach," Master Kenji said. "Fortunately, his armour protected him from worse burns upon his body. Had he not been wearing it, there would have been no hope."

"But there is hope?"

Master Kenji pulled an expressive grimace. "It is hard to say, my lady. We have removed the damaged skin, and although there is a lot of blood, we have applied unguent and linen binding to the blistered flesh, especially on his hands and face. Cold compresses are helping to ease his pain, but I fear it is considerable."

"Will he live?"

"I do not think the burns will kill him."

"You are very specific with your choice of words, Master Kenji," I said. "If the burns won't kill him, what will?"

"Fever, my lady. It is often the case when a man survives a great wound that he is carried off within a few days by fever or chills. Barring that, I suppose one could say the war might kill him, or perhaps, in the fullness of time, old age!"

General Ryoji barked a humourless laugh. "A soldier can hope."

"Is he awake?"

"He was conscious when I left, my lady, but he comes and goes."

"I will see him," I said, rising from my place.

"Hana." Ryoji reached his hand halfway across the table before thinking better of it. "You don't have to do this."

And I knew not whether his care made the moment hurt more or less. Less because he was there to share my pain, or more because I could not accept his help even though I wished to.

"Yes, I do, General," I said. "As for you, I need you out there. I need eyes and ears. The city is too quiet for my liking. Go find out what is going on."

Dismissed, he got to his feet and bowed. "Yes, my lady." A moment later, he was gone, leaving me to face Kin alone.

When Master Kenji slid open the door, a wave of foetid air hit me. Burned flesh. Charred fabric. Honey. The smells scratched at a memory just out of reach.

"I have dosed him with opium," Master Kenji said. "But I fear he is in considerable pain. It is no pleasant sight."

"I am not as weak as you seem to think," I said. "But thank you for your concern."

Like a man beaten, Master Kenji bowed. "My lady. I must check on my other patients, but I will be back soon. Call for one of my boys if you need anything."

He left, but I stayed where I was, courage waning upon the threshold. The room stank of death. It was small but well-lit, dozens of lanterns casting a flickering mantle over its only occupant. Emperor Kin lay upon a Chiltaen-style bed, his eyes closed though his chest rose and fell with reassuring regularity. The trappings of the emperor were gone. Sash, surcoat, armour—all replaced with bandages and thick pats of ointment. Linen wove from hand to elbow like gloves, and patches of thick gauze covered his neck. Blisters surrounded his right eye.

Less than a week earlier, I had pledged myself to this man, but now I wanted to tear what skin he had left. I wanted to clutch his throat and squeeze until his life drained away just as my mother's had so many years before. The man entrusted with her safety had betrayed her.

A pile of discarded cushions sat in the corner. I picked one up. Its silk was soft and light reflected off its shimmering threads. If I ended this now, I would never have to look at his face again, never have to hear his voice or feel the touch of his hand.

Being a leader means having to make hard decisions.

It was too late. Katashi was beyond redemption, and my hold on the empire was too tenuous. There was no heir. If Kin died, his generals would tear the empire apart, unless Katashi destroyed it first in the fury he seemed unable to control, unable to contain.

Kisia needed Kin.

I flung the cushion toward the wall and screamed, the grief tearing at my throat until I had no breath left. Empty, I sagged, angry tears filling my eyes.

"You should have done it. I deserve it."

The cracked voice came from the bed, and I brushed away the

tears to find Kin watching me. His right eye was stuck closed, but the left was open.

"You deserve worse," I said.

"I suffer. By the gods, you do not know how much I suffer."

"But I know it is not enough."

"Then let me die," he said, his face creased with pain. "Take a knife and end this, I beg you."

"No."

His every breath was laboured. "Please, Hana."

"No. You have to live."

"Will you ever forgive me?"

"Forgive you?" I cried. "I never knew my mother because of you. I never knew my father or my brothers, and you have spilled such hate of them upon me, such weights of duty, that I wish more than anything I could finish the job Katashi started, but even with only hatred in my heart, you still have to live, because without you, Kisia falls right now. So you will fight, my emperor, because it is your duty."

Kin tried to lift one bandaged hand and hissed sharply through his teeth. He closed his eye. A spider of blood appeared beneath the gauze pad on his cheek, and I was glad I could not see the broken flesh.

"Did you love my mother?"

He opened his eye again, its dark colour shot with blood. "Yes."

"Being a leader means having to make hard choices," I said bitterly.

"I never meant to hurt you, Hana." Kin took a deep breath, the air shuddering through him. He swallowed, once, twice, the sound dry. "I never meant to love you either, but even with everything that has happened, you have given me more cause for joy than grief."

"I wish I could say the same for you, Your Majesty."

The breath of a mocking laugh passed his lips. "You have a way with words that cuts deeper than any sword."

"You killed my family."

"Yes."

The lump in my throat threatened to send tears spilling down my cheeks again. I pressed a hand to my quivering lips. "Is it so easy to say?"

Kin groaned, clenching his teeth tight. "Yes," he managed between them. "I feel weightless for the first time in years." His words ended in another hiss.

"That only makes me hate you more. I don't want you to be happy."

"Not a day has gone by since I met you that I didn't wish I could undo what I did, however much Kisia might suffer for it. Stupid old fool that I am, I love you more than duty, Hana."

He spoke with such sincerity, with a total lack of the imperial mask I had grown so used to him wearing, that I believed him. But it made no difference. Love had no power to change what had already been done. Whatever his reason had been, whatever the circumstances, there was no forgiveness in my heart.

I swallowed hard, forcing down a glut in my throat. "I have to go."

"Yes, you do. Hold the south bank, Hana, because if he takes the bridge, nothing will stop him burning Mei'lian. Take my sash."

"Your Majesty—?"

"Take it!"

The remnants of his clothing had been thrown in a bucket, every thread peeled from his flesh while he screamed. Only his sash remained, relatively untouched, coiled on the floor like the tail of a sleeping dragon. I picked it up and ran the silk through my fingers. It was not just the crimson sash of a soldier loyal to the Ts'ai, it was the sash of an emperor, blessed by the gods.

"Kisia is yours for now," he said. "Look after her well." Kin closed his eyes, and there were so many things I wanted to say, so many thoughts that jostled for space in my head that I let him rest rather than find voice for them all. I had wanted for so long to sit on the throne in my own right and here was my chance, but it had come at such a time and with such a price that I could take no joy in my success.

General Ryoji was waiting back in the main room, a crumpled lotus prayer cupped in one hand. He had found himself a fresh uniform, surcoat and all, and although he had dispensed with the sling, he held his left arm crooked against his body.

"General," I said. "What news?"

"The truce holds, my lady, but for how long I don't know. We need you. His Majesty's orders were that if anything happened to him, we were to burn the bridge, but General Rini is refusing to take drastic action while the peace holds."

"By the gods, must General Rini always be a thorn in my side? Does no one outrank that man?"

"Only the minister of the left."

"But Kin has been filling that position himself since Darius was dismissed."

Ryoji grimaced. "Yes, and although people were informed he no longer held the position, Minister Laroth was never formally removed."

Despite everything, Kin's trust in Darius had been implicit. And in that last moment, Darius had not let him down. I ran the imperial sash around my waist, tying its knot over my hateful bridal sash. "Then General Rini is going to have to listen to me. What reason does he give for not burning it?"

"There are wounded soldiers crossing now and then," he said. "And of course it should not be destroyed if it need not be. As General Rini has reminded me numerous times, it is more than three hundred years old and was built by one hundred and twenty-one craftsmen, five of whom are interred within its walls."

I took the lotus prayer he was holding and placed it upon the pile of poorly folded flowers, wondering whether the gods listened to shabby ones. There was no time left to fold more.

"Unfortunately, we are all servants of necessity, General," I said. "We burn it."

———————◆———————

Hundreds of soldiers watched us approach. Lanterns lit their intent stares, but even the largest flame was dwarfed by Shimai's crown of fire. It crackled over the north bank, as yet unaffected by the rain.

"They are waiting for Kin," Ryoji whispered as we walked through the silent ranks. "Soldiers need a leader."

"They have one," I replied. "Their emperor lives."

He shot me a meaningful look. Many of these men had seen us bring Kin back unconscious and burned beyond recognition.

General Rini was waiting at the bridge. The Span was the oldest and widest of all the bridges that crossed the Tzitzi. It was an ancient covered construction that had seen the passage of millions of feet, from the daily movement of Shimai's citizens to the trumpeted processions of emperors. Now its tiled roof sang with the rain and its flooded gutters spewed water into the swollen river below.

"General Rini," I said, stopping before him.

"Lady Hana. How is His Majesty?"

"His Majesty lives and has given me the right to rule in his stead until he recovers. By the grace of the gods."

General Rini looked at the sash tied around my waist. "I see," he said. Behind him, the other commanders watched and waited. Endymion was there too, not welcomed but tolerated amid the ranks despite his traitor's brand. Bandages were visible through the tears in his clothing, and all the blood and ash and dirt had been cleaned off his face. He didn't look at all well-rested though, and I wondered where he had been while Darius and Kin had played. Had he been there, would he have been able to save Kin? Would he have tried? It had been his family too that General Kin Ts'ai of the Imperial Guard had plotted to remove from power.

He nodded as our eyes met, but I could not confide in him. He had killed half a dozen men with nothing but a thought and had hardly seemed to realise he was doing it.

"Tell me, General, why has the bridge not been burned?" I asked. "Did not His Majesty give orders to do so if anything happened to him?"

"Yes, my lady, but there has been no movement from the enemy and so no reason to burn it. The first rule of combat is never to back yourself into a corner."

I found myself focussing upon a discoloured patch on the side of his nose, around which drops of rain ran down his face. "Does not being burned alive count as something happening, General?"

"I am sure it does, my lady, but—"

"Then you have backed yourself into your own corner. You have already seen what Katashi is capable of. Burn it."

"My lady—"

"I command you to burn the bridge, General, or I will find someone else to fulfil your duties for you."

General Rini's mouth snapped shut and he bowed. "Yes, my lady, as you command. Though how you expect anything to burn in this rain is quite beyond me."

"I have an idea," Ryoji said, his eyes alight. "Oil. We passed a lamp maker's establishment two streets back. We can break open some barrels and roll them along the boards."

"Do it."

"Yes, my lady."

Each barrel took four men to manoeuvre down the slick black stones of the road. They rumbled like thunder as they rolled onto the Span's wooden boards.

While I watched the rain ease to a drizzle, I found Endymion standing beside me.

"Your sword, my lady," he said, bowing as he held out the weapon. Rain shimmered on the long narrow blade, on a fish and a dragon swimming through steel. The Ts'ai dragon chasing the Otako fish? Or the fish chasing the dragon? Kin had done all he could to wipe out my family completely.

I took the hilt. "Thank you, Endymion," I said.

He turned away, but I held out my hand. "Wait."

"Yes, my lady?"

Kimiko had said Endymion had ways of knowing things he ought not to know. I put my hand on my stomach, a hand covered in the singed remnants of hundreds of tiny hairs. I had been lucky to get away with only minor burns.

"No, nothing," I said. "Thank you."

His gaze darted to my hand, but he just nodded and moved away through the crowd. General Ryoji replaced him. "We are ready, my lady," he said. "Would you like the honour?"

He smiled as I took the unlit torch from his hand. "Thank you, General."

"You have time to reconsider," General Rini said.

"I will not reconsider the fate of my empire, General."

He bowed and said no more.

Together, General Ryoji and I stepped beneath the roof of the bridge. "All yours," he said. The hatch of the metal lantern squeaked open, and I guided the pitch-soaked torch into the flames. It lit with a puff of dark smoke while overhead, rain danced upon the tiles.

I dropped the torch. The oil caught fire with a rush, and flames rose. Ryoji pulled me back, but I cared nothing for the heat, nothing for the smoke, for as the bridge burned, my heart soared. Katashi was not the only one who could play with fire. No number of burned corpses would allow him to cross a river without a bridge.

At my fingertips, the flames danced merrily, licking the thick beams above and catching on the decorative fretwork.

"Set scouts along the length of the river, General," I said. "We take no chances. The moment there is movement on the north bank, I want to know. Any movement at all. Let the others rest."

He nodded.

"And archers. I want every able archer fully equipped and ready. And send a man to the nearest apothecary."

"Apothecary? Are you ill?"

"No, but I want as much jinzen root and yao grass as can be found."

Warily he said, "I fear you must enlighten me. Are not jinzen root and yao grass used to ... evoke desire?"

My cheeks reddened. "A myth, General," I said. "All they do is keep you awake. It has been a long night, and I fear it will turn into a long day. The men could use a boost."

"A unique command, my lady."

"That, General, is because I am this army's only woman."

DAY FIVE

16. ENDYMION

The whispers were too thick for sleep. Too much fear. Too much restlessness. Across the river, dark figures had kept their posts, watching us as we watched them. And in my head, memories clamoured.

I'd stayed away from the meeting, though a hundred times I had been on the verge of going, no matter how much my wound had needed cleaning and binding. Perhaps if I had, things would have turned out differently. Or perhaps everyone would have been dead.

Focus, Endymion. Focus.

Now the sun was rising, and from my rooftop I could see all of Shimai, see the dying fires and the smoke, the hazy, shimmering city surreal in the predawn light. The bridge was still burning. More oil barrels had kept the fire stoked to a roar, but the old timbers held iron-strong.

Whispers ran along the riverbank. The message started as a hiss and grew to a roar.

They're moving.

They're coming.

Vengeance.

On the next roof, one of Kin's archers brushed an arrow fletching across his lips. He was squinting down at the figures on the far bank. All night, the enemy soldiers had lounged at their ease, but now they were shifting their weight and fidgeting.

Something's happening.

I slid down the slick roof until my sandals caught on the eave, arresting my progress with a jolt. From there I rolled, gripped the iron fretwork, and lowered myself onto the broken stones of the road.

It was like dropping into soup. Here the bulk of Kin's men waited, their fear a smell one needed no Empathy to sense. I had climbed onto the roof to get away, but to warn Hana, I would have to go through them. She was with the remnants of Kin's council, a group of shadows against a backdrop of flames.

A parapet ran along the edge of the steep riverbank. The swollen Tzitzi roiled below, but I climbed onto it and jogged along rather than push through the press of soldiers. It was General Ryoji who saw me first, and Hana broke off her conversation to watch my approach.

That boy is mad.

It's a long way to fall.

"My lady," I said as I came within earshot. "They're moving."

General Ryoji scowled across the river. "I can't see anything."

"General! Lady Hana!" An out-of-breath soldier insinuated his way through the crowd. "There's movement on the north bank."

"So ends the waiting," Ryoji said grimly.

"It was only a matter of time, General," Hana said, straining to maintain an outward calm though I could feel the pounding of her heart. "General Rini, rouse the men. Form up the lines."

"Yes, my lady."

General Rini straightened his crimson sash and strode into the mass of soldiers, in his element, while orders barked from his throat. Hana went back to watching the north bank, and I hovered, unsure what else to do. I was running out of time, all of Kisia was running out of time, but I could not reach any of my targets now, could only wait for them to come to me.

"Form up the lines! Form up the lines!"

All around us, the shout went up, and like a drunken wave, the men rose from attitudes of rest.

"Hana?"

She did not look around, did not seem to hear me, so intently did she stare at the opposite bank. Dark figures shifted through the haze, striding through bolts of morning light.

Hana climbed onto the parapet. The wind stirred her crimson surcoat, and in the firelight, her sword gleamed orange. Everything from her straight back and folded arms to the jewelled comb holding back her hair screamed assurance, but I knew her fear like it was my own.

"Hana?" I said again.

General Ryoji looked around. "Lady Hana has rather a lot to concentrate on," he said. "Perhaps you should step back and let us deal with this."

She turned at the sound of his voice as she had not at mine. "What is it?"

"I can't explain," I said. "But I think you need to leave."

"Leave? Why?"

"I don't know. I can't…" Two. Six hundred and forty-three. One hundred and twenty-four thousand and eighty. Whispers. Memories. Words. Sounds. Everything came to me and I was drowning, unable to separate anything from the morass except the ill ease that roiled in my gut. "I think he isn't going to let anything get in his way. There's… intention, a taste of determination. He's laughing at us, and—"

"Endymion," she said, giving me her full attention now in a way I could not reciprocate. "Regardless of where else I am needed, this is where I have to be. I cannot leave this city to its fate."

"Hana—"

She lifted her hand to silence me. "I will not do it."

I stepped onto the parapet beside her. "Hana," I said. "Leave General Rini in charge. If the south bank can be held, he can hold it."

234 • *Devin Madson*

"What are you so afraid of?" she said. "Can you see the future now? Am I going to die?"

"I don't know."

"Wrong answer. General? Are the men ready?"

"Yes, my lady."

She licked her lips. "Good."

Behind us, the men stood silent, statues of fear in the dawn haze. All were watching, craning to see as across the river, the tall figure of a man emerged from the last of the shadows. He was dressed all in black, unmistakable with the tip of an enormous bow rising above his head.

"He is not going to stop," I said. "Fire is not stopped by fire, Hana, you have to get out of here."

Hana sucked in a breath but acted as though I had not spoken. At her side, General Rini said, "If we can hold until General Yi gets here, then we can crush the bastards between us."

There was a gleeful note to his voice, his thoughts converging on victory of the most selfish kind. Katashi's head at Kin's feet would forgive every failure of this night and save his career. Details leapt from his imagination: scores of arrows flying across the river to cut down fleeing rebels; the spit that dripped from Katashi's lip as he begged for mercy; the smell of blood; Kin's approval in a smile and a word, and in the enormous largess that would be his as the protector of Shimai.

"That isn't going to work," I said, speaking to General Rini this time. "His soldiers may not be able to cross that bridge, but you're mad if you think he cannot."

"Nonsense, boy, those flames are too hot now. Nothing can pass. They'll have to go around to another crossing if they want to reach this side of the river."

"You aren't listening," I began, stepping closer. My foot slipped off the stone parapet, sending my heart leaping for safety. A strong hand gripped my arm above the elbow.

"Watch your step, boy," General Rini said, waiting until I had recovered my footing before he let go. "You don't want to be the river's next victim."

Beneath me, the foaming water of the torrid Tzitzi roared through the city, just as the chaos of thousands of thoughts and whispers roared through my head.

On the north bank, Katashi strode forward, his army following like a dark cloud. He stopped at the opposing parapet that protected Shimai's citizens from the sharp drop into the river, and mimicking Hana, he climbed up. His aura had once been golden, drawing all toward him as honey draws ants, but now that same aura distorted the city and the men behind him—a heat haze that made the air tremble.

"All hail my empress," he shouted over the roar of the river. "We are curiously tenacious, you and I. The Otakos that Kin cannot kill, no matter how hard he tries."

"We can stop this, Katashi," she returned. "You don't have to do this anymore."

"Why? Is the great Kin Ts'ai dead?"

She paused, and though she did not turn to look at all the soldiers at her back, her stiffening showed she was more aware of them than ever. "No. Injured. He will live to sit upon the throne again."

In the eyes of the gods, it was wrong to lie. Honesty was one of the five weights by which a soul was judged. That was what the Sixth Law said. It said the gods were always watching. That they can hear the whisper of our souls.

"Then my task is far from finished," Katashi shouted back. "Unless you give him to me. You seem to be in charge now, after all, and you cannot want him anymore."

Such truth that for a moment, Hana closed her eyes, and almost I held out my hand to keep her from falling. All her thoughts were full of hatred for the man who had killed her family. I had told Kin she would never understand, but what I had not seen was just how deeply she had already been grieving. She rolled back her shoulders as she faced what might have been across the breadth of the river and lied to him.

"Unlike you, I am capable of forgiveness. I will not let you burn either Kisia or her emperor."

The heat haze around him thickened. "Where are his generals?"

Both General Ryoji and General Rini stepped up onto the parapet beside Hana, Ryoji with more ease. "We are here, rebel," Rini shouted.

"Who are you?"

"General Esta Rini, first general of the Rising Army."

"You fought for my uncle. But now you fight for my uncle's murderer. Those are not the actions of an honourable man."

Whispers hissed through the crowd of soldiers behind me, as many out loud as in their heads.

What did he say?

Murderer?

I've heard that rumour before, just nonsense put about by the Otakos.

General Rini bristled. "How dare—"

"No," Katashi snapped from the other side of the river. "I will not talk to traitors. General Ryoji, you know the truth. Give me the Usurper and I will not burn you or any of your men. I will leave you alone and leave Shimai the way I came in."

Behind me, imperial soldiers made their choices in an instant, the weight of their emotions so great that I pressed my hands to my head, sure my skull would crack.

Emperor Kin is our god.

Save Shimai.

No.

Let me go home to my wife.

We can't do that. There is no honour down that path even if it would save us.

"We are the emperor's men," General Ryoji replied, not having so much as looked at Hana or General Rini. "We do not treat with rebels."

"Pity." Katashi leapt off the wall and walked toward the burning bridge. "I'll just have to come and get him myself."

"He cannot cross it," Hana said, her voice near a whisper. "Tell me he cannot cross it."

"It's been burning for nearly three hours," General Ryoji replied, but it was no answer. Three hours were not long enough to burn through the centuries-old wooden beams. For over three hundred years, the Span had united Shimai, the endless traffic serving only to wear grooves in its warped boards.

All eyes fixed on Katashi. Disquiet rose behind me, roiling like the Tzitzi River itself.

"He cannot cross it," Hana repeated. "He cannot."

Katashi handed Hacho to one of his Pikes and stepped onto the bridge. The fire swallowed him. His soldiers did not move.

"What is he doing?" Hana said.

"I can see no more than you, my lady," General Ryoji replied. "But it would appear he is standing on the bridge."

"Let the bastard burn," Rini grumbled. "It is no more than he deserves."

The sheer force of hundreds of men holding their breath stung my lungs, and I sucked air fast, growing light-headed as I swam in whispers.

No man can cross that.

The gods can walk through flame.

What's happening? I can't see. Maybe that's a good thing. Oh gods, I want to go home.

The fire. Fuck! Look at the fire!

The flames were shrinking. I stared, sure it was a mere trick of the morning light. Yet at the far end of the bridge, the fire was dying, as though Katashi was drawing the flames into himself. And he was moving.

"Hana, you have to get out of here!" I said, pulling General Ryoji off the parapet so I could take his place. "Come with me, we have to go." Sixteen years ago, blood had dripped from Shin's knife as he halted in the doorway.

Hana ripped her sleeve from my clutching grip. "I'm not going anywhere."

"Then at least order them to get Kin out of the city if you genuinely wish to save him. Katashi is not going to stop."

General Ryoji was scowling up at me from the stones, but Hana nodded. "Get His Majesty out of here, General. Tili too."

"My place is with you."

"No," she snapped. "You are the leader of the Imperial Guard; your place is with your emperor."

Stepping close, he said, "Hana—"

"It was an order, General," she said. "What use do you think you are to me with an injured arm? Get Kin out of here. Now."

General Ryoji bowed. "Yes, my lady."

He walked away, and Hana, grim-faced, turned her attention back to the bridge. The fire was shrinking. Where Katashi walked, flames died and embers ceased to glow. Hisses of fear ran through Kin's men.

"Archers, ready!"

All along the riverbank, arrows were drawn from their quivers.

"Loose!"

Arrows leapt the river like salmon, some making it far enough to fall amongst the rebels on the far bank. Men dropped, some tumbling over the low wall and into the river. It swallowed them without chewing, sucking them deep into the current.

"Aim into the fire!"

A tight group of archers loosed arrow after arrow down the mouth of the burning bridge. When one called for more arrows, Hana lifted her hand. "Hold!"

"He's there," I said. "I can feel him."

"What do we do, General?" Hana asked, her voice hollow. Small. "What if nothing can stop him?"

"Then we fight, my lady," General Rini said. "And we don't let anyone smell our fear. May the gods be with you."

"And you, General."

With the vigour of a younger man, General Rini jumped off the parapet and strode through the lines of his men calling orders. "Hold the lines!" he shouted. "We fear no death. We fear no demons. We will hold this city for Kisia. Loose your arrows at will!"

More arrows flew straight into the flames, desperation in every draw. And still the fire shrank. One of our soldiers broke the last oil barrel and kicked it out onto the bridge. Its trail stoked what remained of the blaze to an epic heat, the curtain of wavering flames obscuring everything in sight.

General Rini raised his hand, and the group of archers at the bridge held again, waiting, watching. The hope was suffocating—hope that they might have gotten him, hope that the fire was too hot, the arrows too sharp, that their luck might finally be turning. I could not move, could not step from Hana's side, so much did I feel like a witness of history.

The oil burned out. The raging flames began to subside, orange fingers sliding back into the timbers from whence they had come. And there a black figure—Katashi, untouched, the god of vengeance who could not be stopped.

A flaming barrel shot out of the bridge's mouth, slamming into the front ranks and bursting into a hundred burning shards. The lid followed, its surface peppered with arrows as it spun out of the smoke. It hit a soldier in the jaw, the resulting crack sending him falling back, dead before he hit the ground.

"Endymion?"

Hana didn't look around. Her eyes were fixed on Katashi as she wallowed in a cloud of putrid emotion. "Yes, Hana?"

"I'm sorry."

"It's not your fault."

"Yes, it is."

Katashi had halted a few paces out from the bank, and through the open arches of the bridge, our eyes met. He nodded to me, an almost friendly acknowledgement, before turning to Hana. He lifted his hands then, his skin bright crimson as he made a series of quick signs.

Move fast. Swim. Then he winked at me, and as heat surged through my veins, I understood what Hana could not. "He's going to vent," I said.

"What?"

"He's going to vent. Move. Now!"

I hit Hana as flames surged toward us. Embers bit. Screams filled the morning. Overhead, the fire bloomed like an orange chrysanthemum, but we were falling. Air rushed past my ears. Floodwater roared. And the water rose to meet us, hitting so hard it beat the breath from my body.

17. HANA

The bridge exploded and I was falling through flames and smoke and steam and spray. Hitting the river burst the air from my lungs and in the inky darkness water roared. Kin's sash tangled about my leg like a slimy hand dragging me down, but whatever its weight, I would not abandon it. Not now. Instead, I fought with my gloves and sandals and kicked with aching legs.

I broke the surface and sucked a great lungful of air—furnace hot. Steam billowed around me. Overhead, a firestorm was dissipating, swirling tongues of orange flame fading to smoke.

"Endymion!"

The current was too strong to fight. All I could do was spin, hunting the haze for any sign of him.

"Endymion!"

Unwilling to so easily relinquish my life, the swirling Tzitzi sucked me back under. Blood thumped in my ears. Again I thought of discarding the sash and again I could not. Kisia belonged to the Otakos, not the Tzitzi. Its dark water pummelled me like a rag doll, but I pushed for the surface again, lungs bursting.

Emerging into the light, I gulped air and water in equal measure.
"Endymion!"

Foam and debris washed around me. Endymion could be anywhere. He could be dead. Since he could kill with nothing but a thought, perhaps that would be for the best. He had wanted me to leave the city and at least in that he had gotten his wish. There was no faster way out than this when the city was in lockdown. Unless...

Siege gates.

The thought arrived mere moments before the gate itself, the black iron grating rushing toward me out of the swirling water. White pain ripped through my skull as I hit it and was pinned to the metal rungs by the force of the raging river.

"Hana!"

Endymion clung to the grating, wet clumps of hair covering the Traitor's Mark that could never truly be hidden. There was another man—a rebel—holding tight to the metal gate. And a third body butted up against the bars, more corpse than soldier, washed against the gate like so much debris.

"You could have killed us," I snapped the moment I had caught my breath.

"*That* could have killed us." He pulled an arm free of the water and pointed back toward the distant bridge. The remnant heat hung above the city like a dense red cloud.

"I need to get back."

"Hey!"

The rebel was edging closer, pulling himself hand over hand along the grating.

"Keep your distance," I warned.

He lifted a hand in surrender. "I mean no harm. My name is Captain Terran, my lady," he said, making a pitiful attempt to bow amid the storm water. "You probably don't remember me, but I fought for General Manshin."

We had been on the same side not so long since but too much had changed. I turned to find Endymion watching, his gaze intent. "Move," I said. "Let's get out of this river."

He needed no further prompting and made his way, hand over hand, toward the edge of the siege gate. I looked up, thinking to climb it, but the iron bars rose into a rounded arch and from there into a stone gatehouse as sheer as the walls. The only way out was to climb the footholds cut into the stone bank.

"My lady!"

The captain's words ended in a pained cry, and Endymion stopped to look back, blocking my progress. "You're injured," he said.

"Grazed by an arrow," the man returned. "Your men are good with their bows."

"You should know," I said. "They were your comrades once."

"I go where my general takes me. It's the law."

"And your general will take you to the hells with Katashi. You ought to have stopped fighting for him when he became like this."

"My general is sick of the stink of burning flesh," he said.

"Then he should do something about it! General Manshin is well practiced at dishonouring his oaths."

I nudged Endymion with my elbow, and he kept moving, more quickly now as we approached the edge of the gate. I glanced back to find Captain Terran following.

When Endymion could go no farther, he swam for the bank, dragging himself through the water like a determined dog. I hesitated. The Tzitzi River had claimed so many lives, the roar of its waters like the voices of a thousand dead souls. But it was swim or stay, and with the rebel captain close behind, I pushed off the gate and made for the footholds. The current was not as strong near the bank, and I soon hit the wall, grazing my hands on the stone. But the handholds were deep and easy to grip, and I pulled myself out of the river, relief overwhelming fear for one beautiful, weightless moment.

Endymion was already climbing, shedding water like rain. It poured off me too, falling on the captain now dragging himself from the water beneath me. It was a long climb, but the stone was warm and the handholds close together. Pulling myself over the parapet at the top was the hardest part.

Endymion was already there, wringing out his clothes, but he offered no helping hand.

Endymion has ways of knowing things he ought not. Kimiko's words haunted me. A touch would be all he needed. All he needed to know what I so desperately needed to know.

He looked up at me, his head cocked quizzically.

I wrung out my surcoat rather than hold his gaze. When the river-keepers cleared out the debris in summer, they might find my sword, but my gloves and sandals would make it all the way to the sea. Both sashes had survived, and I managed a smile at the perverseness. The chastity knot just would not let go.

The captain rolled over the parapet and onto the road with a damp thud. He was breathing heavily, his eyes closed. Blood stained the hand clamped to his side.

"He's badly injured and needs help," Endymion said, kneeling beside him.

"Leave him," I said.

"Leave him? But he's worthy. I cannot leave him to die."

"Then he's all yours. I have to get back to my men."

"They're all dead, Hana."

I would not listen, could not, just strode away along the riverbank, toward Shimai's famous south-bank mansions. These were the summer homes of country lords, each one brightly painted, with window boxes crammed with lavender and white moonflowers. Silence ruled, but screams and shouts and the patter of running feet played in the distance.

"Hana! Wait, stay with us!"

I sped up, rough stones cutting into my bare feet.

"There's no use! Hana!"

I broke into a run.

"Hana!"

Past the summer houses, past barricades and trampled gardens, past packed shrines and empty market squares. Knots of frightened citizens spilled from the steps of a guardhouse, huddled together with their meagre belongings because they had nowhere else to go. Shimai had never been my home and its streets were a confusing mess, but following the roar of the Tzitzi, I needed no map.

Approaching the bridge was like running into the bottom plain of the seven hells. Flames roared from roofs and the stones were awash with debris and bodies. The smell was terrible. Burned flesh, burned wood, burned blood, hair, leather, silk. Smoke choked the streets, so dense it all but obscured people running past. I caught frightened faces and scurrying steps but no sign of soldiers, no flickers of crimson.

Then a black-clad figure sauntered past. Another stood in a doorway, throwing sacks into the street. I darted into an alley, but in the close space between buildings the heat was immense. There were more Pikes in the next street, laughing as they looted an apothecary. Bunches of herbs flew through an open window.

Never had I been so thankful for smoke.

The bridge couldn't be far. I tucked the tail of Kin's sash into my breeches and ran.

The stones were slick and every breath was full of ash and smoke and heat. Always heat. Always the stink of death and the sound of fire and chaos. Again, I heard the roar of the river and turned, unable to see more than a few paces ahead. The river grew louder, and I was alone in the street but for the bodies. Ours or theirs? All I could see was blood. Blood and guts and crimson sashes.

Ours.

And there was the bridge, charred black and smoking. The road was gone, buried beneath a weave of crisped flesh, of sashes and surcoats, of limbs and staring eyes and clumps of scorched hair.

I stumbled back into a doorway, shaking. There was no one. Not one single survivor, just a knot of Pikes picking over the dead like black crows. One of them turned, and I crouched amid the bodies, hoping he would not see me in the smoke. Beside me a blistered arm. Blackened lips. Staring lashless eyes. There was no end to the death.

The Pike peered at me through the smoke. Bile stung my tongue and my heart juddered sickeningly. *Look away. Walk away. Go. Now.*

My mute orders went unheard. The man dropped a charred scabbard. Then he was walking, walking toward me across the sea of dead soldiers without looking where he placed his feet. Arms. Faces. Hair. Still he kept coming.

My hand leapt to my belt but there was nothing. No sword. No bow. No dagger. It had been stupid to come.

"Hey, are you—?"

I slammed into him, knocking him back onto the carpet of flesh. My feet scrabbled to maintain purchase on the slippery bodies as he lunged for my leg, shouting. More Pikes turned. I didn't wait to see if they followed but sped on toward the bridge, no plan, just panic.

Smoke choked the street. Noise. Fire. More shouts. I ran, stones cutting my feet and ash stinging my eyes. The bridge was a dead end, alleys a gamble. I took the next street. It was empty but for the dead. Behind me the Pike shouted, his steps slowing. But there were others, silent like hunters, only the occasional footfall audible over the sound of my own ragged breathing.

I turned again into a narrower street, darting beneath a fallen string of lanterns. Another street, clogged with panicking people. Flames lashed from upper windows and the heat was immense, but turning away was not an option. I ran on, holding my breath, smoke stinging my eyes as I fought to see the shape of the road ahead. No sound of footsteps now, just crackling flames.

A wall appeared ahead of me. No door, just the back of a building that faced onto another street. Two high windows. A rain barrel. And an iron lantern hook. I set my foot on the barrel and started to climb, throwing my hand from hook to sill. *Don't climb with your hands, stupid, climb with your feet.* A nameless boy in an orchard a long time ago. A world away.

I looked down. Two Pikes were a body length below. Panic jolted my heart, but I pushed on, my head spinning like the first time I had breathed in Malice's opium.

My fingers found the eave. I pushed off the shutter, heard it crack as I scrabbled onto the roof and rolled. Into blood. One of my men, the left side of his body burned black. His bow lay on the shingles. An arrow had been nocked, and I nocked it again now and waited, crouched, until the Pike's head appeared above the edge of the roof.

The arrow hit him in the cheek, throwing him back. Not where I had been aiming, but I never had been as good as Katashi.

I pulled another two arrows from the dead soldier's quiver and stepped to the eave. In time to see the second Pike drop back into the smoke, an arrow through the top of his skull.

"And you said I was useless to you injured."

General Ryoji was perched on the eave, a bow in his hand and a pained smile upon his lips.

"Ryoji!" Tears sprang to my eyes. "Oh, thank the gods! I thought you were all dead. Are there others? Where's Kin?"

He pressed a finger to his lips. "No time. We have to go."

So many questions jostled forward, but with enemies all around, I dared not speak.

Moving quickly through clouds of smoke, we climbed and slid down the peaks of Shimai's roofs, my bare feet making no sound on the terracotta shingles. From up above, the city looked different, the smoke thinner and the shouts more distant. Most of the gaps between roofs were little more than steps, and we crossed them with ease, keeping safely out of sight, until a wide road forced us back to ground level.

"We're close," the general whispered as he made to slide over the edge. "We just have to make it to that laneway."

He pointed to where a crowd of Pikes and traitor soldiers milled outside an open door. A cheerful landlord was handing out jugs of wine to the men who ripped the corks out and drank with gusto, spilling liquid onto the stones. He glanced up as General Ryoji dropped into the road. Sharp eyes lifted to me and then fell back as he threw another jug into the crowd like a man feeding rabid dogs. "There's the last. I'll bring up another crate."

Katashi's soldiers cheered, and I dropped down as the landlord disappeared inside. A narrow alley ran alongside the building. There a tiny window allowed for the egress of waste, and it was flung open just as we drew level.

"Quick!" the landlord hissed. "The lady first."

Blood stained the tiny window frame, smearing my already filthy clothes as I slid through. The landlord gripped my legs and half caught, half pulled me inside. Ryoji followed. Then the landlord yanked the window closed and ran the bolt home.

"By the gods, you're lucky, General," he said. "My lady," he added, bowing to me. "Apologies. My name is Loc Hadran, my lady, once General Hadran, commander of the Imperial Guard."

I nodded and would have spoken had he given me a chance.

"I think you had better move quickly," he said instead, already walking away. "Before they drink me dry and come hunting for more."

We were in a basement passage. There were rooms here, stocked with crates and lacquered boxes, with sacks and chests and dusty jugs of wine, and one room, at the end of the passage, containing nothing but a few old pieces of furniture and a moulding bedroll. The landlord had retained the authority of his former station and strode to a pile of rags where one shake disgorged a broken sword.

"All yours, General," he said, handing it over. "I'll put the stone back after you and keep them out as long as possible."

"No one else knows it's here," Ryoji said. "So—"

"Lord Laroth knows," the old general said. "I'd love to hear the rumours of his treachery are in error, but I doubt it. He's always been a cold-blooded snake of a man."

"Lord Laroth is dead."

"I didn't see him die, General," I said.

General Ryoji turned to stare at me, broken sword in hand. "Then we must hope that Otako's anger persists and he would sooner kill him than listen to him. Or Otako will soon be following us." With that, he jammed the broken sword between two identical flagstones. The scrape of steel on stone made my skin crawl, but he just gritted his teeth and rocked the blade back and forth until the edge of the stone began to lift. Awkwardly cradling his injured arm to his chest, he managed to lever the stone up until he could grip the edge with his good hand, blood-blackened fingers straining.

It was dark beneath the stone, the same dense darkness that had surrounded Katashi and I when he led his Pikes into Mei'lian. My heart ached, and I wondered if I might drop into the darkness only to find Monarch waiting to catch me. Would anything have been different had I just told him the truth in the beginning?

"After you," General Ryoji said, propping the stone hatch open with two sturdy rods.

I sat on the edge and lowered myself down, but no one was waiting. This was a different passage and I was with a different man, and yet with the tang of smoke and sweat, I could imagine it was Katashi who landed behind me in the gloom.

"You can walk," Ryoji said. "The floor is level until you reach the light well."

"Is it safe to talk here?"

"In whispers."

"Kin?"

The dim light of the tavern cellar lit him through the hatchway but left his expression hidden in shadow. "Safe."

"Alive?"

"Alive."

"Tili."

A nod.

"Endymion?"

"Yes. He came in with an injured soldier, one of General Manshin's. When he learnt you hadn't returned, he wanted to come find you, but trouble seems to find him wherever he goes so I persuaded him to leave it to me."

Trouble finds him because he's my brother. I wondered if Ryoji knew, or if it was just my little secret now. "How many other survivors?"

There was a beat of silence before the answer, a silence that seemed to suck every hope from my heart. "About three dozen, some badly wounded, others very fortunate."

"General Rini?"

Again the same silence. "No."

Overhead, the stone fell back into place with a heavy thud.

"I think we should keep moving," he said. "Walk toward the light."

I went ahead of him, toward the beacon of a distant light well. I had more questions but wanted no more answers. The last ones had been hard enough. So many dead. All that blistered flesh. All those bodies. All that blood. I had been left to care for the empire and I should have done better than this. Been better. Would Kin have made the right choices?

A cold, bluish light grew around us, brighter and brighter, until we emerged into a large, round room. Two dozen men filled the space, some sitting, some lying, few talking, many silent. Every one of them wore the crimson sash of Emperor Kin, and every one of them smelt of blood and worse. Master Kenji's apprentice knelt beside one—finally a cause for thanks—and Father Kokoro beside another. Of all the people to survive, one had to be this hate-filled man.

"None of these men are well enough to walk the distance," General Ryoji said as I looked upon what remained of my army. "So we are transporting them one by one down the tunnel to Mei'lian."

This was all that remained of my men, ash all that remained of my city. And Mei'lian was next.

"How far is it?"

"A few hours' walk. We should find you some sandals." Together we looked down at my bloodstained feet. "Perhaps Apprentice Yoj should see them."

The pain had been niggling at my awareness. There was no great injury, but a myriad of cuts and scrapes from my run through the streets had left them raw. But they were just feet.

"I am not so weak, General," I said. "I grew up on a farm. It's much easier to climb trees without sandals, you know."

"Yes," he said and smiled without constraint. "I know it is, but I think you should let him look at them all the same, my lady."

I submitted to the ministrations of the apprentice healer, but there was little he could do. He had escaped with nothing but the satchel that was a physician's constant companion, but Master Kenji had taken his better-stocked box through the passage with Emperor Kin. Still, Apprentice Yoj managed to mix up a quick balm before General Ryoji returned with a pair of sandals. I didn't ask the general where he had gotten them and he offered no explanation. Dead men needed no shoes.

We left the light well together, walking into an underground night that tasted old. After walking some hundred paces in the dark, light slowly returned, a stretched, pale sort of light that grew brighter and brighter until it resembled the light of day. Past each well, the night crept back, the pattern the only way to mark the passage of time and distance.

"What do these light wells look like from above?" I asked as we passed our third. "Are we beneath the plains?"

"Not all the way," he said. "When Emperor Kin ordered the passage repaired, most of the wells were still clear, poking up in small villages and copses, made to look like clumps of rock or dry wells."

"Ingenious."

"It's an old idea."

We walked another cycle in silence, from dark to light and back again with only the echo of our steps for company.

"Hana," General Ryoji said after a time, and there in the dark, isolated from the world, the sound of my name on his lips was somehow illicit even though I had insisted he use it.

"Yes, General?"

"I fear that His Majesty is not going to live. And in the circumstances that would follow, I want you to know that I would fight for you. For your right to the throne."

The words hung in the darkness between us as their meaning grew on me.

"General—"

"If you call me 'general' one more time, I swear I will scream," he said in imitation of my past complaint. I could discern his outline but not his expression, yet I was sure he smiled, mocking me. "I think if there is anywhere one can be honest and free of such formalities, it is in the darkness far beneath the earth."

"Very well," I said. "Ryoji."

"Hade," he corrected.

"Hade." His name sat hesitantly on my tongue. "Are you saying you think there's a chance I could rule Kisia without Kin?"

"Yes," he said. "That's what I'm saying."

"And if he lives?"

He stopped walking, light from the next well touching only half his face. "You could still do it if that is your wish. His Majesty is not the protector he claims to be, but you are Emperor Lan's legitimate heir. Kisia is yours if you choose to take it."

They were bold words, even spoken alone here buried under the ground. "That's treason, Hade."

"Not from where I'm standing."

"You gave an oath to serve Emperor Kin."

"And under what circumstances do you consider it acceptable that I break that oath? Must I hold to it even though my emperor is honourless? Even though he lied and cheated his way to a throne that ought never have been his?"

There was sincerity in his face but also such intense attention that I almost looked away. And in the moment I straightened to face him boldly instead, I wondered about this man, this general as young as Kin had been, also the commander of the Imperial Guard, a man from a common background who stood now with a chance to be so much more. Is this what General Kin had looked like, steeped in ambition as he considered a different future?

Perhaps I could use Ryoji's ambition to my advantage. I had accepted the fact that I could not take the throne myself when two stronger claimants already vied for it, had come to want to rule with Katashi at my side, but if I could not have him, then perhaps I need not have a husband at all. With the right allies.

We walked on, my every sense more aware of him now, of his height and his presence, of the way he strode and the sound of his breathing, of the click of his sandals and the smell of blood and sweat and ash that hung about him. It was not the first time I had thought about enjoying his company in a way that could purge memories of Katashi from my skin though never from my heart. Had he ever thought so of me? How difficult would it be to win him completely to my side?

"Hade."

He stopped and turned, the pair of us enough in the light now that I could see every crease on his troubled brow. "My lady?"

"I thought we had dispensed with formalities? Tell me why you want to fight for me."

"Why?"

"Yes. Is it for the honour of your name? Because you truly believe in Otako superiority? Because you dislike being fooled by Kin? Or are you ambitious and see me as the way you might get out of this with your position intact?"

"Is it possible for the answer to be a little of all of them?"

"Your honesty does you credit. Is it at all because you feel sorry for me?"

He reached out on the words, his hand to my cheek. "My lady, I..." His rough fingers ran up into my hair, only to be snatched back. "I'm sorry," he said. "I should not have done that."

"No," I agreed. "You should not have done that."

"You must truly think me ambitious now." His jaw set hard. "We should keep walking."

"Yes, we should."

He started to walk again, but I did not follow. I was as yet unsure what General Ryoji wanted, but that it possessed a physical component was clear enough. History was littered with men whose absolute loyalty had been bought upon a sleeping mat. If I was going to have any hope of taking the throne for myself, I would need him. And need to be sure of him.

"Hade."

He stopped. "Yes?"

"Come here."

He came, frowning. "What's wrong?"

"What's wrong? What's wrong is that a moment ago, you were standing right here, and now you are not." I pointed to the stones where he had stood, and bemused, Hade returned and stood to attention.

"My lady," he said, a laugh in his eyes. "How may I serve you?"

"By standing still."

His grin faded as I closed the space between us. The hollow of his collarbone was level with my eyes, and for a moment I stared at it, resting a hand upon his chest. He didn't move, didn't touch me, just stood there, heart beating fast beneath my palm. Upon his chin, the dark stubble of a rough few days was coarse beneath the trailing tip of my finger. Lips soft, cheek grazed, the rounded tip of his nose gleaming with sweat. His dark eyes were intent, hungry, watching me hunt my way up to meet them. He did not move.

I pressed my lips to his, the first kiss slow, hesitant, unsure how he would respond. Unsure if I could even do this.

"My lady," he said thickly, my kiss sticking to his bottom lip. "Please do not tease me."

"I'm not trying to tease you," I replied. "I'm trying to kiss you." A little groan passed his lips. "Do you have a problem with that, *General*?"

"No, my lady." He swallowed hard, the bump in his throat dipping. "But are you sure you want to do this?"

"I'm sure as long as you are." I pulled back, panic sparking as I tried to read his expression. "What is it?"

"Give me permission to move, please."

"You are free to move."

The words had hardly left my lips before he kissed me, fiercely, one hand in my hair, the other trailing down my back. My body responded to him as it never had to Kin, and I touched his arm, his shoulder, his neck, his jaw—trying not to think of how different he felt to Katashi.

As though hearing that thought, he pulled away, breathing heavily. "Others will be coming along soon," he said, bending to rest his forehead against mine. "We should keep moving."

I swallowed hard, my own breath light and quick. "Damn your good sense."

"I'm damning it too, trust me."

He stepped away, gripping his hair. A long, slow breath passed between his lips. "That was...unexpected."

"Not unpleasantly so, I hope."

"No! Gods, no." More words sat on his tongue, but rather than speak them, he gestured in the direction of Mei'lian. "That way," he said. "We need to go that way."

"That way," I agreed.

My head buzzed as we walked on in step, half intoxicating triumph, half desperate longing for the man I realised in a blinding moment that I had not yet given up on. If any chance remained of getting Katashi back, I would take the risk, whatever the cost.

Because when the world hits you enough, Kimiko had said, *when the gods will not stop spitting upon you, there comes a point when all you can do is be selfish. If I can have but one thing in this life, I would ask for more time to spend with someone who loves me.*

I let out a long, slow breath and walked on.

"What made you want to be an imperial guard?" I asked as yet another light well came and went in a haze of bluish light.

"That's a sudden question," he said.

"Bear with me. I'm trying not to think about how much I want to kiss you again." As a lie, it was a good one.

He groaned and, in the semi-darkness, lifted his hands to his head. "You are cruel."

"Answer the question, it might help."

"You're going to think the answer strange after what just happened," he said, the words disembodied by the darkness.

"Oh?"

"Yes, because you're the reason I chose to become an imperial guard."

My steps faltered. "What do you mean? You were already a general the day we met, when you saved me from the Pit."

I could only imagine his grimace. "A day I will never forget."

"I killed him, you know," I said. "Councillor Ahmet. I poisoned him with Tishwa the night Katashi took Koi. I watched the breath choked from his body."

"After what he did, I cannot say I blame you," he said, though there was a little hesitation is his voice. "He was a pig of a man."

"Yes, but we have digressed. You were telling me why you became an imperial guard."

"I was. Well..." He took a deep breath. "My father is the only farrier in Giana, so everyone who visits the hot springs takes their horses to him whether commoner or nobleman."

"You're from Giana? I grew up on a farm north of there, near the Fork."

A little sound of surprise came from the darkness. "You mean there was a time we lived within a days' travel of one another?"

"So it would seem. How strange the workings of the world sometimes are, but there I go interrupting you again. Your father was a farrier."

"Yes, so as children, we met almost every traveller who came to Giana. I must have been about ten or eleven years old when Empress Li came to bathe in the waters. One of her guards stopped to have his horse shod while the empress was carried about town in her palanquin. My brothers and I chased after it with the other children, and when her carriers shooed us away, she told them not to. So we followed her all the way up the hill to the inn."

He had seemed to be reminiscing with little point, but he turned toward me then with a little smile. "She had to be helped out of the palanquin," he said. "Because she was heavy with child."

It took a moment for this to sink in. "Wait? Me?"

"Assuming my numbers are not out."

"Are you claiming some extra acquaintance with me because you saw my mother carrying me before I was born?"

He laughed. "No. Normally news travels fast to places like Giana because people are always coming and going, but during the storm season the town is cut off. So by the time the news came that Empress Li had given birth to a girl, you were already dead and Kisia was at war."

My gut hollowed and a sudden lump in my throat paralysed speech. "I don't remember" was all I managed.

"Of course not. But I was as devastated as a boy can be. That was the day I swore to become an imperial guard."

I said nothing.

"And now," he went on. "You're here, alive, and the man I swore my oath to is the reason why your mother is not."

I put up my hand. "Don't."

"Hana—"

"I don't want to talk about Kin. Please."

We walked the rest of the way in silence, my head once again filled with troubles. Ryoji made no attempt to reopen the conversation or reignite the desire that had hummed between us, and for that I was grateful. With every pool of light we passed, my pace increased. It was only a matter of time before Katashi marched his men across the plain to another set of old gates and another city incapable of defending against him. I needed a plan. I needed time.

Eventually the tunnel rose. There were more light wells. More turns. Then a rumble of cartwheels overhead.

"We're beneath the city now," Ryoji said, breaking his long silence.

"Where does the tunnel come out?"

"Another tavern, in the Westcourt District near the silk market."

"Why there?"

Another rumble overhead. "My guess is because to go farther into the city would risk breaching the walls of the Waterway."

The tunnel levelled out, and my foot caught something in the darkness. I hissed as I fell against stone steps, losing one overlarge sandal.

"Are you all right?"

"Fantastic," I said, picking myself up. I rubbed my knees, spreading damp soil across my breeches. "I think I have found the stairs."

He went past me up the shallow steps. The light was dim and he had to duck his head, but he seemed to know what he was doing and set his shoulder to the ceiling. The sound of stone scraping on stone filled the passage and light seeped in through widening cracks.

"Who's there?" someone demanded from above. "Answer before you stick your head up or I'll cut it off."

"It's General Hade Ryoji of the Imperial Guard, and Lady Hana Otako."

"My lady!"

It was Tili's voice, but though I heard her scramble through the opening and land beside me, I held up my hand for silence. "Wait," I said, looking back along the passage.

A murmured thank you. A grunt from Ryoji, still holding the slab on his shoulders.

"Quiet. I can hear something."

The soft scent of Tili filled the space beside me, but I did not look around. "Put the stone back," I said.

"But Hana—"

"Put it down," I said. "I think someone is coming but I can't hear anything over the noise up there."

"Probably some of the wounded men, or Father Kokoro," General Ryoji said.

"You said you found Endymion?"

"Yes. He went on ahead."

"Then put the stone back down."

He did so, and as the scraping of stone died away, the distant voice sounded again. It was a voice I knew all too well. Fear and excitement thrilled through me. Perhaps there was a chance I could get everything I wanted after all.

"Draw your sword, General," I said, taking a deep, steadying breath. "We're about to have a visitor."

18. DARIUS

I woke, sucking a breath of old opium. Sick splattered the floor, filling my mouth with the sour bite of self-contempt.

"How pleasant a companion you are, yes?"

A slow breath failed to calm my shaking limbs. The stump of my incomplete arm burned.

"We seem to be making a habit of this," Malice went on from somewhere nearby. "Where you almost kill yourself and I am left to pick up the pieces."

The room wavered as it came into focus. Dim light. Musty old reeds. Faded grandeur. A silk screen so finely embroidered that a myriad of tiny stars peered through the dust.

"Where are we?" My voice croaked.

"Somewhere safe. Your Vengeance has flown the nest. I think enraging him was not the best decision you've ever made, yes?"

The room contained a meagre flock of surviving Vices. At the window, Hope was engaged in wrapping a bandage around his forearm. Avarice hovered close and silent, while Conceit was using his sickle to cut reeds in the old matting. A tapestry covered three others, its dusty, undulating form unsettling.

"Where's Kimiko?"

"What?"

I propped myself up, wincing. "Kimiko was there," I said. "Where is she?"

Malice crouched beside me, and there was real confusion in the lines of his bloodstained features. "Then one can only hope she's dead," he said. "As Katashi loses control, he is capable of anything, yes?"

He was hazy through the sudden sting of tears. "I have been mad." Kin had been as much friend as emperor, Hana like a daughter, and Kimiko the only woman who had ever seen through the façade to the pain beneath and found a man worth saving.

"Stop crying. We are not dead yet." His shock was a twisting, uneasy thing. "You should not have let him win. Must you always play the saviour? It ill becomes you, yes?"

From outside the window came shouts and running steps, but inside the musty little room there was nothing. The surviving Vices watched and listened.

"Ill becomes me?" I repeated, his words gouging deep. "Why do you want me to be a monster?"

"Because that is who you are, yes?"

I had wanted Kin to suffer. I had wanted him to burn. I had manipulated every piece on the board because with control came freedom.

You stupid, broken man.

All I had wanted was to be free.

"Darius."

Malice reached out. Our souls connected for a flash before I slapped his hand away. "Don't touch me!"

"What in the hells is wrong with you?"

"Our father was right."

Malice's brows rose, crinkling blots of dried blood on his forehead. "Was he indeed? What about?"

"The Sight. It needs to die."

"You would have had him succeed? You would have lain down and let the storm take you? You would have let our father bury a knife in my throat?"

My whole body ached. I wanted to lie down, to sleep, but behind my eyes, the memory of Kimiko lurked. She had been my chance at freedom, I her poisoned knight.

"We truly are monsters."

He hit me, the flat of his palm stinging my cheek. "We are gods," he said.

"No, we are men." I touched my smarting cheek. It was a weakness Minister Laroth would never have allowed, but what was self-control but fear by another name?

My poor, sad Darius.

Malice began to pace, his slick ponytail slithering down his back. His Vices watched. Even Conceit radiated anxiety.

"What is it you want, Darius?" Malice said. "We could go anywhere. We could start again, yes? There are always more Vices. We could leave Kisia behind."

I could well imagine that future. It was the past lived over, Malice unwilling, or perhaps unable, to change.

"Wherever I went, it would not be with you."

A vase smashed on the floor beside me, its pieces scattering to every dusty corner. "What more can I do?" he cried. "I have done *everything* for you. You made me what I am and still you cannot abide me." He sucked angry breaths. "Kisia was your dream, yes? To have everyone bow to the superiority of the Sight. In your own words: 'We are gods and we will rule as gods are meant to rule.'"

He had been such a willing student. Together we had hunted, together we had tested the limits of our ability—Mastery and Malice, a shadowy curse upon the landscape.

"You listened to my lessons then," I said, getting shakily to my feet. "Why not listen to them now? I am many years wiser than the boy you idolised."

"The boy with the violet eyes I found in a burning field," he said.

"A romantic image. Did you save me? Is that how you see it?"

"Our father never loved you."

"Our father did his best to crush me, and when he failed, you finished the job," I said. "That is what we do, Malice, we suck life." I spread my arms. "Look at what we have done. Look at these monsters we created."

His hands clenched into fists. "You once thought them beautiful, yes? Concentrated emotion used to unlock lost abilities. And if we had succeeded in creating a Vice with two skills, or three, what then?"

Every mistake thrown back in my face. I had started it all; now Hope, Conceit, and Avarice were the last slaves to our anger at the world. Malice, abandoned by everyone, had marked his Vices so they could never leave. Never disobey. I had just wanted everyone to suffer my pain. Now I was unravelling, no control left, only grief; no mastery, only anger.

"I am tired," I said, swaying on my feet. "I am tired of you, and I am tired of me. I should have died in that maze and never known you."

Malice stepped closer, his sandals making angry snaps. His fingers closed around my throat. "What a paragon I might have been." A sneer lifted his top lip. "Easy to forget that though you may not have marked me it was I, not Avarice, who was really your first victim."

The hand at my throat grew hot as his Empathy tore into me, hunting, caressing, smothering. Owning.

"I want my brother back," he said.

"I am here."

His grip tightened, squeezing the sinews of my neck. The urge was to fight, to push him away, to throw him back with fear and anger and pain, but if I ran, he would follow. So I tried to breathe slowly through my nose and not move. His eyes darted about my face.

"You would let me kill you?" he said. "Do you really hate me so much?"

"I don't hate you." My voice came out strangled. "You are my brother and I love you."

His grip tightened. "Then why? Why did you leave me? Why do you want to leave me again now?"

My violet eyes met his dark, and between us the years of pain and confusion and love and hate and obsession hung unacknowledged. Truth was the only thing we had never spoken.

"Because I hate who I am when I'm with you," I said.

He threw me and I hit the dry matting, breath crushed from my aching body. It had always been weak, and I felt it now in every joint, in the throbbing of my head and the endless pain of my useless stump. All I could do was grit my teeth and breathe, scratchy reeds against my cheek. And there in front of me, the dead Vices covered in their tapestry, the smell half-dust and half-death.

Malice growled, towering over me. "I will break you before you leave me again. You are—"

He broke off with squawk as his head snapped back. Dark hair sprouted from Avarice's fist. "Don't touch him," the oldest Vice said, holding Malice's ponytail.

"Let go!"

Avarice tightened his hold and dragged Malice's head back until the tip of his ponytail touched the small of his back. "Don't touch him," he repeated. "Do you understand?"

"Call off your dog!"

"I can't," I said. "He was not made to obey."

Malice dug an elbow into Avarice's gut, and his skin mottled with stone. Its weight dragged Malice's head back farther still. "Conceit," he said, the word clipped and strangled. "Get this rock off me!"

Conceit drew his sickle.

"Avarice," I said, too tired to lift my head from the floor. "It will make no difference."

Always closed, always wary, Avarice looked from me to Conceit, then let the stone fade back into his skin with a grunt. He let go. Malice lifted his head and stretched his neck side to side, feeling his throat with a tentative hand.

"We will go to Esvar," he said, scratching his head where the hair had pulled. "And spend some time back in the family fold, yes?"

None of my words had made a difference, and now I was too tired to care where I went, but if it ended in death, so much the better.

"We have to get out of here first," Conceit said, hooking his sickle back on its belt. "They'll be looking for us."

"What about back out through the gate Katashi blew up?" Hope said, and it was hope I felt on him. I had called him Malice's toy and mocked his misery, but it was a misery I knew well. Malice had always owned me, though I had been blind enough in my youth to believe myself the master while I tugged and snarled at my chains.

"They'll be guarding that if they're looking for us," Avarice rumbled.

"There's nothing to lead them here," Hope said. "We could lie low until they move on to Mei'lian."

Mei'lian. Katashi didn't know about the passage. He would have to march his men across the plain.

Malice's eyes narrowed. "What are you thinking about?"

"Nothing." I pushed myself up with my one good hand. "Merely that I am rather fond of the capital."

"Fond? You are not fond of anything, yes? That word is not in your vocabulary."

"It must be. I just used it."

Once again, he came and crouched in front of me, this time running a hand lightly through my hair. "You know something, yes? This was your city too. Your empire second only to Kin. What is it you're not telling me now?"

That there's a passage out of the city.

The answer sprang to mind, but I gave it no voice. Instead I held Malice's gaze and wondered how long it would be before he looked away.

He didn't.

"Are we going to play this game again, Brother?"

"What game is that, *Brother*?"

"There's a way out, yes?"

I held his gaze. "Through the gates."

"You want to get caught."

My eyes did not waver from his, their stare a challenge. *Go on*, I heard myself goad. *You're bigger and stronger than I am; just take what you want, you always do.*

He had taken my innocence while my Maturation cursed me to silence. After that first time, I had been too proud, too angry, and I had become the master. He had liked that better, liked to feel wanted. Perhaps if I gave him my body now, he might stall long enough for Katashi's men to find us, but too well could I remember Malice's touch.

It was me that looked away.

The moment I broke eye contact, Malice gripped my cheeks and squeezed. Through his Empathy, he saw the intimate memories upon which I had dwelled and was gratified by their lack of context. I wanted him to stay there, to lose himself in the past, but the screams as Katashi's men sacked the city drifted in through the open window.

Malice let go and I fell back, too weak to support my own weight any longer.

"Pick him up, Avarice," Malice ordered. "We're getting out of here, yes?"

"How?" It was Hope who asked.

"Through the Imperial Cellar, child. If you don't trust me, trust him, yes? Who should know these things but the minister of the left?"

Avarice came to crouch beside me, his leathers creaking. Tears prickled my eyes, but I would not let them fall again. Not now, though his care hurt more than Malice's fury ever could.

He did not speak, but the pause before he picked me up was more permission than Malice had ever asked. I owned no strength to speak, no strength to do more than grit my teeth as he lifted me gently, hefting me over his shoulder as though I weighed no more than the sickly boy he had so often carried.

I must have faded, so little did I know of what followed. Snatches of low conversation; pain in my arm, my legs, my throbbing head. The smell of Avarice: part horse, part sweat. Blood. Smoke. Shouts. Once I woke to feel Malice's hand gripping mine, hunting through me again, but though I tried to pull free, I was already sinking.

"Who are you?"

The words wormed their way into my consciousness.

"This is His Excellency Lord Darius Laroth," Malice said, his tone at its most humble. "Minister of the left in the court of His Majesty Emperor Kin Ts'ai. He is injured, yes? We need to get him out of the city."

"Where are your sashes?"

"You think we could have made it this far wearing our crimson proudly?"

The vaguely familiar voice agreed doubtfully, but there is something about a group of men with sharp sickles that opens every door. With my cheek against Avarice's sweat-stuck tunic, my view of the world was narrow, but I caught a glimpse of Hope beside me, his expression no less grim for being upside down. The smell of blood hung around him. It stained his sickle and the hand that held it, while a contusion on the side of his head was slowly leaking crimson fluid into his dark hair and down his ear.

A door creaked. A bolt shot home.

"How many others have come through?" Malice asked.

"Couldn't say" was General Hadran's cagey reply, the man seeming to have emerged fully functioning from my memory.

"His Majesty?"

"Couldn't say," he repeated.

"You have a very poor memory." Only I knew him well enough to hear the annoyance beneath Malice's light-hearted words. "We'll catch up with them, I'm sure."

"Nah, the last went down a full hour since."

No doubt the general said so to dissuade us from pursuing them, not knowing that the last thing Malice would want was to run into anyone who might stop us reaching Mei'lian, because once in Mei'lian, I was lost. Malice knew the city too well. He would not let me go again.

Avarice kept walking. I faded in and out, cursing my body's weakness. Voices. Jolting steps. Dim blue light came to me between flashes of darkness. Then came a deep, oppressive silence as the earth held us in its hand. Footsteps were the only sound. Three sets. No, four, two of them remarkably in time. Four men. Conceit and Hope were still with us.

We kept moving. Time meant nothing.

It was dark when next I came to myself, and I turned my head, the cheek that had been pressed to Avarice's back emerging damp.

"Put me down," I said.

Avarice stopped walking, his last step scraping on stone. "Master—"

"Put me down. I can walk."

He hesitated, and from the darkness, Malice laughed. "You're like a stone that bleeds, Avarice," he said. "If your puppy stumbles, just pick him up again, yes?"

The old Vice stiffened and slowly, carefully lowered me to the floor. Malice kept walking, though we lingered, letting my legs get used to their old weight. Hope hovered. Behind him, the darkness was deeper than any night. Shimai was long gone.

Avarice leant in close. "Tell me what you need me to do, Master," he said in a low growl. "He wouldn't see my sickle coming."

"No."

The word shot out without thought. There were good reasons to keep him alive, but every one of them was an afterthought.

"Any sign of Hana?" I whispered.

"No, Master."

Malice stopped and turned, his outline aglow with the haze of an approaching light well. "Well? Are you coming?"

More tired than I had ever been, I forced one foot to follow the other. Avarice became my shadow, a wary mother hen waiting to catch me if I fell.

We walked, my legs weak and my hand shaking. The azure glow brightened until I could see Malice ahead. His robe was dirty. His hair was a mess. And the smell that wafted back to me was wrong. No pungently sweet opium lingering about his breath. How long had it been since his last pipe? To my Empathy, he tasted manic. And there was something else, out of reach. Something... familiar.

"Malice," I said, raising my voice so it would carry. "You're dry, aren't you?"

He stopped again and turned, pressing a finger to his lips. "Not so loud, yes? Someone might hear us."

"Like Hana?" I all but shouted the words. "Are you worried *Hana* might hear us?"

"Darius."

"Yes, Brother?"

"Shut up."

"No," I said, as loudly as I could. "I don't think I will."

Malice cocked his head down the tunnel.

"Who's there?" The voice was distant. Male. Familiar. Never had I thought I'd be glad to hear General Ryoji's self-important tone.

Malice scowled. "Well? You wanted attention and now you have it, yes? Go on, answer the man."

I cleared my throat. "My name is Lord Darius Laroth," I called back. "Minister of the left in the court of Emperor Kin Ts'ai."

There was no immediate reply, nothing but the beat of my heart echoing back to me. Then: "Lord Darius Laroth?"

"Don't make me repeat myself, General."

A bark of humourless laughter came next. "That's him."

"Well," Malice said. "Let's go say hello, yes?" He nodded to his Vices, and both Conceit and Hope unhooked their sickles.

As we approached, three figures came slowly into relief, bathed in weak blueish light.

"Darius?"

Hana this time. Malice shot me a warning glance.

"Darius?"

"Yes, my dear?"

"Who's with you?"

"If you are worried about Katashi, we left him behind."

"Is Malice with you?"

A pause, then Malice said, "I'm here, little lamb."

"Good," she returned, hardly needing to shout now we were getting close. "I don't like loose ends."

Malice halted some ten paces from the dimly lit trio. The light well rose above them, its moss-coloured stones forming something like a chimney narrowing toward a distant circle of blue sky. Hana stood in the brightest spot, but it was General Ryoji's drawn sword that glinted with the promise of trouble.

"All we want to do is pass through, lamb," Malice said. "Much better for your general not to end up dead, yes? Let us pass and we'll disappear from your life without bloodshed."

Hana's maid stood behind her, not averting her gaze but staring at each of us in turn. I was reminded of another woman dressed in simple clothes, her demure expression belying ferocity and courage. If Malice got his way, I would never see Kimiko again.

There was another glint of metal as Hana strode forward, a long curved blade in her hand. "No," she said. "Darius is mine."

"No." Malice signalled to Hope and Conceit, and his last two Vices stepped forward. "He belongs to me."

"Arrest them, General."

Malice didn't move. "I don't think you want to do that," he said.

"Why not? Are you going to kill me?"

"No, lamb," Malice said. "*I* could never do that, yes? Conceit, Hope, clear us a path."

Conceit stepped forward, flashing a grin. "Yes, Master."

"Killing us would be pointless," Hana said. "The tavern above is full of loyal soldiers, not one of whom will let you pass."

Malice laughed gently. "Three dozen survivors, most too injured to make the journey. You are outnumbered and you know it, yes? Step aside."

"No."

"A pity."

Conceit skipped forward gleefully, but before Hope could move, Avarice gripped his arm. The boy tried to pull free, but Avarice's fingers had turned from flesh to stone, even the long scar on the back of his hand hardening. Another stony hand clasped Malice's ponytail.

"What are you doing?" Malice demanded, letting out a pained cry. "Let go!"

"Got another hand for me too, traitor?" Conceit said. "Or are you going to hold me back with a glare?"

He danced toward Hana, but it was General Ryoji who met his blade. He stepped in front of her as the Vice swung, his maniacal grin a slice across his features. The sound of meeting steel reverberated through the passage.

A punch of arrogance, and Conceit's twin stepped out of the shadows. He made no sound, but Ryoji must have known, for he turned, shunting the first Conceit off balance as he spun to catch the sickle of the second. A foot slammed into his gut, sending him sprawling.

"You think you're clever," Hana said. "But you just gave away your secret. Now we know which of you is the real one." She levelled the tip of her sword at the first Conceit.

"You think so?" he said. "Surely I know how to use my power better than that. How can you be so certain?" They both spread their arms wide. "We can both talk," they said in unison. "We can both walk. And we can both stab generals through the throat."

They both lunged toward Ryoji, but Hana was there, that quick jab something we had perfected before she had been old enough to hold even half such a sword. Her farmers had not approved, but had not dared do more than mutter about unladylike behaviour.

You're the ones who let her climb trees, I had said. *She needs to work on her bow.*

She is Lady Hana, Orde had pointed out. *Who is there for her to bow to?*

"She's still terrible at it," I murmured, resisting the tug of lassitude. Beside me, Malice snarled, trying to rip his ponytail out of Avarice's hand. "Let go, you stupid beast, or I'll peel that stone off your flesh."

"I don't take orders from you," Avarice said.

There was a terrible crack as General Ryoji hit the stones.

"Hade!"

Hana couldn't get to him. The two identical Conceits were pressing her toward the end of the passage, one slashing, one stabbing, both giggling as she danced. Hana was good, but she was outnumbered and outclassed. Conceit stepped over General Ryoji, his sword left useless upon the stones. I edged toward it, but my weak knees buckled.

A hand gripped the sword. A fine, slim hand with long nails, a hand that shook as its fingers wrapped around the hilt. Hana's maid lifted the weapon with two hands, holding it with neither the correct grip nor the right stance, but with all the assurance of anger.

"Conceit!" Malice shouted. "Watch—"

Avarice yanked Malice's ponytail. One Conceit turned, but Hana's maid did not look at him. She levelled the blade at the second Conceit, stepped in, and with a bestial roar, she thrust it deep into his back. There was no disappearing trick, no vanishing limbs, just the fleshy sound of death. The first Conceit faltered, his gleeful expression slipping into shock. Then Hana stuck her sword into the second's throat.

Malice howled. Conceit wavered like a heat haze as blood bubbled in gouts from his doppelganger's mouth. Hana kicked him, yanking her sword free, and he fell through the fading ghost of his double.

Hana's maid hadn't moved. She was shaking, gripping the sword in bloodstained hands. Hana stared at her. "How did you know?"

"His...his sash," the maid said, breathless. "The other had his tied backward. Like he was in a mirror."

I had never noticed.

In the dream of fatigue, I watched as General Ryoji was helped unsteadily to his feet, his shame spiky. He spoke. Hana spoke. The maid handed back his sword and moved toward the hatchway. More soldiers came. And still holding Malice and Hope, Avarice said, "Give me orders, Master."

He would have fought every soldier Hana threw at him had I asked, but there was only one person I wanted to escape.

"Don't fight," I said. "Let them take us."

Malice snarled and growled and swore, but he could not break free of Avarice's grip no matter what he threw at him.

It was Hana who came for me. "What game are you playing now?" she demanded as she knelt before me.

"No game," I said, holding out my hand and my useless stump. "I'm sick of playing."

"You ought to have thought of that before you destroyed Katashi." There was no anguish in her voice, no hurt, no anger, nothing but a hard determination that robbed me of the strength needed to explain or apologise. "Now you are going to save him for me or you are going to die."

19. ENDYMION

Darius looked half-dead when they brought him up from the passage. Head sagging, legs weak. His stiff, disdainful pride was gone, his beauty soiled inside and out.

The landlord sent for chains and clucked around the cellar, muttering about the world going mad.

"Lady Hana," he said, bowing half a dozen times as Hana climbed out of the hole, all damp armour and ash-smudged cheeks. General Ryoji followed, his gaze caught to her back. The touch of her lips. The smell of her hair. Eyes. Hands. Every bit of her young and supple and sweet.

I barely heard their whispered conversation amid the swirl of thoughts.

All I ever wanted was to fight for my empire.

You think you're so clever, Darius, yes?

I will have him.

I will kill him.

"Endymion?"

Behind Hana, a soldier looked bemusedly from the chains in his hands to Darius's stump. Hope was already on the stairs, being led away ahead of Avarice.

He needs me. I should have killed the shivat years ago.

There must be an end. There must be.

Hana clicked her fingers in front of my face. "Endymion? Are you in there?"

"Sorry, did you say something to me?"

"Did I say something to you?" she repeated. "By the gods, I have more than half a mind to lock you up too."

"Maybe you should."

He's too useful. He has more claim to the throne than I, and I've seen what he can do. If only I could be sure he won't turn against me . . .

"I have no claim to the throne," I said. "I gave it up in favour of Emperor Kin. He is the man Kisia needs."

Hana's hands tightened into angry balls. "If you knew what he did—"

"I know what he did and why he did it."

"He killed my mother," she hissed. "*Our* mother. *Our* brothers."

"And our stranglehold upon an empire of whose needs we were careless."

Only the landlord remained at the bottom of the stairs now, shifting his weight from foot to foot. His ill ease was sharp. Hana turned.

No. No one can know. I have to get rid of him. Kin would do what needed to be done. Oh, how he would enjoy the irony.

"General Ryoji!"

"My lady, I did not mean to—"

An upraised hand silenced the landlord as General Ryoji appeared at the top of the steps. "My lady?"

"Arrest this man," she said, indicating the now quivering man. "He sees no one. Talks to no one. Take care of it."

"*This* man?" The general pointed at the landlord. His gaze flicked to me. Distrust. Bright. Hot. Mingled with confusion.

"Yes, General," Hana said. "He is in possession of . . . undesirable information."

"I promise and swear on my oath that I'll never speak a word of it to a living soul," the landlord begged. "Even a dead soul. I heard nothing, nothing at all."

Hana shook her head. "It cannot be risked. Take him away with the minimal amount of fuss and replace him."

"No! Please, my lady. I have a wife and children. They need me. I have always been a loyal servant of Emperor Kin, and—"

"Lady Hana," General Ryoji interrupted. "This is Lord Tarli. He held the post of minister of the left before Lord Laroth."

At the sound of his former title, the man's face settled into dignified lines and he straightened. Grief poured off him but he hid it well, only his agitated whispers betraying him.

Kin killed the Otakos? That cannot be. No, but those meetings. I'd almost forgotten. It was so long ago.

Once again, Hana was staring at me. She must have spoken words I had not heard, but this time the request was loud in her thoughts. "You want to know if you can trust him," I said.

"Yes."

Whispers streamed in from everywhere, from upstairs and out in the street, from the city and the walls and the plains and the empire, all funnelling toward me.

There was too much noise, his thoughts too restrained. I needed to be closer. The man flinched as I stepped toward him, but I reached out my hand and found him an inch from his skin.

I am loyal to Kin. I am loyal to Kin.

He did not blink, his onyx eyes seeming to cut into my skin.

I am loyal. I am loyal.

My fingers closed around a forearm slick with sweat. Grief and confusion hit me harder than I had braced for, and I tightened my hold. Images of General Kin marched before my eyes, proud, capable, the leader who had given his all for the empire. The leader who had killed for his throne.

Tell me it's not true. Not Kin. No. Not Kin.

I dug, hunting for loyalty, but all that came back was grief. Grief he did not deserve. Grief I could take away from him.

The man tried to pull away, but it was too late. My fingers

tingled. I barely recognised myself, but there we were, Hana and I, as every word of our hissed exchange was sucked from his mind like poison from blood. Then it was gone.

I stepped back, doubling over as fuzzy darkness threatened to floor me. Lord Tarli groaned. "My head," he said. "It feels like someone hit me with a broken bottle. General? What are you doing here? Did I . . . no, you came through the passage, didn't you, and . . . and Lady Hana. Prisoners—"

He stopped talking, confused. "Excuse the mind of an old man. Is everything all right, my lady? Is there something I can do for you?"

There was a long, drawn out silence. My head stopped spinning, but the stolen memory played on, safely trapped inside my head.

"No, Minister, I do not think there is," Hana said at last.

"Minister?" The man chuckled. "I haven't been a minister for a good number of years now, my lady."

"But you are proud of your service?"

"Yes, my lady, no better emperor than Emperor Kin could be found, my lady, Otako god or no, begging your pardon."

There was a spike of embarrassment, but Hana only smiled. "Your opinion is most welcome. Thank you, you may go."

The man bowed and, nodding to General Ryoji, went up the stairs in good spirits. With him gone, I found two pairs of eyes staring. General Ryoji took the last few steps to the basement floor. "What did you do to him?"

"I took the memory," I said. "Of the conversation and of Kin's betrayal. It caused him grief he did not deserve."

"Do you mean he has no memory of it?"

"None."

"You just took the last few minutes of his life?"

"If you wish to think of it like that, yes."

The general seemed to have nothing more to say, but Hana shook her head. "Dear gods but you scare me, Endymion," she said.

"Don't you dare do that to me. Swear it or I will lock you up now and throw away the key."

There is a man called Wen you no longer remember. He was your friend. But now he is mine.

"My lady," General Ryoji said. "We must go."

"Yes, but bring him," she said. "He's too dangerous to leave behind."

20. HANA

The councillors looked like waxen statues in the lamplight. Each owned a troubled face and sleepless eyes and threw back their wine as though it were water. A serving girl circled the table, filling their bowls.

"Only a score of survivors?" Minister Bahain repeated.

"That is what I said, Minister." The words dropped leaden from my lips. "Many are badly wounded."

"So from His Majesty's battalions we have—and let me get this right—eight able men, two injured but able to serve, and the rest either dead or almost dead."

"Yes."

Every wine bowl was lifted in silence.

"Those are heavy causalities."

"Yes, Minister," I said. "They are. We had enough men to hold the city against an army, but not against Katashi."

His name was getting easier to say. On the northern horizon, Shimai glowed like a tenacious ember, and from the walls and towers and high houses of Mei'lian, people had gathered to watch. To wait.

Katashi was coming.

"And His Majesty's war council?" enquired General Vareen of Mei'lian's defensive battalion. "No one else survived?"

"No. Only myself and General Ryoji, who was with His Majesty." I gestured along the table to where the general knelt. I could trust him, but the rest did not like me. They avoided my gaze, frightened by this woman in their hall of men, by this woman wearing the Imperial Sash and sitting proudly at their table. "After he was injured, His Majesty left me in charge."

More silence. Then: "And how is His Majesty?"

I looked at the stocky little man who had spoken. His finicky moustache was twenty years out of fashion, but he was the only one not touching his wine bowl. Darius would have drawn conclusions from such things.

"He is not out of danger," I said. "His injuries are severe and Master Kenji fears fever may prove dangerous. But he will remain with His Majesty at all times and is more confident now he has access to the palace stores and can provide the best possible care."

Another councillor took up the questioning. "And what does Master Kenji say His Majesty's chance of survival is?"

"The answer to that changes hourly. All we can do is pray."

"And if he dies? He has no direct heir. There is Grace Bachita, his cousin, but…" All at the table turned their eyes to the moustached man who had spoken, whose grey hair was thinning at his temples. A worrier? Ambitious? How did Darius see what other people could not?

"I am his empress," I said, interrupting a low-voiced debate before it could take root. "I am his heir. As of this moment, the defence of the empire is under my command."

Their murmurs faded and every man turned to me. It was Minister Bahain who spoke first. "With all due respect, my lady," he said. "If His Majesty dies before the seven days are up, if he dies before your marriage vows can be consummated, then you are neither his empress nor his heir."

I took a deep breath, ready to spill my fury over them, but General Ryoji interjected. "This is not a debate to be had while His Majesty lives and breathes, especially not when we have just lost Shimai and are facing further attack."

"We are prepared for siege," said one of the other councillors whose name was unknown to me. "We—"

"Siege, maybe," Ryoji said. "For Katashi Otako, no."

"You say he brings fire. We have dealt with fire before, General."

"Yes, but you have not seen an entire army burned in a single gout of flame. You may think we are mad, but we are not. Take what you imagine and multiply it a hundred times and then you may have some inkling of the power we are dealing with. The man is merciless."

The flicker of fear in their eyes was there and gone. Again it was Minister Bahain that answered, quietly this time, the hand that gripped his wine bowl not entirely steady. "We saw the smoke," he said. "We saw the flames. We can douse the gates in water. We can—"

"We did that in Shimai," I said. "But the fire Katashi channels is unnatural. He is the embodiment of vengeance."

"You speak as though he has some magic," the minister scoffed.

"There is nothing else to call it but magic. He has been made a Vice."

The councillors shifted uncomfortably on their knees, many reaching for their wine bowls again. I wanted to scream at them, to get up and shake them all one by one.

"Magic, Lady Hana, is not real."

"Then explain the Vices to me. Explain to me how Katashi could burn the gates of Shimai with nothing but his hands. *Explain* to me how he could cross a burning bridge unscathed and unleash its fire upon our army."

"There are many ways to create fire. Oil, pitch—"

I threw up my hands, stopping him mid-sentence. "This problem will not go away just because you pretend it does not exist," I said. "You can shout from the rooftops that it is not real, that it cannot be so, but Katashi will still bring unearthly fire to our gates."

General Vareen leant forward, resting his chin on steepled fingers. "Then what do you suggest, my lady?"

"We cannot fight him," I said, making a direct plea to the council at large. "At the first hint of resistance, he will burn all who stand in his way regardless of their name and rank. If we stand and fight, then Mei'lian will be reduced to a smoking ruin and he will stride to the Crimson Throne over the charred corpse of every man here."

"Are you suggesting we stand aside and give him the throne?"

"What other choice is there, General? There is time to flee, to hide, time to protect ourselves to fight another day."

"Flee?" the general repeated. "Flee to where? His Majesty is injured and the enemy is all but at our gates."

There was only one choice. "Back through the tunnel to Shimai," I said. "He won't leave more than a skeleton force to hold the city. From there we go south."

"While Katashi Otako takes the throne." Minister Bahain cleared his throat. "To speak the words many others here will not, you will accept my apology, my lady, I am sure, but such advice coming from an Otako is not easy to accept as impartial. Katashi Otako is your cousin and the head of your family after all, and not so long since, you rode with his army."

"Are you calling me a traitor, Minister?"

"No! Your loyalty is not in doubt, my lady, but with so tender a heart as yours, it would be impossible to consider the situation with the merciless pragmatism required."

Anger bit at my throat. "A tender heart? Minister, you are not only calling me a traitor but a fool as well," I said. "I am not a little girl. Your emperor gave me his sash and charged me with the defence of this empire. He trusted me. Who are you to refute the choice of a god?"

"There is no refutation intended," Minister Bahain said, all soothing, singsong brightness. "You are His Majesty's chosen representative, but so are we, you must remember. We are his council. We exist to make decisions he cannot and to offer guidance and wisdom. You might have been born to this position, my lady, but you are new to our ways and our world."

"And we have the right to be more forthright in this chamber than elsewhere," said one of the councillors whose name I did not know. "That too is part of our job. We tell the emperor what no one else dares tell him."

Minister Bahain cleared his throat. "Because all men need advice," he said, so mildly and with such a fatherly smile that I wanted to punch him. "And His Majesty is, after all, just a man."

I had argued the same myself. I had thrown Kin's mortality in General Ryoji's face before the battle in Shimai, but here and now, I needed Kin to be more than a man so I could be more than a woman.

"Emperor Kin sits upon the Crimson Throne," I said. "That makes him a god."

"No, it makes him a very powerful man with a very nice chair."

And with those simple words, the smiling minister robbed me of all authority. My hands worked, clenching and unclenching upon the tail of the Imperial Sash. I wanted to scream. I wanted to stomp like a child and smash their wine bowls, but it would achieve nothing. Darius wouldn't. Darius was smarter than that. I had to be smarter than that.

"A very nice chair that will be burned to a cinder if we try to fight Katashi," I said, trying to keep my voice steady.

General Vareen shook his head. "You are forgetting, my lady, that if Otako wants to sit upon the throne and rule this empire, he will not burn Mei'lian to the ground, whatever he might say. And that gives us an advantage you did not have in Shimai."

There was a smattering of agreement.

"You want to call his bluff?"

"Can we hold the city?" Minister Bahain asked General Vareen, ignoring my question.

"We have been working on a plan and pulling in every member

of the city guard and those citizens who wish to fight, and I think we can."

General Ryoji shook his head. "That is exactly what General Rini said before they hit Shimai."

"That's as may be, but we cannot stand aside and let an exile take the throne."

"But we do have a duty to the empire," spoke Governor Ohi. "If there is danger to the emperor, he must be evacuated while there is time. Lady Hana should also be removed from the capital."

"Removed?" I repeated. "Do not speak of me as though I am a thing."

"With all due respect, my lady, you are. As is His Majesty. As you have been at pains to point out, you belong to the empire now, and as such, you must be protected to ensure the survival of the Ts'ai dynasty."

My hands shook like butterflies struggling against the storm.

"I am the only one Katashi may yet listen to," I said slowly, carefully constructing the lies I needed to get what I wanted. "I am the only remaining member of his family. I will not run when I am most needed."

It had not worked in Shimai, but Katashi was no longer in Darius's power. Now I had Darius, and no matter what it took, I would make him help me. I would get Katashi back.

Minister Bahain gave a little grunt. "What you are most needed for is to ensure Kisia has an heir."

I drew myself up. "I am Lady Hana Otako, daughter of Emperor Lan Otako. I am not a broodmare."

"Neither are you a military commander!"

"Minister Bahain," I said, getting to my feet to stand over the minister of the right. "It may be your job to be forthright, but it is not your job to insult and dismiss me. You would not dare do so if Emperor Kin was here."

You think he's going to die, I thought, looking down at a man whose expression screamed false contrition. *You think he's going to die and I will lose all power.*

The realisation stole through me, chilling like spreading ice.

"You must accept my humble apology, my lady," he said, bowing. "These are difficult times."

Again, he had ripped legitimacy from beneath my feet.

There was a smothered murmur of agreement from the other end of the table. "Very difficult times," spoke one of the nameless councillors. "And Governor Ohi is right. We should prepare for His Majesty's evacuation through the passage. Master Kenji could travel with him."

"Agreed." Minister Bahain nodded. "It is our duty to protect him first and foremost."

Your duty to get him out of the way so he can die quietly while you make a play for power. I sat slowly, eyes on Minister Bahain. I wished I knew more about him and his family, knew what power he had. Even if we survived Katashi, there were other ways the Crimson Throne could fall. A commoner had taken it once.

"Master Kenji will not move him again," I said. "That could well kill him before fever or burns get the chance."

"Was escaping not your own plan, my lady?"

I was starting to hate the sound of Minister Bahain's voice. It had been my plan. It was smart. But I couldn't shake this new fear, no longer of Katashi but of the men Kin most trusted.

General Ryoji set an elbow on the table and leant forward. "Moving him might kill him. The man who gives that order bears a heavy responsibility."

Silence at that.

"If we all evacuate and he dies," Ryoji went on, "then it is no one's fault."

More silence. Calculation happened behind every pair of eyes. If one of them gave the order and Kin died, then the others would remember. Lesser mistakes could end careers. Could end lives.

"We have to yield the city," I said, sure there was a change around the table, that maybe, just maybe they would now listen to reason.

"The Imperial Army has never yielded the capital and never will," General Vareen snapped. "We do not run and we do not hide."

They were rousing words, but they filled me with horror. "That is a very honourable sentiment, General," I said, "But you will die. If we must fight, our only chance of success lies with the traitor generals. Their men make up at least half of Katashi's army, the better-trained and -organised half. If we can turn them, we could pinch Katashi between two forces and might be able to crush his army at the gates."

If he was alone and vulnerable, seeing no way to win, then maybe, just maybe, I could get through to him.

"They are called the traitor generals for a reason, Lady Hana," General Vareen pointed out stiffly.

"So I am aware," I said. "I have seen them bow at my cousin's feet. Seen them give their oaths, but that's an oath they also took at Emperor Kin's feet. Loyalty once changed can be changed again. One of General Manshin's own captains told me that his general is angered by Katashi's methods. None of them took their oath expecting their new emperor to burn Kisia to the ground."

"It is a risk we cannot take." Minister Bahain shook his head. "Even if we could get someone safely outside the walls, even if we could get someone into their midst without alerting Otako's Pikes, I would not trust the future of this empire on a chance. No, we must stand and fight with what we have. We are better prepared."

The council were his captive audience. It was a power, once tasted, that he would not easily surrender.

"Have we had any news from the walls?" he asked.

"Only that Shimai is still burning and Otako is not yet upon the plain, Your Excellency," spoke another man, dressed somewhere between a general and a court official.

"Then there is still time to prepare," Bahain said, turning his head to glance at the darkness beyond the window. "It must be nearly midnight."

"Already past, Your Excellency."

"Would he attack in the night?"

Another voice grumbled from along the table. "He's a rebel. He might do anything."

"General Vareen, are our men ready?"

"Yes, Your Excellency."

I watched, silent now, as they fell into a natural rhythm of agreeing with Minister Bahain. My fists were tightly balled beneath the table, but to engage Bahain in open battle would only end poorly. They had dismissed and ignored me at every turn, and every patronising smile and humouring nod was a slight I would never forget. But there were other ways to get revenge. Other ways to hold the empire.

"General Ryoji."

The name snapped me out of my thoughts.

"Yes, Your Excellency?"

"You and your men are entrusted with the safety of His Majesty and Lady Hana Otako at all times," Minister Bahain said, all plans for evacuation apparently forgotten. "General Vareen will take command of the siege."

I smiled upon the company. "And I will sit on the throne and look pretty, and think about children so hard one might magically appear in my belly."

The little man with the out-of-fashion moustache looked as though his eyes would pop. General Vareen reddened like a little boy, and Minister Bahain smiled that same fatherly smile. "My lady is pleased to jest. I suggest you rest and let us worry about the details. If there is no further business, the council is dismissed."

I kept my peace. Whatever further business I had, I would not bring before the council.

Tili was waiting in my apartments. My apartments. This grand suite of rooms all bright silk screens and thick carpets, full of vases of dry cherry blossoms, of hanging lanterns and ornately carved furniture. Rain was falling upon a narrow balcony overlooking the gardens, the smell of damp mixing with the scent of incense.

My mother had been the last empress to inhabit these rooms, and as I stood in the doorway, I told myself I felt her presence, that I could see her moving from the table to the balcony to the enormous Chiltaen bed with its white pillows and crimson silk quilt. Every step she took with grace and decision and a faint smile as though she found something amusing.

"I have laid out a clean night-robe, my lady," Tili said, bowing deeply.

Empress Li faded.

"Thank you."

Falling back into our habitual silence, I let Tili fuss around, removing my stained armour. There had been no time to do more than throw a clean surcoat over it before the council meeting, and now as each piece was removed, I could smell blood and singed leather and damp river stink.

"See what you can do with it," I said as she piled the armour up with a distasteful wrinkle in her nose. "I'm going to need it again."

"Yes, my lady."

Once she had untied the last tie and unclipped the last clip, I went to the washbowl and, taking the cloth, scrubbed my skin until it was red and raw. I stared into the water, stars of lamplight dancing on its surface. Katashi would not wait long before marching on Mei'lian, might even be already on his way. Yet whatever I might persuade Darius to do, we needed the traitor generals if we were to have any hope of protecting the capital if it all went wrong. But even if I could reach them, it would make no difference if I had nothing to offer.

Think, Hana, think, I urged. *Think.*

"My lady?"

I dropped the cloth, shattering the pool of stars. Tili stood in the centre of the room with her eyes downcast.

"Yes? What is it?"

"I'm so sorry about His Majesty, my lady."

"Sorry for his injuries or because he killed my family?" She had been there. She had heard it all. "Neither is your fault."

"No, but I am sorry I was always so loyal to him and not to..."

She could not bring herself to say Katashi's name, and though it had been on my tongue all day, neither could I. I had gotten used to speaking of him as our enemy, as a monster come to burn us all, but the night at Shimai had proved the Katashi I loved was still in there somewhere.

"You had every reason to be loyal to him, Tili, but thank you."

"The servants are all talking about what will happen if His Majesty dies, my lady. Do you think he will?"

I'd had this conversation with the council not so long since and was too tired to have it again so just sighed. "I don't know."

"If... if he does, what will happen to you? And to..." Her gaze flicked to my belly rather than speak the fearful words, rather than acknowledge the single joy that had gotten me through the last few days.

"I don't know," I said again. "Though right now, surviving tomorrow seems unlikely as it is, so..."

With a grimace, she picked up the clean robe she had laid out for me. A simple linen night-robe, not one of mine, as all my clothing had been left behind in Kogahaera. Perhaps it had belonged to my mother. A mother who had died for the ambition of the man whose job it was to protect her.

"I need you to do something for me," I said as Tili tightened the white wedding sash around me once again, its fabric as dry as an hour hanging above the brazier could make it.

"Anything for you, my lady," she said, not looking up from her work. "You know that."

"Fetch General Ryoji to me. No one can see you. No one can see him."

"But, my lady—"

"You said anything. Bring him."

A quick bow, a fearful flutter of her hands, and she was gone. Alone in my mother's old apartments, I paced the floor, back and forth and back again while rain fell on the gardens. It had been raining the night Shin and I had crossed their breadth on that foolish mission. If only I had stayed behind and waited for Katashi to come back, how different—

No, don't dwell on what might have been.

I went on pacing. From here, I could not see the city, nor the walls, nor what was coming beyond, but I could well imagine the sight of Mei'lian more alive than normal for a rainy night, the south gate choked with lanterns as people fled the doomed capital.

For a long time, I stood looking out over the gardens with their lantern-lit groves and listened to the deep silence of the inner palace. No doubt there was activity on the lower levels despite the late hour, but here on the fourth floor there was nothing but the gentle murmur of the guards as they shifted their weight. The guards would see him come, but they were Ryoji's men. If he could not trust them, he could trust no one.

A tap sounded on the door. A vague outline stood silhouetted against the paper panes.

"Come in," I said, the words catching on my tongue.

The heavy frame slid, and upon the threshold, General Ryoji bowed. "Lady Hana," he said, smiling a smile that made me have to push all thought of Katashi from my head. "You sent for me?"

"Yes," I said. "I did. Where have you been?"

"I have been discussing the defence of the city with the generals and gathering numbers from each garrison."

"I believe your orders were to leave the defence of the city to General Vareen."

"Yes, but men prefer to fight for a man they know and like, whatever the risk."

"Fight for you?"

Ryoji had not moved from the doorway. "For me," he said. "For you. The morning could bring anything, and we have to be prepared."

"We have to turn the traitor generals back to our side."

My words cut the humour from his eyes, leaving only tension to hang between us. "I agree that it would be our best chance of survival, but even if the council had agreed, the generals are outside the city, surrounded by men loyal to Katashi. Who would you send to parley with them?"

"Send? No one. I would go myself."

"Go yourself? Hana, that is too dangerous."

"More dangerous than waiting here for Katashi to burn us all if it comes to that?"

"No, but—"

"No buts, Ryoji, I need to reach them before Katashi attacks."

The smile was entirely gone from his face now, leaving only severe lines. "Speaking as the commander of your guard, the whole proposition is insane," he said. "Speaking as an advisor…getting out of Mei'lian unseen is not going to be easy. If you open the gate, Katashi will know you're coming and not let you meet his generals, and General Vareen might refuse to open it at all. There is the passage back to Shimai, of course, but that is a long detour. So short of climbing over the wall at night or walking through it, you—"

"Kimiko."

"Pardon, my lady?"

"Has anyone seen Lady Kimiko Otako since Shimai?"

The troubled cleft between his brows deepened. "Not that I am aware of. No doubt she is with her brother now."

"No...no, it's Darius she wants. Captain Dendzi!"

The door slid, and the guard currently posted as my protection stood uncertainly on the threshold. He glanced at his general. Then he bowed. "Yes, my lady?"

"I want two men posted in every room around Lord Laroth's apartments. No wall is to be left unguarded. When Lady Kimiko Otako attempts to gain entrance to him, you may inform her that unless she comes to me first, Lord Laroth will die. I need to see her."

Again he glanced at his general before bowing. "Yes, my lady. Is that all, my lady?"

"Yes, that will be all, Captain."

He went out, leaving me alone again with a frowning General Ryoji. "I am not sure I understand," he said.

"Lady Kimiko Otako can get me out of Mei'lian unseen. Or even better, can bring the traitor generals to me."

"She can walk through walls, yes, that could work, but how do you plan to persuade the traitor generals to turn on Otako?"

"I don't know yet."

Ryoji let a long slow breath.

"How is His Majesty?" I asked to change the subject.

"You haven't seen him?"

"No."

"He's feverish," he said, "but alive."

"Good."

"Is it?"

It was my turn to frown. "Yes. Sometimes I wish he would just die and put me out of my misery, but though I hate to admit it, as things currently stand Kisia will suffer more from his loss than it suffered from the loss of my father."

Katashi could have ruled the empire. We could have done it together. A few altered decisions and it could have been him standing before me right now, the city ours, but it was not.

General Ryoji stepped into the middle of the floor but no farther. I brushed away tears with the back of my hand. "Excuse me," I said. "It has been a long day."

"There is no weakness in tears," he said. "If you ask me to leave, I will go. Otherwise, I'm going to hold you, with or without your permission."

"If you leave me too, I will never forgive you."

He gripped my shoulders. "Hana, I'm not going anywhere until you order me to, and that's a promise." His hands slid down my arms until he was holding mine. "I'm all yours."

No sooner had he spoken than he was on his knees at my feet, bowing his head to the floor. "I swear on the bones of my forebears, on my name and my honour, that I will do all in my power to protect you from harm. I will mind not pain. I will mind not suffering. I will give every last ounce of my strength. I will give every last ounce of my intellect. I will die in service to you if the gods so will it. I will renounce every honour. I will give every coin. I will be as nothing and no one in service to you."

Less than a minute and it was done, his oath spoken, his honour pledged. It was that easy. But despite his declarations of honour and loyalty, what was to stop him turning against me if I didn't give him what he had no doubt come here expecting? I didn't know him well enough to be sure of him yet.

"Rise."

He did so, unfolding his strong limbs to stand again before me, his cheeks flushed, his eyes burning bright. Tense, ready, yet he said nothing as I put a hand on his sash. Its coils slid smooth and snakelike as I untied the knot.

Not a word, hardly a breath. I did not hear it fall.

A buckle loosened. A strap untied. Four gold buttons on his sleeve. It was excruciatingly slow, a piece of his armour falling away only to reveal another—like a puzzle that would never end.

At last there was skin: warm, golden flesh speckled with scars, every muscle standing proud as I lifted the under-tunic over his head. He had no shame in his bare skin, did not move or blush or look away as I untied his breeches. First one pair, then the second shorter pair, and exhilarated by my own daring, I stared at the completely naked body before me.

He did not move, just watched, heedless of his own arousal. Katashi had been the same, pleased to revel in his own glory—but now was a very bad time to think about Katashi.

I slid the white sash down over my hips, its passage easier now it knew its way. My fingers trembled as I let my robe fall, let my underclothes part company with my skin. His eyes darted down and something like pain creased his face. A groan rattled from his throat as he tilted his head back to look at the ceiling.

"May the gods have mercy on me," he said.

"Is what you see so terrible?"

"No!" He looked back at me and let out another groan. "But I'm fast running out of willpower."

His adoration was a heady joy all its own.

He put his hands on his head and let out a long sigh, his gaze running over me. "You are very cruel, my lady," he said.

"Would you rather I put my robe back on?"

"Gods no, I would rather go on suffering."

I took a step forward, all but closing the space between us. Fear fluttered my stomach, but I touched him anyway, ran my hands over his weathered skin. The breath of his groan danced across my face.

The first kiss was small and tentative, bringing us so close that his manhood was pressed between us. "Hana," he said with a gasp against my lips that ended in a kiss. "I'm all yours. You may do whatever you want with me."

He might not have said so if he knew my initial motives, but though I wanted to be sure of him, wanted to overwrite memories of Katashi on my skin, he aroused enough desire in me for his own sake.

"Then lie down," I said between breathless kisses. "No more waiting."

The bed had been prepared so I could rest, but it was his head that hit the pillow, the contrast of the white sheets seeming to darken his skin and his hair. I threw my leg over his hips, and there for a moment Katashi was lying beneath me.

I must have flinched or gasped, for Hade's hands halted in their passage down my thighs. "What's wrong?" he asked. "We don't have to do this if you don't want to."

"I want to," I said, shaking the memory and grasping at a lie to cover my distress. "But...but you're going to have to help me from here, because I have no idea what I'm doing."

He grinned and ran his hands back up my thighs to grip my hips. "It would be more than an honour to teach you, my lady."

21. ENDYMION

He shouldn't be here."

My head pounded. Somehow I had found myself in the inner palace with what remained of the Imperial Guard. They were wary and hostile and frightened and full of pity.

"Don't worry about him. He's not all there."

"But the brand. He's a traitor."

"General Ryoji accepts him."

Their voices faded back into the small sounds of the inner palace and the whispers of an empire.

No storm tonight. Small blessing.

Not even a breath of wind.

So quiet.

Quiet.

"It's too quiet out there," one of the men said from the fretwork window, open to the humid scents of the garden. "Mei'lian has never been this quiet."

"An army has never marched on our gates."

The soft laughter split my head like an axe.

"At least being under attack will be louder."

Attack.

A collective shudder filled the room. Never would they forget that fire, so hot it burned blue at its heart. Or the screams.

Plates clinked. Footsteps stopped nearby. "Are you sure you don't want anything to eat? There's extra."

I shook my head slowly, afraid of disturbing my brain.

"How about a drink? There's good wine."

"Leave the kid alone," someone else said. "He looks sick."

"Yeah, watch it, Red, you might catch something."

"Shut up."

The soul of Red moved away, a blazing ball of fear and anxiety shrouded in bravado. It was a common theme throughout the room, while elsewhere in the palace, pain was more prominent, dulled only by the tincture of opium Master Kenji carried everywhere.

"Where's the general? Is he still out?"

"No, he came in, but Lady Hana's maid brought a message so he went straight off without stopping to eat."

An awkward silence fell between each throb of my head. More fear. Had it been anyone but their empress, they might have joked and wished their general good hunting. Instead, every thought was strained.

He must be mad.

He wouldn't.

Who am I kidding? I'd risk it.

And if His Majesty dies? What then?

But lust was already seeping into every man's mind and turning their thoughts lascivious. It was coming through the walls.

May the gods have mercy on me.

Is what you see so terrible?

No! But I'm fast running out of willpower. You are very cruel, my lady.

Would you rather I put my robe back on?

Gods no, I would rather go on suffering.

I needed space. Needed air. I got to my feet. Blurry figures eyed me from the table, each one seeming to swim amid faint colours. They watched me go, their whispers trailing after me.

We should run.

First Gerh then Ryo, then the whole fucking army gone. This has to be a nightmare. Please, gods, let me wake.

I dragged my feet along the passage, every step a struggle. But familiar souls called to me from all around—Darius, Avarice, Malice, Hope. Even Kin, fading in and out of my Sight as consciousness ebbed.

Ahead, the air shimmered and shifted, hot with pleasure.

The smell of her.

It had been so long since I had felt pleasure in my own skin.

The feel of her.

I tried not to think about it, tried not to focus on the sensation, though every grunt and breathless groan caught in my throat.

"Excuse me?"

I wrenched my head around, pain shooting through my skull as though I had displaced my brain. A soldier watched me—a captain by his sash, his frown heavy. "Are you looking for something?"

My eyes slid past him to the door at the end of the passage. Weight. Heat. Every breath a gasp. Trapped beneath my robe, I knew I was getting hard.

"No," I managed to reply. "Where is Darius? I want to see him."

"Lord Laroth? No, new orders just came. No one is allowed to see him at the moment."

"Not allowed—"

"If it's a freak you need, the others are in there."

I didn't need him to point out which room. There was something about Malice that could penetrate even the thickest door.

Shaky steps to the door. It slid easily, welcoming me to a small room stinking of piss. There was no furniture, only a square of bare matting, dark and damp, the windows shuttered for winter. But a few shreds of evening light eked through the cracks, enough to illuminate the ghostly forms of Malice and Hope and Avarice. Hope's hands were tied at the small of his back and he seemed to be asleep, curled on the floor with his hair hanging over his face. Malice was even more dishevelled, slumped against the wall with his robe loose.

They were all tied up and none of them evinced any sign of life as I slid the door closed. It shut out the light, but a mere screen could do nothing to dissipate the sensations thickening the air.

I slid to the floor, blood rushing to my groin. There was no thought, only need powering my hand to pluck at the strings of my breeches. My hand was cold, but I gripped myself tight, letting free a groan. They were feeding off each other's pleasure, ecstasy rolling endlessly between them as I stroked myself in time to the sensation, guilt buried beneath desire.

I could not hear the scream but I felt it. Teeth in my shoulder. Hot breath on my skin. The soft flesh of a woman enveloping me, everything about her young body a joy. Her expression a different kind of agony, her groan one that set my skin tingling.

Hana.

I snatched my hand away, but it was too late. It was my own pleasure now leaving my hands hot and slick, the smell reminiscent of so many nights spent sitting outside brothels in Chiltae. Jian had always asked where I had been, and I had always lied. Eventually he had stopped asking.

The smell grew more nauseating as I wiped my hand on my breeches. Avarice watched from across the room. Like the others, his hands were tied behind his back, but between his legs was a hard bulge.

Malice started to laugh, the sound dry.

"Feeling better now, yes?"

My pounding headache was already returning with the whisper of a thousand thoughts. "Not really," I said. Head in hands, I was sure my skull was throbbing.

"Don't worry, she's only your half-sister."

I groaned, and he laughed again, but he owned no true amusement, only despair. "I'm amazed there's enough of you left to get hard," he said. "You're more than half-dead already, yes?" Malice rolled over in the semi-darkness. "When was the last time you ate?"

It hurt to think. His scowl swam in and out of focus. "I don't know."

"And when did you last sleep?"

"I don't know!"

"Darius need never have worried; you're going to the grave faster than either of us, yes?"

I tried to remember what it felt like to eat. To swallow. To taste.

"Did you come here for a reason?" Malice said, trying to wriggle himself upright. "Or just to mock me for being without the use of my hands?"

"You told me at Rina that I would need to be chained up before the end," I said. "What exactly did you mean?"

"I thought that was obvious." Malice's words pulsed in time with his own whispers. *Freak. Killer.* "You've killed a lot of people, yes? So have I. So has Katashi. Even Hope has ended his share, but the difference between us and you is that we won't wake one day to find ourselves the only living soul left because we dreamed the world's destruction."

Wedging his foot against Hope's back, he managed to get himself upright. Sweat stuck his long hair to his face and soaked his robe. Malice swayed, looking for a moment as though he would be sick. "Endymion," he said, tilting his head back and letting out a pained sigh. "I hate you."

"You hate me?"

"Do I really need to repeat myself? With every breath, I curse the day my men brought you to me. I curse the day I first heard your name. Endymion, both Empath and Otako, the perfect weapon. And to think Darius believed you could be virtuous."

He had begun the speech sitting upright and ended it huddled forward. The pain of a thousand pricking needles spread through my stomach.

"Alas that you have fallen, Brother, alas that you turned out to be no better a student than me, yes?" He started to laugh, still crunched forward and rocking back and forth. "The sins of the teacher be visited upon the student," he said. "I guess we've had many generations to perfect our particular kind of evil." He kicked the unconscious Hope. "Wake up! I need you."

"He isn't going to wake up, you rotten waster," Avarice said, oozing contempt. "You've sucked him dry, just like Master Darius. The more he gave the more you wanted." The Vice spat. "Just die already and give us all some peace."

Malice growled and fought his way to his feet only to stumble. Hands bound, he hit the matting hard, and a stomach full of bile and half-digested food sprayed onto the reeds.

Avarice didn't move. "Withdrawal," he said when he found me watching him. "Usually when he gets like this, we get him more tar. Hope was useful for a while."

Curled up, Malice moaned, his long hair half swimming in his own puke. This pathetic mess of a man was the Vice Master. He had struck fear into the heart of Kisia. Malice, the abandoned puppy seeking attention. A man whose obsessive love had nearly destroyed an empire.

Malice's shoulders shook with dry sobs. The tide of his maddened whispers sloshed around me as I crouched beside him and touched a crumpled cheek.

Memories hit me hard. Sounds. Smells. Words. Moments in time he had stored like paintings in his mind. Darius silenced by Maturation. Darius as a boy, lit by burning hedgerows. Darius laughing. Darius smiling. The touch of his hand. Of his body. Of his soul. The click of Errant pieces. The rush of the wind as they rode. The chatter of the city far below, moving like a colony of ants. Darius groaning. Darius undressing. Darius slowly pouring a pot of roasted tea that smelt rich just like him. Darius. Darius. Darius. Everywhere he assailed me, every choice, every second of

Malice's life seeming to hinge upon the brother he adored, every shred of Malice's soul vibrating to the call of another man's voice.

But there were other memories too, locked away deep. They lived and breathed the same, sucking in Darius's soul and never letting go, but here there was anger. Here Darius snarled. He mocked. He jeered. Here he laughed at the pain he caused, grinning as he took out his frustrations on other bodies, with pretty boys and an endless cycle of whores whose heavy, curving flesh had turned Malice's stomach. Arguments. Empathic battles fought with hands to each other's throats. Then Darius's blood poured over my fingers. And as Avarice gave his all to his master, the first Vice was born.

Malice yanked his head awkwardly back, half rolling into his own vomit. "Don't you dare steal him from me!"

I fell back, hands lifted as though in surrender. "Steal him?"

"I can feel you trying. Oh, don't tell me it's an accident." Dry laughter scratched from Malice's throat. "How many people have been sucked into that head of yours?"

"None!" I could not shift my eyes from his face. "Only...only..."

"And you call me a monster." He snorted, the sound superior though his whole body shook with withdrawal. "Well, did you see it all? Go on and judge me, you munted-up little cunt. Put me out of my misery, yes? Put me down like the rabid dog I am."

"No."

"No?"

"I can't. I don't...I can't see anymore. I can't see what's right and wrong. It's all a mess and my head aches." I pressed my hands to my skull, unsure if the horror I felt was his or mine. "The gods will judge. The gods will judge. They will balance the scales. They always do."

"Is that your judgement? Go away and rot!"

"If you'd told him about the child, none of this would have happened," I said, closing my eyes as the room began to spin. "He loves her."

No answer, but each word was a dagger in his heart. In my heart. Anger raged through me, full of chagrin and self-loathing, and Malice wailed like a wounded beast.

"No!" he screamed. "He's mine!"

I reeled back and hit the door. Wood cracked. The paper screen snapped, and in a tumble of shredded paper and shards of wood, I fell into the passage.

"What's going on?"

The captain stood over me, sword drawn, his eyes caught to the room where Malice was still screaming.

Words tumbled off my tongue. "He's mine! Don't you dare touch him! I'll kill that fucking little bitch. I'll cut her up. I'll carve her into pieces and make him eat them."

Through my aching head, the passage was alive with noise, and I could no longer tell the whispers from the spoken word. It was all a mess of shouting while the world spun sickeningly on.

"What's wrong with the freak?"

"Stop that idiot from screaming or they'll hear him in Shimai! Where's the general?"

"Too busy getting well acquainted."

"Endymion!"

My swimming vision locked on the door to Darius's temporary cell, drawn as though by the pool of silence it exuded.

"Endymion!"

Father Kokoro's face hovered overhead.

"I'll cut the bastard from her body," I screamed. "She isn't fit to so much as touch him!"

"What is going on?"

"I don't know, Father, he went in there and came out screaming."

"Shut him up, Captain, he's drawing too much attention."

"Too late."

More whispers were joining the fray as new souls pressed in.

That man has a Traitor's Mark. Who is he?

There's something familiar about him.

Why aren't they grabbing him?

A hand gripped my shoulder. Blood. Fire. A man in my arms struggling for life. "It's all right," I said. "You're going to be fine. Think of Solana, you have to make it back for her."

In the mess of voices, someone swore. "Are you talking about Lian? What happened to him?"

"He's dead. You were there."

"No. No! I wasn't! I can't remember!"

His guts had spilled through my fingers.

A hand grabbed at my sleeve and there was Kokoro again. He was going to arrest me, to have me burned for witchcraft, and he wouldn't even tell me who my father was. I shoved him out of the way and ran, pushing through the mass of souls pressing in. Shouts followed me all the way, whispers clinging.

"They all suspect, but that doesn't matter," I said. "Not one of them would betray me."

"What's going on?"

The landing was awash with doubt and fear, a fog through which I clawed, seeking freedom.

"What's the use in fighting?" I said. "There's no way we can win."

"Stop him!"

More words poured from my mouth. "The gate is closed. He's cornered. We need to knock him out. A scabbard? A stick? I don't want to kill the stupid shit."

I half ran, half fell down the stairs, taking them three at a time, pain jarring my knees. There were people everywhere, limbs, skin, silk, stink, every thought tearing at me as I passed. More stairs, another landing, souls everywhere. Bright light was all that drew me on.

I hit the window head first. Wood snapped. Glass shattered. A myriad of tiny cuts and I hit stones wet with rain. Lantern light shimmered. Every breath was choked with voices.

"Whoa! Are you all right?"

Rain caressed my face. Above me, a lantern lit the golden threads of a dragon flying through crimson silk. Then General Ryoji, raindrops glittering as they fell into his dark tousled hair.

"The gods will judge," I said. "They never leave the scales unbalanced."

"What?"

"Just ignore him, Hade, he's mad." Hana. "Bind his hands and get him out of here."

I tried to run, but pain shot through my leg and I fell, shards of glass cutting into my palms.

"I don't dare touch him."

"Just don't touch his skin. Tie him mid-forearm and put him with the others in a new cell. Father Kokoro can see to them."

"No!"

Hana leant down, her face drawing closer to mine, though she too dared not touch me. "Only the gods can help you now, Endymion. I'm sorry."

Rain hit my face, each drop like a kiss from the sky. "Justice comes to everyone," I said, sucking breaths into my aching lungs. "Even gods."

22. DARIUS

Outside my head, Endymion's screams began between the forty-fourth move and the forty-fifth, around the time my imaginary piece hung in the air over my opponent's imaginary king. I curled up tighter, shutting my Empathy in.

In the passage, the screams turned into shouts before fading into the distance.

I stared at the empty table. For as long as I had called the palace home, my Errant board had sat in this place. I had owned it since childhood, had learnt to play with its well-worn pieces, but it had travelled to Koi with me and was now long gone.

The imaginary piece leapt its fellow, but it turned up blank. I drummed my fingers on the table. Secretaries and councillors innumerable had knelt at my board and let the game reveal their strengths and weaknesses, their fears and their assumptions. Errant was a mirror for life, and in the world of the court, such knowledge was power. Had Kin been my opponent at this moment, he would have taken the obvious risk. Avarice would have attacked, Malice defended, his eyes on me not the game. I had not yet played enough with Endymion to discern a pattern, but Kimiko's style had been clear before the end of our first round. She played the random gamble, because to her, Errant was just a game.

"I wonder if I might have changed your mind," I said, but silence was the only reply.

I continued the game, and outside my head, the palace grew quiet but for voices just beyond my door. One my guard, the other deep and soft. The door slid. The appearance of Hana would have been unsurprising, even Endymion or Malice or Father Kokoro, but it was a hunched and hooded figure that entered. My imaginary pieces clattered about the stranger's feet.

"You have the wrong room perhaps?" I said.

The figure spun, hand on the door. "If you are Lord Laroth, then I am in the right place."

"I am, though you appear to have the advantage, hooded man."

A wrinkled hand pushed back the hood, but the sight of my visitor's face did not alleviate my confusion. Scars disfigured its distinguished features, making a mask from puckers and leathery wrinkles.

"Ah," I said as recognition wormed its way into my mind. "You must be Brother Jian. I ought to have expected you."

"And I ought to thank you."

"For?"

A constrained smile. "Saving my life, though to what purpose I live it I hardly know anymore. I spent the rest of the season imprisoned here at the emperor's mercy."

"It was not I who gave the order to release you, so don't thank me for that."

"No, that was His Majesty. He stopped here on the way to Koga-haera to ask me about Endymion."

Brother Jian had closed the door but remained upon the threshold like a wary animal.

"Your brother doesn't know you're here, I take it," I said.

"No, he doesn't." He advanced into the room then, his gait awkward as though one leg was shorter than the other. "You're in danger, Lord Laroth."

I laughed, though it was a dry, humourless sound even to my

own ears. "You are a master of understatement," I said. "There is a fire-wielding maniac out there with a grudge against me."

"It was not Lord Otako I meant. Kokoro hates you. All of you. It was foolish of me to think I might persuade him to help Endymion."

The Errant game in my head was gone, leaving me no way to escape the old man's pain. I sucked in my wandering Empathy, but the pain did not dissipate. A suspicion had grown too strong in my mind. "He persuaded my father to kill his own children, didn't he?" I said, giving it voice. I hated the tinge of hope in my tone, as much as I hated the held breath with which I awaited his response.

"I was not in Mei'lian at the time so can give you no certain answer," he said. "But I would not be surprised."

I let the breath go. "Then I am in your debt for the care you took of my brother."

"Thank you, my lord." Brother Jian bowed, the movement jerky and entirely devoid of grace. Yet somehow he maintained his dignity. "Though it would seem that what care I took of him was not enough."

"No amount would have been. I tried to teach him to curb his Sight, but I failed as you did. There is nothing more we can do for him."

"He could be granted freedom."

Now the hope was in the other man's face. "No," I said. "His other name is too useful. Were he in his right mind, he could look after himself, but unless there is some plateau of sanity beyond the current incline of madness, I cannot even say he is worth saving."

"He is not mad," the priest said. "I have studied your condition since Endymion first came into my care, not that it allowed me to help him much. But from what I understand, the branding in Shimai triggered what you call the Maturation. Usually it lasts a few weeks or even a few seasons, and a stronger Empath emerges the other side. Rather like a caterpillar from its cocoon, I have always thought."

"Except that we are far from pretty butterflies."

He smiled a rictus grin that twisted his scars. "Kokoro would agree, but he does not know what I know."

"And what is it that you know?" I said. "No, don't speak until you sit, you are giving me quite the crick in my neck." I gestured to the place across the table. The last man to kneel there had been Emperor Kin, for an Errant game that had changed everything.

"Thank you, my lord." Brother Jian settled on the same cushion with none of Emperor Kin's potency. He didn't spread his robe or touch his sash, but he did fix me with an intent stare. "Some years ago, Endymion and I were in Talithan, in northern Chiltae," he said. "I was looking through a discarded collection of prayer books and came across a notebook. It was the most amazing thing I have ever seen." The old man's eyes lit up and he licked his lips. "Every page was covered in words, edge to edge, and not just scribbles but the neatest words I've ever seen. It was as though each letter was formed with no thought of speed, or even time, only precision."

"I think its author was not the only one with no notion of time," I said. "Do get to the point."

Beneath the mess of scars Brother Jian flushed. "Apologies, my lord, but it was truly amazing. Though not as amazing as its contents. It appears to have been a journal used to record experiments and observations. After reading a single page, it was clear the author owned a degree of intelligence few could boast and had spent years on the work."

"What work? I cannot read your mind."

"Studying your kind and others like you. Not only Empaths but also other men and women with . . . special talents. There was mention of a Prescient. And a Kuri. And something called an Aberrant. They were not described in detail, nor was the Empath, but the process by which you came to exist was theorised upon at length."

The fluttering in my stomach made me twitchy. What difference did it make where Empaths had come from? It did not change the fact that I was here. That Malice was here. Always inescapably here.

"I exist because my father put me inside my mother," I said, trying for dry wit and surely failing. "There is nothing mystical about me, Brother."

"No, there isn't, and that's the beautiful thing about it. The theory was that every man, woman, and child upon this world is a soul inhabiting a body. When the body dies, that soul is then reborn into another body."

"Reincarnation, yes, the Chiltaens used to believe in it before they adopted the One True God, but I remember no body but this one."

He smiled a little fatherly smile. "It would be strange if we did remember. But not knowing something does not mean it is not true. The old Chiltaen belief was of an endless cycle, but this notebook said otherwise. Seven times. Seven incarnations of each soul before it is returned to the maker. The first outing a simple soul, the seventh a wise one. But you, you have been reborn *nine* times."

A soul too long in this world. By the ache in my bones, it was an apt description. "It is a nice tale."

"If tale you believe it to be," he said. "I believe you are a beautiful aberration of a natural process, and Endymion is an aberration of an aberration. I don't think his Maturation ran its proper course. It did not end. A stopper left out of the cask, to use another poor metaphor. But like the cask, there is only so much it can be filled."

"If you were hoping for further enlightenment, I'm afraid I must disappoint," I said. "There is little else for a sickly boy to do but read. I've been over every book in our rotting library and never found any mention of reincarnation. As to the mechanics of Endymion's particular malfunction, your guess is as good, if not better, than mine."

Brother Jian bowed, the movement more graceful now he was kneeling. "It would be a lie to say I am not disappointed, but in this situation, Endymion's fate is rather more pressing than his origin. For too many years have I loved him like a son."

"And been a better father than the one who gave him this curse. But you have to let him go now, or he will break you."

It was a wry smile that spread his lips. "I thank you for your warning, but sane or mad, he is worth the risk to save."

"Then I wish you good fortune," I said, bowing to indicate dismissal. He had been nothing but kind and good and worthy, yet I wanted him out of my sight, his tales with him. "I don't know how you got in here, but if you want to see Endymion, I imagine you will need the permission of our lovely Lady Hana."

He took his dismissal with good grace. "Thank you, my lord. May the gods smile on you."

"They need not."

As he rose, the door slid, the sound a soft hush. Father Kokoro entered, glorious in his white and gold. Something in the way he moved made him more spider than I—all soft dainty steps and predatory smiles as his gaze looked right through Brother Jian.

"Lord Laroth."

"Father Kokoro," I returned. "I knew it was too much to hope I might die without seeing your face again."

"Your father was more charming."

"More ways in which we are not alike."

"You're much more alike than you think."

Brother Jian hobbled a step toward his brother. "As are we, if only you would care to remember it."

"You should not be here, Jian," Kokoro said, not looking at the scarred man before him.

Curiosity crept my Empathy from its shell, and it found a lacy web of fear cloaking Brother Jian's broken form. I sucked it back in. For five years, I had held such curiosity at bay and denied what I had been born, but the strength to do so for even a few minutes was fading fast.

"I should be anywhere someone needs solace." They were quiet words, but they owned all the strength I lacked.

Father Kokoro smiled, that cold predatory smile. I felt Brother Jian's inward shudder and once again sucked my wandering Empathy close. "It is time you left," Kokoro said. "One cannot provide solace from a cell." He turned to the guard hovering in the doorway. "Take this man out and I may not mention that you let him in. And send for refreshments."

"Yes, Father. Thank you, Father."

The guard stood aside and waited for Brother Jian. The scarred priest hesitated only a moment before bowing another of his graceless bows. "I am honoured to have met you, Lord Laroth."

"And I you, Brother."

He walked out with his hobbling gait, and having wished him gone, I wanted him back. Rather him and his stories than Father Kokoro and his hate.

The captain closed the door. Kokoro did not move.

"It is customary to enquire whether someone wishes your company before forcing it upon them," I said.

"In this case I come bearing a gift." He stepped toward the table. "It was thoughtful of Lady Hana to imprison you in your former room, but how disappointing to recall you had taken many of your belongings to Koi."

He held out an Errant board, not mine but well-sized in dark wood, its little armies in a separate box. I did not take it.

"Why?" I said.

"I want to talk."

"Talk?"

"Yes, just talk. It's a fair trade."

I nodded. Father Kokoro smiled and put the board down upon the table. "Then this is yours. May I?" He pointed to the cushion Jian had not long vacated.

Again I nodded. "Am I to be graced with your intelligent self or the well-meaning court fool?"

"A stupid man can go everywhere without being watched. You ought to try it sometime."

"I'm running out of sometimes, Father."

The box of pieces clicked as I prised open the tight lid. Kokoro knelt, filling the air with the smell of incense and the rustle of silk.

"Do you wish to know how your brothers are?" he asked.

I did not look up from the pieces, just went on removing them one by one from their wooden prison. "My brothers?"

"There's no need to dissemble, Your Excellency. Lady Hana took me into her confidence. You have two brothers, one of them Lord Takehiko Otako, the other the son of a whore."

"And you have one, who harboured the true heir to the Crimson Throne under Emperor Kin's nose. We've already had this conversation." I took out the last piece and looked up. "Although having now met your brother, I am forced to admit that the world is not entirely rotten."

No smile now. "You know I have no brother," he said. "When we take our oath to the gods, we give up all bonds of blood."

"Yes, that is why you wanted Endymion to take it. You wanted him to give up being an Otako. And a Laroth."

"For which I rather think he might have thanked me."

"Perhaps."

A tap at the door. It was my room, my cell, but it was Kokoro who called permission to enter. A serving girl crept in keeping her head bowed. So had Kimiko, but this one had no curls, just straight dark hair and plump arms. She slid a tray onto the table beside my new Errant board. Roasted tea, by the smell, and a bowl of sugared beans. The girl reached for the teapot, but Kokoro waved her away.

"Your father was a wretched, haunted man by the end," he said, taking a bean as the girl withdrew. "But he accepted the gods, and I pray he died at peace."

"I wouldn't know," I said. "I do know he died in considerable pain, for which I always found myself grateful."

A frown. "And now?"

"That is my own concern."

He crunched the bean between his teeth and offered me the bowl. "What is it you want?" I said, declining with a shake of my head. "If it is to give me the succour of the gods, your brother beat you to it."

"I have no brother," he said, the petulant repetition disappointing. I had expected better. "Although you need all the help you can get. You're a tortured man. Like your father."

"Your brother is the one who was tortured."

No repetition this time. "You can put on a brave face, but I have eyes that see. Your father told me many things. He told me that the curse travels through the male line. He told me it killed your mother when she gave birth to a daughter. He feared the same would happen to Empress Li, you know. That was when he came to me."

Another bean. "It would have been better if it had been a girl and she had died rather than give birth to another monster," he said.

"Better for who?"

"For everyone."

"Even Takehiko?"

"A soul that has never lived cannot grieve, Excellency, but we can lament what became of his life."

"For your brother's sake?"

"For Kisia's. Jian is a sentimental fool. Even after being imprisoned for months, it appears that his heart has not changed."

"A priest who has faith? What a strange notion." I tapped the teacup in front of me with the tip of a dirty fingernail.

Father Kokoro twitched back the sleeve of his robe and reached for the steaming pot, displaying skin puckered with age. "People who believe the gods can give comfort to the living are wrong," he said, pouring the dark brew into my cup. "You can live by their tenets and find solace in their teachings and your own belief, but prayer? You might as well be talking to yourself."

"I've seen you pray."

"You've seen me pray because I'm a court priest. It is my job to be seen in prayer."

"You might not be a court priest much longer."

He placed the teapot back on its tray with a clink. "You mean that I might soon be a charred corpse. So might you if our defence fails. But if not, you and your brothers walk free, carrying your curse." Another bean was crushed between his teeth. "That is just as much a tragedy. You're never going to get a better chance to set things right."

I took up my teacup, trying for grace with my unpractised hand. "Set things right," I said. "You mean kill my own brothers."

The Errant board sat between us, its armies prepared to do battle over the field of black and white squares. Errant was a mirror of life, a window to the soul, but I needed no game to know the man kneeling opposite.

"I was thirteen when my father tried to kill me," I said.

No surprise.

"Not long after, he tracked down my half-brother and tried to put a blade through his throat."

Still no surprise.

"That's what you mean when you say he accepted the gods. He accepted that he was unnatural and ought to be put down, that it was his duty to rid the world of the curse he had loosed upon it."

"Yes," Kokoro said. "He finally realised he was not a god but flesh and blood. He came to me often, troubled, fearing that his soul was poisoned. Abnormal. Invasive. Unnatural. He wanted to take his own life after Empress Li died. He blamed himself. I consoled him, told him the only power he had left was over his own legacy."

Consoled him.

Long ago, I had sworn not to become my father, and yet here I sat, the same tortured man. Life turned in cruel circles, leaving us all following the poisoned steps of our forebears. Katashi. Hana. Even General Ryoji, stepping into a role where every word had already been written. My father had failed to end it, passing the responsibility to me.

I had told Malice that we all deserved to die, but coming from Kokoro, the suggestion was vile.

"Think on it, Laroth," he said, running his finger along the inside of the now empty bean bowl. "You may have no control over your instincts and your urges, but you can seek to change the world for the better as your father once did."

"He failed."

Again that smile. "Yes, but I don't think Darius Laroth ever fails at something he puts his mind to."

"We all have our weaknesses."

Father Kokoro licked the sugar from his finger, and the skin at the corners of his eyes crinkled. "You could end it here, once and for all. One brother a criminal, the other locked up as a madman. But you could finish your father's work. He would be proud."

"Proud," I repeated, with a little snort of air as Father Kokoro sipped his tea. "It would be the first time."

———————

Rain lashed my face, soaking my overlong hair. The grip around my wrist tightened.

"Hurry up."

My father's face appeared in a flash of lightning, emaciated, scowling. His lantern flickered feebly. I tried to dig my heels into the dirt, but weeks of rain had turned it all to mud and I slid along, arm aching. Mud splashed onto my robe.

"Where are we going?"

"To bury this damned curse once and for all." He hauled me through beds of milkweed that caught at our clothes. "The gods must have been angry at man the day they made us."

He had come to my room, had stood in the doorway and looked around as I had always hoped he would. But he was never home, was always away fighting, or doing his duty, or whatever was truly the count of Esvar's job. Iwa always had a glib answer for where father was, and the deadpan way he lied made it easier to believe.

"What are you doing?" Father had asked, though he need not have. His eyes ran over the Errant board. "Where's Iwa?"

"Out in the stables, Father," I had said. "Horses don't like storms."

He hadn't answered, had stepped inside, his sandals making a sound louder than thunder on the old wood. Pinned to the high collar of his robe was the elegant silver eye he always wore. I had asked Iwa what it meant, if it was a symbol of the Laroth house, but he had just shaken his head. Iwa wasn't good with words.

My father had knelt before me then, his hand resting on the hilt of his dagger. He did not look at the game, did not see the Zambuck Manoeuvre I had carefully constructed, did not see the intricate line of defence or the skill it took to play two sides of the same game without cheating. Instead he looked at me, *looked*, not saw, and fiddled with the leather binding on his dagger.

"How old are you, Darius?" he asked.

"Thirteen, Father. It was my birthday last month."

"Thirteen." The word must have tasted foul, for he screwed up his face. "So many years." His fingers tightened around the blade. "Are you happy?"

"Sometimes."

"What makes you happy?"

I stared at the Errant board. "Being smarter than Iwa. He hasn't won a game for months. No one else will play."

"Girls?"

A flush had stolen into my cheeks, and I shook my head.

"Well, that is something."

The leather hilt creaked in his tightening grip. I could not recall ever seeing him smile, and now his lips were pressed so thin they might have been just a line painted on his face. He was pale, and a sheen of sweat covered his brow. He hadn't looked well since arriving from gods knew where he had been for the last two seasons. I found myself hoping he was sick, that mould would settle in his lungs as the doctors said it had settled in mine. Who could be surprised, they said, when the house was rotting.

I stared at the dagger and he followed my gaze. There was some uneasiness in the air, some anguish I could not grasp. Thirteen and I had not yet Maturated. Perhaps it was disappointment I could feel. Once again, his weak and pitiful son had let him down.

Then with an abruptness that made me jump, he tore his hand from the hilt of his dagger and smiled a sickly, awful smile. "Come, let's go," he said, gripping my wrist and yanking me up from my place. A flailing leg kicked the Errant board and sent the pieces rolling across the floor. "While Iwa is busy."

"But it's pouring! Iwa said—"

"Damn it, boy, Iwa is not your father. I am."

DAY SIX

23. HANA

The nightmare was repeating.

From atop the great walls of Mei'lian, we watched the army approach. Not hidden in darkness this time, but marching across the plain in the predawn light, slow, swaggering and relentless, Katashi at their head. He was a tall slash of black and crimson upon the grassland with Hacho rising from his back like a banner.

General Ryoji and I stood in company with the other generals and councillors. Hade had a thumb hooked into his sash and a troubled cleft between his brows. It had not been there the night before when his hands had run all over my body, when I had sat astride him and bit my lip to keep from moaning. I could still feel him there, filling me in a way only Katashi had done before.

I spread my fingers upon the glistening stone parapet and tried not to think about either of them. But Katashi was marching to our gates and there had yet been no sign of Kimiko.

"This isn't going to end well," I said.

"No," General Ryoji agreed. "But the city is as ready as it can be."

"As ready as Shimai was?"

He didn't answer.

All around us, archers clogged the parapet. They and the ranks of heavily armoured soldiers in the street below were all that remained of Mei'lian's standing battalion. The rest of the defence was made of citizens, of labourers and smiths and bakers and scribes and children, so many children lined up in a tangled web of bucket chains running from every well this side of the Silk Quarter.

I had prayed all night that time might halt, but the sun rose steadily in spite of me, its sharp rays gilding the armour of Katashi's traitor soldiers. Many of his Pikes wore black as they had always done and moved like shadows through the sun shower.

A symphony of slamming shutters erupted from the city below. Panicked citizens were taking to the street with their belongings, and I watched them between the obscuring buildings. A family, small children herded ahead like lambs, one bounding around as though this was a new game. An old woman joined them. Then the family disappeared to be replaced by two young men with neatly cropped hair carrying a chest between them. On any other day, these people might still have been asleep, or at breakfast, not running through the streets in fear of their lives.

The Otakos had once been their gods. Now we were their curse.

"He's carrying a white flag!"

My attention snapped back to the advancing army

"A white flag?"

"A white flag!"

I leant forward, elbows on the parapet. It really was a white flag, held aloft. Katashi had tied it around Hacho's upper limb.

A few steps away along the wall, General Vareen chuckled. "He wants to surrender?"

"No," I said. "There is no way he wants to surrender, not after what happened in Shimai. It has to be a trick."

"Maybe he wants to talk," Ryoji said.

The hum of speculation buzzed back and forth along the wall and down into the city. Soldiers who had previously stood still now shifted uneasily. This was not how approaching armies usually behaved.

"He's almost in range," Ryoji said. "Does he want us to take his men down?"

"Maybe he has misjudged the distance," General Vareen replied.

"Katashi Otako is the greatest archer you have ever seen," I said. "He hasn't misjudged the distance."

Minister Bahain shot me a challenging look. "We have archers enough who could make that distance. Kill him."

General Vareen snorted. "And face his full fury when our archers miss?"

"They won't miss."

"At this distance, they will miss. We ought to hear what he has to say first."

"There is little dignity shouting to a traitor on the field, General."

"Then by all means, Minister," came the general's reply. "Go out to meet him. Take a pavilion and some tea."

Katashi stopped, and behind him his army gathered. For a moment no one moved, then a quick burst of flame flared from his hands, there and gone in a breath. Our soldiers flinched back.

"Damn theatrical bastard," General Vareen muttered. He cleared his throat and shouted, "You already have our attention. What do you want?"

A Pike stepped forward. I squinted, trying to make out face or form, but they were all varying sizes of ants from the top of the walls. Only Katashi stood out, his crimson robe glorious.

"Before you stands the victorious army of His Imperial Majesty Emperor Katashi Otako, third of his name, the true emperor of Kisia," the Pike yelled up to us. "I, Captain Chalpo, bear His Majesty's message. Katashi Otako does not want to burn the capital of his empire. But he will."

Katashi stood proud, unmoving while the captain relayed his message.

"Emperor Katashi Otako does not want to kill loyal Kisians, but he will. Emperor Katashi Otako does not want to have to fight for his birthright, but if you make him do so, he will. Surrender Mei'lian. Surrender the Crimson Throne. Surrender the traitor Kin

Ts'ai, and Mei'lian and all its people will go unharmed. Look to the horizon and see the fate of Shimai. Look to your emperor and see that he is lost. If you wish to save your city and your lives, then surrender. If not, take these hours to bolster your defence, and tomorrow we will see whose side the gods are on. You have one day."

A hiss ran along the walls, mingled disbelief and relief rolling off every tongue. It was all too clever a play. Our soldiers would have fought today. But getting their courage up again tomorrow was something else entirely. A day was a long time to dream of surrender.

"We do not bow to threats," General Vareen called back. "And we do not bow to traitors."

Captain Chalpo leant close to Katashi and then returned to his proud pose. "Emperor Katashi is no traitor. Emperor Katashi Otako is the rightful emperor of Kisia."

The words rang out, but before General Vareen could reply, Captain Chalpo leant toward Katashi once again. Every soldier waited in silence, our whole army his captive audience.

"Emperor Katashi Otako also demands the return of his empress, Lady Hana Otako," the captain shouted. "Send her with your surrender, and your city and your families will be safe."

Every soldier on the battlements stood a little more stiffly to attention. I could imagine every eye turning toward me.

General Vareen cleared his throat. "Lady Hana Otako is the empress of Emperor Kin Ts'ai and will not be given up any more than this city."

More whispering down on the plain, then: "Emperor Katashi Otako is loath to have to correct you, General," Captain Chalpo shouted. "But under tradition, Lady Hana belongs to him. The marriage between Lady Hana and Emperor Kin is unconsummated, but as Lady Hana has already lain with Emperor Katashi Otako, she belongs to him by law."

My cheeks burned hotter even than Katashi's fire.

"Whatever lies you spin, we will not surrender this city," the general shouted back.

"Then you have until tomorrow."

Upon the plain, neither Katashi nor Captain Chalpo moved again. The white flag fluttered in the wind and the Pikes shifted restlessly, but there was no sign they meant to attack.

General Vareen gave orders. Half the men to stay, half to rest, eyes on Katashi at all times and frequent messengers to run to the palace with news. Governor Ohi walked past, not even nodding in respect let alone bowing to me. Minister Bahain followed, the depth of his bow belied by the satirical gleam in his eyes.

Unable to bear the weight of so many gazes, I turned, head held high, and strode toward the stairs.

Katashi was playing with me.

In the bright light of morning, Darius was a different man, no longer the godlike image of perfection that had long lived in my memory. He sat in the middle of the floor. His robe was filthy, his face was cut, and his hair was a mess, yet he wore the blood and dirt with the same elegance that had amazed me as an awkward girl. It was infuriating. As infuriating as how he kept on shifting pieces around the Errant board instead of acknowledging my presence, just as though I were seven years old again.

"I wish I could say you were looking well, Darius," I said. "But decidedly you are not."

"I would reply in kind, lamb," he said without looking up. "But it would be a lie. You are glowing. War suits you."

It was a slap in the face, gently spoken. And he kept playing, slowly moving one piece and then another in their purposeless dance across the board.

When I did not reply, he looked up. "Is the Otako motto not 'We conquer, you bleed'?"

"It is certainly Katashi's, thanks to you."

I had not moved from the door, and he pinned me there with his sharp gaze. "Thanks to me? I marked your cousin out of self-defence. Malice has some skill with twisting people's emotions so they develop gifts of use to him, but I have no such talent. Katashi is Vengeance because the need to avenge his father saturated his soul. And that, my dear, had nothing at all to do with me."

Fury at such a dismissal of his guilt seared through me. "Are you trying to justify your actions?" I hissed.

"No. I don't need to justify anything to you. It would be a point-less waste of breath even if I did."

He looked back down at his game, leaping some pieces a little awkwardly with his left hand. Despite the strength of his voice, it was a hollow man who sat before me, dark rings beneath his eyes. Endymion might call it justice. Here a man who had caused so much suffering, tormented at last.

Except that he had been tormented as long as I had known him, I had just never seen it before. Never seen how much Malice had worn him down and suffocated him. How much Malice had bro-ken him.

"How is His Majesty?" he said, focussing on his game.

I tried to remind myself that he had never set out to harm me, nor even to harm Katashi. But I had agreed that night in the Valley that Darius and Malice were too dangerous to be left alive, and see what had come of it. "Alive."

He did not look up again. "And how are you?"

"You ought not ask that question."

"Why not? I'm not the one who put a knife to your parents."

There were so many things I wanted to say, wanted to shout, to scream, but all the words clumped in my mouth. It was too late. He had played his part for better or worse, a truth known only to the gods themselves.

"Kin is my problem now," I said, approaching to kneel on the other side of the Errant board. "But I did not come here to discuss him with you."

"Then why did you come, lamb?" he said, the mocking light in his eyes unmistakable as he went on shifting piece after piece across the board with little pause.

"To make a deal with you."

Click. Click. Click. He didn't look up.

"Darius?"

"What sort of deal?"

No mocking now, no sneering use of my old nickname. The pieces continued their halting dance across the board.

"Your help in return for your freedom."

He set a piece down hard, knocking over a second. There he froze, the wooden soldier pinched between the whitening tips of his fingers. "I don't want my freedom."

"Then what do you want?"

During the long silence that followed, he kept the Errant piece caught to the board. I waited, fascinated. Even his once-so-captivating violet eyes were rimmed with shadows.

Without answering, he started to play again.

I grabbed the board and yanked it toward me. Pieces toppled. Darius snarled, the sound bestial, raw. "Leave me alone," he said and made a lunge for the board.

The wooden soldiers scattered as I tucked it behind my back. "I came to talk to you not to watch you play," I said. "Where did you get this damn thing, anyway?"

Darius returned to his graceful pose like he was curling himself back inside a shell. "Someone took pity on me," he said.

"You do look piteous."

That smile, a shadow of its former self. "And to Hana goes the round."

"Is everything a game to you?"

"Call it a simpler way of looking at the world. And simply put, my dear, I don't want to play anymore. So why don't you take your deal and offer it to someone else."

He held out his left hand for the board. His fingers were dirty and crusted with blood, his once-manicured nails torn.

"I am minded to take the board with me," I said, "if you will not help me get Katashi back."

"The Great Fish is no longer under my control. He too is your problem now."

"You may no longer have any power over him, but there must be something you know that can help. You made him. Can he be... unmade?"

"No."

"You are quick to answer. Are you so sure?"

"Yes." He looked up, no expression beyond fatigue in his eyes. "Katashi is dying."

I almost dropped the board. "What?"

"I said that your great cousin is dying, my dear, and there is nothing I can do about that either. Console yourself with your new conquest and be satisfied."

My cheeks burned and I looked away. "How are you so heartless?"

"Heartless?" he said, seeming to sneer at himself. "I used to think I was."

The words hung awkwardly. I knew a truth he did not, but a child he knew nothing about was a poor bargaining tool for help he could not give me.

Dying. I did not want to dwell on the word, but it filled my heart to bursting and my thoughts to screaming, and I could not keep all that might have been from choking me with grief. Grief I could throw right back at him.

"You will not even try? Not even for Kimiko if you will not do it for me?"

Darius looked up at me, scowling through his lashes. "I told you there is nothing I can do. It is already too late."

"You will not even try for the chance to see her again?" I said, grasping desperately for something, anything that might tempt him. "Or if you are so keen on dying, I could order your execution if you'll help me."

"I can get that without helping."

"Then go die and I will send Kimiko your head! Shall I send her a message as well? Or just my congratulations?"

I wished the words unsaid as they left my lips, but his eyes flashed and I bit down an apology. The first rule of being an emperor was to act like one.

With care, Darius got to his feet, brushing his only hand down the skirt of his dirty robe to ensure it settled correctly, creases and all.

"You think you play hard, little girl?" he said. "You think you are the only one who suffers? I never asked to be your guardian. I never asked to be your god. I looked after you. I fought for you. I lost everything for you, and all you see is what you made me inside that head of yours. And now you want *me* to make reparation?"

I flinched as he thrust out his right arm, sticking his bandaged stump into my face. "Everything Kin said about your family was right. And I thought *my* name was poison."

The neat linen wrappings smelt faintly of liquorice root and scorched hair. I had begged him for help and he had stuck his arm into Katashi's fire.

Darius stepped back. "I can't save him, but I'll tell you how to stop him burning the city if you give me what I want. But it is not Kimiko."

"Then what do you want?" I asked, managing to force the words out through my constricting throat.

"You to let Malice go."

"Let him go?"

"That's what I said."

"And when he attacks us?"

He shook his head. "He won't. I'm the only thing he wants now, but he can't stay. He's in danger here. Endymion too."

"We are all in danger."

"From Katashi, yes, but I'm not talking about Katashi."

"Then who?"

"Father Kokoro. He wants us dead, and trust me I know the look of a fanatic when I see it. He won't let us go now he has us all so close and in his power."

I ought not to have laughed, but I couldn't help myself, so comical was the scene I imagined. Father Kokoro wielding a sword. "I know he hates you, but he's a priest. He wouldn't kill you."

Darius scowled at me. "*Priest* is just a word. He was in here only last night trying to manipulate me into killing my brothers and then myself. I feel he would have done better to fill Endymion with his bile, if he weren't so afraid of him. But regardless of your opinion about our dear Kokoro, my demand stands. If you want information, then you let Malice go."

"Let him go? Darius, he betrayed me. He hurt you. That man is the root of all our suffering and you want me to let him go?"

"Those are my terms."

"But why?"

A little sneer curled his lips. "I will not discuss my reasons with you. We are past that, Hana. Far past. But if I can forgive him enough to make this choice, then so can you. It's the only way you're getting another word out of me."

I threw up my hands. "Fine. He is free to go. If he can manage to walk."

His brows rose into elegant arches that made the filth on his face look so wrong.

"Withdrawal," I said. "Right now I doubt he cares if the city burns to the ground around him."

He made his way toward a collection of large wooden chests against one wall. He opened one, not at random but knowing what each would contain, because this was where he had lived after he abandoned me.

How pathetic that sentiment sounded now.

"Give this to him," Darius said, returning with a narrow box, something like the size of a brush and ink set. He held it out. "Or to one of his Vices if he cannot manage himself."

I tucked the confiscated Errant board into my sash and took the box. "What is it?"

"What he needs."

It was heavy, formed of smooth cedar and delicately painted with hundreds of tiny blossoms and a pendulous bough of wisteria.

"And Endymion," he said. "I know you will not let him go, but the man who looked after him is here, Brother Jian. Let him see the boy. He wants to help."

"Done," I said. "Now how do I save the city?"

Darius returned to the table. "You need to give Katashi what he wants. He is Vengeance, yes? And where does vengeance end?"

I stared at him for a long time, turning his words over in my mind as I turned the box in my hands. "When it is sated," I said at last, not liking those words.

"How fortunate that you picked up some of my intelligence along the way," he said. "Yes, when he wins. The closer he gets to his goal, the faster and harder he is burning. But if you give him the Crimson Throne, if you let him win, the fire will die and take him with it."

"Are you sure?"

"As sure as I am about anything. I don't gamble without good cause."

"And does he know?"

"That he's dying? Yes. That success will kill him? No." He smoothed the fabric of his robe, running his only hand down one thigh. "The councillors will not agree," he said. "But it is the only way. One way or another, you have to give him what he wants." His violet eyes cut unblinking into my soul. "An Otako on the Crimson Throne."

I tapped the wooden box in my hand. "I see."

"You will."

"And you will see Kimiko again whether you want to or not," I said. "She'll come, Darius. If she still wants you, go with her, make a life far away from here."

Again those brows rose. "Relationship advice from a woman who's lying with her husband's general and carrying his enemy's child?"

I stared at that beautiful face with its mocking lilt, all too aware of the thin paper screens in the door behind me. "You...you can feel it?"

"No, I am not Endymion. But you're standing differently, your breasts are bigger, and you keep touching your stomach. It isn't difficult to read people, yet sometimes I think I must be the only one who knows the language."

I snatched my hand away from my stomach, clenching the fingers into a fist. If I gave birth to a son, he would be a full-blood Otako heir to the Crimson Throne.

"For what it's worth, I'm sorry." Darius held out his good hand. "You have my Errant board."

The emperor's apartments were grandly decorated but sparsely furnished. For every ornate fretwork shutter and embroidered screen, there was even more empty space, filled only with the most functional of furniture—a plain lap table, a storage chest, a low desk. It was Kin, this space the full embodiment of his dichotomy.

"Master Kenji?"

There was no answer. The matting crackled underfoot as I made my way on slow steps to next room. No Master Kenji, but his patient lay alone on the bed—a restless figure surrounded by burning braziers.

I slid the door closed behind me, once again shutting myself in with the stink of sweat and the honey-based burn salve I was fast coming to hate. There was no change. Kin's face was as creased and pained as it had been before, aged far beyond his years. Bandages covered most of his wounds, but where they did not, the flesh was angry, red and weeping.

"Damn you," I hissed under my breath, setting a hand on his hot forehead.

As though sensing my touch, Kin muttered and threw his head to the side, crushing his burned cheek to the pillow. He let out a whimper and started to talk, fast and wild, his words nothing but a string of sounds with no meaning.

"Kin?" I said. "Can you hear me? It's Hana."

"There's no point trying to talk to him," came Kimiko's voice, though I could not see her. "People suffering from fever are not really there."

"What do you mean?" I said, spinning slowly to observe the room.

"I mean that they retreat into some other part of their heads, because to be present while the body goes through such pain would drive them mad."

I thought of Darius and his Errant board. He had not spoken a word after I gave it back.

Kimiko emerged from the shadows. Her bright eyes gleamed. "What is it you want from me, Hana? Why threaten Darius's life to get my attention?"

"I need you to do something for me."

"Need me to do something?" she echoed. "Something I don't want to do then, else you might have just asked."

"I'm past asking."

A snort of laughter broke over Kin's restless moan. "Of course you are." She bowed, the gesture just mocking enough to make me seethe. "What can I do to serve you, my lady?"

"You're going to arrange me a meeting with General Manshin, or the next time you see Darius it will be just his head."

"You talk big, but you won't kill him."

"Perhaps not, but Katashi will. The gift of Lord Darius Laroth might buy us some more time. It is a sacrifice I would have to make for Kisia."

She was silent for a moment. "Katashi would be proud of you, Hana. You've learnt to fight for your right to rule even if it means throwing your family under the cart."

"A leader does what must be done."

Kimiko came closer, intricate shadows passing across her face as she stepped beneath a fretwork lantern. "Yes," she said. "That was his excuse too."

"Will you do it or not?"

"What exactly is it you want me to do? I am not in General Manshin's confidence."

"I want you to go into Katashi's camp, unseen, and bring General Manshin through the city wall. I must meet with him. You'll have to find somewhere safe."

"So hardly anything, really," she said.

"Hardly anything," I agreed, ignoring the sarcasm. "And if you are seen, you may pretend you are carrying a message from your brother. No one would risk Katashi's wrath by harming his twin without cause."

For the second time, she clasped my face between her soft, cool hands, and the eyes that looked into mine were so like Katashi's I could have believed him with me.

"I'll do it," she said. "But I don't want just Darius."

"What else?"

"Malice."

There was no kindness in her face. She spoke his name with twisted lips as though it were poison.

"You are not the first to make that request," I said, needing to tread carefully now. "He is no longer mine to trade."

She asked the question with one exquisitely arched brow.

"Darius," I said. "I needed information. In return, I said I would free Malice."

The little woman stood still, considering me with those bright eyes. Despite the plain black robe, Kimiko was all grace, regal in a way I knew I would never be.

"Very well," she said at last. "It does not matter. Wherever Darius goes, Malice will follow eventually. Like my brother, my vengeance knows patience."

I wanted to ask what she meant. I wanted to ask about the child she carried, about her plans, about her feelings, to know where she would go and what she would do, but those were not words to speak. Not here. Not now. Not to this proud woman crushed so often beneath life's heel.

"I will bring your general." Kimiko turned, and walking away added, "But you will get nothing more from me, Cousin. I pity you. Power is a lonely thing."

Without waiting for a reply, she drew a breath and stepped through the panelling as though it were a mere illusion.

Behind me, the door slid. "Oh! My lady, I did not know you were here." Master Kenji, perfectly timed. No doubt he had heard voices, though he would pretend he had not.

"I came to see His Majesty," I said, dragging my eyes from where Kimiko had vanished into the woodwork. "How are your other patients?"

"We've lost another two, my lady. Father Kokoro is with them now."

"That's six since we arrived."

"Yes, it is fortunate that it is a relatively smooth journey through the tunnel, or it would have been more."

"Fortunate indeed. Has there been any change?"

Master Kenji crossed the floor, the skirt of his plain robe dragging with a hush. "He has the fever, as you see," he said, taking up his emperor's slack hand to feel the pulse at his wrist. "Not good, not good," he muttered, replacing the hand and leaning down to lift Kin's undamaged eyelid. "What a change ten minutes can make."

"What is it? What's wrong?"

The man looked up, confusion marring his seriousness. "Wrong? No, my lady, nothing is wrong. He has responded faster than expected to the previous treatment, and I am unprepared. Help me to prop him up."

"There are maids aplenty who could assist you," I said, keeping myself from taking a step back.

"Maids don't mind taking away his dirty sheets and rags; they have qualms about touching their god."

God Emperor. The lie that held Kisia together. The lie that granted so much power.

"Then I'll send in one of his guards," I said, wanting nothing less than to touch the man who murdered my family, to help him. "They have a lot of experience with gods."

He would think me heartless. Kimiko already did, and Darius had all but spat in my face. *Everything Kin said about your family was right.*

Back out on the fourth round, Tili was waiting for me, poised like a statue beneath the hanging lanterns. Their shadows scattered around her feet like beads of jet.

"I need one of those big over-robes the night ladies use," I said before she had completed her bow. "And as soon as it's dark, I'll need a palanquin and four carriers I can trust. No one can know."

Her eyes grew wide and she looked a question at me before dropping her gaze. Doubt crept in. I could be walking into a trap. There was no way to be sure of Kimiko's intentions, no way to be sure she would not gamble Darius on a plan of her own. She was wild. Alone. Desperate.

"I'll need you with me," I added. "Dress appropriately for accompanying a night lady on a visit."

"Yes, my lady."

I nodded dismissal and she left about her mission, leaving me alone with my fears. Down on the third round, servants and courtiers were continuing about their business as though no army camped outside the gates. Mei'lian was the capital. The stronghold. How many of them believed it could not fall to the northern dogs, no matter how many wild stories about Katashi floated through the court? These were people untouched by the everyday world.

General Ryoji came up the stairs. Tili bowed as she passed him, but he seemed not to notice. His steps were loud, hers silent.

"I need two of your most trustworthy men tonight," I said before he had joined me.

"I will give you as many men as you need, but I must ask why."

"A meeting with a general."

Ryoji leant down. "Hana," he whispered. "Manshin is a traitor. It is too dangerous to risk your life on such a chance."

"No, Hade, it is too dangerous not to. Today we are all servants of the empire. Two of your best. I'm taking Endymion too. Make sure your men know. I don't want any trouble."

"Endymion is in no fit state to go anywhere."

"Not yet." I turned Darius's opium box over in my hands. He had meant it for Malice, but Malice could wait. Right now, Kisia needed a prince.

24. ENDYMION

I shivered, cheek to the floor. It was as though ice had replaced every bone in my body and I would never be warm again. Yet despite the cold, my mind was not dormant. There was no silence, no peace. Emotions. Whispers. Numbers. Three in here. Two in the next room. One in the passage outside. Four. Sixteen. One. Eighty-four. I tried to rein it in, but the count just started over. Three. Two. One. Four. Sixteen.

If I could just get my hands around his throat, I'd squeeze, I'd squeeze and squeeze until his eyes bulged. I want to be the last thing he sees before the hells.

Let them come. Let there be an end. Let there be peace.

Help me, Darius. Please. I need you. I need you.

I could no longer distinguish my own thoughts.

The door slid, the hush of the wood running in its velvet groove loud like the thunder outside. Another storm was coming, the rumble rattling the old glass in the window.

"Be careful. If you touch him—"

"I know."

Sullen irritation. Remorse. Pain. A determination that made every muscle ache. I shivered.

"He has been like this since last night?" Hana's voice.

"Yes, my lady, there has been no change." That, Father Kokoro.

"I need him."

I can't take this mess with me.

Pathetic, disgusting freak. All I need is the right time, when everyone is distracted, and I can kill them all. I can rid the world of Empaths.

"You can't take him like that." General Ryoji, though his voice melded with his whispers. *Too risky. Too risky.* "Give up this plan, my lady, I beg you. General Manshin will not listen to anyone but himself."

"He will listen to the true heir to the Crimson Throne. Father Kokoro?"

"Yes, my lady?"

"Fetch your brother."

"My brother?"

"Brother Jian. He tells me he can help."

Going behind my back, Brother?

"Then of course I will bring him at once, my lady."

Brother. The word nagged. It ought to mean something, but though I clawed toward understanding, it was beyond my reach. Seven. Fourteen. Two. Three hundred and four. One million three hundred and ten thousand and twenty-one.

"My lady?"

"Ah, Brother Jian. You said you could help, well now is your chance. I need Takehiko Otako, not this mess. I have opium. Will that help to . . . calm him down? It has always seemed to work well for Malice."

A snort and the glower of Avarice's soul.

"Yes, my lady, I am sure it would, but . . ."

"But?"

"I beg you will let me talk to him first. Let me see what I can do without the drug."

"Very well. You have two hours. I need him dressed and ready to accompany me this evening or this city will burn."

"Yes, my lady."

The door slid, and slid again.

"He's all yours, Brother Jian. Don't let me down."

Again the door.

Souls moved. Seven. Six. Five.

A breeze shifted my hair. Touched my arm. Caressed the rumpled scar of my Traitor's Mark. And in its touch, the taste of another soul.

"Endymion?"

My poor boy, what has happened to you?

It was hard to focus on the blurred face above me, but a red scar glared through the fog, like a hook caught over a dark eye.

"Jian?"

"It's time to wake up," he said.

"Why? Where are we going?"

"Home."

I shook my head slowly, vaguely aware of the stink of vomit nearby. "I don't have a home."

"Home isn't always a place."

"He isn't a child anymore, Jian," Kokoro said. "He Maturated, remember?"

"Yes, but that doesn't make him a monster."

Three. Two. One. Four. Fifteen. One. Eighty-five. *He's both a monster and a freak, just like the other two. Look at this pathetic sack of bile. At least he'll be easy to get rid of.*

"He's killed at least a hundred people in the last month just by touching them," the same voice said out loud. Kokoro again.

"Two hundred and forty-one," I said. "All unworthy of life. I gave them justice." Two hundred and forty-one, and how many of their memories lived within me now? How many of them had I stolen? Had I become?

My teeth began to chatter. I was shaking, my bony shoulder grinding against the floor.

Can you hear me, Endymion? You're a monster. Your father ought to have killed you and rid the world of your curse. You think you're a god? You spit on the gods just by breathing.

"Endymion?"

I did not answer.

"He's cold. Can you send for blankets and hot soup? None of them look well."

A grip on my elbow fought to drag me up, and my vision floated into focus. Jian. Different. Lined. An angry scar marred his face and his hair was gone but for a few stragglers that had escaped the torture. He looked older, more worn, but the look in his dark eyes was the same as ever, the same pity, the same tenderness.

My child, I wish I had done better by you. I wish I had known what you needed.

His hand reached for mine and I slapped it away, scuttling back across the stones.

"Stay away," I said. "Don't touch me."

"Endymion—"

"No, he's right, I'm a monster. You ought to have strangled me as a child and thrown me to the crows." Back to the wall, I clasped my knees, still shivering. "Oh gods, what is wrong with me?"

Jian hushed me, the old man hunched over, approaching on slow, shuffling feet. "You are sick and tired and hungry and nothing else."

"No! You don't understand. I don't know who I am. Who is Endymion? Did I steal his memories?" I held up a shaking hand to hold him off and he came no closer. "I was there the day the Chiltaens tried to take Riyan Bridge. I watched men die, watched their corpses boil beneath the sun, and I can remember the smell. But I remember being told the story too, by a farmer's boy while I sat in the fork of an apple tree. He said six hundred of the emperor's men had been thrown from the bridge to crack their skulls upon the rocks. And I remember you telling me that war with Chiltae would make travel difficult. There was a priest in one of those villages between the Ribbon and the border who wouldn't stop talking about it, and you sent me to feed the ox a second time just so I wouldn't hear what he was saying. But I was there; I'd already seen it. How can I have been there if I was with you? How can I have been with you if I was sitting in an orchard, taking a bite out of a crisp yellow apple before I threw it at the boy's head?"

Every breath rushed in and out of my chest with the fury of a gale and I could not slow it. For a panicked moment, I wondered if it was possible to choke on air.

A fierce slap sent me sideways, my Traitor's Mark stinging. It wasn't Jian before me anymore but Father Kokoro's scowl.

I should never have left him to Laroth back in Shimai. He might have been ruthless in everything else but weak when faced with the truth. Just like his father.

"You're wrong," I said, a trembling hand caught to my stinging cheek. "Darius is not weak."

The slap came back the other way, hitting the opposite cheek. "Your precious brother is as much a freak as you are," Kokoro said. "And he will fail and die like his father."

"Come over here and say that to me," came Avarice's voice from outside my frame of vision.

"Kokoro," Jian warned, and the court priest straightened, uncurling his fingers from fists.

"My apologies, Endymion, that was uncalled for," the man said, his features slipping back into a waxen, empty smile. "It is hard to remain calm when there is an army at the gates and we are running out of time." *This is not over yet, freak; if your brother doesn't kill you, I will.* He stepped back, ushering Jian into the foreground. "He's all yours, Brother. Lady Hana wants him functional, and perhaps if he can help save two hundred and forty-one lives, he might manage to balance the scales."

Who's the whore going to bed to get us out of this mess, I wonder? Manshin would sell every shred of honour he has left for a chance at her, give him—

"—would sell every shred of honour he has left for a chance at her, give him a feisty little whore and he'll nail her down hard. Damn little shit! Get out of my head or I'll make sure you lose yours."

Kokoro did not move and did not speak, just glared at me from beyond arm's reach.

"I think you should leave, Kokoro," Jian said quietly. "Unless you want your *feisty little whore* to be disappointed in you."

He grunted. "You take my words out of context. She is not *my* feisty little whore."

"Perhaps not, but Lady Hana has charged me with—"

"Be careful, *Brother*," Kokoro growled. "Much more of this and I will make sure you end up back in that cell."

"Out. Do not make me call Lady Hana back to kick you out herself."

Father Kokoro did not say farewell or wish Jian luck, just went out in a cloud of fury. The door slid closed on hushed feet behind him.

"He serves the gods in his own way," Jian said after Kokoro had gone. "Emperor Lan appointed him but never let him do more than officiate at court functions. Emperor Kin was kind enough to keep him and give him more scope. But he didn't like your father and he doesn't like your brother. I'd hoped he would see that you aren't like them, but I was wrong."

How could I have been so naïve? All those years trying to stave off the Maturation and now this.

Amid the sea of thoughts that broke around me, his words stood out. "Maturation?" I said. "You know about Maturation?"

"I . . . yes."

He felt as troubled as he sounded. "You don't have to speak," I said. "I can hear everything. 'As if the late lord wasn't enough, the master had to fall in with a leech who would suck him dry if given half a chance.' I think that's Avarice. And the guard outside the door is thinking about the maid who just walked past. There is one man in the next room, six on the landing. Two. Sixty-four. Two hundred and nine thousand six hundred and fifty-five souls in the city. One million three hundred and ten thousand and fifteen in Kisia. One million three hundred and ten thousand and nine. Eight. Five. One. Two. One million—"

"Stop, please!"

"I bet the general wouldn't even notice if I wasn't here for five minutes. I could be dead by tomorrow. Like the man who's rutting the empress can complain about me taking a maid."

"Endymion."

"They can't all be dead. You can't burn a whole battalion. I wonder if it hurts. I've heard men scream when tied to the stake. One million three hundred and nine thousand nine hundred and ninety-eight. One million three hundred and nine thousand nine hundred and ninety-eight. One million three hundred and nine thousand nine hundred and ninety-seven. One million three hundred and nine thousand nine hundred and ninety-eight. One million—"

"Stop!"

Brother Jian's shout filled the room, and when the word was done, he stood before me breathing fast, tears streaking his cheeks. "Dear gods, Endymion, please don't do this."

He had a box in his hands.

"That belongs to Master Darius," Avarice said. "His stash."

Jian turned his attention on the old Vice. Beside him Malice lay asleep or unconscious, his whispers silent. *Is he one of them? I can't do it. Maybe he can. Maybe he can.* "Do you know how it works?"

"Yes. But you'll have to untie me."

Can I trust him? I don't want to do this. Please, Endymion, just listen to me, you need to calm down. Focus on everything I taught you.

"You taught me that I was fragile," I said. "But you're the fragile ones. You're just numbers. I'm a god. One million three hundred and nine thousand nine hundred and ninety-five. One million three hundred and nine thousand nine hundred and ninety—"

Jian dropped the box at Avarice's feet. It cracked upon the floor and an opium pipe rolled free of its blue silk cage. Lamp. Spare bowls. Another box.

"Help me."

For a price. Avarice nodded. "Only if I can keep what's left."

"It is not mine to give away."

"Neither is it Lady Hana's."

Their words were like flashes of light through the mire of numbers. One. Sixteen. Four. One million three hundred and nine thousand nine hundred and ninety-two.

"Do it," Jian said. "I need my boy back."

25. HANA

It was dark inside the palanquin, only shreds of light creeping in from the street, from lanterns and torches and the windows of passing buildings. It fell upon Endymion's side, illuminating the Traitor's Mark on his cheek. I stared at it, at the raised ridges and the red skin, some edges puckered, others stretched. It might be healing, might eventually fade to a flat pale scar, but there had been so little skill, so little care expended in its creation, that it would always be ugly.

He hadn't spoken since joining me, had barely moved. Brother Jian had done his job well. The boy was dressed in layers of crisp silk and a pair of fresh sandals, his hair brushed and pinned and his face cleaner than I had ever seen it. Even the smell of the opium had been all but washed away, discernible only to a nose that knew it was there. He looked like the prince he ought to have been. Like the prince I needed him to be.

The carriers slowed to a stop, and one of Ryoji's guards drew back the side curtain. Rain dripped down his face. It drenched the black headscarf he wore as a member of a night lady's entourage, sticking it to his forehead. "We're here, my lady," he said. "There's no sign of anyone."

The man touched the hilt of a knife concealed in his tunic. It was not discreet, but it was not unusual for a night lady's companions to be armed with more than just a modest dagger.

"No one at all?" I said. "Lady Kimiko?"

"I'm here."

She stepped through the door, the latch appearing from her gut. The soldier stared.

"Good," I said and stepped out of the palanquin. Tili was immediately at my side, pulling forward a hood wet with rain. Her skilled hands worked quickly to straighten my voluminous robe, black from its tight collar to its wide shapeless hem. With broad bell-shaped sleeves, it was as hideous as it was distinctive, the whole thing little more than a black silk tent, easily able to hide a sword. Common whores might need to show off their wares to get business, but a high-class night lady showed hers to no one who could not pay. It was an exclusive business, entertaining Mei'lian's nobility.

Tili did not speak while she worked. I had warned her we could be walking into a trap, but night ladies always travelled with an entourage, with a maid, a guard, and an assistant to broker each contract and deal with the money.

"Wait here," I said to Endymion once Tili had finished. "If you hear nothing within ten minutes, the carriers will take you back to the palace. If the captain returns, then I'm ready for you."

He nodded, but whether he truly understood I could not tell.

"Don't trust me, Cousin?" Kimiko's smile was broad and amused, her eyes sparkling in the torchlight. "I wonder why not."

"Because I can't rely on trust."

Rain fell on my hood as I strode between the mounting block and the door. Next to the house, the wall of Mei'lian rose, imposing. "It belongs to the sister of one of Manshin's most trusted officers," Kimiko said. "Apparently she married a physician, so they live on the edge of what Manshin called 'society.'"

She held out her hand. "Shall we?"

"I think I would rather ring if it's all the same to you." I gestured to Tili to pull the bell. She did so, gripping the elaborate chain to send a pair of bells jingling on the other side of the door.

Footsteps thudded beyond. I pulled myself up to my full height and let out a slow breath, my heart seeming to race in time with the rain dancing at my feet. The door opened. A lantern was lifted into my eyes, and there in the light was a familiar face. I had last seen it drenched and pale, lying on the riverbank at Shimai.

"You!" I said.

Captain Terran was taken aback. "Me?"

I put back my hood, heedless of the rain, and his jaw went slack. "Lady Hana!" A hurried bow followed, a hiss proving his injury had not entirely healed. But the bow was a good sign.

"The general—?"

Captain Terran pressed a finger to his lips. "Come inside."

I stepped past him, Tili and Captain Dendzi right behind me. The house was dark but for a pair of night lanterns, their thick fretwork covers cutting the light into intricate shapes. They flickered on my sleeve as I strode the length of the passage to a reception room at the end, its closed screens lit gold from inside.

Once again, Tili bustled around me, this time untying the strings of the over-robe with quick, practiced tugs. I had spent hours preparing for this moment, standing still while Tili and two other maids constructed the imperial face around me—full armour, longsword, my white wedding sash, and Kin's Imperial Sash, tied in a complex nest of luck twists worn only by the emperor himself.

The robe fell away. Tili straightened the pin in my hair and the fall of my sash, before pronouncing me ready with a nod. She slid the doors and stepped aside, leaving me to stand upon the threshold, head raised, channelling every shred of Otako arrogance I could muster.

A little chuckle was the first response. General Manshin sat alone at a low table, one elbow resting on the wood and his eyes alive with amusement.

I lifted my chin. Calm was the only response worthy of an

empress. His smile did not fade, but he got to his feet with all the awkwardness of a portly man getting on in years.

"Lady Hana," he said. "I am honoured that you have gone to such great lengths to impress me. Last time we met, I was rather beneath your attention."

"General Manshin," I said. "Who, beside Katashi Otako, is not?"

His second laugh was humourless in tone. "Indeed. I hope you mean to join me for refreshments."

"Yes, but if you will remain standing for a moment longer, General, I have someone to introduce to you." I nodded to Captain Dendzi, and he went back along the passage.

"I am all curiosity, my lady."

Back along the passage, Captain Terran held open the street door. Rain darted in, golden needles in the lantern light. Then Endymion came, a hollow shell of a man dressed in the finest silk.

"You might already have met him with another name," I said as Endymion came slowly along the passage. "But allow me to introduce my brother, Lord Takehiko Otako."

I entered the room so Endymion could follow, but he too stopped in the doorway. This time General Manshin did not laugh, not at this boy with his crimson sash standing out like a bloody gash, with his Traitor's Mark and his midnight-blue robe shining with dozens of tiny silver stars. It was impossible to hide how ill he looked, how emaciated, but he neither blinked nor turned aside his gaze under the general's sudden scrutiny.

"Takehiko Otako?" General Manshin said. "That is not possible."

"It is possible because when faced with two young children, the man who assassinated my mother, my father, and the rest of my brothers found he had a conscience after all," I said.

"You'll excuse my confusion, my lady, I'm sure," the general said. "But I have seen this young man before. He is the illegitimate son of Nyraek Laroth."

"Yes," I agreed. "He is. But whatever his blood, my father acknowledged him as an Otako and as his true-born heir. To argue that is treason."

No longer amused, General Manshin once again indicated the place opposite him at the table. "I am already called the traitor general, I believe. Treason is my forte."

I knelt, Endymion beside me, silent and staring. General Manshin nodded to the serving girl. "I think tea would be a good place to start," he said. "And while I drink, you can tell me what it is that you want, my lady."

The girl poured tea, and Manshin's eyes swung to appreciate the curve of her hips. There was nothing the girl could do but keep serving, feigning innocence though her cheeks burned.

"I don't think Kisia would take to an emperor with the Traitor's Mark branded on his cheek," he said abruptly, not shifting his gaze from the girl.

"They won't be called upon to do so," Endymion said. It was the first time he had spoken since arriving, and I was glad he didn't slur. "There is only one man who can rule Kisia, and he is already on the throne."

"Which throne?"

"The only one that matters."

This was not the conversation I had planned. It had been a risk to bring him, but Endymion had something I did not, something that made him more worthy of being listened to. A cock.

"So you are a supporter of Emperor Kin, Lord Takehiko," the general said. "I can understand your sister taking such a stance when Emperor Katashi failed to give her what she wanted"—I clenched my fists rather than correct his assumption—"but you I do not understand. You're a bastard-born freak with more power in your signature than any man alive, why not take it?"

"Because I don't want power. I want freedom. Justice. Hope."

General Manshin chuckled, finally turning his eyes from the

poor girl. "He's a pretty boy, Lady Hana, a pretty stunt, but I am not so easily impressed. I did not join your cousin for ideology."

"Neither did you join him to watch Kisia burn to the ground."

The general reached for his tea. "No," he said. "But in that regard, I appear to have picked the winning side."

My tea remained untouched. "And when he dies?" I asked. "What then? Who will he leave the throne to then?"

"His son, one might assume, once he marries and produces heirs."

I tightened my hands to fierce fists. "If his chosen bride survives beyond the sevenday. And he had better find one quickly. He's already dying."

It was a hit. General Manshin froze, his features caught in a half smile.

"He didn't tell you?" I said. "How careless of him. I suppose he feared you might abandon him if you knew you were fighting for nothing."

"Who told you he is dying?"

"Lord Laroth. And since he made him what he is, I rather think he should know."

Silence fell over us like a smothering cloak. General Manshin's fingers tightened about his tea bowl. They were long fingers with neatly kept nails, and if he'd ever owned battle calluses, they had long since succumbed to the prevailing fashion for washing in wine and goats' milk. But he would have to fight if Katashi died—if Kin died. Without heirs, there was no strong candidate for the throne beyond Kin's absent cousin, leaving the generals to scrap amongst themselves for power.

"I do not come here to ask you to fight for Emperor Kin, General," I said after sufficient time had passed. "I come to ask you to fight for me."

"For you?"

The room was hot and still and I was sweating. Again I let a beat of silence pass before I answered. "I am the legitimate daughter of Emperor Lan Otako. I am to be the empress of Emperor Kin Ts'ai. And perhaps most importantly, I am the cousin of Emperor Katashi Otako and the mother of the only child he will ever have."

General Manshin put his bowl back on the table with a snap. "Child?" he said.

"Yes, General. You know how long I rode with Katashi's army. How often he came to my tent. You need not act surprised."

As though invited, he ran his gaze down my body, halted only by the presence of the table between us. "Not surprised," he said, his stare lingering. "But what assurance can you give me? It may not survive. It may be a girl. One does not change allegiance on a chance."

"Lord Takehiko is an Empath, ask him if you don't believe me."

This brought his gaze from my body. "More witchcraft? Even if I accept that there are many things I do not understand, he is your brother. He is on your side. He would lie to me."

"I don't lie."

The words were quiet but as hard as stone.

"No?" General Manshin leant his elbows on the table. "Tell me then, my lord, where have you been these past sixteen years?"

"Lord Nyraek Laroth placed me with a priest called Brother Jian, and we travelled as priests do. When I came of age, he wanted me to take the oath and renounce my family, but I wanted to know who they were first. He took me to Father Kokoro, his brother, hoping I might meet Lord Darius Laroth. Father Kokoro refused. I was imprisoned. I was branded"—he pointed to the ugly branding on his cheek—"and sent into exile. The Vices came for me. I helped Katashi take Koi. Then Katashi sent me to Kin as a test of his honour. Now I am here."

"A colourful life. How many women have you been with?"

"Two."

"Do you like women?"

"Yes."

"How about boys? Do you like boys?"

"Yes."

"How many have you had?"

"None."

"None?"

"None."

"How about your sister?"

"She feels good."

My cheeks reddened, but though General Manshin's eyes crinkled with contained laughter, I sat straight and still, chin resolutely lifted.

"You've had her then? I wish I could say the same."

"Not me. General Hade Ryoji, but I am an Empath. I feel everything."

I gave General Manshin back stare for stare. He was deliberately digging now, but if he thought he owned me, thought he held every card, then he would fight for me. The shame did not matter, only Kisia.

"You're fun, Lord Takehiko," Manshin said. "We should go out and find you a boy to sate that curiosity of yours."

I thought to bring him back to the point but did not speak. Better to let him play out his game, to let him think me vulnerable.

"So, Lord Takehiko who does not lie," he said, swirling the dregs of his tea. "Tell me what your beautiful sister is brewing in that stomach of hers. Digestive distress? Or the first pure-blood Otako for over a hundred years?"

Endymion touched my surcoat, just beneath my paired sashes. "May I?"

"You may," I said.

Fingers splayed, he pressed his palm to the silk. It felt different without the touch of his skin on mine, not the same ingress of cold I had felt back in Kogahaera over the body of the dead Pike. Through the cloth, the sense of intrusion was gentler, the connection different, all muted whispering like a world of secrets at the edge of my hearing.

After a time he sat back. "She is carrying Kisia's future," he said. "And Katashi's heir."

Katashi's heir.

"That is interesting," General Manshin said. "And in an ideal world, a pure-blood Otako would be worth fighting for. But this is not that world. I'm afraid I cannot help you."

The words were a slap. My gut twisted.

"He's afraid," Endymion said. "Captain Terran was not expecting us because General Manshin does not even trust his own men. He is as afraid of them as he is of Katashi. We are the only ones he is not afraid of."

"You are hardly fear-inspiring," Manshin said. "Emperor Kin lies on his deathbed and Mei'lian is all but lost. Katashi might be dying, but on his side of the wall, I am unlikely to do so myself. It will be a massacre. You have offered me nothing but a greater chance of death."

"Marriage," I said.

"Pardon, my lady?"

"You once told me about your granddaughters."

"I have four, the youngest barely out of the cradle."

"And I am carrying Katashi's son. A pure-blood Otako warrior who will sit on the throne when Emperor Kin dies. How many great families in Kisia can claim so close a relationship with the Otakos? Three generations of Chiltaen empresses have left our connections rather thin on the ground, don't you think?"

An open stare. Hungry and intent. "Sichi is my son's eldest. She'll be three at the beginning of the summer. She's a pretty little thing, like her mother. And wise and strong like my son."

"A perfect bride. If you send Captain Terran for parchment and ink, we can draw up the contract now."

For a time, General Manshin did nothing but stare from me to Endymion and back, his gaze eventually coming to rest upon my stomach, his finger tapping the edge of his empty tea bowl.

Betrothal to a prince could elevate a whole family and protect them from the repercussions of his betrayal to Katashi's cause. Yet it was no small thing I asked.

The air was oppressive, thick with the smell of tea and incense and warm coals in their braziers. My head spun like I had drunk too much wine, but I had already done all I could. Now Kisia's fate rested on this man with his thinning hair and his clever eyes, long fingers tapping on his empty bowl, not absently I was sure, but with all the deliberation Darius brought to such a task. Tapping. Tapping. Then suddenly tapping no longer.

"Bring wine," he ordered. "And Terran?"

"Yes, General?" The man was by the door, no emotion discernible in his stance or his expression.

"We need parchment and ink and a discreet scribe."

"Yes, General."

"And a map of Mei'lian."

"Yes, General."

Captain Terran bowed and went out, and in full view of the general, I leant toward Endymion. "Can I trust him, Brother?"

"Yes, Takehiko, do tell us," General Manshin said. "Can I be trusted? Or am I a traitor to the core?"

Increasingly listless and unsteady, Endymion shook his head. "No, you cannot trust him," he said, the words a little slurred. "He is all self-interest. But for now he means to keep his word."

General Manshin smiled broadly. "I really do like this boy," he said. "Such honesty is sadly missing at court. Well, my lady? Do we have a deal?"

"We do."

"Are you sure you want to do this?" Endymion said, his whisper warm against my ear. "There are always other ways."

"This time there is no other way," I said. "Being a leader means making hard choices. I can only hope that one day my son will understand that."

DAY SEVEN

26. HANA

Back in the street, the sun was rising, edging the dark clouds in gold. Again I had hoped that morning would never come, that I could push the sun back below the horizon, but its glow continued to creep across the city.

It was still raining. Water dripped from the palanquin's rain cover and its saturated carriers, each staring ahead like a statue.

"It looks like my time is up," I said as Tili and Endymion joined me in the street. Thanks to Tili, I was once again attired in the shapeless black over-robe.

"My lady," Captain Terran said, bowing as he joined us. "General Manshin has commanded me to remain with you for your protection."

Hoping to appear coldly formal, I lifted my brows. "My protection, Captain? Am I not safe inside my own city?"

There was a pause before he replied. "I will escort you back to the palace. I have my orders."

"If the general is right, then it could happen any moment," Endymion said, his tone dead flat and his eyes flickering. "We can't be standing here when the gates open."

"What?" I turned on him, but his eyes darted about the street.

"It's all right, the walls are tall and strong and the soldiers are here to protect us."

"Endymion?"

"I'm scared. I wish the bad people would go away."

"Endymion!"

"He's coming. He's coming. We can't just stand here. He's coming."

I gripped his shoulders and shook, glad of the silk between his skin and mine. "Endymion!"

The boy frowned and looked down at my robe. "Hana," he said. "You should not stand in the street. Night ladies don't do that."

"To the hells with night ladies," I snapped. "What did you say about the gates?"

"They are going to open."

"How do you know?"

Endymion looked over my shoulder, and I followed his gaze to the fidgeting form of Captain Terran. For a long moment, he stared at me and I stared at him.

Then I said, "Katashi has men inside the city."

A nod, the slightest of movements that might have been little more than a twitch, but it was enough for me.

"One million three hundred and nine thousand eight hundred and ninety-one," Endymion chanted. "One million three hundred and nine thousand eight hundred and ninety-one. One million three hundred and nine thousand eight hundred and eighty-nine."

I thrust Endymion toward the palanquin. "Get in," I said. "You have to get out of here. Tili, you too."

"No, my lady, I will stay with you."

"The city is about to be overrun, Tili, I—"

"Yes, my lady, and my place is at your side." There was a fierce light in her eyes. I could have ordered the guards to take her back to the palace, but I knew all too well how it felt to be powerless.

I nodded.

Captain Dendzi stood waiting. "Go with the palanquin back to the palace," I said. "Don't stop. Don't let anyone get in your way."

The captain bowed. "My lady, our orders are to protect you."

"No, Captain, your orders are to do as I command. You have

to get Endymion back to the palace before the opium wears off, because gods only know what mess he could create out here. And General Ryoji must be warned to prepare immediately for an attack on the palace. Katashi has men inside the city."

Another bow. "Honoured lady, we will take you back to the palace."

"Go with them, my lady," Captain Terran interjected. "There is nothing you can do."

I turned on him. "Damn you, what do you know?"

"No more than I am told."

"And what did Manshin tell you that he didn't see fit to tell me?"

It was his turn to bow. "Apologies, my lady, but there is little to say. Emperor Katashi does not take his generals into his confidence. All they know is that he is expecting no fight at the gates. It is General Manshin's belief that the Great Fish may have used old passages to get men inside the city. It is my job to ensure you return safely to the palace before they can complete their mission."

"No, there's still time to stop them," I said. "We can lock the gatehouse and double the guard."

My silk over-robe tore as I yanked at the fiddly clips and ties like a butterfly pushing through a stubborn cocoon. "I gave you orders, Captain," I snapped at Ryoji's men. "Get that palanquin out of here."

"Lady Hana, I beg you to reconsider," Captain Terran said as I threw the ripped black silk onto the step. "It's too late."

"We don't know that."

I strode into the rain. It was falling heavily and had made the road slick, its shining surface reflecting the light of lanterns left to burn out on their own. No lantern boy was coming to douse them this morning.

Mei'lian's streets were a maze to me, but Tili led the way on quick feet, leaving Captain Terran and I to keep up as best we could. From the broad avenue, she turned along the wall through a nest of narrow alleys edged in narrow houses. Dozens of water barrels had been dragged here from their corners, a smattering of young boys left to man them. A pair were filling buckets as fast as they could and throwing the contents over each other, laughing.

"Stop wasting the water!" another shouted at them.

"It's raining," said a fourth. "The city isn't going to burn if it's raining. Lighten up."

Captain Terran stopped and snatched the bucket out of one's hands. "Quit playing," he said. "Get out of here."

"We've been given orders to bring water."

"There isn't going to be a fire." He thrust the bucket back into the boy's arms. "Get far away from here while you can."

Tili kept on through crowds of waiting soldiers, making always for the northern gates. Outside, Katashi's army. Inside a broad thoroughfare choked with soldiers.

A line of city guards blocked access to the gate, but no one was attempting to break through; no one was even close.

I looked at Captain Terran. "Where are they?"

"I don't know, my lady," he said. "I am not in Emperor Katashi's confidence."

The arc of gate guards eyed us as we approached, our weapons sheathed to show we were no threat. Some recognised me and bowed.

"Who is in charge here?" I asked.

"Captain Hakuri, my lady," one of the guards said, bowing again.

"Where is he? I must speak to him." I looked around, and my gaze skimmed past a pair of soldiers in conversation with a guard farther along the line. Familiarity gnawed at the back of my mind.

"The captain is in the gatehouse," the guard said. "But we have our orders not to let anyone pass."

"Then I will see him here."

"Yes, my lady."

Tili had joined me. "My lady," she said, staring at the pair of soldiers. "What about them?"

I looked around again, and in my mind's eye, their imperial garb melted away to Vice's black. Ire and Rancour.

"You!" I said. "Arrest them!"

Rancour lunged, grabbing Tili around the waist and sticking a dagger to her throat. "If it isn't the master's damn little cunt," he snarled. "Always getting in the way."

My grip on my sword hilt was slippery. "Let her go," I said, aware of guards shifting around the edges of my vision. I looked to Ire, standing beside him—he ever the kindest of the Vices. "Ire, don't do this."

"We have orders," he said, everything about his bearing exhausted as though he was ready to drop. If he'd had to do the whole journey through the passage again with only his ability, then it was no surprise.

"You want me to let your friend go, then open the gates," Rancour said, taking a step back and dragging Tili with him. His knife hovered, its tip dancing back and forth.

"You know I can't do that," I said.

He sneered. "See that?" He gestured at Ire. "That's the sort of loyalty we got too. The bitch won't lift a finger to save you, girl."

"Killing my maid isn't going to get you anywhere, Vice," I said, and the sound of that title sent hisses of fear through the watching crowd.

"No, but taking something from you will give me great satisfaction."

"Rancour, leave it," Ire said. "Let's just do the thing and go."

Tili's fists were balled, her back straight. "Don't do it, my lady," she said, wincing as he tightened his grip.

"I'm sorry I could leave Malice and you couldn't, Rancour," I said, edging a step closer. "But that's anger you should take out on him, not me."

I couldn't tell if Tili was crying or it was just rain running down her face, but she set her jaw and did not speak again. Behind the two Vices, archers were moving along a sheltered balcony, arrows nocked. No Spite here to turn them back on themselves as I had seen him do before, but Ire could destroy them if he had enough energy left.

"This is your last chance," I said, hoping Rancour might consider his own safety.

"No, *my lady*, it's yours. Order them to open the gates."

I looked again at Tili. She stared back at me. But an empress could not bargain. An empress could not compromise. The archers were waiting for an order, but even with his back peppered with arrows, there was no guarantee she would be safe.

There was such anger in Rancour's eyes and a cruel lilt to his lips. "Tick-tock, Captain Regent," he said. "Too late."

"No!" I cried, darting forward, but Ire was already there, gripping Rancour's knife arm. The Vice screamed as smoke rose from his sleeve, the smell like that of decaying flesh. The knife clattered on the ground and Tili broke free, snatching it up with a shaking hand.

A soldier swung at me from the crowd. Instinct moved my feet and threw up my blade, but it was Captain Terran who ran the man through. Blood sprayed over my arm. More concealed soldiers charged the line of gate guards, felling one with a mace. Another didn't move in time and took the backswing of his comrade in the chest.

Of course the Vices had brought Pikes with them, and with no difference between them and our soldiers, the fight descended into chaos.

"It's a diversion!" I yelled at Terran. "Get to the gate. Stop them opening it!"

Captain Terran did not move. "No. My orders are to protect you."

"Stop them opening the damn gate or I will run you through myself!"

"Then you will have to run me through. I will not disobey my general."

"Damn you!"

The captain gripped my arm as I turned to the gate. "It's too dangerous. We need to get out of here."

His grip was too strong. I swung at him, but he caught my blade on his. "Stop this!" he said. "We need to get out of here or you'll be dead. And if you die, General Manshin won't fight for you and Emperor Katashi wins. Is that what you want?"

"Damn you!" I hissed again.

In the desperate scuffle before the gates, no one had eyes for the injured and the dead. Soldiers, both friend and foe, trampled Rancour as he writhed, stepping on his arms, his legs, his hair, his face. There was no dignity, only blood and dirt and a blanket of mangled limbs. And still the rain fell. Ire had disappeared.

"The gates!"

A deafening creak screamed out over the fighting.

"They're opening the gates!"

Captain Terran held out his hand, beckoning furiously. "We have to get out of here, my lady. There is nothing more you can do."

I wanted to stay and fight, to sate my fury with blood, but he was right. Manshin would only fight for me. For my child.

"Now, my lady!"

"Yes," I said. "Yes, I'm coming."

I grabbed Tili's hand, and though it trembled, she squeezed mine, and for a moment I did not feel so alone.

27. DARIUS

The inner palace was too quiet, the gardens too still. Footsteps. Hushed conversations. Even my Empathy gave me no clue what was happening beyond these walls.

I had left an Errant game unfinished. It wasn't working anymore, my legs too restless to sit, my thoughts too restless to scheme. This room had once been my sanctuary, but now it was my cell.

Rain ran down the rippled glass window.

"Good evening, Lord Laroth?"

I shivered and did not turn. Did not speak.

"That's what I said, wasn't it?" she asked. "The first time we met. And you didn't even have to open your eyes to know who I was."

I held my Empathy close, the pain of it like stones settling in my stomach. Perhaps if I did not turn, she would remain nothing but a voice. A memory.

A soft step on the reeds. A rustle of fabric. And her smell, dragging forth unwilling recollections with its sweetness. We had held one another in the darkness like children hiding from a storm.

"Is that not what I said?"

Her voice was closer now. Too close.

I turned, and there she was, real, solid, standing in the centre of my room with her thick brows arched in question.

"That's what you said," I agreed, the voice not sounding like my own. "You should have left me to die that night."

"As I recall, I tried to. It was you who was too soft-hearted, Darius."

She came toward me, slow steps crunching old reeds. Even without my Sight, there was anger and hurt in the lines of her face and the set of her brows, her hands stiff and her back proud. There was a cut on her cheek and a bruise on her jaw, but the eyes that looked steadily up at me had not changed.

"It is you who looks worse for wear, Darius," she said quietly, and I flinched as she touched my right arm, drawing back the sleeve to look upon the stump I hated. It had been well-tended, had been healing for weeks, yet the sight of it filled me with disgust.

"It hurt a lot," she said, a little smile turning her lips. "Thank you for sharing it with me."

I had known it would be bad, but not this bad.

"Don't thank me," I growled, snatching my arm from her grip. "And for the gods' sake, don't act as though I was giving you a gift."

"Like when you destroyed my brother's life even more than Malice destroyed mine?"

I fought the urge to turn away. How much easier it would have been to die without putting myself through this hell. "Exactly like that."

"I didn't know he was coming, Darius." I didn't need the name to know who she meant, to be once more back in that room at Esvar as the borabark slowly stole my voice. It seemed wholly broken again now.

She set a hand on my cheek and I could not move, wedged between her warmth and the rain-splattered window. "I hurt you." Her other hand found my scarred cheek, and she turned me ruthlessly to face her. "I'm sorry."

I slid along the wall, pulling from her hold. "Where is your anger?" I said. "Don't forgive me, hate me. I am a freak. I am a curse. I'm a fool who has survived on lies because I could not face the truth."

"Do you love me?"

"Kimiko—"

"No, don't try to wriggle away behind your mask," she said. "Just be honest."

"I like my façade better."

"I don't. Malice made Mastery, not you. You gave Mastery a face and a voice and took joy in controlling every little twitch, but you wouldn't have needed to if Malice hadn't forced you to retreat into yourself, to build Mastery layer by layer as each new injury scarred over."

"How pathetic you make me sound," I said. "I assure you I hurt him as much as he hurt me. Laroths don't breed happiness."

She stepped back then, the better to see my face. "No, but we could make each other happy, Darius. I love you enough to try."

"You cannot. Everything I have done. Everything I am. Kisia is burning because of me."

"And you hurt because Malice destroyed you. Because your father hated you. Because of everything Kin did before you were in his service. When the trail of wrongs stretches back as far as you can see, its consequences cannot be laid solely at the feet of the last person to err. They must be carried by all."

"Don't make excuses for me."

"I have to."

"Why?"

She lifted a brow. Mocking. "Come now, Darius, you're better than this. I half expected you to tell me you already knew. You're going to be a father."

The weight of the word dropped through me, crushing every bone.

Father.

It sat wrong, the shape of it filling my mouth with hatred. Until Kimiko, I had been so careful. First only Malice, then other boys, and then a discreet whorehouse that knew how to manage its women. I wanted to call her a liar, but the same signs were there as they had been in Hana, the same change to how she stood, more loose, her grace impaired, her breasts shifting her weight ever so slightly forward.

Father.

"You're pregnant."

She neither nodded nor spoke, but her silence was answer enough. I stared at the rough fabric of her servant's robe.

My child.

The gods tell me it will be a boy, my mother had said. She had seen me peering around the screen and had come to kneel before me, her stomach bulging beneath her robe. *Don't worry, Dari*, she had said, her hand warm against my cheek. *By tomorrow, you're going to have a little brother.*

She had screamed long into the night, and in the morning, my mother lay covered in a silk shroud. It hadn't been until later, reading through the lives of my ancestors, that I had seen how common it had been for Laroths to have many wives and lose them in childbirth. Could we be any more monstrous?

I had never before considered how my father must have felt, but as I stared at Kimiko now and imagined how I would suffer to lose her, I couldn't shift him from my mind. Had he blamed the Sight for my mother's death? Had it just been too hard for him to look at me and see her face? How different the world looked when I was able to believe, even for a moment, that my father had loved me.

How ironic it would be for fate to deal me the same blow as it had him. Each generation living out a pain mapped before us.

Or perhaps we could be the first to change it.

Kimiko stood before me, framed by the rain-battered window.

"You said you love me enough to try for happiness," I said, closing the space between us with a single step. "Gods know I'm a walking curse. I'm a broken mess of a man who has no right to even breathe the same air as you, but..."

I knelt at her feet. My head was spinning, and my heart pounded with fear and joy and desperate hope. Maybe this was what it felt like to be truly alive. To be free.

"Get us out of here and I'm yours," I said. "Every ragged shred of soul that's left is yours if you will have me. We could leave all this behind and build something new. We could go wherever you want to go, do whatever you want to do. We could be free of all this." I looked up. "Will you marry me, Kimiko?"

I flinched at the soft, caressing touch of her hands upon my cheeks, so used to Malice's gentleness being the precursor to an attack. "Yes, Darius, I will. But only if you give all this up. All of it. The ministerial position, the power, Kisia, the Vices, Malice, Mastery, Esvar, all of it."

Mastery. The Monstrous Laroth. Dari, my mother had called me. Master Darius, on Avarice's tongue. So many names, but all I had ever been was a boy lost in a storm, hoping for a rescue that never came.

"All of it," I said, though the words were difficult, emotion threatening to clog them in my throat. "All of them."

28. ENDYMION

Whisper by whisper, souls were sneaking back through the opium clouds. Thoughts. Memories. Intentions. Fear. The fear stank as the palanquin was carried through the crowded streets like a silken fish swimming through rising panic.

"He carries the fire of the gods," someone shouted beyond the curtain.

"They say he can set things alight just by looking at them."

Rumours flowed, spreading more stinking fear.

"Clear a path!"

The palanquin slowed. Through a slit in the curtain, there were glimpses of silk-clad shoulders and pinned hair, of brown peasant sashes and merchant-green, the whole seething mass shouting as one as they pushed against lines of soldiers blocking their way to the palace.

The city guard was here in force.

"Clear us a path!" one of Ryoji's men shouted to them as the palanquin rocked and jolted.

An elbow broke through the curtain, and I tucked myself into the corner, pressing both hands to my pounding head. Out there, a man was preaching.

"The wrath of our gods bears down upon us," he shouted. "At Kisia's birth, the gods made the Crimson Throne for the first divine Otako. Now we have turned from their choice, turned from our gods, and we are paying the price. Lord Otako visits their wrath upon us, and he will not stop until we give penance, until an Otako once more sits upon the Crimson Throne."

We deserve to burn.

Treason!

Get him out of here.

We're doomed. The city is going to burn. We're all going to die.

Where is our army? Why aren't we fighting?

Against the palanquin, the mass of people swelled like a tide. A rotten persimmon hit one of the carriers, adding a pungent odour to the emotional din.

"Ignore their warning and Mei'lian will burn too!" the man shouted. I peered out in time to see him rip the hem of his robe away from grasping hands. "All for pride. Our pride in believing a man could ever do the job of a god. All hail the Otako gods!"

One of the imperial guards shoved someone away from the curtains. "Get back!" he growled.

The freak will eat you alive. Lady Hana is mad to keep this dog to heel.

Three hundred and eighty-seven. Four. Seven thousand and two. One million three hundred and nine thousand eight hundred and seventy.

"They are coming," I muttered. "Why didn't I leave last night like the Katos? I should have gone with them. They asked. Too proud. Too stupid. Now it's too late. Everyone says the gates are locked. There's no way out. Maybe I can hide. There's always the waterway. Even if the stories about giant rats are true, I'd rather face one of them than Katashi bloody Otako. Oh gods, we should never have let a commoner take the throne. The Crimson Throne isn't for ordinary people. It's for gods. What am I going to do? What am I going to do?"

The soul faded as the palanquin moved on, slowly pushing its way toward the palace gates. Another soul drew close. "At least if the city burns, the records will burn with it. No one need ever know what happened. I could make sure. I could go to the court and make sure they burn."

One of the guards tugged the curtain back and glared in. "What are you muttering about?"

"You scare me," I said. "I wish the general did not pick me for this mission. If he thinks this freak is safe, then Lady Hana has blinded him. Oh shit, he's reading my mind."

The man threw himself away from me and the curtain fell gracefully back into place.

I heard he can kill with a touch.

One million three hundred and nine thousand eight hundred and sixty-eight. Kill with a touch. Not kill. No, I didn't kill. I judged. It was my duty.

"Keep them back! Keep them back!"

Who is that?

Is Emperor Kin really dead?

Lords burn the same as peasants. Your silk palanquin won't save you. We're all meat in the end. Or tinder. Ha!

The palace gates clanked open.

I had never been to Mei'lian before now, not as Endymion. Prince Takehiko had called this city home, this palace, and had I still been His Imperial Highness, I might have been carried toward the gate in just such a fashion, flanked by guards while the crowds pressed in upon me. His Imperial Highness Prince Takehiko Otako—the life Kin had stolen from me.

Running steps followed as we drew away from the crowd and into the greater peace of the courtyard. Here servants and soldiers bustled, but their whispers were less panicked. Here there was purpose.

Buckets. There might be more in the lower storeroom. Have to be quick. They're already coming.

If he's going to burn the gate, we need an open formation. Bucket chains through the centre.

I hope the stress doesn't cause her to miscarry. Poor Lady Hinton, this is not what she needs right now. Food. Water. Smelling salts. Captain Rill says the library will be the best place to hide.

There has to be another way out.

I'll just play dead.

One million three hundred and eight thousand nine hundred and ninety-one.

The palanquin hit the mounting stone with a bump.

"Lady Hana, Minister Bahain is requesting—"

"Not Lady Hana, my lord," one of the carriers hissed. "The boy."

A man with a single thick eyebrow yanked aside the curtain and scowled in at me. "Him," he said, that brow wriggling like a black snake. "Where is Lady Hana?"

"I could not take it upon myself to say, my lord," the same carrier said. "But she ordered this boy brought back safely." *Pompous shit. Mama always wanted me to become master of the court. No thank you, not if you have to look down your nose as though everyone is a worm.*

How is he important to the Otako bitch?

The master of the court held out his hand to help me from the palanquin. It was his job. As judgement was mine.

I took his hand, laying his soul bare. Self-importance. Pride. But he had been nothing once. A younger son, destined for the priesthood until he stole gold from the temple. Fear. No one could know. No one could ever know.

I threw the fear back. His knees buckled. He let go of my hand, but I did not let go of his. Tightening my grip, I stepped from the palanquin. "You shouldn't have done it," I said. "That money had been collected for the poor."

"What are you talking about?"

"The gold you stole. You didn't need it. You weren't starving.

You had clothes on your back and a noble name, but you wanted more."

I squeezed and the fear bled into him, bitterly cold. He slumped into a puddle, gasping for breath, trying to yank his hand from mine. "No," he cried. "No, no I needed it. I couldn't let them throw me away like rubbish. I—"

The master of the court grasped at his throat with his free hand. His eyes bulged. The rhythm of his pulse quickened. Faster. Faster. Eyes wider. Breath caught.

Then silence. His hands stilled. I let go.

Is he dead?

What just happened?

"Someone get help! He's not breathing!"

"He's dead," I said, stepping over the body as it slipped farther into the puddle. "He deserved death. He was a fraud and a thief. I am a god and I have judged him unworthy of life."

"Who are you?" someone demanded.

"My name is Takehiko Otako," I said, not turning around. "And I bring justice."

Shouting broke out behind me as I strode away. Hana's two imperial guards ran to catch up. "Stop! Did you just kill him?"

They didn't touch me.

"I don't kill," I said, striding on into the bamboo court. "I judge."

"Takehiko Otako is dead."

They jogged along beside me, keeping their distance.

"I'm breathing," I said. "My heart beats. What other signs of life would you like?"

Anxiety oozed off them like the sweat dripping from their brows. "What proof do you have?"

"What proof would you accept?" I stopped walking and turned on them. Both jumped back, hands close to their sword hilts. "If I had something with the Otako crest on it, you would say I stole it,"

I said. "Papers I could have forged. And if someone were to vouch for me, you would call them a liar."

"But if you're Takehi—"

I hadn't needed skin back in Shimai, only needed to let the shell of Endymion go and become the god I had been born. Now their souls screamed to me, and I threw their judgement back. Cruelty in one, perversion in the other. They dropped, crumpling like unwanted dolls.

Nausea crashed over me in the aftermath and I fought to catch my breath. Shouts echoed from the central courtyard, while out in the city, the crowd roared. "Burn!" the preacher was screaming. "Burn all you sinners who reject the gods, our divine Otakos. Throw wide the gates and welcome Lord Otako, bringer of justice!"

His delight tingled through my limbs. The man was unworthy, bringing fear for his own ends.

My nausea doubled, but I staggered on while out in the square, shouts turned to screams. Justice was my duty. It would come to everyone in time, even gods.

My brothers were waiting.

Deep memories directed my steps from one courtyard to the next, through reception rooms and small gardens, gates and walls. The outer palace was a maze built to confuse enemies, to force them into narrow passages where they could be picked off one by one, but I knew this building in my bones, born to it as I had been born to my duty.

The next guard I passed eyed me warily. "State your business," he said, resting a hand upon his gold-edged crimson sash.

"My name is Takehiko Otako," I said.

His first reaction wasn't one of disbelief but of amazement. "Really?"

The man had drawn no weapon. Mine lived within my skin,

invisible to the eye as I walked toward him. "Really," I said. "Let me show you."

Perhaps he thought I might bring forth papers or marks of the Otako family, for certainly there was eagerness in his face, but he flinched as I took his wrist.

Frustration. Dread. His thoughts upon a family he feared he would never see again. Friends in Shimai. Friends among Kin's army. Doubt. There was no cruelty, no vicious desire for violence.

He was worthy.

I let him go, and he reeled back into a door. Its paper ripped and its frame cracked beneath his weight, and he fell into the room beyond. There was a sharp cry from inside, but I was already moving.

Memory guided my steps to a grand archway edged in blocks of white stone. The story was they had been a gift. Who from and why had long since been forgotten, but each ruling family had been given one to carve with their crest so it might be used in this symbolic construction. I had run my hands over them as a child. Or had that been another boy? Someone else whose memories now squatted in my mind.

"That is the Toi family's stone," my mother had said as I ran my hand over the carved lily. *"And this one is the Kato family. And the Bahain family."*

A spider had stretched its long, smooth legs beneath my fingers. "And this?"

"The Laroths."

"Where is ours?"

Had she paused? Had there been a moment of indecision? I could only imagine so now. "Up at the top," she had said, pointing to the keystone. "The Otako family holds Kisia together. We are Kisia."

From the archway, a long colonnade led across the gardens to the inner palace. Rain poured from its roof, singing as it bounced down rain chains and along gutters. A week of storms had drowned the gardens, turning ornamental ponds into lakes and fountains into waterfalls, the weight of so much water causing thin branches to droop.

At the end of the colonnade, the inner palace rose magnificent. There were guards here too, but no one stopped me. Not at the doors where imperial guards were checking little-used defences, not on the stairs where I swam against the current of soldiers and servants and courtiers, and not outside Darius's room where there were no longer any guards at all. I didn't need to press my hand to the wooden frame to know the room was empty.

There was another door not so far along the passage, and as I approached, the smell of opium grew stronger, preceding raised voices.

"Just get out of the way," Avarice growled, his voice the first to penetrate the fog that surrounded my head. "You can suck his cock when I've cut it off."

Hatred washed over me, and I slammed the door back on its runners. In the centre of the room, Avarice and Hope stood shouting at each other, while Malice, barely moved from the position he had occupied before I left, was getting his fix with the leftover opium. The smell of it was so cloying I blew air up my nose in an attempt to disperse it.

"You've had your fun," Hope said. "Now I need him to be able to walk so I can get out of here."

"You can stay here and burn for all I care, sycophant," came the replying growl from Avarice.

"Damn you and your arrogance," Hope spat. "You think I want to do this? You think this is what I wanted for my life? *I must obey*, but you, Avarice, you are here by your own choice."

"Shut it, and get out of the way."

"No."

Avarice prodded the air in Malice's direction, sending smoke swirling. "You're going to protect that rotten—"

"Yes, I am," Hope interrupted. "Not because he deserves anything from me, but because right now, I would do anything to stand between you and what you want. You've made my life hell since I was marked, but how does having free will make you so much better than us? If I could leave, I would. If I could fight for what mattered, I would. But you? You're so damn hung up on Master Darius this and Master Darius that, you haven't noticed your little boy no longer exists. You still think you can save him? Well guess what, Papa Avarice, you failed."

Hope leapt back as Avarice lashed out. Not entirely absent, Malice chuckled, the sound dry and pained. "Want to kill me, Avarice?" he said, smoke eking between his lips. "Your Master Darius wouldn't thank you for that."

"Is that what you think?" Avarice's fists were clenched, shaking at his sides, his anger so thick it blanketed the room. "Is that what you really think, you shit? You're a pathetic leech, squeezing and squeezing until there is no air left in his lungs let alone love in his heart. I knew a boy who used to dream of walking barefoot to Chiltae with nothing but a bushel of pears and the clothes on his back. But trapped as he was he used to pray, every night, that he would not wake upon the morrow, that sickness would take him." Tears ran down Avarice's ravaged face, flecks of spit flying at every impassioned word. "And every night, I sat and listened to him want to die. 'At least the dead are free,' he used to say. So don't you dare lie there and act as though you know him. You see what you want to see. You created a monster, but I remember a boy who wanted to be free."

With his big hands splayed, he shunted a stunned Hope out of the way, and the boy stumbled back, slamming his head against the wall. Avarice gripped the front of Malice's wretched robe and dragged him up amid the curls of smoke. He was conscious, but Malice lacked his old strength and looked like a broken doll in Avarice's hands. Yet he was laughing, the same slow, humourless chuckle—the laugh of a man at the end of his sanity.

I had been so sure, had been filled with such purpose, but now their whispers drowned out my own.

I only ever wanted to help Master Darius. No one else loved him, not like me.

Oh gods, let me die.

"Avarice," I said, finally stepping into the room. "Leave him."

His head turned, a sneer so like Darius's twisting his features. "You too?" he said. "Why does everyone leap to protect this pathetic rat?"

"Because he already has his justice," I said, putting a hand out but finding nothing to steady myself on. "There is nothing you can do to him that is worse than what he has done to himself. It's over. Just let him go and break himself in whatever way he sees fit."

"No. I will repay my years of service."

"But it wasn't him you were serving, was it?"

Avarice didn't answer. Tears stood in his eyes. Behind him, Hope stared, open-mouthed, as the realisation hit him. Avarice had stayed so Darius could be free.

More footsteps. The click-clack of sandals in the passage.

They must be put down. Like rabid dogs.

Hatred shook my limbs, its bile burning my tongue. More steps. Louder. I tried for numbers but found nothing, not even clear intentions—there was too much revulsion.

Father Kokoro stepped into the doorway, blocking the light from the passage. Two guards stood behind him, and Brother Jian hovered.

"That's him," one of the guards said. "He called himself Takehiko Otako. He killed the Master of the Court and two of our men."

"But you were worthy," I said.

"What right have you to judge?" the man demanded.

He was shaking. I shook too, fury dammed inside me. "The blood of gods runs through my veins, and I will judge. The empire will bow to justice."

"Endymion." Brother Jian. I could barely see his expression

through the opium haze that sparked with anger, but I could feel his horror. It added to the chaos filling me head to foot, beginning to burst from the seams like stuffing from a doll.

"I am Justice!" I shouted. "You must all be judged."

"Endymion!"

Father Kokoro laughed. "I told you he was a monster, Brother, you ought to have listened. We should have done away with them all years ago. But it is not too late."

"Avarice I have judged," I said. I could only see his aura, not his body. Sacrifice, love, and deep sadness. He had done everything he could.

"Hope—"

"No!" The boy flinched.

"Is worthy."

"Enough of this," Kokoro snapped. "Kill him."

The two guards pushed into the room. One aura red, the other yellow-tinged blue. One already judged, the other I read in a heartbeat. The worthy was pushed aside with a thought. The unworthy's heart I squeezed until it burst inside his chest. Both hit the ground.

He didn't even touch them. Oh gods. We are all dead.

I told you you'd need to be chained before the end.

"The world is rotten, Endymion," Malice croaked. "You can't save it. Even those you deem worthy will sin before long. That is the nature of man, yes? Just destroy it. Destroy it all."

"Shut up!" Hope kicked him.

"See?" Malice said on a pained cough. "Even Hope, the perfect paragon of virtue, will turn to violence. Kill him."

He was right. It was there, deep in Hope's soul. Anger. Hurt. Revenge. He wanted to see the world burn just like Katashi.

"Men hate, yes?" Malice said. "It's what we are all made to do."

Jian came toward me. "No, Endymion, you don't want to do this."

"Yes," I said. "I must. I am Justice."

"No, Endymion, please."

"You said yourself that the gods say a man is made the way he is for a purpose, and to seek to alter that—"

"And you said let the gods live a day in your skin before they judge you!" he cried. "Yet you judge without living. You judge without understanding. This is not true justice."

"I will judge. I am a god. I—"

Jian pressed his hands to my cheeks—skin on skin—and though I tried to pull away, I was up against the wall with nowhere to run. The connection flared, his thoughts, his memories, his feelings drowning out an entire world, drowning out everything I thought I was until there was nothing, nothing but this man and his pain. Aches, injuries, angers, but more than anything a heart that cried for the boy he had taken in and cared for as his own, for the father he had failed to be, and for the world slowly crumbling around him.

If only they would understand him. If only they would let me find him, let me take him back. I worked so hard. You warned me he would Maturate, that it would increase his ability, give him urges and turn his thoughts from serving the gods, and by the grace of the heavens, I did everything I could to stop it from happening. I made sure he did not suffer, that I was always there, but I failed.

Tears ran down my cheeks as they ran down his. Memories leaked through his fingers like water. Racing to the beach with my brother. He always won and would turn back laughing as I caught up. My dead father, his neck broken as he was thrown from a horse. The weight of the oath upon my tongue. The voice of the gods on the wind.

"Stop," I begged, the words coming out on a sob. "Let go!"

"Not until you judge me," he returned, teeth gritted tight. "Do it, Endymion, judge me. Am I worthy?"

Sacrifice. Devotion. Striving. Love.

"Yes!" I screamed, trying again to pull out of his tightening grip. "Yes. Let me go!"

"No. Judge yourself."

"What?"

"Judge yourself, Endymion. I'm not letting go until you do."

The memories kept pouring out, filling my head as they emptied his. Now I was trying to protect a young, hollow-eyed boy with tousled brown hair from hearing the story of the battle of Riyan Bridge. The damn priest wouldn't stop talking about it, all that bloodlust in him, all that hate.

Jian's hands shook. "Do it. Trust me, Endymion. Judge yourself."

In all the numbers, I had never counted myself.

Closing my eyes, I turned the Sight in.

One.

Anger. Justice. Revenge. Pain. It all whirled at me like leaves in a gale. Two hundred and forty-five souls in the name of Justice. One hundred and four on the road to Rina with Hope's skill running through my veins. The men who had tortured me in Shimai. Darius. Kimiko. Hana. Kin. Every one of them a victim because of me.

"The memories that haunt us are the ones that linger," Jian said. "They are the first you see. You are judging insecurity, not truth—self-doubt and fear, not guilt. These are not the memories that make us who we are."

Nyraek Laroth had held me before him on his horse. It had been dark, but I could smell the blood on his hands and on his cloak, but not upon his sword because he had been too late to save the woman he loved.

"We are all of us our own worst enemies," Jian said, though it was more a whisper than real words, a whisper like a thought inside my head. "We judge more harshly, we expect more and are disappointed the most at our own failure. And that is what you feel, Endymion, that is what you hear, what you smell and what you taste, it is what you have become. You have drunk poison until there is nothing left of you, until all you can do is listen to Kisia screaming."

One million three hundred and eight thousand eight hundred and twelve.

"You are the only one you have the right to judge."

29. HANA

B arricade the palace gates! The city has been breached!"
Imperial guards swarmed the main courtyard.

"Prepare for siege! The city has been breached!"

I walked through the preparations blindly until General Ryoji approached. Ryoji was outwardly calm, but he eyed the blood on my sleeve. At another time, the space between us might have been there and gone in an instant, his thumb smoothing the skin of my cheek, his breath warm, his lips soft. But there was no place here for our forbidden tryst. Perhaps ought never to have been at all.

"General," I said, inclining my head in proud greeting. "Are we ready?"

"As ready as it is possible to be, my lady. Unfortunately, the First Battalion was on the walls. The Second was deployed in the city under General Vareen. They might thin Otako's numbers—"

"Or die trying. What men do we have here to protect the palace?"

"We have half of the Imperial Guard and the soldiers of the Third Battalion that survived Shimai."

"That is not enough."

There was a beat of silence. Then: "No, my lady. But my men know this palace very well. They train in its defence. We could hold off a siege by ordinary soldiers but not Otako. Without knowing something of his weaknesses and limitations, it is only a matter of time."

Preparations continued around us, all noise and bravado. The Imperial Guard had never failed to hold the palace against any and all enemies.

"There's a way," I said. "But you're not going to like it."

He raised an eyebrow.

"We let him win. We give him the Crimson Throne."

More silence. General Ryoji was not as skilled as many others at maintaining a blank expression, and he failed now as incredulity crept across his features. "Your pardon, my lady," he said. "Give him the throne?"

"Yes, General, give him the throne. He is living vengeance, and the only thing that douses the flame of revenge is success."

"I cannot counsel strongly enough against such a gamble, my lady. I understand your theory, but what guarantee do we have?"

"Only the word of Lord Laroth."

A grimace.

"I told you that you wouldn't like it."

"And nor do I," he said. "Even if I trusted the minister, allowing Katashi Otako to sit upon the throne would still leave us with hundreds of Pikes and traitor soldiers inside the palace."

"Not the traitors. General Manshin will fight for me."

Another scowl. "Why?"

"Because he cares about his name," I said, keeping my voice low. "Do you think he wants to be labelled a traitor all his life? To have his family suffer that stigma? Under Emperor Katashi, he might have been a hero, but Katashi is dying and Kin will not forgive traitors."

"General Manshin is...unpredictable," Ryoji said. "I trust him as little as I trust Lord Laroth."

There was distance between us now, distance between his hand and mine, between our lips, our bodies, and our hearts. The rest of my plans were too fragile to risk on trust.

"Then your only recourse is to stop Katashi getting in," I said.

"He will be here soon. He doesn't care about Mei'lian. The Crimson Throne is his only goal now."

"We will do our best, my lady."

I kept my doubts to myself, holding close the hope that they would fail to stop him, that Darius had been wrong, that there was still a chance of getting Katashi back. "Very well. Now I need six of your strongest men."

He had been about to bow, about to return to his preparations, but he froze now with that same crease dug between his brows. "I can ill spare even a single soldier," he said. "What are you planning?"

"To protect the emperor."

"The best way to protect the emperor is to keep the bastards out. Even six of my best men could do little to protect His Majesty against Otako once he's inside the walls."

"I am not after guards, General, just six men for an important task. You will get them back."

He bowed, perhaps knowing argument was pointless. "As you wish, my lady."

"Good. That will be all, General."

He bowed again, his brows set low over dark eyes. Those eyes had run over my naked skin. Those lips had parted in a gasp as he slid slowly inside me. I had wanted to take his face in my hands, to kiss him, to own him completely, but like so much else I had touched, I could already see it spoiling.

I did not stay to watch him go; there was too much to be done and I was running out of time. The Crimson Throne was not the only thing Katashi wanted.

"Come," I said to Tili, resolutely glued to my side. "I have a job for you too."

As I entered Kin's rooms, I took a deep breath of poisoned air, not only smelling but also tasting of Master Kenji's hateful salves. A sheen of sweat covered Kin's exposed skin, his body wasted such that every muscle showed like a rocky landscape.

"He is not getting better, my lady," Master Kenji said, looking sidelong at me as he stirred a fresh salve with a wooden spoon. "He is in the hands of the gods now."

"Katashi is inside the city."

Master Kenji paused in his stirring. "Then we are all in the hands of the gods."

"Gods." My laugh was more snort than chuckle. "What a pleasant fiction that is."

Kin flinched and rolled his head restlessly on the bloodstained pillow. Kisia's emperor was dying. One more day and I might call him husband, might inherit his throne. He had to live one more day.

"There are no gods, Master Kenji," I said. "You are the one who has to keep him alive. I don't care what it takes. He has to live."

"I can only do so much, my lady," the court physician protested. "The rest is up to him."

"That was an order, Master Kenji, not a request."

His lips parted but he did not protest again, just bowed deeply. "Yes, my lady."

The emperor's rooms might have been sparsely furnished, but Master Kenji was leaving his touch. A half-eaten tray of food sat upon a side table, its teapot having long since ceased to steam, and what looked like the entire contents of the palace's medicinal stores now colonised a section of the floor. All bottles and packets and bundles of herbs, bowls and spoons and incense sticks, and metal instruments that made my skin crawl.

"Do you have everything you need?" I said.

"I believe so, my lady."

"Food. Water. I assume there is a chamber pot."

Master Kenji once again halted his stirring. "If there is something else I require, I can always call for the servants."

"No. I'm going to barricade you in. Tili, my maid, will be remaining to help you."

"You're going to…"

"My lady—"

Ignoring Tili's protest, I said, "You are a physician, not a soldier. I have ordered you to keep him alive, but if Katashi makes it this far, there is nothing you can do to stop him."

For the first time, I saw real fear in his face. This man who had dealt with death every day, who lived amid blood and screams, was afraid of what was coming.

"Do you have everything you need?"

"Yes, my lady."

"Good." I turned to leave.

"My lady?"

"Master Kenji?"

"No barricade will keep out Katashi Otako. Fire can burn through any amount of wooden furniture."

His hand had completely stilled. He was no longer even looking at the salve, his mind alight with flames.

"You are right, but it just needs to slow down his men. I will keep Katashi out."

He did not ask how, just bowed. "Thank you, my lady."

Tili hovered, unsure. "I would rather stay with you."

"Yes, but as I would rather not lose anyone else today, I beg you will stay here where it is safest. Master Kenji may have need of your help."

She looked for a moment as though she would argue but nodded stiffly. "As you wish, my lady."

I could only hope she would have reason to thank me for it later.

Outside the emperor's apartments, dust motes danced in the morning light. General Ryoji's six strongest men stood waiting in silence.

"Barricade them in," I said. "You have permission to use any and all furniture you can find. I want this hallway impassable."

No time was wasted. They left and returned carrying divans and chairs and sleeping mats, then tables, shelves and armfuls of books, more bedding, ornate sideboards, travelling chests, and even a pair of enormous canopied beds. I watched as they piled it up, not just dumping but stacking strategically to create a dense tangle until there was no way Pikes could easily get in and no way Master Kenji could get out.

The floor shook to a thunderous boom. Beyond the window the gardens looked peaceful, but above the outer wall smoke was rising.

"He's in the square," one of the soldiers said, and I could hear his fear.

Another boom shuddered the floor. Flames ripped through the palace gatehouse and smoke poured into the sky. Screams echoed up from the lower levels of the inner palace, and my stomach twisted into knots.

"Finish here," I said. "Then return to General Ryoji."

The men bowed, gleaming now with sweat and with their chests heaving. "Yes, my lady."

I looked at the door, but my feet would not move. "Come on, Hana," I said. The first step was like dragging myself through swamp ooze, but the second was easier and I began to walk, step after step, toward the landing.

"Keep walking," I hissed. "Come on!"

At the end of the passage was another narrow window. The view had not changed. Rain was putting out the flames and dampening the smoke while servants and courtiers fled like jewelled ants across the sodden gardens. Dying flames meant Katashi was not remaining to sustain them.

He was already coming.

30. DARIUS

As we slipped through the wall, it occurred to me to wonder whether Kimiko's skill allowed her to move through objects or allowed objects to move through her. Perhaps it was one and the same, both resulting in a fuzzy sensation throughout my body and the taste of sawdust.

"Might I request we do that as little as possible?" I said as we emerged into the next room.

"I never used to enjoy it," Kimiko said, touching the now-solid wall we had just passed through. "But I'm used to it now. It certainly allows one a freedom not available to ordinary people."

"I'm always afraid you'll get stuck part way. Having seen it once was enough for me."

"Well, when you say it like that." She shuddered and went to the door, but it was locked from the outside. "Damn. I guess we'll have to do it my way."

Kimiko held out her hand and I took it, keeping my Empathy close. With so much raw fear in the air, it was hard not to connect, not to read. But I was determined not to do so, determined to make the right choice as though one good deed now could atone for a lifetime of wrongs.

While I could hold back from all else, the deep sadness she resonated to fade was impossible to ignore. I faded with it, and together we stepped through the wood into the next room. It had once belonged to my head secretary, a clever and all too ambitious little man who had always dressed rather too finely for a civil servant. No doubt he had already found himself another patron.

This door was locked too. Outside, the storm was attempting to drown the gardens, and beyond the outer palace, plumes of dark smoke rose to a grey sky.

"He's already inside the city," Kimiko said, joining me at the window. "Shimai put up more of a fight."

"We wanted a fight in Shimai," I said. "We needed to demonstrate his power and draw Hana out."

"Did you plan this attack for him too? If you know his plans, that might help us get out."

I touched my stump to the rippled glass. "I don't think he's planning much of anything anymore, just intent on reaching the throne. Before we marched on Shimai, he sent some Pikes and Vices through the tunnel though, no doubt to open the gates of Mei'lian for him when he got this far."

"You knew that and didn't tell Hana?"

"What would she have done if I had? Stopped them, and then Katashi would have burned his way in and killed thousands more people than necessary to reach his goal. I told her the only piece of information she needed to save the empire."

Kimiko tilted her head in that birdlike way she had.

"Your brother is dying. Vengeance is all that sustains him now, but no amount of vengeance can survive revenge."

She closed her eyes a brief moment, and I wished I had not spoken.

"You recall now what I monster I am?" I said. "I have been given every opportunity to die, and every time I fight to live. If I had been less afraid, your brother would have retaken his throne with Hana and been happy. Think better of loving me while you can."

"You have a right to live, Darius," she said, though her smile was tight, forced through the lies she was determined to hang happiness upon. "Come." She held out her hand again. "We can leave all this behind, we just have to keep moving."

I took her hand and caught a flash of hurt and anger and grief before the sadness engulfed us. Those emotions had been impossible not to feel, I told myself, but it was a lie.

On the other side of the wall lay another office and a door not only locked but barricaded. "We must be getting close to the landing," Kimiko said.

"A few more rooms."

"Is it? I never spent much time in this part of the palace. Princesses don't have much to do with administration."

It was easy to forget that she had once been a princess of imperial blood. She had the grace, but the youth was gone from her face, leaving lines bred by hardship. "This is the last private office," I said. "There's an anteroom and a library that has a back stair to the archive vault, but it doesn't lead out. The main stairs will be our only option."

"Shall we brave the stairs together then?" Once again, she held out her hand. "We can hope Hana's soldiers are too preoccupied to give a damn about us."

Hana's soldiers. "His Majesty may come to regret his choice of bride," I said.

"If he lives."

"If he lives," I agreed, and I lived that night in Shimai over in my mind. Fire. Noise. Hana had begged, and Kin's face had blistered and burned. In the aftermath, Avarice had bandaged my stump well, but I had been shedding pain ever since.

A distant scream tore me from my memories, its shrill tone sliding into the guttural growl of a trapped animal.

"Katashi cannot be here yet," I said, failing to keep the alarm out of my voice. "So what is that?"

We both turned our heads to better hear, and the scream rose again upon a tide of babbled numbers, the panic in the familiar voice far more frightening than its usual monotone.

"Endymion," Kimiko said. "The opium Hana gave him made him dopey, but it must be wearing off."

"Opium? Where did she get it?"

"I don't know. Why does it matter?"

"I gave her some," I said. "I gave her the box I always kept for Malice in case he ran out, and she gave me her word she would give it to him and let him go. Without it, he wouldn't get far."

The screaming rose again, then as abruptly as it started, it ceased. Hana had been so fierce, so determined, so desperate. Perhaps I had taught her how to lie well after all.

"I have to go back," I said.

"What? Why?"

"Because if Malice is still here, then he's about to die. If your brother doesn't kill him, Father Kokoro will."

Silence. Even the scream had ended and not returned. There was just Kimiko, just the sound of her quick, shallow breaths and the ever-intoxicating smell of her hair.

"Darius," she said, once again taking my face gently between her hands. "You promised you would walk away."

"And I will, but I cannot leave anyone to die when we could save them."

"Malice destroyed you. He stole your freedom and twisted you and sucked you dry until all you could do was retreat behind that face. He deserves whatever is coming to him."

I covered her hands with mine. "I will walk away from him, but I don't want him dead. He's my brother."

"Malice *broke* you, Darius, doesn't that make you angry? He has hurt everyone I care about and he will just go on doing it until he's dead. He's an empty pit sucking in every shred of love and happiness he can, but it's never enough."

"Of course that makes me angry, but he's my brother! Isn't that why you dosed me with the borabark in the first place? Whatever Katashi had done, he was your brother."

"And now he is dying thanks to you," she snapped, pulling away and drawing her blade from her sash. "If I kill Malice, then we even the score."

"No!" I reached out my only hand. "Don't do it, Kimiko. Please don't."

"If we let him survive, he will just follow us."

"Then we go somewhere he can't find us."

"There is no such place! That's why you're so afraid of him. You will never be free while he lives and you know it, yet you will not stand aside. Well—" She took another step toward the wall. "If you cannot do it, then I will, and I dare you to tell me you won't forgive me for freeing you from him after all you have done, after all I have forgiven. I dare you!"

The blade trembled in her hand as she took another step toward the wall. "Kimiko, don't do this, he's dangerous. He could kill you."

"Not while suffering opium withdrawal."

"He will still fight."

"I hope he does! It will give me joy to kill him, not just see him die."

I closed the space between us with a single tentative step. "You said you wanted to walk away, then let's walk away. Both of us, now, together. Don't risk your life to end his."

Silence hung a dreadful moment before she smiled at me. "You fool," she said. "If this is my last chance to free you from him, I will take it, because by the time he tracks us down again, I may not be around anymore to protect you."

"What?"

"You don't think I read all those books about your family without figuring out there's no such thing as a female Empath, do you?"

I'm sorry, Master Darius, but it was a girl, the woman had said. *Lady Laroth has passed on. She is laid out if you wish to see her.*

At the mere thought that history might repeat itself, my legs seemed loath to hold my weight, and I dropped to my knees. Tears squeezed through eyes shut tight. I tried to force them back, but they kept coming, kept falling, wetting the dark fabric of her robe, into which I buried my face when she drew close, every gasp of breath full of her smell.

They had covered my mother in silk and let me kneel at her side. My father had never encouraged tears, but at five years old, I had not been able to hold them back. I had cried until I could not see, cried until I could barely breathe, mouth sticky, nose clogged, my whole face awash with grief. No one had tried to stop me. They had let me sit at my mother's side for hours, let me touch her still face, her pale lips, her brow, her hair, her cheek, let my tears fall on her skin until there were none left to fall. Beside her, my baby sister was equally still, her limbs curled and uncomfortable, her head an ugly shape with sparse dark hair stuck in clumps. She had been cool to the touch, all except her tiny hands. They had maintained some warmth, as though somehow my mother was holding her close.

Kimiko touched my hair and started to sing as she had often done at Esvar. It was the song of Saki, the daughter of the goddess Lunyia, and the mortal man she had given up her divinity to love.

It ought, perhaps, have made me wary, but grief has a way of swallowing one whole.

From my hair, Kimiko's hands ran down my neck. Outside, someone started to shout. I could not hear the words and could feel nothing beyond my own self-pity.

"I'm sorry, Darius," Kimiko said at last, letting the strains of her song fade to an echo. "You will never be happy while he lives. I'm sorry."

She gripped my collar. Her hand was hot and her knuckles dug into the side of my neck. She gripped the other side of my robe before I could move, and yanked hard, her wrists crossed. Pressure mounted around my throat. There was silence but for her quickening breath as the black of her servant's robe grew blacker still. My tongue felt fat and tingly, my brain sluggish. And like a repeating species of nightmare, I was sinking once again.

"I guess Otakos don't breed happiness either," came Kimiko's muzzy voice. And then there was nothing.

———————◆

The smell of matting came first. Then small sounds—distant shouting and the crackle of the dry reeds beneath my good hand as I pushed myself up. The room spun into place—the office of an unknown administrator, its screen door barricaded with an upturned table and a pair of sleeping mats.

Recollection soaked into my mind. Kimiko was gone. It could only have been seconds, but it felt like an age, the world different on this side of waking. Here, shouts echoed through the closed door and a thunderous boom made the whole building shake.

Here, every word took on a new meaning.

I guess Otakos don't breed happiness either.

"But we were going to try," I murmured, trying to fight memory's urge to play its awful theatre across my eyes. I had wanted death, but now life danced across my skin, imbued by her touch. If anyone could find a way to stop the curse from taking her, I could, and if anyone could fight it, it was her. But she had gone before such words could be spoken.

Another boom shook the floor. Closer this time, and my heartbeat sped to a sickening pace. We were all running out of time.

Four steps to the door. The sleeping mats were easy to shift, but the upturned desk would take an able-bodied man to move. Lifting was not possible, even pushing would be difficult, but I knew exactly what Malice would do to Kimiko if he found out she was carrying my child.

I threw my weight against the side of the desk and it rocked. Another push, then another, shoulder bruising. Then at last it toppled, falling heavily onto one of the sleeping mats and smashing a lap table into a pile of splintered wood.

The door was locked. No key, but it didn't matter. Wax paper was thick and strong, but it was only paper, and one of the panels snapped when greeted with my fist. Reaching through, I found no key on the outside either. Whoever had barricaded the door must have taken it with them.

I found I was gripping the doorframe hard, but the passage was empty except for floating dust and the chatter of voices. Stepping back, I slammed my foot into one of the thin crossbars in the frame, and it cracked. Another kick. Then I rammed bodily into it. The door splintered—not quite enough to escape, but it was a start. Despite everything Kimiko had said, I did not want Malice to die.

They say the god Dokei can read a man's true name in his heart, that he knows where we all belong.

One day I would have to ask him.

31. ENDYMION

My lifeless eyes stared up at me from the matting. Brown, their sockets crinkled like old paper and edged in grey lashes. My eyes? I shook my head, but the fog didn't clear. My throat was raw.

"Jian!"

Father Kokoro knelt on the matting beside me and touched my lifeless face. Me. I shook my head again. He had never shown such care when I had been alive, but now I was dead I could see his hands shaking.

No. Not me. It was Brother Jian lying there. I knew his face and his voice, and the smell of old incense that hung about his robe—not even the stink of wet ox could drown it out completely. For all those years, we had travelled around Kisia and Chiltae with no greater goal than to help the people we met and bring the gods to where they were needed. But while I could remember him as though he sat right beside me, I could also remember sitting beside myself, remember the furrow between my brows and the messy brown curls I had run my fingers through while Endymion slept.

"He's dead."

The words fell leaden from Father Kokoro's lips and he glared at me. From elsewhere in the room came the sound of Malice laughing. There was strength in the sound now as the opium brought him back to life.

"You judged him unworthy?" Kokoro roared.

"No," I said. "I just... I just wasn't quick enough."

"You mean you killed my brother *accidentally*?"

"Yes. No."

He gripped the front of my robe. "Don't you dare tell me my brother wanted to die, you little shit."

"No." My head was thick with fog. "I don't think anyone ever truly wants to die," I said, my tongue feeling fat and slow. "But there are good times and right ways and this was his. For a long time, Endymion was all I lived for, Brother."

He threw me back against the wall. "Don't call me brother, you freak," he said, the wrinkles of his face making deep, harsh frown lines.

"But Kokoro," I said. "I am your brother."

His scowl didn't shift. Malice laughed again, harder now. "I don't think your brother is dead, so much as... consumed, yes? You never disappoint, Endymion."

Hope stood between Avarice and the Vice Master, his eyes darting. The guard in the doorway looked—no, felt familiar. The screen door had cracked under his weight. He had been worthy.

I blinked. "I can't... can't feel as much... The world is not so loud anymore. And the numbers... I can't quite reach them."

Kokoro's hate was familiar. I'd seen that expression the day he crept up on the kitchen cat, a smirking boy stalking through the grass toward the animal that had stolen his last rice ball. My attempt to protect it had left a scar. Endymion had once asked how I got it, and I'd prayed forgiveness for the lie.

"Kill the others," Kokoro said. "This one is mine."

The guard didn't need a second order. He strode into the room of unarmed prisoners with nowhere to run. Confident. Too confident. Malice might only have just picked himself up off the floor, but he was still dangerous.

The guard went straight for Hope. Avarice shouted. A shadow flickered in the doorway and, hovering there with her curls loose and wild, Kimiko swore. She hesitated while every occupant of the room stopped to stare at her.

"You," Malice said. "I've been hoping I might see you again, yes? You've got something I would like to take away from you." He gestured to his own stomach, his lips leering cruelly.

"Well I was hoping never to see you again," she said. "But Darius wants you dead, and what Darius wants, I will give him."

"Liar!" Malice took a step toward her, but the guard blocked his way.

"Liar?" Kimiko advanced into the room. "He hates you. Why do you think you've never been able to keep him? Grab him," she said to the guard. "Hold him while I gut him like the animal he is."

Whether recognising the voice of authority, the face of an Otako, or just someone on his side, the guard strode toward Malice.

"Hope!" It was an order through gritted teeth, and the young Vice did not hesitate. Could not. Before the guard could stop him, Hope had yanked the man's own dagger from his belt and stuck it into his side.

Vicarious pain filled my body. It was enough pain to kill, but though I could have touched Kokoro's hand, his face, his neck, I could not find the power to judge. In his own way, Jian had chained me.

He hurt you too.

I know, but that doesn't change anything.

Kokoro kept his dagger levelled at me, but Kimiko's arrival had caught his attention. In the middle of the room, she spread her arms wide like a player upon a stage. Even Avarice watched soundlessly from the shadows, waiting, watching lest Kimiko fail at the job he had long wanted done.

"Don't send your Vices to do your work for you, Malice," Kimiko said. "Fight me yourself. Winner gets Darius? Oh no, wait, he doesn't want you."

Malice snarled. "I will make sure you die as you lived, on your back and begging for it, yes?" He advanced as though in acceptance of her challenge, the expression on his haggard face like nothing I had ever seen. "You will keep your filthy hands off him."

"Says the man covered in his own puke."

"Poor work," Malice said. He held out his hand toward Hope, who had armed himself with the dead guard's sword. "Hope. Kill her."

His chin jutted. "No."

Kokoro started laughing.

"What did you say?" Malice demanded.

"I said no."

Hope stood trembling between them, over the body of the dead guard bleeding out at his feet. "Do it yourself." To disobey hurt him more than the dagger in the guard's side, but he did not move.

The building shook. Shouts echoed beyond the doorway. Numbers would once have sprung to my tongue, but now my mind was silent.

Are you really in here, Jian?

There was no answer. His body lay lifeless at my feet, its eyes staring. I knelt, touched his face and his hair, and closed his wide dark eyes. The only person who had ever truly cared for me was dead by my own hand.

A hot tingle shot through my shoulder, its blooming pain sharp and paralysing. I gulped air. A hilt protruded from my flesh, a hilt connected to a hand, connected to the white sleeve of a priest's robe that ran all the way to an old face, its many lines seeming to smile. "Please don't do this, Brother," I said. "Endymion is no threat to you anymore."

"He is an abomination and a threat to everything and everyone in this empire."

"Kokoro—"

"No, don't even think about trying to talk me around, Jian," Kokoro said, spittle flying. "I should have done this years ago. My mercy has only made things worse. Your boy dies now."

He yanked out the blade, liberating my blood.

32. HANA

Emerging onto the highest landing, I left peace behind. It looked like half the court was gathered outside the throne room, a sea of glittering silk robes and jewels interspersed with clumps of servants. Captain Terran stood waiting. "Lady Hana!" he said, causing dozens of heads to turn my way. "They've breached the outer gate."

"What are we going to do?" a lady with elaborate curls wailed.

"We are all doomed! He will burn us alive!"

Another blast shook the palace. In the weak storm-light, the gathered mass huddled together, silenced by the sound of screams rising from below.

"Where is General Ryoji?" I asked.

Captain Terran pointed in the direction of the stairs. "Down at the garden gate," he said. "Losing men by the dozens."

"Take me to him."

"My lady, I don't think that's wise."

"I will not hide in a corner and wait for death," I said. "I am the only one Katashi might listen to. Take me to him or I will go without you."

He went ahead, pushing his way through the press of people, of scented courtiers and their maids, of ambassadors clutching papers, of lords and ladies and even children awaiting what would come with the air of martyrs. They bowed when they saw me, the effect like reeds bending in the wind.

Shouts came from the third round. "It is the gods' vengeance!"

"They gave the empire to the Otakos. Who were we to cast them aside?"

More shouting. The sound of a scuffle. "The Otakos deserved what they got!"

"That happened years ago. Why now?"

I halted at the top of the stairs. Below, some two dozen frightened men argued, shoving and snapping and snarling at one another like dogs rather than the civilised secretaries, servants, advisors, and lords that their clothing proclaimed them to be.

"Stop!" I shouted, but the roar of opinion only rose as they sought someone to blame for their fear.

"But the Otakos are our gods!"

My shrill whistle made them all stop and turn, immediately prostrating themselves as the others had done. "I *am* an Otako!" I said, removing my fingers from between my lips. "And I am your empress. Katashi Otako does not burn you for any vengeance save his own. The gods have smiled upon His Imperial Majesty taking the oath in their presence for sixteen years, and today is not the day to doubt him."

The silence went unbroken.

"I know you are afraid," I said, no longer needing to shout in the reverential hush. "But we are Kisians. Today we fight to whatever end the gods make for us, loyal always to the oaths we spoke in their names."

There was too much fear clogging the air for cheers, these people no battle-hardened soldiers. All I could hope for was that they had listened.

"Get these people out of here," I said to Captain Terran, still at my side. "I don't care where you put them. Find unused rooms, servants' stairs, anywhere but here, and tell them to wait quietly and pray."

"That is a job for someone else. My orders are to protect you. I will not—"

"Disobey my general," I finished for him. "You are frustratingly persistent, Captain, but I can respect your loyalty. Give the job to someone else then and let's go."

Together we went down the stairs into the noise, into the smell of smoke and singed hair and blood. It was more than the smell of death now—it was the smell of Katashi.

The entrance floor was a large round space edged in columns and screens, in lanterns and silk-covered divans and doors that led to passages and distant rooms I had never seen. Wounded soldiers were propped up against the walls while others were bringing furniture from those distant rooms to throw against the tall lacquered doors—tables, sideboards, great sheets of decorative fretwork, anything that would thicken the wood and make it harder to burn.

General Ryoji was there, blood dripping down his arm. "Lady Hana," he said. "They blew the main gate. I've lost over half my men and there is no sign of General Manshin."

"Katashi won't stop until he sits on the throne."

Ryoji dropped his voice to a growl. "Hana, we cannot just stand aside and let him take it."

"Then the only thing we can do is keep fighting until we are all dead, His Majesty included."

He ought not to have stared at me so directly, challenge in his stance and the set of his jaw, but appearances meant nothing so close to death. "If we let him in, we will all die," he said, ash raining from his hair as he bent his head close. "His Majesty included."

I held his stare. I could have given him a direct order to open the doors, to surrender, to let Katashi stalk uncontested up three flights of stairs and take the throne, but how sure was I? Darius had been sure, but Darius had been wrong before. My own desperate hope was not enough.

"I will speak with him."

"What?" he said. "With Katashi?"

But I was already striding toward the door. The soldiers stopped piling up furniture before it. "Let me through," I said.

"But, my lady, we cannot open the doors." Respect, but no reverence, not like the courtiers on the fourth round. Soldiers had a far more pragmatic approach to gods.

"Are they out there? Bang on the door with the butt of your spear and get their attention for me."

Bewildered, he looked to General Ryoji, who said, "Do it."

The soldier did so as I climbed into the tangle of table legs and divan cushions, hunting a place where I could put my cheek to the wood. I motioned for the soldier to bang again.

"Are there Pikes swarming outside my door?" I called.

"Is this Captain Regent in a pretty robe?" someone shouted back, his voice muffled by the door.

"This is Lady Hana Otako and I want to speak to my cousin."

There was a growl and some hissed words, but even pressing my ear to the lacquer, I could not make out their meaning. Someone laughed. Then against my ear, the wood grew warm. "Katashi?"

"Hana."

His voice crackled like a brazier, but it was still his voice, his warmth, and for a moment I could do nothing but press against the wood and think of all that had been. All that might have been. Seconds passed into minutes, yet I could not form the words I needed. Beneath my hand the wood stayed warm.

"Hana?"

Was that concern? Was the man who loved me still in there even now?

"Katashi, I—" Words clogged my throat like so much wool. *Katashi is dying*, Darius had said. *And there is nothing I can do about that.*

"Katashi, I know you're—"

Shouting started beyond the door.

"What?" Katashi's voice grew distant and the door cooled. "What did you say?"

I knocked. "Katashi?"

More shouting. Then the crimson lacquer glowed with sudden heat. "Congratulations," Katashi said, his voice close and crackling again. "General Manshin? A masterstroke to be sure. How did you manage to turn him to your side?"

I'm going to have our child—words I could not say while there was anyone else who might hear me. "He didn't want to fight for you anymore," I said instead, relief that Manshin had not failed me palpable in my voice. "Didn't want to burn the empire down. You don't have to do this anymore, Katashi."

"Why? Is he dead?"

It would be no use to lie. "No, but..." I lowered my voice as far as I could while ensuring he could hear me. "He will probably die soon. Master Kenji thinks so. So you could just...leave this now, just...let him die."

"I...must...have my vengeance," he said, and the crackle in his voice grew more vicious like a roaring fire, the door hot under my hand. "The Crimson Throne is...mine."

"Katashi, please listen to me, I—"

"Hana, move. Get away...from the door."

The heat rose sharply, and I scrambled up and out of the jumble of furniture, shouting, "Brace the door!"

"Did that go as well as you hoped?" General Ryoji said as I rejoined him.

"General Manshin has turned."

Ryoji's brows went up. "A win. I look forward to hearing how you achieved that at a more appropriate time. If we survive that long. You should get out of here."

I drew my sword. "No, General, you need me," I said as smoke curled out through gaps in the barricade. "He won't blow the door while I'm here. The risk of hurting me is too great."

"If you're sure, then that gives us more time. Not a lot, but if we can hold them off long enough, General Manshin might be able to get them from behind." Ryoji turned, shouting to his men. "Get those buckets and the wet sheets on the door. Everyone else, ready your arrows."

Water came, but slowly, a single bucket at a time carried from the kitchens below. Steam hissed as each was thrown on the heap, but like in Shimai, the water barely slowed the flames.

The burning lacquer stank.

All too soon, the door was completely aflame, the wood burning as red as its lacquer had once been. Steam and foul smoke filled the air, causing our soldiers to fall back, their buckets discarded upon the floor. And then the hammering began, as though dozens of spear butts were slamming against the outside, slow and steady at first, then picking up speed until it roared like heavy rain.

"Archers, ready!" General Ryoji shouted above the artificial storm.

Chunks of the door burst inward.

"Everyone back!"

Soldiers scrambled away, drawing their swords. Beyond the door, men were chanting now. "Burn them all! Burn them all!"

The mass of furniture lit as one piece, filling the hall with blinding light. Chunks of charred wood scattered.

The chanting stopped. The hammering died, leaving nothing but the collective pant of our breath in the smoky haze.

And from within the smouldering remains of the door, Katashi smiled.

33. DARIUS

Muffled shouts guided me along the passage, a cry leading me to the right room. I slid the door as Kokoro yanked a knife from someone's shoulder—a shoulder clad in midnight-blue silk. Messy brown hair was thrown back, and it was Endymion who howled.

Kimiko. Malice. Hope. Avarice. They were all there, watching as Endymion's hair was grasped and his head pulled back to expose the jagged line of his throat.

I charged at Father Kokoro, and he overbalanced, flapping white silk wings. Endymion toppled beneath us, and we fell in a tangle, the tip of Kokoro's blade scratching my cheek.

"You're supposed to be locked up," he said, leaping to his feet.

"Planning to kill me too when I couldn't fight back and couldn't run?" I said, righting myself less nimbly. "And you said my father was a coward."

Without turning my head, I could just make out the small form of Kimiko in the side of my vision. Avarice too, a larger bulk to the other side, the whole room lit by ghostly grey light.

"Damn you, Darius," Kimiko said. "You weren't supposed to follow me."

I kept my eyes on Kokoro. There was no sign of the foolish court priest left in his face. Avarice stepped into his field of vision and he spun, threatening the Vice with his blade. "Ah, one of your slaves.

This one is called Avarice, I believe. Why is that? Why name your freaks after undesirable traits?"

"Because we have a sense of humour," I said. "Katashi Otako is in the palace, come to burn it all, and this is what you choose to do? Kill us?"

"You are unnatural, Laroth," he said, keeping his blade levelled at Avarice. "Unnatural and uncontrolled and drunk on power. I have let this coven of evil exist too long. As a man of the gods it is my duty to see it eradicated."

"Your precious gods made me what I am," I said, the presence of Avarice as calming as it had always been. "Think on that before you destroy their handiwork."

Kokoro spat at me, his saliva catching the edge of my jaw. "The gods no more made you than they gave this empire to the Otakos. The Otakos conquered Kisia by force, and you, Your Excellency, are a freak of nature."

"So is a perfect diamond, yes?" Malice said.

I didn't need to be able to see him and Kimiko to know they were watching Kokoro as I was, the pair briefly aligned in a desire to keep me safe. Kokoro seemed to sense it too and licked nervous lips.

Avarice took another step toward him, and the priest slashed wildly in his direction, a manic grin showing too many teeth. "You're a big man, Avarice," he said, slashing the air. "Go on, you can take an old priest."

Kokoro lunged with the next slash, catching Avarice's arm. His skin mottled in immediate response, hardening its crust. Stoned up, his movements were slow, but I had seen that fist crush a horse's skull, shattering bone. Now it flew for Kokoro's face. But the priest darted out of the way faster than I had ever seen him move. He ducked under Avarice's arm and struck, snakelike, ramming his dagger straight into the Vice's eye.

Blood spurted from the socket. It dribbled down the hardened skin of Avarice's cheek toward grey, mottled lips and I could not breathe, could not move, my mind numb and stupid. The man who'd been more father than servant fell back. No scream, nothing but a sucking silence as the blade pulled free of his skull and he hit the floor heavier than flesh.

Kokoro's laugh broke the silence. "You were right, Laroth," he said. "You all have weaknesses. He certainly did." He indicated the dead Avarice, his skin slowly warming back to flesh but not to life. "Our eyes are the windows to our souls, did you know that, Your Excellency? That is written in the Book of Qi."

I returned his stare, not daring to look again at Iwa lest the knot in my gut choke all strength from me.

"No bodyguard now," he went on, his manic grin the centre of all attention. For the first time, I caught a picture of the room. Two dead guards, Endymion bleeding in the corner, and the slim figure of Hope standing between Malice and Kimiko like a fragile screen.

"What is your weakness, Laroth?" Kokoro asked. "Or rather, who is your weakness? Kisia's bastard prince? How about your brother?"

I did not flinch or twitch or grimace but kept my expression in the dead lines of the Monstrous Laroth. I needed him now more than ever.

"No, but of course, it's your lover. She has your child."

"So could any other woman I chose to bestow that honour upon," I said, managing my old chilly tone better than I had thought possible.

Malice laughed. Malice, his hair caught in filthy clumps, his robe stained with sick and piss. Malice, the brother I loved and pitied and hated in equal measure.

In blood-splattered silk, Father Kokoro advanced. "Your father's weakness was pride. I hated him for what he was, but it never occurred to him to wonder if I had another motive for wanting him dead, never occurred to him to wonder why Emperor Kin had kept me on though I had been Emperor Lan's priest. Never occurred to him to question what was in the tonics I gave him to calm his grieved mind."

"You helped Kin take the throne and you blackened Grace Tianto's name." My voice sounded dull with shock that I could not hide. I had thought I knew it all now, had uncovered every secret, every lie, but as Kokoro's glittering eyes laughed at me, I felt little wiser than the child who had stood back and watched his father die. "And then you killed my father."

"I did. I had to get rid of the only man who knew enough to put all the pieces together. Easy when he was so very tortured."

"He died in a puddle of his own filth."

"Fitting."

Another step and I backed into Avarice's foot, my heel hitting his sandal. *Only peasants walk around without sandals, Master Darius. It's a long way to Chiltae and the roads are rocky.*

So many memories came unbidden. The smell of the oil he had used on the saddles; the dry grass in the high field; sweat mixed with the foreign spices he chewed while he worked.

There had been so much left to say.

"Father Kokoro, that is enough." It was the tone of someone used to being obeyed, but the priest did not even look at Kimiko. "Stand down."

He advanced, eyes blazing with righteous fury. I was sure I held him by a thread, that the moment I looked away or even blinked, he would lunge forward like a snake and stick me like he had stuck Iwa, through the eye or the throat or the heart. Malice had done that once. The blade had slid between my ribs but had found no beating organ.

"Did you know?" I said, looking at Father Kokoro though my question was not for him. "Did you know my heart was on the wrong side?"

"What?" Malice said, his voice proving he still existed.

"Did you know?"

There was a beat of silence, but I could not look at him, only at the hatred in Kokoro's eyes. Then: "Of course I knew. I could never have lived without you, yes?"

I hardly knew whether to be relieved or angry.

"Kokoro?" Endymion's voice came from the corner, but he paid the boy as little heed as he had Kimiko.

Another step.

"Kokoro?" A flash of midnight blue moved behind him. "If you judge them this way, you're no better than Endymion," the boy said, the voice hardly his own.

"I am a man of the gods, Jian," Kokoro said without turning. "It is my job to see their mandate carried out here as it is in the heavens."

I stepped back. And hit the wall.

"Brother?"

Father Kokoro smiled. "Jian?"

"I forgive you."

Kokoro frowned, half turning, and I gripped his hand as it swung up. I pushed everything through, emptying myself of all pain for one blissful moment. Shock froze him, and Hope clamped one hand over the old man's mouth, smothering a cry.

"Pious shits like you are the reason there are freaks like us," Hope said and jammed the tip of a blade into the side of Kokoro's neck. I let go, ducking as he ripped the knife out. Blood gushed down Kokoro's white silk robe like the bile he had spewed.

Another corpse was added to the floor. Endymion collapsed beside him, and Hope, dropping his blade, began tearing strips from Kokoro's robe to bind Endymion's shoulder. There the last patch of sanity in the room, there the last true empathy. But without Hope to stand between them, Kimiko and Malice eyed each other like beasts ready to spring.

"I am going to slice that rat out of you," Malice snarled. "Then

I'll send your head to Katashi. That's what I ought to have done when I marked you, while you were begging for help."

"You think there is anything you can say to me that frightens me now?" she said. "You think you can make yourself more of a monster than I already know you are? You took the man you loved and destroyed him."

Malice circled around her, eyes for no one else. "I set him free! I gave him everything."

"Everything *you* wanted, without ever once thinking about him."

"Shut up, both of you," I snapped, stepping in close enough to be seen. "I am not a child that needs defending, not a child to be fought over. Put down your weapons and let's just get the hells out of here before the whole palace is on fire."

"It's too late. He's inside."

The words came from the middle of the floor, from the pale form of Endymion, dry lips parted as the echo of his words rippled through the room.

"Then we may as well have this out, yes?" Malice said.

"No," I said. "Kimiko, let's just go before it's too late."

"He will keep chasing you."

"Let him. I don't care. My Empathy need not define me, remember? Well neither should he."

"You're right." She stepped back, ready to leave with me, to walk away into another life, another future. "Your Empathy isn't a disease, Malice is."

"How dare you, you little bitch." Malice slashed almost drunkenly at her abdomen and she leapt back. "I am going to make you bleed." His gaze flicked my way. "Without this whore, you'll be my Mastery again."

"No," I said. "I won't. We're done."

Kimiko retreated from his wild, fatigued slashes, seemingly pressed though she moved with ease.

"You will not touch me," she said. "You will not hurt me. I will not risk you ever coming after me again. No, Darius," she held out her hand as I stepped in. "This isn't just about you. It's me he wants dead. It's me he would see suffer. I will not live in fear."

His attacks got wilder and he staggered, seeming to trip on his own exhausted feet. She was letting him tire himself out and he could not see it. Neither did he see her draw the dagger. Or change her stance.

Grounding both feet, Kimiko darted around Malice's guard at his next wild strike.

Her sword slid into his shoulder. His went for her throat. Sadness swelled. Ethereal, Kimiko moved through the steel, through death, a dagger aimed for Malice's heart.

"No!"

I slammed into Malice's injured shoulder. He tripped. Fell, letting out a pained cry and leaving Kimiko before me, anger gritting her teeth.

A numb tingle spread through my stomach. Shock broke her sadness, and the tingle turned to pain. It burst through my gut, stealing my breath, my words, my thoughts. I looked down. Her sleeve protruded from my robe, my silk giving way to her dark linen. Blood ran down my leg.

I tried to speak, but there were no words. I tried to move, but there was only pain. Night teased the edges of my vision. A night laced with screams.

Come, Master Darius, it's just the horses afraid of the storm. You're safe here with Iwa. I'll never let anything hurt you.

34. HANA

Katashi filled the charred doorway as he filled my past, my present, and my future. On a shouted order, arrows flew for his eyes, his throat, his chest, but it was Pikes who fell, their bodies thrown aside as more swarmed into the hall. Our archers backed up the stairs, but no matter how many arrows fell into the mass, Pikes kept spilling in.

The head of a mace swung all too close to me, crushing a guard's skull. Blood. Brains. Shards of bone. A Pike leered at me as the dead man fell. Dran. His name came to me with the stink of the Fen. I lunged, but another Pike stepped in, deflecting my strike, and when he didn't turn his blade on me, he died for it. The full length of mine slid into his flesh, into sinew and organs, spilling blood as I yanked it back out.

They had been given orders not to kill me.

Another Pike whirled past. I went for his throat, but he was quick and brought his blade around. His eyes met mine, widened; his arm jolted back and he yanked his thrust off course, letting it glance off my leather sleeve, slicing gold fasteners. They scattered, flashing as fire flared.

"Pull back!"

Ryoji's voice cut through the noise, but I couldn't see him for the press of struggling men. "Pull back to the second round!"

I caught sight of Katashi as I mounted the stairs. No fire now, just a sword in his hand, its blade melting through flesh and sending blood splattering onto already red skin. So much simpler to flame us all, but like the Pikes, he would not risk my life. In a way, I was everyone's protection.

A Pike rushed toward me up the stairs and was thrown back, the fletching of an arrow in his forehead like a third eye. Dran was there again, pushing past as his comrade fell. Captain Terran dodged the first swing of his bloodied mace by a hair and would have caught it on the return had I not jabbed the tip of my blade through Dran's side, enjoying the moment of resistance as it cut through the thick leather, through skin, glancing bones and curving into flesh. He howled, turning into the blade as I ripped it out through his stomach.

"Pull back!"

"Go, my lady, quickly," Captain Terran yelled, holding off another rebel as I pulled my sword free.

Someone shunted me in the back as another mace came out of nowhere. It clanged upon the metal stair rail. "Go!"

I went, turning to sprint up the stairs, dodging the injured and the dead. General Ryoji stood at the cusp of the second round, bow in hand. He scowled as he let go the string, and behind me a scream was cut short. I turned in time to see a Pike thrown back over the railing.

"Don't ever turn your back in battle," the Captain snapped as he joined me. "What were you thinking?"

"That Katashi will kill anyone who harms me."

"Small blessing."

The Pikes had not followed us but stayed on the stairs and in the hall like they were frozen in place, chests heaving.

"Hana!" Katashi's voice rose above every other.

"Don't acknowledge him," Ryoji said, turning me to face the stairs to the third round. "Don't answer."

"Hana!" Katashi called again, his crackling voice breaking upon the tense peace. "Don't ignore me, Hana. I'm here to take my throne and save you from your murderer, love."

Ryoji was close, a hand on my arm speaking the caution he didn't allow his lips to utter.

Silence filled the hall. Then: "Should I tell them all the truth?" Katashi said, and I could imagine him standing there amid his men, amid the dead, his gigantic presence crowned by the black arm of Hacho. "Should I tell everyone that it was me you were going to marry? That we were lovers? That their Traitor Empress is a traitor in every way."

Eyes bored into me, accusing, judging. I had to force myself to hold Ryoji's gaze, challenging him to speak. There was no answering smile, no reassurance, just a hard look that cut to the bone.

"Haaa-naaa." Katashi sang this time.

With a pounding heart, I stared at the top clasp of Ryoji's tunic. "Order the archers to loose," I said. "Now. We have to stop this before he tells everyone Kin's secret."

He moved away, and around me the soldiers continued to stare.

"Oh Haaa-naaa."

My cheeks burned.

"Yes, my beloved Katashi?" he said in imitation of a female voice. "I'm here."

Laughter filled the entrance hall. Out of sight along the railing, seven archers were crawling into position. Arrows were pulled from quivers. Nocked to bows. And in another breath, they leapt up and loosed, laughter turning to cries of pain.

"Not even aiming for me," Katashi said, laughter rasping in his throat. "How sweet a show of love."

I stayed where I was, unable to see him, though everyone could see me. I clenched my fists and stood proud.

The archers had crouched back down against the railing to nock again, but they leapt up yowling as waves of heat haze rose above the ironwork.

"Do you really want me to kill all the men you have left under your command?" he said. "There are so few it seems such a shame."

The wooden lantern hanging over the landing burst into flames. It dropped, scattering fire and screams.

"You wanted to talk," Katashi shouted over the noise. "Give me Kin and we'll talk."

Kin, buried behind a thick barricade. I could only pray it would be enough.

"I think we're past talking now, Katashi," I said as my soldiers kicked the flaming chunks of wood off the edge of the round and into the hall below.

"Ah, there you are, love. Tell me, are you really going to marry the man who killed our family?"

Every soldier stared. "That's a lie," I said, fighting tears. "You are the murderer, Katashi. How much of Kisia will you burn before you are sated?"

"As much as I have to, Cousin, to see the Crimson Throne restored. As many as I must to see the man who destroyed us suffer."

"He already suffers enough," I shouted back, staring at the air wavering above the iron railing. "Let it go."

A chunk of smouldering wood hit the floor and skidded toward my feet, bright shards scattering. Another fell, raining embers and pieces of cloth, then the leg of a table and a chunk of the lacquered door. Our soldiers ran for the stairs, arms over their heads, and into the chaos came the Pikes, weapons flying.

"You can't hide, Hana!" Katashi yelled above the noise, and for a moment I saw him at the top of the stairs, his bare chest red and blotched with burns. Never far away, Captain Terran pushed me toward the next flight of stairs. "Go!" he said. "They won't hold this landing. Go!" He turned, catching a blade upon his with a terrible scraping. Caught there, he kicked the man in the chest and brought his sword down into the neck of another Pike, every one of their faces all too familiar.

"Pull back!" General Ryoji shouted over the grunts and scrapes and broken cries of battle. "Pull back to the third round!"

We were running out of space and running out of men.

"Pull back!"

I ran with the rest, leaving our dead and our wounded. The Pikes followed hard on our heels, the stairway all chaos and blood. Captain Terran pushed me on, his bloodstained hand in the small of my back shoving me toward the next landing.

"Pull back!"

Katashi was close to his goal now. Up the last stairs and through the doors, killing all who stood in his path and that would be the end. The end of the war. And the end of him.

Katashi's dying, Darius had said. *And there's nothing I can do.*

"We have to let him take the throne," I shouted at Ryoji as we reached the third landing. "We have to surrender."

"Surrender? Are you insane?"

"No, trying to fight him is insane. Too many people have died, Hade. It's time to do it my way."

There was a proud, mulish set to his jaw. Here a man who would not back down, would not give up in the heat of battle, and in that moment I hated him for it. "General Hade Ryoji," I said. "I order you and your remaining men to surrender."

"Hana—"

"I am your empress and I am giving you an order."

A scowl. Then a nod and a bow. I did not wait, only heard his orders break behind me as I darted up the last stairs two at a time. The fourth round was empty, but beyond the first pair of doors, the antechamber was full of wounded men. Apprentice Yoj was performing quick, brutal triage, on his own here without his master.

No sounds of battle followed. Here were just the moans and cries of the injured and the dying.

"My lady, is it over?" a wounded soldier asked as I strode through the antechamber.

"No," I said. "But it will be soon. Katashi and his men are coming. Don't try to fight them. Just let them come."

"But...my lady?"

"Let them come. I will deal with them alone."

Panic erupted, but I could not stay. Ahead, the double doors to the throne room called to me, tall and heavy, their engraving so detailed a full day would not suffice to examine them. Two patches at shoulder height shone with wear, and I set my palms to them and pushed. They opened slowly, crimson light pouring through the gap. The throne room was empty. Still. Streams of dust hung in the shafts of light.

With the weight of history upon my shoulders, I crossed the floor toward the Crimson Throne. It had belonged to my ancestors, and now it belonged to me.

As I climbed the dais, the first sounds interrupted the peace. Men shouting. Heavy footsteps. Terrified screams. Katashi was coming. Darius had said that giving him what he wanted would kill him, but perhaps there was another way. One final desperate chance to get my Katashi back.

"Hana!"

He was not singing now.

Placing my sword at my feet, I lowered myself onto the throne that had seen many emperors come and go, but in that moment, I was its first empress.

"Hana!"

Katashi stood in the doorway, heat wavering around him. Pikes fanned out as he entered, dragging imperial guards with them. They were bloody and disarmed, injured and singed. Ryoji was amongst them, blood running down his face from an ugly wound on his forehead. He hit the floor, dazed, holding close the arm he had injured in Shimai.

"It's over," Katashi said, slowly advancing.

"Kneel," I said as he reached the Humble Stone.

Katashi stopped and looked down. "Kneel?"

"I am the Empress of Kisia, and you will bow before me."

His lopsided smile turned ugly. Dark charcoal patches marred his skin like scabs. "You are no empress," he said, stepping off the stone. "You're still wearing that white sash. You have taken no oath. You are more mine in flesh than his."

"The gods do not judge by flesh. Kneel."

"You are sitting on my throne."

"No," I said. "I am the last surviving heir of Emperor Lan Otako. This is my throne."

He snarled, flames licking up his skin. For a moment, he seemed to glow from the inside, red-hot like the interior of a bake oven. There was a wildness to him, a desperation, and I wondered then if he knew how fast he was dying.

"Give it to me," he said slowly. "Or I will remove you by force."

Swinging out my leg, I kicked my sword to the edge of the dais where it lay out of reach. "That could turn farcical. I could hold on to the arms. I have quite a strong grip. Better you just kill me."

"If you try my patience much further, I will grant your wish," he growled, so animal a sound there seemed no trace of the man left, and it took all my courage not to flinch. "This is what I've fought all my life for, Hana, don't get in my way."

"So you would murder another Otako to take the throne? How does that make you better than Kin?"

One more step brought him to the edge of the dais, and he put his sword down beside mine. Shouts came through the open door, but I dared not look at our audience, dared not break eye contact with the man I loved.

Muscles bulged beneath blood-red skin as he hoisted himself onto the dais. He would have towered over me, but with one hand upon each arm of the throne, he bent his face to mine. It was like standing too close to a brazier, even the smell like hot ash and embers. Up close, his smile was a grimace.

"Hana, my love. Get up."

"No."

Katashi lifted his hand to my cheek. The heat of his bare skin seared but I would not pull away.

"This is your last chance," he said with that crackle of embers once more in his throat. "I have come too far to let this be the end. Give me my throne."

"No."

The flare of angry flame did not come. Katashi's skin roiled like an angry sea, each black patch an island of death upon his flesh. He gripped my chin. "Hana," he growled. "I will kill you unless you move."

"Then you will kill me."

Again no angry flare. "Hana!"

I ran my hand down his cheek, the prickle of singed hair seeming out of place on skin that glowed like hot coals.

"You're in pain," I said. "This is killing you."

"I know. For the gods' sake, Hana, allow me my vengeance! Allow me my throne."

Behind him, his victorious Pikes were growing restless. One of them called out to his captain, but Katashi did not turn.

"Sometimes the best revenge is the quietest one," I said, unable to hold back my flood of tears. "An Otako of your blood will sit on this throne again."

He let go of my chin. Licked dry lips. "My blood?"

"Yes. You made me promise our son would sit on the throne when you were gone, and I meant it. How is that for vengeance?"

His bright-blue eyes burned trails down my chest to dwell upon my stomach. "My heir?"

"Damn you, Katashi," I said softly, pressing my other hand to his burning skin. "Can you let this go now, can you come back to me? We could do this together. Rule together."

"It's too late for that, love." His bloodshot eyes glistened, but there were no tears. "All too late."

Shouts penetrated our bubble of suspended time, and I let him go, his face blurring through my tears. "Then if you want to take the throne, you had better do it now, while you can."

The Pikes were panicking now, their noise rising to a furore. From outside came sounds of battle.

"Captain!"

Katashi seemed not to hear them. Lines were appearing like fissures in his flesh. Stiff-jointed, he dropped to his knees and sank his head into my lap. I touched the tangled hair of his once glorious mane. Every strand was singed. "It is almost over, my Monarch," I said, the words thick with tears.

Manshin's soldiers came, and the Pikes fought, each man dancing his last steps as death tiptoed through the vaulted hall, his bony feet snapping like the finest sandals. But it all seemed so far away.

"It is…it…it is…all daa…arr…" Katashi struggled to speak, forcing out sounds as though his mouth was the wrong shape.

"Shh." I stroked his hair. "Go to your father."

When the last Pike fell, there was silence. And there amid the ever-growing crowd of soldiers filling the room stood General Manshin. He did not speak or approach, just stared at us like everyone else, not daring to break the spell.

My legs began to ache beneath the weight of Katashi's head. He was breathing slowly now, little puffs of smoke escaping with each exhale. Smoke that stank of burning flesh.

"Goodnight, my love," I said. "May you find peace."

I took his hand and pressed it to my stomach. His body was stiffening and his skin flaked beneath my fingers, turning to ash. The charcoal patches on his skin hardened, spread, while every shallow breath was little more than a sigh through black lips. And then the fire was gone with his life, and he lay like a beautiful coal statue, his eyes closed and his lips faintly smiling.

35. ENDYMION

Kimiko screamed. And when she ran out of breath, she screamed again, unable to escape the man impaled on her outstretched arm. Piss pooled around Darius's feet.

"No! No!" Hope grabbed Malice around the waist as he threw himself toward them.

Kimiko's screams became words as she cupped Darius's cheek with her free hand. Blood stained his lips bright red. "No," she pleaded. "Darius. Please."

Blood dripped into the piss at his feet. I couldn't move, every part of me numb as though I were no more alive than the wall, just another inanimate witness to the brief passing of men.

Malice thrashed in Hope's grip, howling like a wounded beast. The sword Kimiko had thrust through his shoulder was stuck there, ripping flesh as he fought his last Vice.

"Endymion, help!" Hope called. "Get this damn sword out of him."

I forced my feet to move.

There were no words in Malice's scream, just spittle and lank hair falling into eyes raw with tears. With more speed than finesse, I gripped the sword hilt and yanked the blade free. Blood soaked Malice's shoulder, but he went on screaming like a man demented.

Tears streamed down Kimiko's face. "I will walk away from this with you. I will marry you, Darius," she said. "We can go anywhere, everywhere, see the world with our little Saki. It's going to be all right."

Pale, shaking, broken, Darius barely seemed to be there at all. Rattling breaths shook his fragile frame, and with every convulsive swallow, he gagged and spluttered.

Kimiko's intrusion had caused the wound but was also plugging it, prolonging his pain.

"Let him go," I said. "Kimiko, please."

"No. We need a physician!"

Darius's knees buckled and she fell with him, her hand shifting inside his body. Blood spurted, splattering her face and the floor and soaking up her sleeve. Kimiko howled.

"Give her the sadness, Endymion," Hope said.

Sadness. It seemed so meagre an emotion, once so weighty, now pathetic.

Malice sank to the floor, but Hope did not let him go, just rested his pale face against his master's silk-clad back. The Vice Master convulsed with sobs, each growing weaker as blood drained from his shoulder wound. Perhaps it was a kindness to let him bleed out. It was either that or live without Darius, not only without him, but with no chance of ever getting him back. Never again would Darius give me that deadpan stare, never again would he mock or laugh or smooth the imagined creases from his robe, eyeing me over an Errant board. His game was over.

I touched Kimiko's cheek. All at once, my hand was hot, enveloped in blood and pulsing organs. There was joy in the sensation of living tissue, and a terrible, pathetic hope not yet extinguished.

Sadness.

Kimiko faded. Her hand slipped from Darius's gut, and she fell back, wailing, leaving behind a bloody, tangled mess framed in expensive silk. And there Darius lay upon the matting, still and beautiful and staring at nothing.

Malice rose with a roar and lunged at Kimiko. "You stinking whore!" he screamed, slamming his foot into her chest. "He's mine. Mine!"

He kicked her again and again before Hope was on him, pushing him away. "He's dead!" Hope shouted. "It's over!" But Malice lunged at Kimiko again, and once more, Hope thrust him back. Malice's face was pale and he staggered, clutching his shoulder as though finally realising the wound was there. His hand came away bright red and his legs collapsed beneath him.

"Damn you," Hope hissed, catching him awkwardly.

He set the man down but did not stay. Decisive steps took him to the door. "He needs a physician," he said, looking back at me. "I'll go find out which emperor I need to ask for help."

He was gone before I could beg him to stay, leaving me alone in a room full of the dead and the dying. A pitiful moan came from the filthy mound that was Malice, but he did not move again. The two guards had been all but forgotten, their names unknown, their fate bringing no sorrow. I wanted to mourn them, but when my eyes turned to Avarice, I knew there would be no space left in my heart. The original Vice lay face up where he had fallen, blood tears streaking his cheek. Kokoro and Darius were less tidy, their organs spilled and their blood soaking into the matting.

At my feet, Kimiko had curled into a ball. I crouched, lips too numb to form words.

"Wake me up," she whispered. "Please, wake me up from this nightmare."

"I can't." The stink of blood filled my nose, blood and vomit and urine shoved so far up there I doubted I would ever get them out.

Her wail rose from a groan and she gripped handfuls of curls, tearing them out. "No," she sobbed. "Oh gods, Endymion, kill me." She dug nails into my arm. "Please!"

Her face was blotchy, and tears streaked from red raw eyes. It would have been so easy. There were abandoned blades in abundance and no one to stop me, but I did not reach for one. "I can't," I said, looking at my hands. "I can't."

She rocked back and forth, hands on her stomach. I wanted to tell her that focussing on life would get her past death, that there was always something worth living for, that she was young, strong, and healthy, but all the words that spilled from Jian's consciousness were as pathetic as the sadness had been, useless to a situation that was beyond words.

"Just one more," she pleaded. "One more! You've killed hundreds, what is one more who is begging for your help?"

She was right. I had killed hundreds without so much as a blink, what was one more? But the day I died, the gods would weigh my heart upon their scales and find it heavy if I did not atone. Atone by carrying the burden for her until it grew lighter.

The idea was sudden. Blinding. I knew not whether it was my own or Jian's, but there was no time to think lest fear steal my resolve.

"Kimiko."

She looked up and I took her face in my hands. She did not flinch, did not pull away though she must have known my purpose, must have felt her own thoughts fleeing. The heat of his guts, life draining from that porcelain face, light from his eyes, those lips I had kissed, that skin I had touched, those eyes I had looked into and seen a soul capable of carrying my weight.

It was slow, every memory a struggle to extract now, allowing time to hunt for Darius, to find the traces he had left on a heart long battered. Touching me, holding me, laughing as I moved an Errant piece across the board pinched between two toes. Katashi was there too, and Malice, their memories interlinked by pain.

Kimiko closed her eyes, her breathing taking on the even rhythm of one asleep as I pulled the last of Darius from her mind. Tears dripped from my chin. They were flowing freely as again and again, I felt my hand solidify in his body, felt his pulse quicken and his body tense. My lips parted in a silent scream at the enormity of what I had done.

Footsteps heralded Hope's return. At sight of him, I tried to speak, but all that emerged was a cry more creak than scream as though my throat was too narrow. He knelt before me. "What is it?" he asked, trying to catch my fluttering hands. "What happened?"

More figures darkened the doorway.

"I don't think you should see this, my lady."

"And I think we've had this conversation before, General."

Figures moved about us, but I had no eyes for them, no thoughts but for the grief that had no voice.

"Malice is alive." That was Hana, something in her tone catching my attention. "Take him to the antechamber and get Apprentice Yoj to look at him."

"Yes, my lady."

Men moved behind Hope. Their steps were heavy on the matting as they worked to lift the unconscious Empath from his pool of blood. He looked dead already, and I envied him the chance at freedom. All the pain in the room was nothing to the agony of unspoken words welling inside me. Of unlived moments and fractured memories.

Hope gripped my hands, but there was no leap of his mind to mine, no instant connection, just a subtle warmth like sunshine upon my skin. "Endymion, talk to me."

Nothing would come.

"Oh gods…"

Horror trembled in Hana's voice. She stood over Darius's body, a hand caught to her mouth. General Ryoji was at her side, protective despite the turmoil his soul threw into the air. I didn't want to look at Darius, but his abdomen drew my gaze as it drew the gaze of every soldier Hana had brought with her. They all stared at the bloody hole. One turned away, his vomit barely adding to the stench of the room.

Hope squeezed one of my hands. "Endymion?"

"We need to move them," Hana said, turning her gaze around the room, brushing briefly over me to Kimiko, Kokoro, and Avarice. "We can't leave them here. General, do something."

"Yes, my lady." He nodded to two of his men, both faces drained of colour. "Carry Lord Laroth to his room. His body needs to be washed."

"No!" I cried. "Don't touch him!" I tried to pull away from Hope, but he tightened his hold. "Leave him alone! Oh, my Darius, what have I done?"

Hope wrapped his arms around me. "You took her memories," he said, his voice close to my ear. "Why?"

I could not explain, not here, not now, not when all I needed was to purge the grief in scream after scream, tears obscuring everything but the memories that played inside my head. Darius had knelt at my feet. Had smiled, for the first time open and real and alive. Free.

Hope's hair tickled my neck. "I think he's taken Lady Kimiko's pain," he said. "She might not remember Lord Laroth at all."

I little cared who he was talking to, could hear no answer beyond my own gasps for air. "Endymion." Hope was in front of me again, gripping my face between his hands. "Endymion," he said, speaking though I cried. "I'm going to take you to get your shoulder looked at, and then you need to rest."

"Don't leave me," I sobbed. "Don't leave me."

"I won't." He smiled, the comforting sight undiminished by the blood at his temple. He stroked my cheek with the pad of his thumb. "I won't leave you. We'll get through this together."

DAY EIGHT

36. HANA

It took seven days to become a man's wife. But seven days could change the world.

I had not moved from the Crimson Throne for hours. Members of the court had come and gone through the red-hued light, and the guards had changed twice, but still I remained, sitting proud while men bowed at my feet. Each one stopped at the Humble Stone and brought prayers for the emperor, requests for reparation, oaths, or counsel.

General Manshin had been one of the first to bow his head to the floor. He had done the same to Kin, and to Katashi, and had betrayed them both. But for now he was mine.

"His Grace Arata Toi, duke of Syan," the servant announced as the last of Malice's Vices crossed the floor to the Humble Stone and knelt. I had summoned him and he had come, still in his blood-stained clothes.

"You sent for me, my lady?"

The *my lady* smarted, but although seven days had passed, Kin had not woken. People were swearing their allegiance to him at my feet, but I yet stood in some strange shadowed area where I was not quite an empress and not quite a lady. If he died, I would have to fight for the throne. And if he lived...I wasn't sure anymore. In just one day, I had almost drowned in new reports of plague outbreaks and food shortages. How much damage could further conflict deal the empire?

"Yes, I did, Lord Toi," I said, trying not to think about my crumbling empire or Katashi kneeling before me, about the weight of his head in my lap and his cold skin. "You must be aware that you are the only surviving member of your family. As such, you naturally inherit the title, lands, and responsibilities of your father. But...is this what you wish?"

Another bow. "I fail to understand, my lady. Is it not the law?"

"No, the emperor is law. Everyone believes you to be dead, which presents you with a unique opportunity should you not wish to return to Syan and take up your birthright. Syan needs a duke. It is an important position. But that man does not have to be you."

"Are you offering to bestow my family's property upon someone else, my lady?"

"I am informed your property is substantial. The castle would, of course, have to remain with the new duke, but I am open to the possibility of dividing other assets so you could maintain a portion of your family's income."

Hope shook his head slowly. "I'm afraid I cannot answer you, my lady. I am not sure what I want from one moment to the next. It seems I have grown unused to freedom."

The simple words made my heart ache. Not once had I questioned Malice. His Vices had just been a part of his life. Of my life. Noblemen paid guards and retainers, Malice had Vices.

"I understand," I said. "I will not press you for an answer yet, although I will need one soon. How is Endymion?"

"Not good. I would like to return to him now if there is nothing else you wish, my lady. I do not like to leave him alone for long."

"This palace is well enough stocked with servants who could sit with him if he needs such constant company."

"It is not the company, my lady; he would harm himself with

anything he could get his hands on if I let him. One of your guards found him climbing onto the parapet last night when I fell asleep."

"Caring for him ought not to be your responsibility," I said. "You have done enough. Take your freedom."

"Thank you for your concern, my lady, but it is my responsibility if I choose to make it so. Even if I did not care for him as I do, I do not believe I could adjust well to the freedom you speak of if I had nothing to live for, nothing to work toward."

Beside the dais, General Ryoji shifted his weight from one foot to the other. Guards all around the hall might have done the same, but he was the only one I noticed, the only one my mind was attuned to.

"You are a remarkable young man, Lord Toi," I said, choosing to use his real name rather than the epithet Malice had given him. "Endymion is fortunate indeed. And...and Malice?"

"I hear he will live, but he is not...himself. He no longer seems to have any hold over me, as though some part of him is truly broken."

"Will you see him?"

Arata shook his head. "No, my lady."

There was nothing more to be said, though my heart bled for the man who had once been my guardian as much as it bled for all those whose lives he had damaged and destroyed.

Hope bowed again and went out. No doubt there were more people who wished to see me, but I needed a moment alone before I could face anyone else.

"General?" I said.

"Yes, my lady?"

"Please ensure your men keep an eye out for Endymion. We've had enough bloodshed."

"Yes, my lady."

I stared at the empty Humble Stone and adjusted the set of my dual sashes. "I can't even begin to imagine what it would be like to have all of that inside your head," I said, more to myself than to him. "Memories that aren't your own."

"It might be kinder to let him throw himself off the highest wall and clean up the mess, Hana."

We were alone but for the two imperial guards inside the door, but his use of my name stiffened my back. "I know I gave you permission to use my name in private, General," I said. "Do not make me rescind it."

He took a step closer to the dais. "Hana—"

"General."

"Nearly every member of the court has pledged his allegiance to you," he said, ignoring this. "You will never have a better time to move."

"You are overstepping your position, General."

Unbidden, the chancellor parted the doors and entered, bowing once upon the threshold before coming forward. "A message, my lady," he said as he walked. "From Master Kenji. One of his boys ran all the way here."

"And what?" I said, shifting to the very edge of the throne, "did he have to say?"

"It's His Majesty, my lady. He's awake. He's asking for you."

Kin and I stared soundlessly at one another. I had prayed for him to live as often as I had hoped he would die, and now the gods had granted one of my prayers, I knew not what to say. He looked pale, weak, nothing like the emperor I had first faced that night on the upper landing. Fever had wasted him to a wraith.

"Ah, my lady," Master Kenji said, noticing me in the doorway. "You got my message."

I entered the room under his expectant gaze. Even with the window thrown wide, the foul smell was second only to what had met my nose when I had followed Hope into a room of death. That was another job that would fall to me—explaining to Kin what had happened to his favourite minister. His only friend.

With his apprentices needed elsewhere, Tili had remained to help Master Kenji, and he glanced at her when neither Kin nor I spoke. The physician cleared his throat. "Your prayers have been answered, my lady. You ought to have seen how many lotus prayers Lady Hana folded in your honour, Your Majesty. I have seldom seen such devotion."

"I thank you, Master Kenji," I said, holding my anger close, protecting it. I wanted no one to take it from me. "To pray for His Majesty is the duty of every Kisian. You may leave us, Tili. You too, Master Kenji; if you are needed, I will call."

A bow. "Of course, my lady. I shall check in on my other patients."

"My lady," Tili murmured and went out with him, her little smile grim with understanding.

Kin had not shifted his surviving eye from my face. The door opened, the door closed, and still there was silence. "Prayers for life or death?" he asked eventually, the distance between us more than an arm's length.

"Both."

His laugh was dry. "Honesty. We're going to need a lot of that, I think."

"Yes. I'm sure Master Kenji has informed you that Katashi is dead."

"Yes, he told me. He told me how you got me here and that we lost almost the whole army in Shimai."

"We did. We lost General Rini and all but some three dozen men. And when Katashi stormed the palace, we lost about three-quarters of the Imperial Guard by our last count and would have lost everything if not for General Manshin. He betrayed Katashi to fight for us."

Kin scowled, but he did not interrupt.

"Most of the court survived," I went on. "Although Father Kokoro is dead. And Darius."

The scowl softened, but he did not speak.

"He...he fell protecting his brother. I..." Tears choked my voice as they had not done before, and I could not finish my words. Kin tried to reach out but hissed in pain. The distance between us was too great anyway.

I swallowed the lump suspending my voice and turned away, a trembling hand pressed to my lips.

"Hana—"

"Don't," I managed to say. "You think I need comfort from you? I cannot even look at you without thinking of my mother—her life gone. Just like Darius. And Katashi. No, don't tell me it's all right. Don't tell me they're at peace, or free, because I don't care. They're still dead."

"You think my heart is made of stone."

"Isn't it? How else do you order a whole family murdered in their beds?"

"Do you really imagine that I don't hate myself for it? That I didn't cry and wish it undone when it was too late? But before I met you, I would have done it again in a heartbeat because there is nothing, *nothing*, I would not do for Kisia."

Every word became a struggle as though his throat was drying up, but his words resonated to the very core of my being, and I realised that although I could never forgive him, I understood him. I had lost so much that all I had left to cling to was Kisia. Duty. Honour. Sacrifice. The fate of a whole empire would be decided in this moment.

I stepped close. He watched me, his single uncovered eye fixed on my face, his whole body tensed in preparation for an attack. It would have been so easy to finish him, just like when he lay screaming in Shimai, but I hadn't done it then and I wouldn't do it now.

"Then we have something in common, Your Majesty," I said,

taking his right hand gently in my own as I came to my final decision. "Because there is nothing I would not do for Kisia."

I set his hand upon my white sash.

"Hana," he said, trying to pull his arm away and letting out a sharp cry. "Hana, don't do this. I will not have a wife who hates me."

"Yes, you will," I said, pulling the first loop free with his bandaged hand.

"Hana!"

"No. This is what Kisia needs. Stability and peace, not war and plague and famine. That is what you said the first time you asked me to marry you." Another loop came free, and the knot looked more like a lopsided bow now than the flower it had been.

The second-last loop of the ragged flower took a hard tug to free, and Kin winced. Tears welled in his eyes but whether they were from the pain or my words, I couldn't tell. Didn't care.

"But you said we needed honesty," I said. "So here is your honesty. I'm pregnant with Katashi's child, and to secure General Manshin's loyalty, I have promised your pure Otako heir to his granddaughter."

The last of the knot fell apart on its own, and the white sash uncoiled from about my waist, leaving only the Imperial Sash holding my robe closed. The Imperial Sash I was not ready to give back.

"Child?" He tilted his head back and laughed until it turned into a hacking cough that left pain lining his face. "You stupid woman."

"Not as stupid as you," I said. "Falling in love with the daughter of the man you betrayed and murdered."

"How fortunate for Kisia then, that it has two fools to lead it through what is to come, two fools and a bastard heir."

He closed his eyes. For a moment I had forgotten just how injured he was, how close to death he had been. "When you're stronger, I'll come to you so we can consummate our marriage."

"How pleasantly businesslike you make it sound."

"I told you, there is nothing I would not do for Kisia."

He did not answer.

"I will leave you to sleep now. Tomorrow we lay Katashi to rest with his father."

Kin did not open his eyes. "Then by all means, do not let me keep you, Your Majesty."

I left, taking my loose bridal sash with me.

The main room had been empty when I entered, but now General Ryoji stood waiting. His gaze snapped to the untied sash. "You completed the ceremony. Why? He murdered your family. Hana... You could have had the *empire*!"

"And how many more people would have had to die for that?"

I went to walk past him, but he thrust out an arm to halt my progress. "And me?"

"You? You are the commander of the Imperial Guard."

"That is not what I meant. I swore an oath that I would protect and serve you and *that* I will never betray or abandon, but I gave you my heart as well as my sword."

I glanced back at the closed door and pulled him away from it, still clasping my white sash. "What would you have had me do?" I hissed. "I learnt the hard way that love is a dream for a perfect world, a world in which we don't live. I am an Otako and you are a commoner who owes his entire career and fortune to Emperor Kin. Marriage—"

"Marriage? Don't treat me like a fool," he snapped. "Even if you held this empire in your own right, marriage to a commoner, as you put it, would only weaken your position. I know that, better than you imagine, but we could have achieved much together."

"We still could, if your ambition yearns for it. It is not like Kin is in any position to rule Kisia as he is right now. Better to rule from the shadows than risk everything in further war."

"Is that your plan?"

"Yes, but if you mean to be a part of it, then you have to know Katashi was telling the truth."

Bewilderment added to his impatience. "About what?"

"That I loved him. That I was going to marry him. That he was my lover. You wondered how I enticed General Manshin to fight for me." I gripped his hand, just as I had done to Kin, and forced it to my abdomen. "A pure-blood Otako heir to the Ts'ai throne."

Honesty was a strange thing. It lightened the body and allowed the soul to breathe, but sometimes letting go that weight only transferred it to another. Kin had taken the burden of my admission, and now it was General Ryoji who grimaced, perhaps feeling my lies all the more keenly. For a tense moment, I knew not if he would stay or go, until he let out a loud laugh. Fearing Kin would hear him, I pushed him toward the door.

"Nothing is ever simple with you," he said, holding up his hands in surrender and lowering his voice. "Have you considered that it might be a girl?"

I stared at him. I had not, not after what Endymion had said, not after the promise I had made Katashi. It could not be a girl, but I put up my chin and said, "Either way, my child will sit on the throne."

"No empress has ever ruled Kisia in her own right. I would have fought for you to do it, as Emperor Lan's daughter, and off the back of a civil war in a time of change, but to name a girl Kin's heir…" He shook his head. "You would face opposition from every quarter."

"Then the day might come when I will need your sword, General, but it is not today."

I dressed in the pale dawn light the following morning, bemused by so ordinary an activity. Tili had set out robes for me and waited to tie my sash, fussing about every detail as she always did—a single familiar thing to anchor me in my grief.

Breakfast came, and I picked at it and wrote letters while

listening to the rain. I would have to learn to play with words if I wanted power without bloodshed. There were decisions to be made too, and a meeting with the Council to prepare for, all the while trying not to think about the two bodies laid out in the shrine, covered in crimson silk.

"Your Majesty?" The chancellor bowed in the doorway.

"Yes?" It didn't sound like the voice of a majesty, but it was the only one I had.

"The carpenter is here with the burial boxes, Your Majesty. You said you wished to be informed. Lord Laroth has been taken down, as you instructed."

"Thank you, I'll come at once."

At the door, Tili gave my hand a squeeze. "It's going to be all right," she said. "Do you want me to come with you?"

"No." I squeezed back. "I think I want to be alone."

"As you wish."

The palace courtyard was a mess of charred wood and strewn debris, but people were going about their business as though the rain was the only inconvenience. From the doorway, two serving maids followed me with a canopy, the dregs of the storm running off the canvas to drench them where they stood. It was a stupid custom, and while Lady Hana might have sent them away and stood in the rain, I was learning fast. Power was all in its perception.

"Your Majesty." The new master of the court bowed. Lord Rota had been an early visitor to the throne room. I had watched them all, trying to discern their true allegiance from their demeanour. It was not always clear, not always obvious, but I mentally stored every little twitch and false smile for later assessment. Darius would have been proud.

"Has a caretaker been appointed?" I asked, letting my gaze slide to the box on the back of the wagon. Black lacquer inlaid with gold and nacre, with hundreds of tiny pieces of pink quartz making up the blossoms on the wisteria boughs. It would have to be his beautiful face now.

"Yes, Your Majesty," Lord Rota said and indicated a small man in old leathers, rain running from the downturned points of his hat. "Vaxun Dale. From Giana."

"How fortunate that we are sending you part of the way home," I said, addressing the man.

He bowed low, murmuring thanks and wishing me good health and a long life.

"There will be two bodies in your care, Vaxun Dale from Giana," I said when he didn't rise. "One is Lord Darius Laroth, the sixth count of Esvar. There is a small graveyard in the back garden at the Court, and he is to be buried beside his mother, Lady Melia Laroth, do you understand?"

"Yes, Your Majesty. Of course, Your Majesty. With his mother, Your Majesty."

"The other body belongs to a servant of Lord Laroth. He is also to be buried in the family graveyard, do you understand this as well?"

"Yes, Your Majesty. Buried with the family, Your Majesty."

"Thank you. You may rise."

The man straightened a little reluctantly, and when he risked a glance at me, I smiled. It was such a simple way to reward a simple man. "You see," I said. "It is important to me that this is done. Family is all we have in the end."

"Yes, Your Majesty. Of course, Your Majesty."

I found my gaze drawn back to the box on the cart. "Is he in there now?"

"Yes, Your Majesty. All ready to go."

"I will have a moment alone."

The man bowed again and left me to touch the smooth surface of the burial box. "Goodbye, Darius," I said quietly. "I was more fortunate than I knew to have you for a guardian. I will never be able to forgive you for everything you took from me in the end, but... if there is peace in death, I hope you find it."

He had never set out to harm me, never sought to injure. But what can a broken man do but sow seeds of further destruction wherever he goes? He had been in pain to the depths of his soul his entire life.

There were no tears left to cry, not then and not later when Katashi was lowered into the ground. Another black lacquered box containing a past I could never retrieve.

In the drizzling rain, Kimiko and I stood together, the only mourners of a man once admired by so many. Tears ran down her cheeks. Katashi had been her brother, but it took all my self-control not to shake her, not to scream and shout that she was mourning the wrong man. But no words could bring Darius back. He was nothing to her now.

Once the priest had finished his prayers, Kimiko and I were left alone to the silence of the imperial graveyard. Generations of Otakos had been buried here, and now Katashi lay beside his father and mine, my mother and my brothers. Katashi's mother was the only one absent, and I wondered what had happened to her body, lost beyond the borders of her homeland.

"Goodbye, Brother," Kimiko said and knelt to place Hacho upon the burial box.

An awkward silence gathered. "How are you?" I asked when she stood, not sure what else to say.

A dark bruise marred her collarbone, like a star peeking from beneath her robe. She touched it, self-conscious, thick dark brows drawn together. "How am I?" she repeated as though it was a strange question. "I'm... I'm well, I think, at least I feel well."

And back along the blossom path and up the stairs of the inner palace, Endymion had screamed all through the night.

"I think it hasn't sunk in yet that Katashi is gone," she went on. "I hadn't seen him for so long, but I think there is always a bond between twins. Now you and I are the only Otakos left. No, only me, I forget that you're a Ts'ai now." She was frowning again. "Things keep slipping out of my mind. I don't...I don't even remember how I came to be here. Sometimes I think I remember, but then it's gone."

"You're here because you belong here," I said. "Because you're my cousin and you're an Otako. You deserve to live the life to which you were born."

"And you married the Usurper," she laughed, genuine amusement in her voice. "I don't think Katashi would have approved."

I stared at her, jaw dropped. The sentiment was so absurd, so understated, that all I could do was laugh. And Kimiko laughed with me, each of us infecting the other until we could hardly breathe.

When the laughter faded, there were no words left. Kimiko spoke another prayer over her brother's grave and left me with him. I envied her peace, envied the little smile that turned her lips as she ran a hand down her belly.

Rain started to fall again. It was a soft, caressing rain that dampened my skin and my hair and the skirt of my crimson robe as I knelt beside Katashi's grave. His body had shattered as it cooled, sending hundreds of glowing embers scattering across the dais. Ash had slowly settled in the silence, and I had held in my scream of anguish though it tore through my body.

I had cried the night through, and alone once again, I let my tears fall, let them join the raindrops chasing down my cheeks. "There was still so much left to say," I said, just spilling the thoughts that clogged my mind. "Still so much left to do. I wanted to grow old with you, fighting over every little thing we could find to fight over. I wanted to watch you teach your son to use a bow. To ride. To rule. I wanted—"

I stopped, tears all I had left when the rest of those thoughts were torture.

Once I could speak again, I said, " 'Before you embark on a journey of revenge, dig two graves.' You almost made it true, but when I am laid to rest beside you, it shall be as a victor."

Katashi would have smiled his lopsided grin and run his hand down my cheek, but now there was only the rain.

"Our son will sit on the throne, Katashi, I promise."

Lying atop Katashi's casket, the unstrung form of Hacho looked strangely misshapen without her string. Her wood was no longer a delicate brown, but shiny, waxed black, most of the leather grip singed to tatters.

I looked around, hunting for colour amid the grey, but Kimiko had gone. I reached into the grave and picked Hacho up. The naked bow was heavier than I had expected.

"Call it a bequest," I said, and unable to stay longer for fear of succumbing to the grief tearing at my soul, I turned away. "Goodbye, beloved Katashi."

EPILOGUE: ENDYMION

Screams echoed through the inner palace. It had been a long night, but now weak morning light leaked in through the high windows, gradually dispelling the darkness. Beside me, Hope had found sleep, curled up in the corner with a woollen blanket brought to him by one of the many servants unable to rest but at a loss for what more they could do. Some went in and out with bowls of water and rolls of linen, but it was always blood and crimson cloth that came out, each maid's expression grimmer than the last.

Hope snuffled, his cheek smushed against an inlaid panel. He had often fallen asleep just so, propped in the corner of my room like a piece of furniture upon which I had come to depend. I envied him his ability to sleep now as I had every day since the war ended. I had spent many hours examining the lines of his face and holding silent conversations with his slumbering body while the night hours dragged past. I was getting better: better at relaxing, better at sleeping, better at forcing down food. Hope stayed with me for every meal. Even after all these months.

A maid rushed past. The door slid open. The door slid closed. The earthy scent of blood found its way out.

The next time the door slid, it was Hana who appeared. These months had changed her from the fierce young woman I had first seen in Koi to one fast developing the dignity of the empress she called herself. Her blonde curls were swept up and pinned with a comb, and her face glistened with sweat. Dark rings framed dull eyes, and she shook her head. The screams had faded to low moaning.

"I don't think there is any more we can do," she said, not really talking to me but to the world at large, though no one else was there to hear.

Through the winter, Hana and Kimiko had become close, Hope had told me, bringing me news from the world I could not face. I had not seen Kimiko more than once since I took her memories—a chance encounter on the stairs that had left me crying for hours. She hadn't even known my name.

Tears welled now in Hana's eyes, but she did not let them fall. I had warned her how it would be if it was a girl.

Silence crept upon us. The pain that had been battering my defences slowly began to dissipate.

Hana was gone in a flurry of crimson sleeves.

Sun streamed through a window at the end of the hall. Through the rippled panes of glass, cherry blossoms waved their bright leaves. Spring had brought Kisia back to life. It had been a harsh winter. Word had come that the tributaries west of Esvar had frozen over and half the winter harvest had been destroyed. The stress of ruling was aging Hana even faster than motherhood.

"What's going on?" Hope rubbed the back of his hand across damp lips and blinked bleary eyes.

All I could do was shake my head. The silence had not broken.

Casting off his blanket, Hope got to his feet. Whispers came from the room. True whispers, not the thoughts of others that had once filled my head. Hana returned. The door opened, letting free a new smell. Incense. Death sticks, burned for a departing soul.

"She will be buried with her family," Hana said, once again speaking without directly acknowledging us.

"The last Otako gone," I said, and Hana looked at me then, scowling. Hope cleared his throat, and there was some awkwardness, my brain too sluggish to remember why.

"As you say," she said at last. "And so she will be buried with her family."

"And the child?"

"A girl. Master Kenji has her."

"Where will she be buried?"

Another scowl I could put no meaning to, my once-so-powerful Empathy clogged with memories and the pain that lingered on the air. "She will not be buried as she is not dead. You said she would die."

"Alive?" I wasn't sure if it was Hope who spoke or it was my word, but either way it hung there in front of us, unsure.

"She can't be alive." Those were my words, interrupted by the guttural sound of a baby's first cry. My heart skipped what felt like a whole minute's worth of beats. Alive. A girl. "The mark?"

"What mark?"

"The Empath Mark!"

Thrusting her out of the way, I strode into the dark room, hit by the stench of blood coming from saturated sheets. In shadows, Kimiko lay upon the bed, eyes closed. A maid was washing her face and hands.

"Endymion." Master Kenji greeted me with a nod. We'd had many conversations about the curse and how it would present itself when this day finally came. "I did everything I could."

In the corner of the room, a middle-aged woman was cradling the tiny, screaming bundle, gently rocking it back and forth. "The baby is sickly?"

"No. After your warning, I am impressed. She needed no great assistance to start breathing."

"And you're sure it's a girl?"

It was sometimes hard to understand the looks shot at me without my Empathy's old strength, but I understood this one— amused, tolerant. "I've been a physician for more years than you have been alive; I know a baby girl when I see one. She has all the right parts, I assure you."

Alive. Healthy. But how could she be when her mother was dead?

The woman eyed me warily as I approached the calmed baby. "Excuse me," I said, bowing deeply. "May I see the child's left arm?"

The woman said nothing, just stared at the Traitor's Mark on my cheek before turning to Master Kenji for her answer. He must have nodded, for the woman reluctantly unwrapped the child. Immediately, it started to scream, growing crimson of face. Tiny fingers were balled into fists, and it was a struggle to get her to stretch out her limbs. She seemed to want to remain as curled as she had been in her mother's womb, disliking this strange, bright new world.

The woman held out the baby's left arm. I took it gently, sure a stronger grip would break the tiny thing. Three horizontal lines crossed by a single diagonal stared up from her wrist, mirroring my brands and the mark I had always carried. I let go, allowing the child to curl itself back up.

A female Empath.

"If you're finished, I will feed her now," the woman said, swaddling the child.

"Yes, of course," I said, numb, bowing again. When I turned, Hana was right behind me, Hope in the doorway.

"She'll stay here of course," Hana said, her imperial pride shining through, straight-backed, stiff, expecting capitulation.

"No."

"You are in my palace. My empire. Are you going to give me orders now, Brother?"

"You can't raise an Empath, and you're a fool if you think you can. You think you know what she needs but you don't. What she needs is to be with her own kind."

Hana managed to look down her nose at me while having to look up to my face. "She needs to be with her own blood."

My hand whipped out and closed around her throat. Master Kenji gasped, but Hana barely flinched.

"Really, Endymion? What are you going to do if I refuse? Kill me? You wouldn't get away even if you did."

"I would kill for her," I said. "Tell me you wouldn't do as much for your children."

"She isn't yours."

I tightened my hold. "Give me my daughter."

Hana's eyes widened. "Kimiko?"

"Give me my daughter, Hana, or I will kill you before anyone in this room can move."

She stared back, unblinking. "On one condition."

"And what is that?"

"That Endymion takes the Oath of Word and becomes a priest. You must renounce your family. Both of them." The words were cold, shrewd. "If you do that," she went on, "you may take her and get out of Kisia and never come back. If she even survives."

"I'll do it."

"Endymion." Hope took a step into the room and stopped. I had forgotten he was there, forgotten anyone else was present. Master Kenji cleared his throat but did not speak.

"I'll do it," I repeated.

"Good," Hana said, my hand still at her throat. "Let me go and I'll send for a priest."

I let her go, my hand cramping, tight, unwilling to fully release and relax. But she stepped back out of reach, watching me. "Her name is Saki," I said.

"Like the story?"

"Just like the story."

She went away on the words, and I looked back down at the child in the wet nurse's arms. The nurse was scowling at me, waiting to feed the child, but it wasn't anger or annoyance I felt. It was an ache in my heart for the parents Saki would never know. Perhaps in another life they might have met, the count of Esvar and a princess of the empire. There would have been nothing to bar such a marriage, nothing to keep them apart, but with all the time in the world, there would have been no fury to their love. They had met and loved in a moment, loved fiercely, and then they had been gone, leaving behind only the beautiful child sleeping now in the crook of a stranger's arm.

Not for us to grow old. Not for us to grow tired. Without life to weary it, our love can live forever, weathering every storm.

I looked up at Hope. "Will you come with me?"

A nod and the flicker of a smile. "I'll come. You know I will."

"Then I have a family. Somewhere to belong. I need no name."

I thought of a day at the end of a long summer, sitting behind a stalwart ox as it walked a shimmering road. The day had been listless yet alive with the buzz of a thousand insects. Jian had sat beside me as we travelled toward Shimai and an inescapable future. If only I had known then I already had all the family I needed.

In my thoughts, Jian laughed. *You said you would make a very poor priest.*

"We'll let the gods judge."

Acknowledgements

It has been four years—it is amazing how much life can change in four years—since I started this journey (more like eight now, past Devin, but we'll let it slide), and a difficult and emotional journey it has been. There are always so many people to thank, so many people who make a book happen, whether by putting in their own hard work or merely by existing to provide some flicker of inspiration, but there are an important few without whom there would be no book.

ahem (Here come some additions from the future...)

Enormous thanks to my editor at Orbit, Nivia Evans, who has worked so hard with me to polish these books to the beautiful things they are now. In fact the whole team at Orbit are just wonderful to work with, with extra special thanks to Emily Bryon, and to publicity extraordinaires Ellen Wright and Angela Man. And these thanks wouldn't be complete without a huge nod to my diligent copy editor, Maya Frank-Levine, and to cover goddess Lisa Marie Pompilio. AND AND...the art. The stunning art. Without the skills of Gregory Titus, these books just would not look so beautiful.

ahem (You may now continue, past Devin.)

Firstly, there is my team (from the original release in 2015, people without whom the original version of this book would not have existed). I would, as always, like to thank my wonderful (and extremely patient) editor Amanda (J. Spedding…you know, I feel she deserves a full name after putting up with your nonsense for years, past Dev), without whom my work would never be its best and my life would be sadly lacking in poop emoticons (we call them emojis now, you know). Also Dave (Schembri), my wonderful designer and typesetter who takes on every extra job I throw at him with a smile. Geoff (Brown) for ebooks and matchmaking (Not as weird as it sounds; I met my partner Chris at a writers' retreat he ran. Although it was at a haunted insane asylum, so maybe it's still creepy) and honest answers to endless questions. And Viktor (Fetsch, geez Devin, what is with the lack of last names in here) for the art that gave this book a face.

Next I must thank my ever-supportive and long-suffering parents, who might not always understand the drive or the goal but always accept it and get behind me (Still very true; present Devin's parents are just as awesome as past Devin's parents at this but are now extra especially proud to be able to walk into bookstores and see my books on the shelves). Also my three beautiful, frustrating, delightful, and challenging children who never cease to teach me things about myself that I'm not always sure I want to know (HARD AGREE, PAST DEV). Thank you to all the friends who have helped me through the difficult times with listening ears, advice, and patience, you know who you are.

An enormous thanks is due to my partner, Chris. It has been a long and difficult slog to get this book finished (and then re-finished again), and every step of the way, you were there to catch me when I fell. And thanks to Devin (NOT myself, that's my ex-husband… yes, I used his name for my pseudonym, with permission, when I first started out. Yes, it's a bit weird now, let's move on…) for beginning this amazing journey with me four (eight…wow) years ago when everything was different.

But more than anything, I would like to thank all my wonderful readers for being so patient with me as the release date for this book got pushed further and further back (my life absolutely collapsed between the release of *The Gods of Vice* and this, and it was a struggle sometimes to remember why I had started and why I needed to finish, so every bit of support was hugely appreciated). Thank you. The care and support I have received throughout the journey have kept me going.

There are many stories yet to tell, and really the journey is only just beginning.

—Devin Madson

extras

www.orbitbooks.net

about the author

Devin Madson is an Aurealis Award–winning fantasy author from Australia. After some sucky teenage years, she gave up reality and is now a dual-wielding rogue who works through every tiny side-quest and always ends up too over-powered for the final boss. Anything but Zen, Devin subsists on tea and chocolate and so much fried zucchini she ought to have turned into one by now. Her fantasy novels come in all shades of grey and are populated with characters of questionable morals and a liking for witty banter.

Find out more about Devin Madson and other Orbit authors by registering for the free monthly newsletter at www.orbitbooks.net.

if you enjoyed
THE GRAVE AT STORM'S END

look out for

WE RIDE THE STORM
The Reborn Empire: Book One

by

Devin Madson

Seventeen years after rebels stormed the streets, factions divide Kisia. Only the firm hand of the god-emperor holds the empire together. But when a shocking betrayal destroys a tense alliance with neighboring Chiltae, all that has been won comes crashing down.

In Kisia, Princess Miko Ts'ai is a prisoner in her own castle. She dreams of claiming her empire, but the path to power could rip it, and her family, asunder.

In Chiltae, assassin Cassandra Marius is plagued by the voices of the dead. Desperate, she accepts a contract that promises to reward her with a cure if she helps an empire fall.

And on the border between nations, Captain Rah e'Torin and his warriors are exiles forced to fight in a foreign war or die.

1. MIKO

They tried to kill me four times before I could walk. Seven before I held any memory of the world. Every time thereafter I knew fear, but it was anger that chipped sharp edges into my soul.

I had done nothing but exist. Nothing but own the wrong face and the wrong eyes, the wrong ancestors and the wrong name. Nothing but be Princess Miko Ts'ai. Yet it was enough, and not a day passed in which I did not wonder whether today would be the day they finally succeeded.

Every night I slept with a blade beneath my pillow, and every morning I tucked it into the intricate folds of my sash, its presence a constant upon which I dared build dreams. And finally those dreams felt close enough to touch. We were travelling north with the imperial court. Emperor Kin was about to name his heir.

As was my custom on the road, I rose while the inn was still silent, only the imperial guards awake about their duties. In the palace they tended to colonise doorways, but here, without great gates and walls to protect the emperor, they filled every corner. They were in the main house and in the courtyard, outside the stables and the kitchens and servants' hall—two nodded in silent acknowledgement as I made my way toward the bathhouse, my dagger heavy in the folds of my dressing robe.

Back home in the palace, baths had to be taken in wooden tubs, but many northern inns had begun building Chiltaen-style bathhouses—deep stone pools into which one could sink one's whole body. I looked forward to them every year, and as I stepped into the empty building, a little of my tension left me. A trio of lacquered dressing screens provided the only places someone could hide, so I walked a slow lap through the steam to check them all.

Once sure I was alone, I abandoned my dressing robe and slid into the bath. Despite the steam dampening all it touched, the water was merely tepid, though the clatter of someone shovelling coals beneath the floor promised more warmth to come. I shivered and glanced back at my robe, the bulk of my knife beneath its folds, reassuring.

I closed my eyes only for quick steps to disturb my peace. No assassin would make so much noise, but my hand was still partway to the knife before Lady Sichi Manshin walked in. "Oh, Your Highness, I'm sorry. I didn't realise you were here. Shall I—?"

"No, don't go on my account, Sichi," I said, relaxing back into the water. "The bath is big enough for both of us, though I warn you, it's not as warm as it looks."

She screwed up her nose. "Big enough for the whole court, really."

"Yes, but I hope the whole court won't be joining us."

"Gods no. I do not wish to know what Lord Rasten looks like without his robe."

Sichi untied hers as she spoke, owning none of the embarrassment I would have felt had our positions been reversed. She took her time about it, seemingly in no hurry to get in the water and hide her fine curves, but eventually she slid in beside me with a dramatic shiver. "Oh, you weren't kidding about the temperature."

Letting out a sigh, she settled back against the stones with only her shoulders above the waterline. Damp threads of hair trailed down her long neck like dribbles of ink, the rest caught in a loose bun pinned atop her head with a golden comb. Lady Sichi was four years older than my twin and I, but her lifelong engagement to Tanaka had seen her trapped at court since our birth. If I was the caged dragon he laughingly called me, then she was a caged songbird, her beauty less in her features than in her habits, in the way she moved and laughed and spoke, in the turn of her head and the set of her hands, in the graceful way she danced through the world.

I envied her almost as much as I pitied her.

Her thoughts seemed to have followed mine, for heaving another sigh, Lady Sichi slid through the water toward me. "Koko." Her breath was warm against my skin as she drew close. "Prince Tanaka never talks to me about anything, but you—"

"My brother—"

Sichi's fingers closed on my shoulder. "I know, hush, listen to me, please. I just…I just need to know what you know before I leave today. Will His Majesty name him as his heir at the ceremony? Is he finally going to give his blessing to our marriage?"

I turned to find her gaze raking my face. Her grip on my shoulder tightened, a desperate intensity in her digging fingers that jolted fear through my heart.

"Well?" she said, drawing closer still. "Please, Koko, tell me if you know. It's…it's important."

"Have you heard something?" My question was hardly above a breath, though I was sure we were alone, the only sound of life the continued scraping of the coal shoveller beneath our feet.

"No, oh no, just the talk. That His Majesty is seeking a treaty with Chiltae, and they want the succession confirmed before they talk terms."

It was more than I had heard, but I nodded rather than let her know it.

"I leave for my yearly visit to my family today," she went on when I didn't answer. "I want—I *need* to know if there's been any hint, anything at all."

"Nothing," I said, that single word encompassing so many years of uncertainty and frustration, so many years of fear, of knowing Tana and I were watched everywhere we went, that the power our mother held at court was all that kept us safe. "Nothing at all."

Sichi sank back, letting the water rise above her shoulders as though it could shield her from her own uncertain position. "Nothing?" Her sigh rippled the surface of the water. "I thought maybe you'd heard something, but that he just wasn't telling me because he…" The words trailed off. She knew that I knew, that it wasn't only this caged life we shared but also the feeling we were both invisible.

I shook my head and forced a smile. "Say all that is proper to your family from us, won't you?" I said, heartache impelling me to change the subject. "It must be hard on your mother having both you and your father always at court."

Her lips parted and for a moment I thought she would ask more questions, but after a long silence, she just nodded and forced her own smile. "Yes," she said. "Mama says she lives for my letters because Father's are always full of military movements and notes to himself about new orders and pay calculations."

Her father was minister of the left, in command of the empire's military, and I'd often wondered if Sichi lived at court as much to ensure the loyalty of the emperor's most powerful minister as because she was to be my brother's wife.

Lady Sichi chattered on as though a stream of inconsequential talk could make me forget her first whispered entreaty. I could have reassured her that we had plans, that we were close, so close, to ensuring Tanaka got the throne, but I could not trust even Sichi. She was the closest I had ever come to a female friend, though if all went to plan, she would never be my sister.

Fearing to be drawn into saying more than was safe, I hurriedly washed and excused myself, climbing out of the water with none of Sichi's assurance. A lifetime of being told I was too tall and too shapeless, that my wrists were too thick and my shoulders too square, had me grab the towel with more speed than grace and wrap it around as much of my body as it would cover. Sichi watched me, something of a sad smile pressed between her lips.

Out in the courtyard the inn showed signs of waking. The clang of pots and pans spilled from the kitchens, and a gaggle of servants hung around the central well, holding a variety of bowls and jugs. They all stopped to bow as I passed, watched as ever by the imperial guards dotted around the compound. Normally I would not have lowered my caution even in their presence, but the farther I walked from the bathhouse, the more my thoughts slipped back to what Sichi had said. She had not just wanted to know, she had *needed* to know, and the ghost of her desperate grip still clung to my shoulder.

Back in my room, I found that Yin had laid out a travelling robe and was waiting for me with a comb and a stern reproof that I had gone to the bathhouse without her.

"I am quite capable of bathing without assistance," I said, kneeling on the matting before her.

"Yes, Your Highness, but your dignity and honour require attendance." She began to ply her comb to my wet hair and immediately tugged on tangles. "And I could have done a better job washing your hair."

A scuff sounded outside the door and I tensed. Yin did not seem to notice anything amiss and went on combing, but my attention had been caught, and while she imparted gossip gleaned from the inn's servants, I listened for the shuffle of another step or the rustle of cloth.

No further sounds disturbed us until other members of the court began to wake, filling the inn with footsteps. His Majesty never liked to linger in the mornings, so there was only a short time during which everyone had to eat and dress and prepare for another long day on the road.

While I picked at my breakfast, a shout for carriers rang through the courtyard, and I moved to the window in time to see Lady Sichi emerge from the inn's main doors. She had donned a fine robe for the occasion, its silk a shimmering weave that defied being labelled a single colour in the morning light. Within a few moments, she had climbed into the waiting palanquin with easy grace, leaving me prey to ever more niggling doubts. Now I would have to wait until the end of the summer to discover what had troubled her so much.

Before I could do more than consider running down into the yard to ask, her carriers moved off, making space for more palanquins and the emperor's horse, which meant it wouldn't be long until we were called to step into our carriage for another interminable day on the road. Tanaka would grumble. Edo would try to entertain him. And I would get so bored of them both I counted every mile.

Tanaka had not yet left his room, so when the gong sounded,

I went to tap on his door. No answer came through the taut paper panes and I leant in closer. "Tana?"

My heart sped at the silence.

"Tana?"

I slid the door. In the centre of the shadowy room, Tanaka and Edo lay sprawled upon their mats, their covers twisted and their hands reaching across the channel toward one another. But they were not alone. A grey-clad figure crouched at my brother's head. A blade hovered. Small. Sharp. Easy to conceal. Air punched from my lungs in a silent cry as I realised I had come too late. I could have been carrying fifty daggers and it would have made no difference.

But the blade did not move. Didn't even tremble. The assassin looked right at me and from the hoarse depths of my first fear my cry rose to an audible scream. Yet still he just sat there, as all along the passage doors slid and footsteps came running. Tanaka woke with a start, and only then did the assassin lunge for the window. I darted forward, but my foot caught on Tanaka's leg as he tried to rise. Shutters clattered. Sunlight streamed in. Voices followed; every servant in the building suddenly seemed to be crammed into the doorway, along with half a dozen imperial guards shoving their way through.

"Your Highnesses, is everything all right?" the first demanded.

Sharp eyes hunted the room. One sneered as he looked me up and down. Another rolled his eyes. None of them had seen the man, or none of them had wanted to. Edo pushed himself into a sitting position with his arms wrapped around his legs, while Tanaka was still blinking blearily.

"Yes, we're fine," I said, drawing myself up and trying for disdain. "I stepped on a sharp reed in the matting is all. Go back about your work. We cannot leave His Majesty waiting."

"I hate being cooped up in this carriage; another day on the road will kill me more surely than any assassin," Tanaka said, stretching his foot onto the unoccupied seat beside me. "I hope His Majesty pushes through to Koi today. It's all right for him, getting to ride the whole way in the open air."

"Well, when you are emperor you can choose to ride wherever you go," I said. "You can be sure I will."

Tanaka folded his arms. "When? I wish I shared your confidence. This morning proves that His Majesty still wants me dead, and an emperor who wants me dead isn't likely to name me his heir."

It had been almost two years since the last attempt on either of our lives, and this morning's assassin had shaken me more than I dared admit. The way forward had seemed clear, the plan simple—the Chiltaens were even pressing for an announcement. I had been so sure we had found a way to force His Majesty's hand, and yet...

Across from me, the look Edo gifted Tanaka could have melted ice, but when it was returned, they were my cheeks that reddened. Such a look of complete understanding and acceptance, of true affection. Another day on the road might kill me too, if it was really possible to die of a broken heart like the ladies in the poems.

Edo caught me looking and smiled, only half the smile he kept for Tanaka. Edo had the classical Kisian features of the finest sculpture, but it was not his nose or his cheekbones or his long-lashed eyes that made the maids fight over who would bring his washing water; it was the kind way he thanked them for every service as though he were not the eldest son of Kisia's most powerful duke.

I looked out the window rather than risk inspiring his apologetic smile, for however imperceptive Tanaka could be, Edo was not.

"His Majesty will name Grace Bachita his heir at the ceremony," Tanaka went on, scowling at his own sandal. "And make Sichi marry him instead. Not that Manshin will approve. He and Cousin Bachi have hated each other ever since Emperor Kin gave Manshin command of the army."

Edo hushed him, his expressive grimace the closest he ever came to treasonous words. He knew too well the danger. Like Sichi, he had come to court as a child and was called a guest, a member of the imperial household, to be envied such was the honour. The word *hostage* never passed any smiling courtier's lips.

Outside, four imperial guards rode alongside our carriage as they always did, rotating shifts at every stop. Sweat shone on the face of the closest, yet he maintained the faint smile I had rarely seen him without. "Captain Lassel is out there," I said, the words ending all conversation more surely than Edo's silent warning ever could.

In a moment, Tanaka was at my shoulder, peering out through the latticework. Captain Lassel could not know we were watching him, yet his ever-present little smirk made him appear conscious of it and I hated him all the more. The same smile had adorned his lips when he apologised for having let an assassin make it into my rooms on his watch. Three years had done nothing to lessen my distrust.

Tanaka shifted to the other window and, looking over Edo's shoulder, said, "Kia and Torono are on this side."

The newest and youngest members of the Imperial Guard, only sworn in the season before. "Small comfort," I said.

"I think Kia is loyal to Mama. Not sure about Torono."

Again Edo hushed him, and I went on staring at the proud figure of Captain Lassel upon his horse. He had found me standing over the assassin's body, one arm covered in blood from a wound slashed into my elbow. At fourteen I had been fully grown, yet with all the awkwardness and ill-assurance of a child, it had been impossible to hold back my tears. He had sent for my maid and removed the body and I had thanked him with a sob. The anger had come later.

The carriage began to slow. The captain rose in his stirrups, yet from the window I could see nothing but the advance procession of His Majesty's court. All horses and carriages and palanquins, flags and banners and silk.

"Why are we slowing?" Tanaka was still peering out the opposite window. "Don't tell me we're stopping for the night— it's only mid-afternoon."

"We can't be," Edo said. "There are no inns within three miles of Shami Fields. He's probably stopping to give thanks to the gods."

Removed as we were from the front of His Majesty's caval-cade, I had not realised where we were until Edo spoke, but even as the words left his lips, the first kanashimi blossoms came into view, their pale petals spreading from the roadside like sprinkled snow. A flower for every soldier who had died fighting for the last Otako emperor. Though more than thirty years had passed since Emperor Tianto Otako had been captured here and exe-cuted for treason, it was still a fearful sight, a reminder of what Emperor Kin Ts'ai was capable of—an emperor whose name we carried, but whose blood we did not.

Mama had whispered the truth into my ear as a child, and with new eyes I had seen the locked gates and the guards, the crowd of servants and tutors, and the lack of companions for what they were. Pretty prison bars.

The assassins hadn't been coming for Miko Ts'ai at all. They had been coming for Miko Otako.

"Shit, Miko, look," Tanaka said from the other side of the carriage. "Who is that? There are people in the fields. They're carrying white flags."

"There's one over here too," I said, pressing my cheek against the sun-warmed lattice. "No, two. Three! With prayer boards. And is that...?"

The carriage slowed still more and Captain Lassel manoeuvred his horse up the line and out of view. When the carriage at last drew to a halt, I pushed open the door, stepping out before any of our guards could object. Ignoring their advice that I remain inside, I wound my way through the halted cavalcade, between mounted guards and luggage carts, hovering servants and palanquins bearing ladies too busy fanning themselves and complaining of the oppressive heat to even note my passing.

"Your Highnesses!" someone called out behind me, and I turned to see Tanaka had followed, the gold threads of his robe glinting beneath the high sun. "Your Highnesses, I must beseech you to—"

"Some of those men are carrying the Otako flag," Tanaka said, jogging to draw level with me, all good humour leached from his expression.

"I know."

"Slow," he whispered as we drew near the front, and catching my hand, he squeezed it, gifting an instant of reassurance before he let go. I slowed my pace. Everywhere courtiers and councillors craned their necks to get a better view.

Some of the men blocking the road were dressed in the

simple uniform of common soldiers, others the short woollen robes and pants of farmers and village folk. A few wore bright colours and finer weaves, but for the most part it was a sea of brown and blue and dirt. Their white flags fluttered from the ends of long work poles, and many of them carried prayer boards, some small, others large and covered in long lines of painted script.

Upon his dark horse, His Imperial Majesty Emperor Kin Ts'ai sat watching the scene from some twenty paces away, letting a black-robed servant talk to the apparent leader of the blockade. The emperor was conversing with one of his councillors and Father Okomi, the court priest. They might have stopped to rest their horses, so little interest did they show in the proceedings, but behind His Majesty, his personal guards sat tense and watchful in their saddles.

In the middle of the road, Mama's palanquin sat like a jewelled box, her carriers having set it down to wipe their sweaty faces and rest their arms. As we drew close, her hand appeared between the curtains, its gesture a silent order to go no farther.

"But what is—?"

I pressed my foot upon Tanaka's and his mouth snapped shut. Too many watching eyes. Too many listening ears. Perhaps it had been foolish to leave the carriage, and yet to sit there and do nothing, to go unseen when His Majesty was mere days from announcing his heir . . . It was easy to get rid of people the empire had forgotten.

Only the snap and flutter of banners split the tense silence. A few guards shifted their feet. Servants set down their loads. And upon his horse, General Ryoji of the Imperial Guard made his way toward us, grim and tense.

"Your Highnesses," he said, disapproval in every line of his aging face. "Might I suggest you return to your carriage for safety. We do not yet know what these people want."

"For that very reason I will remain with my mother, General," Tanaka said, earning a reluctant nod. "Who are these people?"

"Soldiers. Farmers. Small landholders. A few very brave Otako loyalists who feel they have nothing to fear expressing such ideas here. Nothing you need worry about, my prince."

My prince. It wasn't a common turn of phrase, but we had long ago learnt to listen for such things, to hear the messages hidden in everyday words. Tanaka nodded his understanding but stayed his ground, tall and lean and confident and drawing every eye.

"General?" A guard ran toward us. "General Ryoji, His Majesty demands you order these delinquent soldiers and their company out of his way immediately."

Ryoji did not stay to utter further warning but turned his horse about, and as he trotted toward the head of the procession, I followed. "Miko," Tanaka hissed. "We should stay here with—"

"Walk with me," I said, returning to grip his hand and pull him along. "Let's be seen like heirs to the Crimson Throne would be seen at such a time."

His weight dragged as Mother called a warning from behind her curtains, but I refused to be afraid and pulled him with me.

Ahead of our cavalcade, General Ryoji had dismounted to stand before the protestors on equal ground. "As the commander of the Imperial Guard, I must request that you remove yourselves from our path and make your grievances known through the proper channels," he said. "As peaceful as your protest is, continued obstruction of the emperor's roads will be seen as an act of treason."

"Proper channels? You mean complain to the southern bastards who have been given all our commands about the southern bastards who have been given all our commands?" shouted a soldier near the front to a chorus of muttered agreement. "Or the southern administrators who have taken all the government positions?" More muttering, louder now as the rest of the blockade raised an angry cheer. "Or the Chiltaen raiders who charge into our towns and villages and burn our fields and our houses and murder our children while the border battalions do nothing?"

No sense of self-preservation could have stopped a man so consumed by anger, and he stepped forward, pointing a gnarled finger at his emperor. Emperor Kin broke off his conversation with Father Okomi and stared at the man as he railed on. "You would let the north be destroyed. You would see us all trampled into the dust because we once stood behind the Otako banner. You would—"

"General," His Majesty said, not raising his voice, and yet no one could mistake his words. "I would continue on my way now. Remove them."

I stared at him sitting there so calmly upon his grand horse, and the anger at his attempt on Tanaka's life flared hot. He would as easily do away with these protestors because they inconvenienced him with their truth.

Slipping free from Tanaka, I advanced into the open space between the travelling court and the angry blockade to stand at General Ryoji's side.

"No blood need be shed," I said, lifting my voice. "His Majesty has come north to renew his oath and hear your grievances, and if they are all indeed as you say, then by the dictates of duty something will be done to fix them. As a representative of both the Otako family through my mother's blood and the Ts'ai through my father's, I thank you for your loyalty and service to Kisia but must ask you to step aside now that your emperor may pass. The gods' representative cannot make wise decisions from the side of a road."

Tense laughter rattled through the watchers. They had lowered their prayer boards and stood shoulder to shoulder, commoners and soldiers together watching me with hungry eyes. Their leader licked his lips, looking to General Ryoji and then to Tanaka as my twin joined me. "You ask us this as a representative of your two families," the man said, speaking now to my brother rather than to me. "You would promise us fairness as a representative of your two families. But do you speak as His Majesty's heir?"

General Ryoji hissed. Someone behind me gasped. The man in the road stood stiff and proud in the wake of his bold question, but his gaze darted about, assessing risks in the manner of an old soldier.

"Your faith in me does me great honour," Tanaka said. "I hope one day to be able to stand before you as your heir, and as your emperor, but that is the gods' decision to make, not mine." He spread his arms. "If you want your voices heard, then raise your prayer boards and beseech them. I would walk with you in your troubles. I would fight your battles. I would love and care for all. If the gods, in their infinite wisdom, deem me worthy, I would be humbled to serve you all to the best of my ability."

His name rose upon a cheer, and I tried not to resent the ease with which he won their love as the crowd pressed forward, reaching out to touch him as though he were already a god. He looked like one, his tall figure garbed in gold as the people crowded in around him, some bowing to touch his feet and to thank him while others lifted their prayer boards to the sky.

We had been careful, had spoken no treason, yet the more the

gathered crowd cried their love for their prince the more dangerous the scene became, and I lifted shaking hands. "Your love for
my brother is overwhelming," I said to the noise of their prayers
and their cheers. "But you must now disperse. Ask them to step
aside, Tana, please."

"Isn't this what you wanted?" he whispered. "To let His Majesty see what he ought to do?"

"He has already seen enough. Please, ask them to disperse.
Now."

"For you, dear sister."

"Listen now." He too lifted his arms, and where the crowd
had ignored me, they descended into awed silence for him. "It is
time to step aside now and make way for His Imperial Majesty,
representative of the gods and the great shoulders upon which
Kisia—"

While Tanaka spoke, I looked around to see the emperor's
reaction, but a dark spot in the blue sky caught my eye. An arrow
arced toward us, slicing through the air like a diving hawk.

"Watch out!"

Someone screamed. The crowd pushed and shoved in panic
and Tanaka and I were trapped in the press of bodies. No guards.
No shields. And my hands were empty. There was nothing I
could—

Refusing the call of death, I snatched the first thing that came
to hand—a prayer board from a screaming protestor—and
thrust it up over our heads. The arrowhead splintered the wood.
My arms buckled, but still vibrating, the arrow stuck. For a few
long seconds, my ragged breath was all the sound left in the sultry afternoon.

"They attacked our prince under a flag of peace!"

The shout came from behind us, and the leader of the

blockade lifted his arms as though in surrender. "We didn't! We wouldn't! We only ask that His Majesty name his heir and—"

An arrow pierced his throat, throwing him back into the men behind him, men who lifted their prayer boards and their white flags, begging to be heard, but imperial guards advanced, swords drawn. One slashed the throat of a kneeling man, another cut down someone trying to run. A few of the protesting soldiers had swords and knives, but most were common folk who had come unarmed.

"Stop. Stop!" Tanaka shouted as blood sprayed from the neck of the closest man. "If I do not—"

"Back to your carriage!" General Ryoji gripped Tanaka's arm. "Get out of here, now."

"But they did not—"

"No, but you did."

I followed as he dragged Tanaka away from the chaos and back to the cavalcade to be met with silent stares. Mama's hand had retreated back inside her curtained palanquin, but His Majesty watched us pass. Our eyes met. He said not a word and made no gesture, but for an instant before doubt set in, I was sure he had smiled, a grim little smile of respect. Wishful thinking. No more.

Edo stood waiting at the door of the carriage but slid out of sight as Ryoji marched Tanaka up to it and thrust him inside. He held the door open for me to follow, and I took my seat, trembling from head to foot.

Still holding the door, the general leant in. "Do you have a death wish, boy?"

"I was the one trying to stop anyone getting killed, General, if you didn't notice."

"And painting a great big target on your back while you did it."

"They loved me!"

General Ryoji snarled an animal's anger. "You think it was you they were cheering for? They weren't even seeing you. That was Katashi Otako standing before them once more."

"And I'm proud to look—"

"Your father was a traitor. A monster. He killed thousands of people. You—"

Words seemed to fail him and he slammed the door. A shout to the driver and the carriage lurched into motion. Tanaka scowled, ignoring Edo's concerned questions, while outside, more people willing to die for the Otako name bled their last upon the Shami Fields.*Photo Credit: Leah Ladson*

Enter the monthly
Orbit sweepstakes at

www.orbitloot.com

With a different prize every month,
from advance copies of books by
your favourite authors to exclusive
merchandise packs,
we think you'll find something
you love.